A former au pair, bo[illegible] seafront trader, **Jessic**[illegible] onmental charity in [illegible] daughter, one fluffy do[illegible], she spends her time avoiding housework and can usually be found with her nose in a book. Jessica writes emotional romance with a hint of humour, a splash of sunshine and a great deal of delicious food—and equally delicious heroes!

USA TODAY bestselling and RITA® Award–winning author **Marie Ferrarella** has written more than two hundred and fifty books for Mills & Boon, some under the name Marie Nicole. Her romances are beloved by fans worldwide. Visit her website, marieferrarella.com.

Also by Jessica Gilmore

Her New Year Baby Secret
A Proposal from the Crown Prince
The Sheikh's Pregnant Bride
Baby Surprise for the Spanish Billionaire
Summer Romance with the Italian Tycoon

Also by Marie Ferrarella

The Cowboy's Lesson in Love
Diamond in the Ruff
Her Red-Carpet Romance
Coming Home for Christmas
Dr. Forget-Me-Not
Twice a Hero, Always Her Man
Meant to Be Mine
A Second Chance for the Single Dad
Christmastime Courtship
Engagement for Two

HONEYMOONING WITH HER BRAZILIAN BOSS

JESSICA GILMORE

THE LAWMAN'S ROMANCE LESSON

MARIE FERRARELLA

MILLS & BOON

First Published in Great Britain 2019
by Mills & Boon, an imprint of HarperCollinsPublishers,
1 London Bridge Street, London, SE1 9GF

ISBN: 978-0-263-27228-4

0419

MIX
Paper from responsible sources
FSC™ C007454

This book is produced from independently certified FSC™ paper to ensure responsible forest management.

For more information visit: www.harpercollins.co.uk/green

Printed and bound in Spain
by CPI, Barcelona

HONEYMOONING WITH HER BRAZILIAN BOSS

JESSICA GILMORE

For Nana and Papa.
I wish I didn't know so much about how
dementia robs us of loved ones too early,
and I wish you had both been spared.
I hope you're happy and at peace now xxx

CHAPTER ONE

'COME ALONG, HATTY. Leave that!'

Harriet Fairchild looked up from her computer screen, eyes full of spreadsheets and numbers and projections, and smiled at the petite woman jiggling impatiently from foot to foot by the side of the pretty antique desk.

'I just need to finish this and I'll be right there. Five minutes, Amber, I promise.'

'You said that ten minutes ago,' Amber pointed out. 'Our guests will be here in fifteen minutes and we haven't had our private toast yet. Those spreadsheets will still be there in the morning.'

'Along with everything else I haven't managed to do yet. I can't believe I'm so behind, when we haven't even opened the agency.' But Harriet was saving the documents as she spoke, closing down the laptop and shutting the lid with a sigh she did her best to hide from the bubbly redhead. Her new business partners—and best friends—had been more than understanding when Harriet disappeared across London most days to sit with her father after yet another fall, but with the Happy Ever After Agency due to open its doors imminently she knew it should have been all hands on deck back at the elegant Chelsea townhouse where they now lived, worked and dreamed.

'I can't believe it's actually happening.' Amber bounced up and down on her trainer-clad tiptoes as Harriet slipped her laptop into the desk drawer and locked it. 'That we've made it.'

'We're not there yet; we need some clients first.' But although Harriet was trying to maintain her usual calm and sensible manner, excitement fizzed inside her like the champagne Emilia was getting ready to uncork on the other side of the room.

'Well, that's what tonight's about. Launching the business. After tonight we'll have more work than we can cope with, you'll see.'

'We will if the other two have anything to do with it. Between Emilia's event skills and Alex's PR skills, how can our launch event be anything but a success? And if it isn't, well, we can live off canapés and champagne for the next week!'

She followed Amber through the office and into the freshly decorated reception area, where the other two co-owners of the Happy Ever After Agency were waiting for her. As she joined them Emilia finally let the cork go with a resounding pop, Alexandra deftly holding a glass under the bottle to catch the first rush of golden bubbles, handing the filled glass to Harriet with a smile.

'Thank you!' Harriet took the glass and held it out, waiting till the other three each held their own to join her in the toast. 'To dreams coming true and happy-ever-afters,' she said.

'To happy-ever-afters,' Emilia echoed, her answering smile for once full and frank, the shadows that usually haunted her eyes nowhere to be seen.

'And to all our dreams.' Alexandra could never be anything but cool and collected, but her even, polite smile was genuinely warm, the excitement in her voice unfeigned.

'To us.' Amber was never less than sunny and her smile lit up the room. 'We've done it. I'm so proud of us!'

Harriet turned to Alexandra, her heart full of gratitude. 'And earlier than planned, thanks to you, Alex.'

The tall, slim girl shook her immaculately coiffed head. 'Thanks to my godmother, you mean. She left me this place. Without her, our dreams would still be just that, only dreams.'

'To your fairy godmother, then.' Amber raised her glass in another toast and the small group responded with a respectful murmur. They all knew how lucky they were. Alexandra's inheritance meant that not only were they opening the agency a couple of years earlier than planned, they didn't have to worry about renting premises or any of the overhead costs starting a new business usually entailed.

Harriet took a sip of the champagne, trying to work out just what it was that made this vintage twenty times more expensive than her usual brand of corner shop Prosecco, and looked around the room, unable to stop herself critically surveying it, looking for flaws or potential problems. Her stomach settled, the squeeze in her chest relaxing as she saw nothing out of place. They were ready, and after tonight's launch the great, good and wealthy of Chelsea would know that they were here and that they were open for business.

Luckily the small Chelsea townhouse Alexandra had inherited was structurally perfect, if outdated in decor, but between them they had saved just enough to knock down the wall between the front sitting room and back dining room to create the light, inviting reception and office space they now stood in. Wooden floorboards shone with a warm golden glow, the replastered walls were freshly painted matt white above the picture rails and a light grey below and the original tiled fireplaces had been scrubbed until they shone. Two comfortable-looking sofas sat opposite each other at the front of the room, inviting spaces for potential clients or staff to relax in, and their own desks, an eclectic mixture of vintage and modern classic, faced the reception area in two rows, paperwork neatly filed in the shelves built into the alcoves by the back fireplace. Flowers and plants softened the space, a warm floral print on the blinds and curtains, the same theme picked up in the pictures hanging on the walls. They wanted their public-facing space to look professional and yet unique. Like the services they offered.

The door at the back led to a narrow kitchen and a sunny conservatory extension they used as a sitting/dining room. Usually the door would remain closed, keeping the area private, but today it was flung open to welcome their new neighbours and potential clients to their launch party, the fridge filled with a much less expensive champagne than the one they were currently drinking, the tables and counters covered with an array of tempting canapés baked by Amber over the last two days. The scent of warm spices and fresh bread mingled aromatically with the beeswax polish and fresh flowers.

Upstairs, each of the two floors housed two bedrooms and a bathroom. Thanks to Alexandra's generosity, this was all theirs. The bills were to be paid out of the agency profits, each partner only drawing enough salary for simple needs, the rest to be pooled back in until they had enough for what each of them truly dreamed for—security. Security and a home. Harriet inhaled, letting the unique scent fill her lungs. Security, home and a family.

'Ten minutes, girls.' Emilia brought Harriet back to the here and now. 'Are we ready?'

'The office couldn't look more perfect,' Harriet said. 'And we're all looking presentable, too.' She grinned at the understatement. As usual her friends looked stunning; they had agreed to all wear black, and if Harriet's sensible wrap dress looked dull next to Alex's elegant shift, Amber's vintage-inspired swing dress and Emilia's pretty floaty skirt and lace top, well, she was more than used to fading into the background. Preferred it in fact.

'I've been chatting up all the neighbours,' Amber said. 'They've all been invited personally and I managed a subtle sales pitch at the same time. I've identified several in need of an emergency childcare provider, dog walkers and housekeeping and I've already been approached for some light cleaning and shopping for a couple of elderly residents I spoke to in the park. And while chatting I made sure they know that I have all the contacts. I reckon we'll hear from some time-poor, cash-rich families wanting their date nights organised from babysitters to impossible-to-get-into restaurants before the week is out…' Amber specialised in providing bespoke concierge services. At Aion, the company they had all recently left, her role had been to run the small team who ensured VIP clients wanted or needed for nothing, no matter how short the notice.

'And I've already got a couple of events lined up and the clients are, of course, invited tonight. First up a charity brunch and then two birthdays; one is for a child, Amber, so maybe we can combine on that? Children are definitely more your thing than mine.' Emilia smiled over at her friend. 'I can't wait to get going. If we can pull these off then we might have a chance at some of the Christmas balls, and they will really get our reputation out there.'

'There's a new restaurant opening up the street and I have offered to do their PR. It doesn't pay much but it's a nice story for our launch.' Alexandra was all about the story. Even after four years Harriet wasn't sure what was real and what was manufactured about her friend, but it didn't matter. The truth was they were four kindred spirits, four lonely souls who had found each other one Christmas Eve and slowly formed a semblance of a family.

'I have temps coming in to interview all week,' Harriet contributed. 'I had hoped to be further along by now but…'

'But nothing. We have the time and space to build the agency up carefully and properly. The right staff, the right clients and the best service,' Alex reassured her. 'We're in this for the long-term. Your dad is important, Harriet, more important than anything else. Never apologise for being with him.'

'Thank you.' Harriet's whole body warmed with affection and relief. She didn't have to make excuses here, hide her emotions and needs. She belonged. It was all she had ever wanted. 'Hang on, was that the bell? It sounds like our first guests have arrived…'

Deangelo Santos didn't often read magazines. He certainly didn't read gossip magazines. And since the day he'd first set foot on British soil, twelve years before, all his reading material had been in English. The bright, gaudy Brazilian magazine lying on his desk was as out of place in his severely modern and austere office as a child's teddy bear. But he hadn't bought the magazine to read it. He'd bought it to allow himself one glorious moment of anticipation.

Three faces smiled out of the front cover. All in their forties, all sleek and self-satisfied in the way that only inherited privilege and extreme arrogance could instil. And all completely unaware that in just a few weeks their entire lives would be turned upside down, inside out and ripped apart. Deangelo allowed himself just one moment of looking at the magazine, the faintest semblance of a smile curling his lips, before picking it up between his thumb and forefinger and tossing it into the recycling bin. He stalked to his office door. It was time to put the final pieces of his plan into play.

He threw open the glass door and stifled a sigh as the slight woman who occupied the desk outside jumped. It was a tiny jump, almost imperceptible, but there all the same. 'Good evening, Mr Santos. Is there anything I can do for you before I leave?'

There was nothing wrong with the question or the way she asked it. Just as there was nothing wrong with her work. For the last two weeks she had been sitting at this very desk when he arrived at work at seven thirty a.m. after his usual ten kilometre run and half-hour workout. He would walk into his office to find his computer switched on and waiting for him, his task list neatly printed out and waiting on his keyboard, the bitter dark coffee he preferred brewed and waiting. Everything as it should be.

Equally she had been right there, at her desk all day, taking less than half an hour for lunch, managing his inbox and diary, booking flights and arranging meetings, making sure he was only disturbed when he needed to be.

Just as he liked it.

Now here she still was, ten hours after starting, not complaining about her long day or showing impatient signs of wanting to get home.

Although, to be fair, she would be handsomely paid for exactly those kinds of hours.

Really, in the grand scheme of things one small nervous jump wasn't anything to complain about.

Except…

Except it was Monday. Which meant the woman sitting at his PA's desk had been here for two weeks and one day.

And that one extra day was unexpected. Deangelo didn't like unexpected. He planned and schemed and went through every possible contingency to avoid the unexpected. Having your life ripped away from you before you hit your teens would do that to a person.

Instead of answering her question, Deangelo wheeled round and walked back into his office, pulled his phone out of his pocket, pressed a button and waited, foot tapping impatiently until the call was answered.

It took less than three seconds. Good. 'Hello, sir. How can I help?'

'Where is Harriet?' he demanded.

There was a pause before his head of HR responded. 'Harriet?'

'Yes. Harriet. Tall. Blonde hair.' Or was it red? He could never decide. Not that her hair colour mattered, the only thing of any import was that Harriet Fairchild kept his life smooth, in order and seamless. As it should be. 'She's had two weeks off already. When is she due back?'

'Mr Santos, Harriet left.'

'Left?'

'Left the company.'

She had *what*? Deangelo paused, trying to remember the last day he had seen her. Come to think of it, she had looked a little expectant when saying goodbye. Maybe even disappointed? It was hard to remember;

he had been putting his final plans together for Brazil that week, his head, for once, nowhere near business as usual.

But how could he have not realised she was leaving? At least that explained the flowers on her desk…

'Where has she gone? I assume you offered her appropriate recompense to stay?'

'I did, naturally. I know how you dislike your routine changing but she is setting up her own business; I don't think there was any inducement we could have offered to make her stay.' Sue, his head of HR, sounded a lot more sure of herself now and Deangelo couldn't blame her. It was a different matter losing his valued PA to her own business than losing her to another company. Still inconvenient, though. Especially with the biggest deal of his life, if not his career, coming up. A deal he had counted on her help to pull off. Deangelo cast a quick look through the open door at the nervous replacement as she sat typing diligently but unable to shield the worry in her eyes, biting her lip as she pretended not to listen in. No, with those kind of acting skills she wouldn't do at all and it was far too late to train anyone else.

'What kind of business?'

'An agency. She has gone into partnership with three other ex-Aion employees. They are providing an all-round service, I believe, from event management to PA temps, household management to reputation management.'

Deangelo seized upon the one piece of information that was relevant. 'They provide PA temps? Excellent.

Then hire her back. For the next month. I'll pay double the going rate.' Everyone had their price and a fledgling agency would be more eager than most for business and income. 'Tell her to make sure her passport is up-to-date; we leave for Rio in two weeks, but I want her back in tomorrow.'

He ended the call and stalked across the office to stand at the full-length windows, staring out at the London skyline beyond. Views like this were worth millions, buildings like the one Aion occupied—occupied and owned—in the heart of South Bank were worth more. He lived right here, in a penthouse apartment, his office took up the floor below, his private gym and swimming pool were in the basement, right next to the garage which housed his beloved collection of vintage sports cars. The rest of the building was a thriving hub of some of the world's leading minds and they all worked for him. He had come a long, long way from the *favela*. But when he set foot in Rio would he be Deangelo Santos, founder of Aion, tech billionaire, philanthropist or would he revert to the street rat, illegitimate son of one of Rio's oldest families? Discarded and left out like the rubbish they had deemed him.

His hands curled into fists. He had the power now and in two weeks he would show them just who he was. And for that he needed everything to be perfect. He needed Harriet.

As if on cue, his mobile rang. Glancing at the screen before he answered, Deangelo began to relax. Sue with the news of Harriet's return, no doubt.

He answered the call with a curt 'Yes?' then listened

to the apologetic voice for a moment, incredulity creeping over him. 'What do you mean, she can't do it?'

'She says she hasn't got time. Give her a week and she'll find you a new replacement for Jenny, although she thinks you should give the poor girl more of a chance—her words not mine—but she's too busy setting up the agency at the moment to take a month away. They only opened today, sir; they're holding their launch party tonight. I was just on my way there now.'

Deangelo stilled. 'Launch party? What's the address? I'll see you there. I'd better speak to Harriet myself.'

He ended the call, cutting off Sue's polite but clearly panicked protests. If Rio was to go to plan then nothing could go wrong and that included Harriet Fairchild's presence. And if he had to go to Chelsea and persuade her himself then that was exactly what he would do. His gaze stole towards the recycling bin and the gaudy magazine cover peeking out the top. He had a deathbed promise to fulfil and nothing—and no one—was going to stand in his way.

CHAPTER TWO

THE HOUSE WAS pleasantly full, closing in on crowded, a steady stream of curious neighbours, local businesses and carefully selected potential clients passing through to sample Amber's spectacular canapés, have a glass of champagne and toast the Happy Ever After Agency's launch. Harriet had watched Alexandra and Emilia turn on their cool, professional charm, while Amber tempted people with tray after tray of delicious treats, disbelief that it was really happening looping around her stomach. This was it. They existed. Their future was entirely in their hands—it was both thrilling and terrifying. Had they really thought when they'd first come up with the idea that it would actually happen? For so long it had seemed a nice pipe dream, not an actual plan.

No more dreaming. Things had just got serious and for the agency to work they needed clients and fast. This party was just the start. It had to be a success.

Leaning against the wall, Harriet pushed away the misgivings that liked to whisper in her ear; she could be at her desk right now, clocking off for the evening, earning a good salary, pension, benefits—safety. It was time she struck out and dared to do—to be—someone new. No longer the mousy little PA, more part of the office furniture than warm flesh and blood. Of so little significance that after three years Deangelo Santos hadn't even said goodbye. She swallowed. She was a fool to be disappointed by the omission, a fool to care. Just because, occasionally, very occasionally, that keen stare had seemed to see her, seemed to know her, didn't mean the connection she'd imagined was real. She might be a Jane Eyre type but that didn't make him Rochester—which was a good thing. Harriet had never visited Deangelo's penthouse suite but she was pretty sure he didn't keep a wife hidden away there!

Enough. She had clients to woo and impress and moping over her old boss's indifference would help nobody. She smiled even though there was no one there to see it, tilting her chin and pushing her shoulders back. *Fake confidence if you don't feel it* was Amber's mantra. It was one she was going to adopt.

Harriet's own job for the evening was, by choice, greeting guests at the door, handing out brochures and booking in appointments and jobs. Small talk had never been her forte; she much preferred having an actual task to do. Besides, this *was* her job, just as networking and promoting was Alex and Emilia's. She would be managing the office for all four of them as well as recruiting and placing the army of temps she hoped to have in place before too long, providing emergency PA cover herself if necessary. She liked the tidiness of admin work, sorting and solving problems, organising. She liked to be needed.

Outside this house there was nobody who needed her any more, nobody who even noticed her. Somehow, between school and now, she'd turned into the invisible woman. She would never regret the decisions that had taken her to this place. Never regret the years she had spent as her dad's carer, the dates she had turned down, the potential friendships that had never come to fruition, the two fledgling relationships that had never progressed beyond possibility, the university place postponed until she had finally, regretfully withdrawn her application. She had no one but her father, and he had no one but her.

But now his dementia had progressed to a level in which she didn't even exist. So where did that leave her?

Harriet summoned up a smile as a couple of guests passed her on their way out, copies of the agency's promotional brochure in their hands. *Stop being so self-pitying.* She had her friends now—and more. She had a new way forward. Thanks to Alex's inheritance she had a new job, a new home, a new purpose and with it a new resolve: that it was time to stop living on the sidelines, time to step out, actually try living not merely existing. To try and live a life that was more than work and responsibility, now that her father didn't know who she was, now she no longer needed to spend every spare hour by his side. She would start by signing up for the evening language courses and the local book group and see about local volunteering opportunities. Not the wildest activities for someone just turned twenty-six, but a lot wilder than a night in alone with a herbal tea and a book.

And maybe while she was in this spirit she should stop skulking in the hallway with a tablet and a handful of leaflets and go and circulate as the other three were so effortlessly doing. She'd been to many work receptions while she worked at Aion, all over the world. She could do this… Resolutely she turned around but, as she did so, the old-fashioned doorbell rang its sonorous chime.

Pausing, Harriet cast a quick glance in the mirror to make sure she still looked like the professional, aspirational businesswoman stroke hostess that she was trying to be. Okay. Her strawberry-blonde hair hung in a silky sheet, the frizz ruthlessly tamed and controlled, and a discreet coating of lipstick still covered her overly generous mouth. Her wrap dress wasn't gaping and she hadn't spilt anything down it. All that counted as a win. For the umpteenth time in the last two hours Harriet pinned an appropriately pleasant yet professional smile onto her face and opened the door. 'Welcome to…' She looked up before she could complete the sentence and her gaze met a pair of hard amber eyes. She faltered, the door swinging back as she stepped back in shock.

Was she dreaming? Imagining things? Tentatively she reopened the door and looked again. No. No imagining. Tall, broad, the body of a street fighter, face of a fallen angel, marred—or enhanced—by the scar that ran right down one side of his face, temple to chin. A face she knew as well as she knew her own—better, she'd seen it every day for the last three years. 'Deangelo? I mean, Mr Santos, what are you doing here?'

'You're holding a party, aren't you?'

'Erm…yes,' she managed.

'Then aren't you going to invite me in?'

'I…of course.' Harriet was hurriedly running through the many invitations they'd sent and no, she didn't recall the billionaire businessman's name on any of them. Aion's HR staff of course, some of their old colleagues, but not the man himself. He wasn't exactly the party type—and, even after working in close proximity with him, they weren't on invite terms. But, invite or not, Deangelo Santos was not the kind of man to leave cooling his heels on a doorstep, not even a Chelsea doorstep. Besides, she would be mad to turn a man with his money and influence away, and the gleam in his eyes told her he was well aware of the fact. Harriet stood back and nervously, as if she were inviting a predator into her home, said, 'You'd better come in.'

The air seemed to shift as he stepped into the hallway and Harriet was reminded irresistibly of the old vampire movies and the dangers of inviting the powerful over your doorstep. 'Okay, the party is this way. We're actually expecting a few people from Aion.' She smothered a smile at the thought of the shock on their faces when they walked in to see their famously reclusive boss at the party. 'Let me show you around.' She started towards the open partition which linked the hallway to the reception area but Deangelo made no move to follow her.

'Why did you say no?'

Harriet stopped and turned back to face him, startled by the abrupt words. Was *that* why he was here? Surely not. She was a good PA but not that good. 'No?

You mean to the temping offer? Because I work here now. It was kind of you to think of me…'

He brushed away her words as if kindness was a foreign concept. 'You are a temp agency. I am in need of a temp. I want to hire you. It makes no sense for you to refuse.'

'But you have a PA. I trained her myself.'

Distaste flickered across Deangelo Santos's face. 'She rustles. And she jumps when I speak.'

'She *rustles*?' Harriet blinked. Maybe she had fallen asleep at her desk and this was some kind of surreal dream. It wouldn't be the first time she had dreamed about her dangerously distracting ex-boss. But the pinch at her toes from Amber's too-small shoes and the noise from the office and reception area were all too real. 'Look, come and get a drink; we can't discuss this in the hall.' And there was safety in numbers.

Safety? Where had that come from? She'd never had even a cross word from the formidable Brazilian before. But then she had never thwarted him before either.

Lightly, lithely for such a tall and muscled man, Deangelo followed her into the office and reception room and the hubbub quietened as he entered. Nobody there would know who he was; he shunned all publicity. Not for his gushing newspaper profiles or charity galas—he protected his privacy with the fierceness of a secret agent—but his sure, confident presence was enough to cast a spell over the moneyed gathering. Avoiding her friends' curious gazes, Harriet led him to a chair in a quiet alcove at the very back of the room. 'I'll get you a drink.'

She didn't need to ask what. It was past six at night which meant no more of the dark, bitter coffee he favoured; instead he'd settle for ice-cold water. No alcohol, not unless entertaining and even then he rarely drank more than one glass. She knew his habits better than she knew her own. She walked quickly into the kitchen and pulled a bottle of sparkling water from the fridge, pouring it into a glass and adding ice and lemon.

Any hope that Deangelo would be on the back foot in Harriet's own space disappeared as soon as she walked back into the office. He sat at perfect ease, his penetrating gaze raking sharply over every object, person and detail in the room, assessing and adding and coming to goodness knew what conclusion. Harriet had never been able to read him. She set the water down in front of him and leaned against the desk opposite. 'Welcome to the Happy Ever After Agency.'

Slowly his gaze returned to meet hers. 'This is a nice house. Yours?'

'No, it belongs to Alex—Alexandra Davenport?' She looked down the room until she located Alex. 'There, by the fireplace. She was your head of media.'

His eyebrows drew together. 'You set up a company with another Aion employee?'

'Three, actually.' Harriet's incurable honesty had her babbling answers to questions he hadn't even asked. 'Emilia Clayton, who headed up events, and Amber Blakeley, who was your client concierge manager.'

For a moment Harriet thought she saw incredulity cross his face, but when she checked again his expression was shuttered as usual. 'You didn't earn enough at Aion?'

'It wasn't about money.'

'Everything's about money,' he said flatly.

'We all earned far more at Aion than we will earn here for several years; maybe we'll never make what we made there. But we all wanted to try to own our own destinies.'

He nodded slowly. 'I can respect that, I suppose, even if I think the risk foolish.'

'You set up your own business.'

His expression closed down even further, just like it always did when she inadvertently touched on anything personal. 'But I had nothing to lose. You had security, a good salary, a good pension. What do you have to gain from this freedom?'

'A family. The four of us, we're like a family.' Harriet snapped her mouth shut. Why on earth had she said that?

Luckily he didn't press it any further. Why would he—what did family have to do with business? 'Tell me, Harriet. What's your price?'

Three years, three long years, she had spent every working hour with this man and not once had he looked at her this way, so intently, as if he could see right into the beating heart of her. She swallowed, fingers itching to grab one of the flutes of champagne Amber was offering round and down it to try and cope with the magnetic focus of Deangelo Santos's full attention.

What was wrong with her? She'd never felt so wrong-footed, so unsure of herself around him before. But then she'd never been quite so aware of him. Never allowed herself to notice how his shirt strained across the broad planes of his shoulders, the barrel of his chest, how physically imposing he was. How magnificent. Her stomach dropped. *Get a grip.* Straightening, Harriet sat up as tall as she could, trying to exude authority and wishing she wasn't perched on a desk. This was her business, her office, her home, after all. She was in charge here.

'I can't help you, I'm afraid. There is too much for me to do here. But I could spend some time with Jenny and help train her in how you like things? Or we do have some excellent temps already signed up. Would you like me to find you someone suitable while HR recruits someone permanent?'

She mentally ran through the CVs she had already received. Deangelo needed a certain type of temp. Someone strong enough to cope with long hours, no thanks or gratitude and brusque interactions, but also someone calm enough to deal with abrupt volte-faces, exceedingly high standards and comfortable working with extremely privileged information. Someone prepared to travel. And, most importantly, someone who wouldn't develop a crush on the very rich, very masculine man lounging opposite her. That was why Jenny had seemed the ideal candidate—experienced and newly married. No rustling, she added to her mental list—whatever that might mean. And no jumping. Maybe she could test for both at interview.

Deangelo leaned forward, his penetrating gaze still fixed firmly on her. 'I want you to come back.'

Heat suffused her cheeks. 'That's very flattering…'

'I have no interest in flattering you.' That was her told. 'It's a fact. I have an extremely important trip coming up and I need everything to run seamlessly. I don't have time to train someone new or worry about details.'

'The trip to Rio?' She couldn't stop curiosity creeping into her voice. Harriet had no idea why Deangelo had turned his attention to buying a chain of hotels an ocean away. He was from Brazil, but had left at the age of eighteen to take up a scholarship to Cambridge and, as far as she knew, hadn't been back in the intervening twelve years. 'The paperwork was sorted before I left, the jet already notified of your timings, all that was left to do was book the hotel and…'

'I need you to accompany me.' He cut her off ruthlessly. 'All I ask is a month of your time. Then you are free to do whatever you would like.'

Harriet managed to bite back a retort that it was very kind of him. If they could start to supply temps to Aion then that would be a huge coup, exactly the kind of contract that would propel them straight into the top league. But could she really take off when she'd just started up her new business—and, more importantly, did she want to take a step back, even for just a month?

'Why me?'

'This assignment is very—' he paused '—unusual.'

The curiosity she was trying to keep at bay flared. 'Unusual?'

'I need someone I can trust. This is not simply a matter of accompanying me as my PA.'

'Then…' But before she could formulate the question her phone rang. Pulling it out to silence the jaunty tune, she caught sight of the name of the caller, her heart stopping as it flashed on the screen: her father's care home. 'I'm sorry; I really need to take this.'

She barely registered the surprise on Deangelo's face—he probably hadn't been asked to wait once in the ten years since he'd set up Aion as an undergraduate—getting to her feet and walking out of the office and into the mercifully empty kitchen. 'Hello? Harriet Fairchild.'

Numbness consumed her as she listened to the home manager explain that there had been another incident, another fall, that her father's physical health was beginning to deteriorate along with the disease destroying his brain. Blinking back tears, Harriet tried to concentrate as the manager calmly took her through the options for stepping up his care. It was so unfair! So wrong that this should happen to her brave, strong, funny dad, who had cared for her after her mother's death, after already raising her half-sisters alone before that. He'd deserved the most relaxing of retirements, the travels he'd never had a chance to go on, the opportunity to play golf and drink fine wine and read all the books he had planned to get around to. Harriet had never cared that he was older than her friends' fathers, that people often mistook him for her grandfather. He was her wonderful, loving father and she'd do anything for him.

But the truth was she had done all she could; now he needed her the most she had no idea how not to fail him. She'd only got enough for six months' fees as it was. The extras the manager was detailing were bound to be way beyond her reach.

'Yes,' she said at last. 'I understand. Of course. If you could send me a forecast of how much extra you think the enhanced care will cost I would be very grateful.' On autopilot she thanked the manager for the home's quick response and promised to be there in time for the doctor's visit in the morning. As she finished the call Harriet stood still for a moment, blinking rapidly to stop the threatened tears, trying to get her face back to cool and professional.

But it was hard to turn her hostess persona back on, not to think about how much this new level of care would cost. Hard not to panic when even six months no longer seemed possible. She could try her sisters again, see if this time they would help out with the cost. Beg them if need be.

They were her last hope. And she knew that meant that she had no hope. 'Damn,' she whispered, the tears this time refusing to be kept away, no matter how she swallowed and blinked.

'Why are you crying?'

How had she not heard Deangelo creep up behind her? Harriet half jumped, swiping her eyes swiftly. 'I'm not,' she lied.

Before she had a chance to compose herself properly, Deangelo had taken hold of her elbow and marched her through the galley kitchen and into the room beyond. The kitchen had been purposely made a contrast to their calm public space, the walls of the narrow room a bright, warm pink, polka-dotted crockery in the same colour on the white-painted dresser. It opened out into a bright glass-roofed conservatory, furnished with a red velvet sofa and chairs and a round table set with four dining chairs. It wasn't a huge space for four grown women to cook, eat and relax in but so far it had done very well. Deangelo deposited her on the sofa before sauntering to the fridge, returning with a large glass of white wine.

'Drink this,' he commented as he handed it over.

'That's Alexandra's; she's the only one with any palate between us.' And the only one happy to spend her hard-earned cash on luxuries like expensive wines and luxury make-up brands.

'Why were you crying?' Deangelo asked again, small talk and niceties dismissed now the tears had stopped.

'It's nothing,' she said, desperate to get the conversation back on track, the thought of the commission from the Aion millions slipping away filling her with panic. 'I'm sorry; this is so unprofessional. Let's go back to the office and begin again. You said this was an unusual assignment?'

'Is it your father?'

Harriet stared. 'My father?'

'He's in a home, no?' The brusque voice was gentle, Deangelo's usually subtle accent stronger, as if the effort cost him.

'I...yes. How did you know?'

'Harriet, you worked less than six feet away from me for a long time; the door is not soundproof.'

Oh. God. She had always thought him oblivious. Did that mean he had heard every tear-filled begging phone call to her sisters, every long conversation with the healthcare professionals? 'I'm sorry. I always made the time up.'

'Harriet, your professionalism was never in doubt.'

'No.' She closed her eyes for a brief moment, rallying herself. 'My dad has dementia,' she said, the hated words sticking on her tongue. 'He needs specialist care and just before I came to work for you I had to make the difficult decision to put him in a home. I sold his flat to fund it, saved all I could, contributed my own money, but that kind of care is just so expensive and I'm almost out of money, which means I'm going to have to find somewhere a lot cheaper. The problem is he's so settled there. It's like he has a new family. He doesn't ever recognise me any more but he knows his care workers,' she finished sadly.

'And yet you left your job? Why not ask me for a pay rise?'

She couldn't help laughing at that. 'There's no way, even if you doubled my salary, that I could afford to keep him there, not even if I slept in the office and lived on noodles. In a way, knowing there is nothing I could do made my decision to leave a little easier.' The only tiny positive in all the darkness.

'I'll make things even easier. Come with me to Rio and I'll pay for your father's care for as long as he needs it. Do we have a deal?'

'I…' Harriet put the wine glass down carefully, aware she was shaking, hope and grief and adrenaline combining. 'Deangelo, that's very generous.'

'Not at all. You need money and I have plenty.'

'This could be thousands of pounds, tens of thousands.'

But he shrugged as if the vast sums were insignificant. Which for him, she supposed, they were. 'So do we have a deal?'

Yes, her heart cried, but she couldn't agree, not just like that, not without knowing more. 'Just how unusual is this job?'

For one tiny moment Deangelo's gaze shifted, and foreboding stole over her as he spoke.

'I need you to pretend to be my wife. Now, do we have a deal or not?'

CHAPTER THREE

ORDER WAS RESTORED, for now at least. Harriet was back in her rightful place, at her desk, her little cactus by her screen.

Life was back to normal.

Almost…

Deangelo glanced through the open office door to the foyer where Harriet hummed as she typed. On the surface she was her usual efficient self, but something was different and Deangelo couldn't quite put his finger on what it was. Aside from the humming.

She had a sweet, tuneful voice. He'd never realised that before. But then again, she had never sung in front of him before. Maybe that was what was different. Harriet was perfectly respectful, but she was acting more like his equal, business owner to business owner rather than his diffident PA.

The new confidence suited her, added a glow to her usually pale cheeks and a spring to her step. A step now headed towards him, tablet in hand.

'I just want to check the final timings with you before I head home to pack.' Harriet glanced down at the itinerary she had been adjusting for the last two weeks. 'I can't believe we fly tomorrow. I've never been to South America. Are you looking forward to going home?'

Deangelo frowned. 'Home? London is my home.' He'd created his home, carved it out of grit and stubbornness and flashes of brilliance—or desperation.

'Yes, now, but you grew up in Rio, didn't you?' Her blue, long-lash-fringed eyes were alight with curiosity. 'You must have family and friends there, people you want to catch up with.'

Deangelo had no idea how to answer. His past was a closed book and that was exactly how he wanted it to be. He didn't court publicity, invite questions or disclose any personal details to anyone and there were very good reasons for that. He wasn't ashamed of his rags-to-riches story, or of his climb out of the Rio *favela* to a penthouse on the South Bank. No, it was the other side of his life story he was ashamed of. The side he had taken for granted until it had been ripped away from him. The spoilt boy who had lived in luxury, utterly ignorant of the poverty just feet away from his air-conditioned life.

'We're not there for family.'

Only that wasn't true, was it? His return was all about family. The family that had denied him. The family who had turned their back even as he had swallowed his pride and begged.

'I've been reading up on the city and it sounds incredible; I can't wait to explore a little. Surely there will be time for some sightseeing. Revisiting old haunts?' she pressed.

Haunts was the word. Anywhere he visited in the city

would be crawling with ghosts and the kind of memories he had locked away years ago. Deangelo stared out of the window, mouth compressed. Going back was a risk, he knew that. He also knew it might finally set him free. If he dared to reach for it. Funny, he usually thrived on taking risks, but this freedom from the past seemed like a step too far.

'I lost touch with my friends long ago,' he said stiffly. 'I will try and make time to see my aunt, my cousins. If possible.' But it was unlikely. He hadn't even told them he was returning. He knew his aunt wouldn't approve of what he planned to do. He couldn't bear to see disappointment in eyes so similar to his mother's.

Besides, Harriet didn't need to know about his aunt or his cousins, or the work they did for him, work he managed away from the office, away from his PA. Nor did she need to know about the low thrum in his veins, the tingling in his nerves, at the thought of Rio. England was the place where he had reinvented himself, London the city he had conquered, but there was a tinge of grey in his life—grey buildings, grey weather and a grey formality. It suited him, but part of him, the impulsive, hopeful part of him, a part he kept well and truly squashed down, would always hanker for the vibrancy of his childhood home, the colours and the smells and the music. The ability to turn any gathering into a party.

Enough. Deangelo pushed the past back into the past, where it belonged. 'So the itinerary is finalised at last?'

A swift wrinkle between her eyes showed that Harriet had noted the abrupt subject change, but she didn't comment, merely placing her tablet on his desk, the timetable displayed on the screen.

'Yes. You wanted to arrive in the late afternoon so we leave Heathrow early tomorrow morning. A car will meet us on the airfield and it's booked to take us straight to the hotel and your first meeting with the Caetanos is scheduled for the following day. I can't believe how much chopping and changing they've done. I wouldn't be surprised if we get another three rearrangements between now and then.' She didn't add anything else but Deangelo knew she was confused by his acquiescence to the Caetanos' ever-changing schedule when normally such capriciousness would make him walk away.

She placed one delicate fingertip on the screen. 'Okay, hotel. I changed the booking as you requested. I guess it makes sense to stay in the hotel you're buying into but, I have to warn you, it's not up to your usual requirements.' She swiped and a picture of a huge white building studded with balconies and overlooking a golden sweep of sand filled the screen. 'Here you are, The Caetano Palace. As you can see, the position is great, although the hotel is apparently a faded version of its former grandeur; the reviews are less than enthusiastic. I've done some digging on the Caetanos—they're like something out of a soap opera, an old Brazilian family, practically aristocracy. Until around twenty years ago one man, Augusto, controlled the whole business: all the hotels, investments, the lot.' She pressed on a link and the screen changed, Deangelo's chest tightening painfully as he looked down at the photo displayed there. A man in late middle age. Upright, silver-haired, a shrewd look in the laughing eyes.

Augusto Caetano had controlled the company until twenty years ago this very week, the date engraved on what remained of Deangelo's heart. He stayed silent, the old toxic mixture of grief and anger bubbling inside. Grief for the life he hadn't appreciated until it was gone. Not the money, but the safety, the family he had taken for granted. And anger that the safety had been nothing but an illusion. That the man on the screen hadn't cared enough, not when it counted.

'As you have arranged, we're meeting his heirs, the current owners. There are two sons and one daughter, Isabela,' Harriet continued. 'Rumour has it that the business was all they managed to inherit; none of them have the old man's brains. They expanded quickly into luxury island resorts. They aren't popular with the locals or environmentalists from what I can tell. There are claims of bribery and extortion, and complaints of poverty wages for the locals who work at the exclusive resorts, along with some pretty worrying environmental infractions. All this has cost an absolute fortune and so they've been allowing investment by outsiders in order to continue with their spending spree and to keep up their lavish lifestyles.' Harriet's forehead crinkled. 'It doesn't sound like a very good investment, not financially or reputationally.'

'Investment? No. Takeover? Yes.'

'Takeover?' Her eyebrows arched with surprise. 'But the contracts only specify two per cent.'

'When have you known me to bother about two per

cent of anything? Fly across the world for something so insignificant? No, Harriet, this is no investment. The Caetanos have been careless. Not only did they sell off a share of the business overall, they've each been chipping away at their own bits, selling a little here and a little there independently. The result? None of them know how much in total has been handed over to outsiders.'

'But you do.' It wasn't a question. He answered it anyway.

'Forty-nine per cent. And even if they knew it was so much, they would assume the majority was held by hundreds of investors all over Brazil and South America, that they can carry on as majority owners unchallenged. Their assumptions would be very wrong. That forty-nine per cent is currently owned by Aion subsidiary companies. Oh, the trail is clear enough, if they had ever bothered to look. I have done nothing illegal, nothing shady. But here we are. They are ready and willing to woo me, not knowing that if they convince me to invest this week, I will hold the controlling stake.' Deangelo's chest tightened in anticipation.

'It seems like a lot of effort for a chain of failing hotels. I mean, yes, the buildings are gorgeous old world creations, but I've been on the review sites and they need a lot of updating. And the islands are incredible, but they're riddled with corruption and bad feeling. If you're planning to own your own hotels wouldn't you be better off starting from scratch?'

'It's not about the hotels, Harriet. It's about justice.'

Justice and fulfilling the promise he'd made to his mother.

Without quite meaning to, he reached up and traced the line of his scar as it bisected his cheek, running his finger along the thin line that ran from forehead to chin. He would make them pay, every one of them, and wipe the Caetano name from the city. No price was too high to pay for that. Abruptly, he changed the subject. 'Anything else?'

'Yes, at least…' She paused. 'It's just when you hired me it was because…' She paused again. Harriet wasn't usually chatty, nor had Deangelo ever seen her lost for words.

He tried to hide his amusement at her uncustomary colour and the flustered way she was wringing her hands. 'Because I need you to pose as my wife?'

'Yes. That.' Her colour heightened even more. 'At least, as Marcos Santos's wife. That was the name you wanted me to book the room in?'

'It's still me, I'm afraid,' he said drily. 'Marcos is my middle name.'

As was Deangelo. Luciano, his first name, he'd left behind him in Brazil. Only his father's family had ever used that name anyway; to his mother he had always been Deangelo. Her angel.

'Right. I'm still not clear. Why the name change?'

'Think, Harriet. I have managed to stay out of the press, but this way I can be sure the Caetanos have no idea who I am. If they think Aion are interested in their hotels the price will inflate, but Marcos Santos, CEO of a small tech firm, won't raise any suspicion.' Deangelo clenched his hands into fists. In a way he would have preferred suspicion. Preferred them to remember his middle names. To see him and instantly know who he was. But they had always ignored him. Thought him beneath them. Denied his very existence and claim to kinship. Why, sixteen years after their last encounter, would they suddenly remember his mother's surname, his own full name? Recognise the skinny boy in the man he had become?

Well, the Caetanos would remember. Remember and rue the day they had disowned him and disinherited his mother. He'd make damn sure of that.

Harriet still looked unconvinced. 'The tech firm is one of your subsidiaries, I suppose? Okay, I concede the name change, but I don't understand why you need a wife.'

'To make the meeting seem more like a social gathering, to put them off guard.'

'Right.' She picked up her tablet, her hair falling across her face, a rose gold cloud. 'I hope you don't mind me saying that this whole plan seems utterly insane.'

'You can say whatever you like, as long as you perform your part properly. Just remember we're on our honeymoon and everything will be fine.'

Harriet was already at the door, but as he spoke she stopped and pivoted, eyebrows arched. 'I'm sorry. For a moment I thought you said *honeymoon*.'

'I did. It's the perfect cover. As far as the Caetanos are concerned we are in Rio for our honeymoon and the investment talks are just a side project. I'm ensuring they won't be tempted to look further. I've covered my tracks well, but I'm more comfortable with an extra layer of safeguarding.' Deangelo wasn't sure what the incredulous look on Harriet's face meant, but it didn't seem wholly positive. 'You already agreed to pose as my wife,' he added. 'I'm not asking you to do anything we haven't discussed.'

'*Honeymoon?*'

Surely he'd been quite clear. 'Yes.'

'But—' she gestured wildly, the most exasperated gesture he had ever seen from the usually cool and contained Harriet '—a honeymooning couple is quite, *quite* different to a married couple, you must see that. If we'd been married for ten years or even two, then some kind of coolness, or lack of physical affection wouldn't be noticed. But people expect honeymooners to be, you know, *honeymoony*.'

'Honeymoony?' Was that even a word?

'Yes!'

Deangelo stared at his PA, who seemed uncharacteristically agitated. Her cheeks were flushed a delicate tinge of pink, her lips full and red, her blue eyes brighter. Indignation and embarrassment had stripped her of her professional air and it was as if a veil had been lifted, the full force of her personality shining through, turning conventional prettiness into something deeper and more vibrant.

Something—someone—infinitely more dangerous.

Harriet swallowed and, fascinated, he watched her throat move. When she spoke her voice croaked. 'Does it have to be a honeymoon? It's so intimate. Exposing.'

Intimate. Exposing. Was it getting hot in the office? Deangelo pulled at his collar. 'We're not going to be spending the whole two weeks in Rio with the Caetanos, just the initial meeting when they try and convince me that they're not conning me to invest in a failing business, and the shareholders' meeting a fortnight after. The honeymoon is just a cover, not a role-play. I am recently wealthy, from the wrong side of the tracks, desperate to ally myself with the right people and with my eye firmly off the ball thanks to my new bride. It's not complicated.'

'Even so…' She paused again, biting her lip. 'A honeymoon is really tricky to pull off. If we act just like we usually do then no one will believe that we're newlyweds for more than a minute. You need to convince anyone looking at us that you're mad about me and I need to do the same. Just where people can see us,' she added hurriedly. 'Obviously.'

Deangelo had never been mad about anyone in his life. Never even been tempted to allow a relationship to progress beyond mild desire and liking. But he'd insisted on having Harriet with him for exactly this kind of feedback: not just because he trusted her, but because he also respected her opinion.

'Obviously,' he echoed. 'And how do you propose we convince people we're mad about each other?' The words felt strange on his tongue, heavy and sensuous, and as he spoke them he had a sudden vision of Harriet smiling at him, her hand in his, her lush body warm against him, and with that vision a sense that he was stepping over a line and into the unknown. That the walls around him suddenly didn't feel quite as solid as they always had. He breathed in deep and slow, willing the walls to solidify.

'Well…' She walked back into the office, placing her tablet onto his desk. Deangelo stilled, very aware of her wild strawberry scent, of the curve of her hips, the grace in her long limbs. 'I've not actually been on a honeymoon, but I suppose it's about showing that you're together, standing a little closer than normal, touching each other's hands or arms.' He watched her hand as it fluttered close to his shoulder before jerking firmly away, but he could feel a warm sensation on the tip of his shoulder blade, as if her fingertips rested there.

He straightened, trying to dislodge the ghostly caress. 'Is that how you behave when you're in love?' He both did and didn't want to know the answer to that question.

'I… I've never actually been in love. I've dated,' she added, chin tilted and eyes bright. 'Obviously. But this isn't about me; it's about what other people do and what they'll expect. Like always looking into each other's eyes. Pet names…'

'Pet names?'

'Yes, you know, like darling or honey or something…'

'In Brazil,' he said, 'we would say *querida, minha amada, me amor.*'

Where had that come from? He never spoke Portuguese any more. Thanks to the private international school he'd attended for his first ten years he'd grown up bilingual, unusual in Brazil, and as soon as he had moved to the UK he'd worked hard to speak, think and even dream in the language of his adopted country. When he could control his dreams that was.

So why was it so easy to imagine saying such words to Harriet?

'Yes,' she said a little unsteadily, stepping back. 'That's the kind of thing. So you see why it would be easier to forget about the whole honeymoon thing.'

'I disagree, *querida.'* Again the endearment slipped out with ease. 'I'm sure we can manage, if we try.'

'Plus—' another step back '—we haven't factored in a honeymoon wardrobe. I own nothing that says bride or rich husband—and I would be surprised if you have a single item suitable for a beach holiday. We're much better sticking to what I assumed was the original script, a wife accompanying her husband on a business trip and dressing accordingly.'

'What do you need?'

'Need?'

'For a honeymoon?'

'Dresses and swimsuits and nice shoes. I don't know, clothes that make me feel special. Sexy.' She bit her lip on the last word as if wanting to recall it, but it hung in the air, thickening it, until Deangelo could hardly breathe.

'Okay then. Take the rest of the afternoon and buy whatever you need. You still have your company card?' Harriet nodded mutely. 'I'll meet you once I've finished here. We can put in some practice at being newlyweds. Book us in somewhere appropriate. That will be all.'

He didn't allow himself to look up until Harriet had finally left the room, but he could feel her wide blue eyes fixed disbelievingly on him, her scent lingering along with the echoes of that word. *Sexy.* Harriet was bright, incisive, tactful. She was tall and curvy and too demure. She hid her attractiveness behind shapeless clothes and her glorious hair spent most of its life tied up in a tight bun but Deangelo had always seen—seen and resolutely ignored—her potential for real beauty. He had never considered her sexy, though, but now the thought was in his head there was no recalling it. And tonight they would be getting to know each other as newlyweds should.

Only this was all business, and the blood rushing around his body, the thrum of his pulse beating through every pressure point, needed to remember that. Attraction was one thing, acting on it quite another. Not that he had any intention of acting on anything. Fake honeymoon or no fake honeymoon.

CHAPTER FOUR

'THIS WASN'T WHAT I was expecting.' Deangelo turned to the large mirror and grimaced. 'I look ridiculous.'

Harriet suppressed a grin. 'Come on, you weren't born in a suit. You must have worn shorts when you were growing up.'

'Nothing this lurid.'

The shorts were bright, streaks of pinks and oranges and yellows edged with navy. They looked surprisingly good. Deangelo was in fine shape but he wasn't lean; his muscles gave him breadth, his strength apparent in every move. With an effort Harriet pulled her gaze away from the toned brown legs. Thank goodness he was wearing a T-shirt. She couldn't have coped with a bare torso. Which just went to show how crazy this whole honeymoon idea was. Hopefully Deangelo would come to his senses and realise that.

'Pierre is the most sought after personal shopper in London. Amber had to pull in every favour she had to get this appointment as I didn't think you'd want me to use your name. If he says this is what's hot in Brazil right now then you need to trust him.'

The look he gave her from underneath lowered brows promised retribution. 'When I said we would meet to practice being comfortable with each other, I did not mean shopping.'

Harriet was well aware of that. Completely aware that he had expected her to book some exclusive restaurant so that they could sit in an uncomfortable silence and poke at their food. The thought made her stomach twist in panic. Far better to be busy while they sorted out the parameters of what to say and how to be. 'I realised when I was sorting out my clothes for the trip earlier that you could do with a refresh as well.'

'I have clothes.'

She folded her arms. 'Deangelo. You travel, a lot. You must notice that people on holiday do not wear wool suits.'

He shrugged. 'I don't take holidays.'

'No. You don't. But you are claiming to. That means you should be wearing shorts and loose shirts or T-shirts, maybe a couple of light suits but not that…' She waved her hand at his perfectly tailored suit hanging in the dressing room behind him. 'I am completely kitted out now; you need to match.'

Harriet's initial plan to buy just a couple of dresses had been dismissed by Amber, who had accompanied her into Sloane Square and the high-end shops along the King's Road. 'You need to feel the part completely,' her friend had said and, although Harriet had stopped short of the whole new wardrobe Amber had urged on her, she had bought enough clothes for the entire two weeks with cosmetics, accessories and shoes to match, and designer luggage to pack it all in. It was all waiting for her back at the townhouse; tonight she was defiantly wearing one of her own long skirts and baggy blouses, despite Amber trying to persuade her to slip on one of the pretty new dresses for the evening.

She felt safer in her own clothes. More confident, which, after those peculiar moments in Deangelo's office when she hadn't been able to catch her breath, when her chest had seemed to tighten till she could barely speak, her stomach dissolved and her cheeks caught fire, was important. If the mere discussion of pet names and physical closeness could discombobulate her in such a way, what would actually acting as a lover be like? Tonight was supposed to be a practice for the next two weeks and she had agreed to that, but it would be on her own terms. And she would be her own person. Straight, boring Harriet in her boring clothes. It was safer that way.

Hopefully the shopping trip that preceded the practice would be the cure she needed, the magic tonic to restore her to her normal professional self. Surely nobody could be attractive in lurid board shorts and a matching pink tee, no matter how he was built? She allowed herself another peek at Deangelo and stifled a sigh. He had to be the exception that proved the rule. Maybe it was the way the board shorts clung to strong thighs, the T-shirt moulded itself to impressive chest and stomach muscles.

'Stop complaining. This whole escapade was your idea; I'm just trying to make it work.' There, no nonsense and slightly bossy. The perfect PA tone. Boundaries firmly set.

She pretended not to see the gleam in his amber eyes. 'Harriet, you could have ordered me these clothes online. Are you just trying to put the reason for this evening off?'

'Not at all,' she said as airily as she could manage. 'I'm completely prepared for Project Rio.' Giving the next fortnight a codename made it all seem a little easier.

'Project Rio?' But anything else he was planning to say was curtailed by the arrival of Pierre, wheeling a rail which held several pairs of light trousers and a dazzling array of brightly coloured shirts. Harriet sat on the plush sofa designated for waiting friends and family while Deangelo was ushered back into the thickly carpeted and mirrored dressing room. A reprieve. She'd better make the most of it.

Pierre had wheeled all the clothes into the privacy of the dressing room and Harriet suspected she had a lengthy wait in front of her. Taking a sip of the champagne she'd been presented with, and popping one of the delicious dark chocolate truffles into her mouth, she reopened the book she'd started earlier during the suit fittings. But for once the words didn't grab her, absorb her. Instead, every time the hero spoke she saw Deangelo, heard the way his voice had turned to molten honey as he called her *querida*.

Harriet sat back, the book half-closed in her hands. Alexandra was right when she teased her for living through books instead of in the real world. Why wouldn't she? In the books she read families were re-united and dreams came true and love conquered all. Sisters didn't stay away and leave all the burden on one small pair of shoulders, lovers didn't fade away, put off by too many cancelled dates and the reality of dating someone with caring responsibilities. She needed, craved the happy-ever-after she got from books, from her imagination. It was much safer than risking her happiness with someone else. Other people left, even when they didn't mean to. And not always physically or intentionally. Sometimes they just drifted away.

But what wasn't safe was casting her boss, no matter how inadvertently, in the role of hero. Deangelo's longest relationship she knew of had lasted three months—and he had been in Australia for half of that time. His proximity might make her body heat up, but she had to stay cool. She'd been doing so for three years; what difference would another two weeks make?

Suddenly restless, she jumped to her feet and walked to the door of the personal shopping suite, opening it to peer outside. The exclusive department store stayed open late to cater to its demanding customers, and to the tourists who came in to buy small gifts and marvel at the baroque elegance and the designer goods and prices. Her gaze fell on a couple, a few years older than her, flicking through jumpers. The woman pulled one out to hold against the man, desire clear on her face as she surveyed him, before leaning in for a long, lingering kiss. Harriet leaned against the door. Had she ever looked at anyone that way? Had anyone ever looked at her? Had she ever kissed anyone like that, been kissed like that, as if there was nobody else in the world?

The answer was a resounding negative. Nobody had ever treated her as if she was everything. She was safe and reliable—she'd had to be; her father's health had demanded it. But she wanted more. She just needed to be brave enough to step away from her books and find it. Maybe she could practice a little in Brazil, while she was busy being someone else. The kind of woman who owned bikinis and little dresses and whose new husband was mad about her. A taste of the world she was nearly ready to step into.

Harriet was uncharacteristically quiet as they exited the shop, the clothes Deangelo had picked left behind to be delivered straight to his apartment. His car was waiting for them outside and he directed it to take them back into Chelsea.

'You were right,' he said as the chauffeur pulled out into the lighter than usual evening traffic.

Harriet looked up, surprise widening her eyes. 'I was? Can I have that in writing?'

She smiled, but it seemed forced, not her usual grin, the smile that seemed to come from nowhere to light up her whole face. For the first time Deangelo couldn't help wondering if he had done the right thing. The idea of pretending he was on honeymoon had occurred several weeks ago. He knew his tracks were pretty well covered business-wise, and was as sure as he could be that the Caetanos wouldn't remember that Marcos was his middle name—if they ever spared him a single thought.

He doubted it; they'd never come looking for him, after all. But the scar was a problem. Bruno Caetano hadn't stayed around to see what damage he'd inflicted after lashing out at the just fourteen-year-old Deangelo, but the scar was the first thing anyone noticed about him, one of the reasons he preferred to stay in the shadows. He didn't want them to be sidetracked by it and start wondering…

Plus there was the family resemblance. Deangelo had enough of his mother in him to dilute the fierce hawklike Caetano genes, but he couldn't rely on the famously self-absorbed Caetanos not to notice his eyes, the shape of his jaw. He needed a decoy, a distraction—and another person seemed the best way. Someone who would automatically draw their attention. Who better than a bride, especially as the Caetanos wouldn't want the conversation to be too businesslike or for him to start asking any awkward questions that might reveal just how tangled their affairs really were?

But asking someone to step into the role of pretend wife meant allowing them unprecedented access to his life, to his past. Even if he concealed his relationship to the Caetanos, his real reason for the takeover, and stayed away from his mother's family and the projects they ran for him, he would still be returning to Rio de Janeiro for the first time in twelve years and that made him vulnerable. Plus, he wanted the whole affair to be as discreet as possible, his role in the Caetanos' downfall hidden. And the only person he trusted absolutely was Harriet.

But he was asking a lot of her. She had her own burdens, burdens he'd watched her carry uncomplainingly, with grace and courage. And one of the reasons she was perfect for the role was that she was as perennially alone as him. There was no jealous boyfriend to protest the charade. But that loneliness made her vulnerable. He had to be aware of that. Work hard to keep the professional distance between them, even as they pretended intimacy.

Good. Now to put his new resolve into action. Deangelo deliberately lightened his tone to something as near to playful as he could manage. 'You're right as in I did need new clothes. The kind of clothes Marco Santos might wear.' The kind of clothes he might have worn if he'd stayed in Brazil and made his fortune there.

'See, you should always listen to me; life is much simpler when you do.'

'It would be easier if you hadn't resigned.'

'True, but you could retain me as a consultant. A couple of hours of advice every week.'

'I might just do that.' Although he kept the light tone the idea appealed to him. Deangelo knew all too well that all relationships were transient, personal and business, but he wasn't ready yet to lose Harriet's quiet common sense. If she wasn't around to be his PA any longer then maybe some kind of consultant role would work.

'At an appropriate hourly rate of course.'

'Naturally. Now, unless you think I need a haircut or new socks or anything else, maybe we could get to the purpose of this evening.'

'Right, Project Rio.'

'Project Rio,' he confirmed. 'Pretending to be newlyweds.'

'Yes. So…er…how do you want to do this?' Her voice trailed off without specifying what *this* actually was.

'It might help if we find out a little more about each other,' Deangelo suggested.

'Or about our personas?' She turned to face him, eyes lit with enthusiasm. 'I mean, I'm not pretending to be married to Deangelo Santos, famously private Brazilian billionaire, CEO of Aion and workaholic, but Marcos Santos. Who is he? And who is he marrying? Not a boring woman of twenty-six whose idea of a fun weekend night is a new book and a clean pair of pyjamas.'

Harriet's words conjured up an irresistible vision of her in simple white pyjamas, curled up on a sofa in front of the fire, book in hand. It wasn't the sexiest vision he'd ever had, but Deangelo's whole body ached with a wish that his life could be so simple and perfect, that his evenings could be spent with something, someone, so uncomplicated and pure.

And that ache, that need, was dangerous. He'd trained himself not to need or want anything other than safety and security. Maybe her idea of being someone else entirely, not just in name, was a good one. A safe option.

'Okay, personas it is. Who is Harriet Santos?'

She sat back, eyes half-closed as she thought. 'How did we meet? Where did we get married?'

Deangelo already knew the answers to her questions, dropped into emails to the Caetanos when setting up the investment. 'We married at the weekend, in New York. We live there.'

Harriet's eyes flew open. 'But I don't know New York!'

'You've been there many times.'

'Yes! But I don't know it; how could I? We get a limousine straight from the steps of your private jet to the hotel. We always stay in some exclusive luxury hotel right in the financial district. We might get another limousine to a Michelin starred restaurant but otherwise you hold all meetings in the hotel. I could be anywhere. I've never actually walked around New York. There's no way I can act like I live there. What's wrong with London?'

'London is too close to the truth.'

She stilled in a way he knew all too well, a way that meant she was thinking furiously, her brain coming up with solution after solution. Her ability to think on her feet was one of the reasons he had employed her, despite her youth, barely in her twenties when she'd started at Aion. 'Okay. I work for a business contact of yours. We met when I was on a business trip with him in New York and you pursued me back to London. We've carried on a long-distance courtship, weekends in Paris and Rome and exclusive resorts where we barely set foot out of the bedroom.' Her cheeks reddened. 'Not that they need to know that explicitly, but we can infer it if they ask too many questions. I haven't had a chance to see New York yet; it's all been so whirlwind. We had a private ceremony at City Hall, but plan to have parties back in New York and London after our month-long honeymoon.'

'Good, that will work.'

'Great. What about you, *Marcos*? Why this investment?'

'Because I want to impress you. I'm not secure in my wealth. I grew up in São Paolo, lower middle class.

We got by, but now I have money I want to buy my way into the upper circles of my country, show my bride that I am someone.'

'And how much money does my new husband have?'

'A few million. He founded a tech firm which he's sold on so he's sitting on the profits. The newlyweds are very comfortable indeed.'

'But not in your league?'

'No. And although Marcos Santos probably is richer in real terms than the Caetanos it's not enough to wipe away his nouveau riche stain. Expect the Caetanos to be very condescending.'

'I can cope with condescending.' Harriet's mouth folded in a way that suggested she had first-hand experience.

'Good. Because we are easy to please and slow to take offence. Overwhelmed with our good luck.'

She nodded and as she did so the car drew up and the chauffeur got out to open her door. 'This isn't my house,' Harriet said in surprise as she exited the car and looked around.

'No.' He followed her out of the car. They were in a pretty tree-lined street, the mighty River Thames just visible in the distance. 'We are about fifteen minutes' walk from your home. I will accompany you there. Maybe we could have a drink on the way. I'll see you back here in an hour,' he told his chauffeur. It wasn't often he walked. Ran, yes. But that was exercise, done for health and to ready his brain for the day ahead. Just to walk, for the sake of the air and the view, with no discernible purpose? He couldn't remember the last time he had done that.

Nor could Harriet, judging by the puzzled look on her face as he turned towards the river. It was a clear spring night, a chill still hanging in the air, stars bright in the purple sky. 'Only two months until the summer equinox,' shc said. 'I love this time of year, every day a little more light, a promise of warmth.'

'April showers, wind…'

'It just means we appreciate summer more.'

'I may have lived here for over a third of my life, but I still can't consider what you call summer to *be* summer. A few weeks of humidity and everything coming to a standstill because there's no air conditioning isn't a real summer.'

'That's the true joy of a British summer. You have to plan for rain and cold, hope you get humidity and warmth, but occasionally the skies clear and everything is perfect. Like life, I suppose.' They reached the end of the road, the river path before them, and Deangelo turned left towards Harriet's road, she in step beside him. 'So, it's not that I don't appreciate this starlit walk,' she added. 'But it would have been a lot quicker to just drop me off.'

'But Project Rio isn't finished yet.' Business, just business, he told himself as his heart began to thump. He stopped and held out his hand in silent invitation. Harriet's eyes flew to his. He expected to see uncertainty, distaste, maybe even fear, but instead curiosity gleamed in their blue depths.

'Is this the physical proximity and pet names part of the pretence?'

'That's the one. *Querida.*' He added the endearment as an afterthought, the word thick on his tongue.

'*Querida* sounds so much more romantic than darling or honey.' She made no move to take his hand. 'Which do you prefer?'

Deangelo shrugged. 'Whichever is easiest?'

Twisting her hands together, she looked up at the sky. 'I loved acting at school, wanted to take it further at one point but my dad, well, you know. Anyway, when I was sixteen I was in a play and I had to kiss this boy. I didn't fancy him at all, and he certainly didn't fancy me, that was very clear. It made me realise just what acting meant, the physicality of it. Being put in situations you might not choose. How exposing the business was.'

Of course she didn't want to touch him, not even in pretence. He was monstrous, inside and out. He curled his other hand into a fist, the urge to touch his scar, that physical reminder of his mental wounds, strong.

'But on the night itself it was fine. Somehow we managed this amazing chemistry on stage, despite never interacting off it. And then I realised that acting made you take risks, go places, inhabit feelings you would maybe shy away from. It's a long time since I've done that.' And with that she slipped her hand into his.

Her hand was smooth and cool and fitted into his as if it were meant to be there. Deangelo inhaled. This was acting; she was right. A chance to be someone else for a moment out of time. He started walking again and she fell into step beside him, their conjoined hands between them, an anchor and a barrier. Deangelo was preternaturally aware of her every movement, the swing of her step, the way her hair moved, the swish of her skirt around her ankles. Harriet always dressed like she wanted to fade into the furniture, but the shapeless beige and grey she favoured just set off her hair, her porcelain skin, moving with her body, not concealing it.

Deangelo's pulse sped, beating faster and faster. He wasn't supposed to be thinking of her body, but it was impossible not to when she was near enough to feel her warmth, smell her fresh strawberry scent. What had he been thinking about? Harriet was right. A honeymooning couple was a ridiculous idea—how could they pull it off for even five seconds? How could he remember who he was and what he needed to do with her so close, the boundaries they so carefully maintained blurred?

'This is my street. You don't need to see me to my door.'

'Fine.' He hadn't noticed that they had reached the road. 'So I'll see you at the airport. A car will come for you at six tomorrow morning.'

'Good. Thanks.'

He nodded brusquely and yet he was exquisitely aware that her hand was still in his. That she had turned towards him, her face tilted towards his, and that same glint of curiosity and adventure danced in her eyes.

'I think,' she said in a low voice, her gaze still fixed on his, 'that you're not really a *babe* or a *hun*, or even a *darling*. *Sweetheart* doesn't work; you're more savoury than sweet. I think I'll keep it simple. How does *love* sound?'

How did it sound? Foreign. Alien. Nobody had spoken a single word of love to him since his mother had died. His aunt had been affectionate in a no-nonsense way, various girlfriends had been romantic when they'd felt it necessary, but love? No. And he preferred it that way. Usually.

Somehow he managed to speak. 'That will be fine.'

Understanding warmed her eyes. 'Okay, love. In that case I'll see you in the morning.' And she rose on her tiptoes and kissed him, a quick, sweet caress on his cheek. Deangelo froze as the warmth from the kiss spread through him at lightning speed and he caught her hand as she pulled away, so she turned to face him again.

'Thank you.' He leaned in only to return the brief kiss, to seal their unspoken contract, but instead of her smooth cheek his mouth found hers, warm and sweet and lush. He froze, every sound, every sensation fading except for her hand in his, her mouth under his. He needed to step back now, apologise, call an end to this whole crazy idea, but before he could move Harriet sighed and, leaning in, deepened the kiss, her free hand creeping up to his shoulder, his own resting on the curve of her waist. It was a sweet kiss, tentative, a millimetre space between their bodies apart from those touch points. The urge to deepen it further thrilled through him, the roaring of his blood drowning out all other sounds, wanting, needing to pull her against him, to feel her curves pressed close, to possess and learn her. But with the thought warning bells sounded loud and clear. He needed nobody, wanted nothing. It was safer. Necessary. He stepped back, releasing her, and instantly the evening chill hit him.

'There,' he said, trying not to notice the dazed look on her face, her sweetly swollen lips. 'I think we're prepared. I'll see you tomorrow.'

He turned without another word and walked away, fighting the urge to go back with every step. Revenge. That was what mattered. And nothing and no one was going to get in his way.

CHAPTER FIVE

'CAN I GET you anything else?'

The receptionist smiled brightly and Harriet summoned up all her courage, stepping closer to Deangelo and slipping her hand through his arm. *Think newlyweds*, she told herself as she leaned into him. *This is quite normal.* But the fizz zipping up her spine was far from normal. Nothing about this situation was normal.

Take her floral sundress, for instance. Not only was it bright and yellow—two words that hadn't described her clothes since she had hit her teens—but it was cut daringly low for a day dress, the pattern louder than she was comfortable with, her wedge sandals precipitously high.

At least Deangelo was also in unfamiliar clothes, his usual handmade suit replaced by chinos and a short-sleeved shirt in a bright blue that contrasted nicely with her yellow dress. He looked good casually dressed, more relaxed. Women still looked at him, not because he exuded wealth and power but because of his sheer attractiveness, the scar and muscle adding a dangerous vibe to his good looks.

No. That was not a road she was going down. Not

after the humiliation of last night. Could it have been only yesterday when she had lost herself in a kiss that was nothing but a pretence? Shame and embarrassment engulfed her. But as long as Deangelo didn't suspect the kiss had affected her she could keep her chin high and pretend the whole thing had never happened.

At least neither of them had alluded to it today. They were very much business as usual, the flight taken up with business for the first few hours before Harriet had retired to the smaller cabin, ostensibly to nap and read, in reality to lie on the narrow bed and relive every kiss and brief caress over and over until she'd had to have a Stern Word with herself.

'*Senhora...?*' the receptionist prompted her and, pulling herself together as much as was possible under the circumstances, Harriet looked up at Deangelo with her best imitation of a besotted gaze. She just hoped she didn't look ill instead.

'Thank you, but I think we have everything, don't you, my love?' and if there was an infinitesimal pause before the 'love' and if Deangelo tensed up at her touch just as Harriet tensed up touching him, she didn't think it was too bad an attempt at marital affection.

'*Sim, querida. Obrigado,*' he added to the receptionist, giving her the benefit of his most charming smile, one that was usually only unleashed when he was about to pull off a business coup. Which, Harriet supposed, he was.

'And can I make you dinner reservations for tonight? We have a very fine restaurant here or I could recommend somewhere?' The receptionist's smile widened even further, revealing brilliant white teeth in her perfectly made-up face, her glossy mane of dark hair more suited to a catwalk than a reception desk. But then again, Harriet was beginning to realise that beauty standards in Brazil were very high indeed. Even if she hadn't needed a new wardrobe to play her role as the new Mrs Santos, her sensible work clothes simply wouldn't have cut it here.

Deangelo turned to her, his smile warm and intimate. '*Querida*, what would you like? If you're tired we could always order room service?'

Did he have to make room service sound so very indecent? Harriet wanted to concentrate on the conversation but she was far too aware of the solid feel of Deangelo's arm under her hand, of his hip pressed close to hers, the way she could feel the rise and fall of his breath and how her own breath responded, her heart speeding up at the proximity. If only she didn't know how it felt to hold his hand in hers, how he tasted, decadent and dark and yet tinged with sweetness. Like a sinful dessert, wrong yet so very right.

'Room service sounds perfect. Is that everything? Great, then let's go.'

With an exhaled breath of relief Harriet pulled him away, not caring if the receptionist thought that Harriet was pulling her new husband away from the desk and up to their honeymoon suite with indecent haste.

It took a few minutes for the old lift to reach the top floor where their penthouse suite awaited them. The bellboy escorted them to the ornately gilded door and Harriet waited until Deangelo had tipped him before speaking, doing her best to sound amused rather than hurt. 'I'm not sure you're supposed to flinch when I touch you.'

On the one hand, if Deangelo flinched every time they were in touching distance, then she was in no danger of repeating yesterday's mistake. On the other, no woman wanted to make a man recoil in horror.

'I didn't flinch.'

'Okay. You didn't flinch, you reacted negatively.'

'Harriet, let me make one thing clear.' Harriet's stomach dropped at the low purr in Deangelo's voice and she took an involuntary step backwards, towards the door. 'My reaction was one of surprise, but it was in no way negative.'

'Fine.' Oh, my goodness, was that an actual squeak she'd just emitted? 'I mean, that will make things easier. If we can be positive about this, I mean.' She inhaled, a long deep breath designed to stop her babbling on as much as to try and settle her jangled nerves. 'Okay. I'll set up the office and unpack. Shall I unpack for you, too?' It wasn't one of her normal duties when they were abroad, but then usually they had separate suites.

She would have preferred separate suites this time—with several floors and acres of corridors between them. A safe space where she could hide with her book and her daydreams.

'I can manage, but thank you.'

'Great!' Another squeak, but at least this one was audible to human ears. 'I'll just check out the rest of the suite.'

It was all going to be fine, she reminded herself.

The kind of hotel suites Deangelo stayed in were bigger than most people's flats. Houses in some cases. She would have her own room and bathroom and office and he would be comfortably tucked up in his own bed and everything would be perfectly normal and she just needed to stop thinking about beds before she sent herself crazy…

Grabbing the new designer bag that cost more than her own entire wardrobe, Harriet took a look around the suite. The sitting room was opulent but dated, the heavy velvet curtains and soft furnishings and the bronzes and golds too heavy for the sunny, nature-heavy city she'd passed through, eagerly taking in every sight on the sun-drenched journey from the airport. The furniture was good quality but dark and chipped in places and as she looked around the signs of neglect were clear, from faded paintwork to a missing light bulb. Five-star on the outside, three in reality.

Frowning, she noted that the dining area was situated in an alcove off the sitting room and there was no sign of a separate study. That was going to be awkward; she needed to have some space away from Deangelo. He was so overpowering his presence took over every space. Hopefully there was a desk in her room…

She also didn't see any kind of hallway or corridor, just one door the opposite side to the alcove. She walked slowly to it, dread creeping over her as she turned the ornate glass handle, opening the door to see one huge bedroom. One huge bedroom, with one bathroom, dominated by a bed big enough to sleep an entire family. If, Harriet thought numbly, she was ever called upon to design a nineteenth century bordello, she would be able to draw on the room for inspiration. It featured a lot of red and gold velvet, the bed swathed in heavy curtains.

'Deangelo?' She tried to suppress the quiver in her voice. 'There's only one bedroom. Only one bed. I'm sorry, I should have made myself clearer when I booked. I'll call down to reception and get them to find us another suite.'

Deangelo stilled. *Dammit.* The last thing he needed was for this trip to slip out of his control in any way. He needed Harriet focused and on game and *he* needed to be focused on the end result as always—and that meant forgetting just how soft Harriet felt when she leaned into him, the way her hip tucked perfectly under his, the light touch of her hand on his forearm. And it certainly meant forgetting about the trusting way she'd accepted his kiss last night, the way she'd returned it, stoking it to a heat he hadn't dared contemplate. What would have happened if he hadn't broken it off? He'd not been able to banish the thought all through the sleepless night.

And that was a big problem. Thoughts and feelings that were nothing but distractions—worse, they were dangerous. Whoever had said that no man was an island was wrong. Every man and woman was exactly that and if they were sensible they stayed that way.

Striding to the door, Deangelo stepped into the oppressively decorated room, his gaze bouncing from gilt mirror to heavy chandelier to oil portrait before finally resting on the huge bed dominating the space. 'How many throw pillows do they think a person needs?' he asked, mentally totting them up and arriving at twelve.

Harriet folded her arms and glared at him, one foot tapping the floor. 'Never mind the pillows, what about the bed?'

He eyed it critically. 'I bet the mattress is soft.'

'Soft or not, there's only one. I didn't think to check. They offered us the best suite in the hotel and that usually means at least two bedrooms. I'm sorry. I'll phone down and see if I could get another room, but I can't order us a new suite or a second bedroom without alerting the kind of questions you need to avoid so either we tell them that you snore so loudly I need a different room or I'll sleep on the sofa.'

'Nonsense. I will sleep on the sofa.'

'No.' Her glare intensified. 'That's ridiculous. I work for you—and this was my mistake. There's no way I am allowing you to sleep anywhere but in that bed.'

'Harriet, I have slept in many places much less comfortable than that sofa, I assure you. Please don't think that I will allow any woman under my protection to not take the bed.' And with that an old memory came unbidden to his mind. He, snug in the one small bed whilst his mother curled up on a pallet on the floor. Shame engulfed him once again and he straightened. 'This conversation is over.'

She glared for one long second. 'Fine. You're the boss.'

'Yes,' he said silkily. 'I am.'

'In that case—' her smile was anything but conciliatory '—I'll leave you in peace. Please close the door behind you.'

To his surprise, Deangelo found himself in retreat for the first time in many years, the bedroom door closed firmly in his face.

He stood there for a second before shrugging and turning away from the firmly closed bedroom door. It was unlike Harriet to show her feelings so clearly, but he preferred annoyance to the dangerous spark that seemed to have ignited between them. Striding over to the curtained windows, he wrenched the heavy drapes aside, cursing the stupidity of people who cloaked such magnificent old windows in overly fancy fabrics. It was one of the many contradictions of Rio that the best views were often to be found in the poorest, most dangerous parts, the *favelas* clinging to the hillsides looking down at the city and sea beyond, but, Deangelo had to admit, this view of Copacabana Beach was gut-wrenchingly beautiful. Miles of golden sand, never-ending blue sea matched by never-ending blue skies. He found the window catch and flung it open, letting the sweet, salty air permeate the room. The air of home.

He was home.

The stone balcony looked as neglected as the rest of the hotel but, after testing it with his foot, Deangelo stepped out, gripping the wrought iron rail as unwanted, long-pushed-away feelings assailed him: nostalgia, grief, anger and a fierce pride at the beauty of his city. A city of contrasts, stunningly beautiful, unbelievably ugly, wealthy beyond belief and horrifically poor. Fun-loving and violent… Rio was all this and more. There was nowhere else like it.

Right now Rio was at its most beguiling. Beneath him, gorgeous people of both sexes sunbathed and paraded perfectly toned bodies shown off by the flimsiest of swimsuits. Children played football on one area of the beach, teens threw a volleyball right next to them, whilst people of all ages swam or waited, surfboard in hand, for the perfect wave. Once he'd been one of those footballing urchins, but never a surfer or a volleyball player and definitely not a beautiful beach boy with no thoughts beyond the sun and the sea. This Rio wasn't his. Could never have been. That was why he had had to leave, to reinvent himself, to lock the part of him that needed and wanted and hoped deep down. He'd thought the chains rusted and the key long lost, but last night, during the brief moments of that kiss, the chains had slackened and for a few beautiful seconds he had needed and wanted and hoped…

'It's beautiful.' Deangelo half turned at the soft voice to see Harriet on the neighbouring balcony gazing wistfully out at the view. 'I've never seen anything like this.'

'You've travelled all over the world.' He didn't mean to sound so brusque, but he also didn't want to get drawn into a talk about Rio, not when his defences were so unexpectedly lowered. He'd thought he'd be able to come here, wrapped in the layers of cynicism and blankness that had kept him safe for all these years, but the combination of revenge so tantalisingly in reach and his new vulnerability around Harriet were battering away at his defences. Made him realise how tired he was of always keeping everyone and anything other than business at arm's length. A curiously hollow feeling ached in his chest. Who knew what would motivate him once he'd achieved his vow, the years stretching ahead devoid of purpose. Making even more money no longer his driving force.

He didn't know how to do anything else, be anyone else.

Harriet stepped closer, her hand still on the stone wall, gaze directed out to the view. She was almost within touching distance; he could reach over the partition that separated them and cover her hand with his. But he wouldn't, no matter how much he wanted to.

'I have been all over the world, you're right. But it's like I said yesterday about New York. I've flown to every continent on your private jet, where we get picked up at the airport by a limousine with blacked-out windows. We're driven to some gorgeous five-star hotel, eat in their world-renowned restaurants and the view from my window is usually the hotel gardens. Sometimes I forget where I am. But this place, despite the Victorian English vibe in there, is real. I'm in Rio. I can't wait to explore. You know—' her voice was wistful and, turning to look at her fully, Deangelo was surprised to see her face was equally so '—everywhere else I went with you I was so busy being the perfect PA I didn't take a single chance to actually see the cities we visited. Sydney or New York, Bangkok or Beijing? Just a hotel room. I'd order room service, use the gym and then read, even when I knew you were busy for hours and wouldn't need me. I think I was just too afraid to venture out alone. But no more. I have to go out and live my life; it's the only one I have and I just can't spend it afraid of what might happen. There's a city out there waiting to be explored and I am going to explore it.'

Wait. *What?*

Deangelo narrowed his eyes, noting the light wrap she'd added to the sundress, the change of shoes from vertiginous sandals to flatter, more comfortable-looking espadrilles, the bag clasped in her hand, her sunglasses. 'You can't go out alone. It's not safe.'

'This is a tourist mecca.'

'Exactly. Where tourists are, so are those who prey on them.'

'Oh, come on. It's early evening, I won't take any expensive jewellery or all my money or anything silly. I'm just going to walk down the street and find somewhere where I can eat and watch the world go by.'

Deangelo could feel the muscle pulsing in his cheek. His plan was simple. Come to the hotel. Get to know his prey up close. Pounce, bite, win. Watch the expression in their eyes as they conceded defeat. Strip all they had from them, including their name, and then return to London—his real home—with his past firmly, once and for all, behind him. What his plan did not include was any kind of engagement with the city which had allowed him to be slung out like trash, the city which had allowed his mother to die for want of affordable treatment.

But he couldn't allow Harriet to go out into Rio's uncertain streets alone. Nor could he forbid her, although that would certainly make things easier. He stood there for a moment, knuckles whitening as he grasped the top of the balcony, contemplating insisting that they had work to do and she would need to do her outing some other time, with a guide he would hire for her. But then he glanced over again and saw the anticipation shining on her face, the excited smile as she stared down at the beach. 'I will come with you,' he said instead, the words almost as much a shock to him as they evidently were to her.

'You don't need to do that.'

'No. But I would like to. If you would allow me?' He made himself add the last part. He had every intention of accompanying her, whether she was comfortable with him there or not.

'It would be nice to have some company,' she said. 'And I suppose it would look a little odd if we went out separately on the first night of our honeymoon. Thank you. I appreciate it.'

'Be ready in five minutes.' Deangelo gave a curt nod before walking back into the hotel room, stomach tightening at the thought of the evening ahead. But whether he was more nervous about going back out into the Rio streets or it was the prospect of spending the evening in an informal setting with a woman he had vowed to maintain a strictly professional relationship with he wasn't sure. Either way, he needed to keep his guard up this evening. The walls he'd erected were there for a reason, to protect him, to protect others from him, and a balmy evening in the *cidade maravilhosa* wouldn't change that, no matter how beautiful and enticing the view—or his companion.

CHAPTER SIX

'I CAN'T BELIEVE I am actually walking on Copacabana Beach.'

Harriet skipped with excitement, her eyes drawn everywhere. For the first few minutes she'd felt self-conscious in her low-cut, floaty dress, her skin so pale that even in the early evening she'd slapped on the factor fifty and a wide-brimmed hat, miserably aware that all those mornings she'd decided on an extra fifteen minutes sleep rather than getting up to run, all those second biscuits and her cake habit meant she would never be able to achieve the toned goddess-like proportions of the women parading up and down in itsy-bitsy bikinis, held up more by luck than gravity. But the sights and sounds were too exciting for her to feel down for long.

Deangelo merely raised a disdainful eyebrow. 'It's looking a little better than the last time I was here, but Copacabana is for tourists. The beach scene is better in Ipanema and some of my favourite beaches are out beyond Leblon. We should be there, or a little north of here, Gávea or Botafogo. Or maybe Santa Teresa.' He slanted an unreadable look her way. 'I think you would like Santa Teresa.'

Was that a good or a bad thing? Harriet made a note to look up Santa Teresa as soon as she got back to the hotel room. 'So why aren't we staying in any of those places?'

'Because the Caetano family offered us a free stay at their flagship Rio hotel and under the circumstances it would have looked odd to refuse.'

'It's a little faded glory.' She watched him carefully as she spoke. Deangelo had made it very clear that they were here to take the hotels over, but he hadn't said why, just stated something obscure about justice. Despite herself, Harriet slid a glance to his scar. She'd been careful when she first went to work with him not to look at it, always keeping her gaze direct and at eye level, and then in time she didn't notice it any more. It wasn't the scar itself that was so shocking, it had healed to a thin, puckered white line; it was more the length of it that jarred. At some point Deangelo's face had been torn apart and no one she knew had any idea why. Was that the justice he spoke of? Were the Caetanos responsible for the scar? For the closed-off way he lived, alone and shut away?

If so, she would happily take everything they owned away from them herself.

Because it was increasingly clear that whatever, whoever had shaped him had scarred him inside and out. But he hadn't been closed off last night. Try as she might, she couldn't forget the moment his hand had slipped around her waist and the kiss had caught fire. He had wanted her, she was almost sure, even in her relative inexperience. There had been something about the careful way he had held her—and released her—that had suggested that he was only just keeping control.

Or was that wishful thinking on her side? Allowing her imagination to run away with what might have meant nothing at all?

Either way, she had made that happen. Hadn't stepped back in shock after his brief caress. No, she had demanded more and for a brief time had got it. It was a lesson to her to be bolder. What was the worst that could happen? She was used to rejection. She shouldn't fear it. She tried to imagine taking hold of his hand, strong and tanned and so close, but her imagination, usually so vibrant, failed her.

Coward, she told herself.

'Back in the nineteen-twenties the Caetano Palace was one of the most prestigious hotels in the city, if not the country,' Deangelo said, and Harriet turned her attention back to the conversation with some relief. 'It's that name, that history they want me to invest in. And,' he added, 'the kind of businessman naïve enough to want to make this kind of investment is the kind who would think staying right here is the epitome of sophistication. Still, once the deal is complete we'll move somewhere more appropriate.'

'Well, I think Copacabana is beautiful. Everyone seems to be having a good time. You know, I still can't get my head around how big Brazil actually is. In my head there's Rio and then the Amazon, but that's like saying Europe is Paris and the Danube and missing out on all the other cities and coasts and rivers. Is there anywhere I should try and visit while I have the opportunity? There's a few free days in the itinerary and if you can spare me I'd like to see something of the country.'

This was the start of a new page—she was going to live her life, not just read about other people's.

Deangelo didn't answer for a long moment, as unreadable as ever. She'd worked for him for three years and still knew nothing about him apart from his coffee order. He never took leave so she didn't know the kind of holiday he enjoyed, she'd never seen him read a book, heard him listen to music. When he finally spoke, his voice was so quiet she could barely make out the words. 'I don't know anywhere in Brazil but here; the first time I left Rio I was eighteen and on a plane to England.'

Harriet opened her mouth but could find no words, so shut it again, feeling a little like a landed fish. Deangelo was so sure of himself, he was the very epitome of sophistication. She knew nothing about his past, but she'd assumed he came from money, or at least a comfortable existence. Everything about him exuded privilege, from the way he wore his handmade suits to his austere but impeccable taste. He'd been educated at Cambridge, for goodness' sake.

But he'd never mentioned his family, or even a single childhood anecdote. Maybe the slight hint of street fighter, one amplified by the scar on his cheek, was more than a hint. Harriet glanced around again, her gaze alighting on a gaggle of boys kicking a football, their clothes old and worn, feet bare, hair cropped close to their heads. She looked back at Deangelo and saw his gaze also fixed on the boys, a bleak sadness in his eyes, and realised with a jolt he saw himself in their skinny limbs and dirty clothes.

'Come on,' she said, desperate to change the subject

and wipe that sadness out of his amber eyes. 'Let's get some food. I'm hungry.'

Harriet swiftly overruled Deangelo's suggestion that they look for one of the new crop of critically acclaimed restaurants that had recently opened up as Copacabana tried to shake off its slightly seedy tag. 'You came along on my evening out, remember?' she said. 'And I don't want fine dining. I want to sit and soak in the atmosphere. In fact—' her eye was caught by one of the kiosks that were prevalent along the golden strip of sand '—let's eat here.'

'At a kiosk? Outside?' He couldn't have sounded more outraged if she'd suggested stealing food out of the hands of the small group of children picnicking nearby.

'Sounds perfect, doesn't it? Let's see what they're serving.'

They had passed several of the iconic beach kiosks, some the traditional wood, others, like the one they were approaching, a silver metal glinting in the sun. The large round kiosk was surrounded by several tables, each shielded from the sun by a huge umbrella, all with an unparalleled view of the sea. From the kiosk itself an enticing smell wafted out and Harriet realised just how very hungry she was. She peered over at the menu, squinting as she tried to read the scrawling handwritten sign. 'They serve *espettos*—they smell good, whatever they are.'

'Kebabs,' Deangelo told her. 'Usually meat or fish, sometimes vegetables.'

'Perfect. I'll get these; what would you like?'

It took a few minutes to convince Deangelo that she

both could and would buy dinner, his argument that she'd only be claiming the dinner back on expenses waved away. 'It doesn't matter that I'll be using the corporate card. I want to go up and order the food.' She knew it sounded a little pointless, but Harriet had spent so long *not* doing, waiting for life to start, she just didn't want to wait any more, just like she hadn't wanted to spend another night waiting for room service in an anonymous hotel room.

The young man in the kiosk was perfectly charming, praising her halting phrasebook Portuguese, his appreciative gaze resting on her in a way that managed to combine respectfulness with a playful flirtatiousness and a sense that if Harriet was willing the flirtatiousness would be amped up. She'd never been flirted with quite so expertly before and carried the cold beers back over to the table where Deangelo sat glowering, feeling sexier and more feminine than she had for a long, long time. 'I ordered a selection so we can try all the different types, along with bread and salad; is that okay? What's wrong?' she asked, as his glower intensified.

'Was that boy being disrespectful?'

'What? Who? No! He was being nice. He's not really interested in me, I'm at least a decade older. But I appreciated the gesture, he flirted so charmingly.'

'As far as he is aware you're a married woman.' The glower intensified and a sense of the absurd mingled with a weird moment of wishing this was real, that she really was carrying the drinks back to someone who cared deeply about her, deeply enough to mistake practised flirtation for genuine interest. Harriet inhaled, trying to quell that note of wistfulness. Deangelo was being overprotective, that was all.

'Actually, there's one thing we forgot.' She held up her bare left hand. 'No ring, so he couldn't have known about any marriage, real or fake. But I was thinking we'd say we left the rings behind because of safety concerns, so there's no need for us to buy any.' Harriet wasn't comfortable about accepting valuable jewellery, even temporarily, and the thought of wearing rings on her fourth finger made her uncomfortable in ways she didn't know how to articulate.

Deangelo's frown merely deepened. 'It's been taken care of; they will be here tomorrow.'

Wait, what? 'No, no, there's no need. Honestly.'

His brows drew together but, before he could respond, the waiter brought over a bowl filled with delicious-smelling bread, a mixture between a dough ball and a bread roll, and the conversation stalled as the delicious aroma floated towards them. Harriet managed to remember her manners and wait until the bowl had been set down before picking up a roll, her stomach gurgling in anticipation. The roll was still warm as she bit into it, the texture crisp on the outside, soft in the middle and filled with cheese. 'Oh, my goodness. These are amazing.'

She looked over at Deangelo for confirmation and, to her surprise, his face had softened to a melancholy nostalgia. '*Pão de queijo.* My mother used to make them. I haven't had these since I left Brazil.'

'There must be somewhere in London you could buy them. Now I've discovered them I'm not going to let them simply walk out of my life. This is a long-term relationship, I can just tell.'

But Deangelo was shaking his head. 'In London I like to forget about Brazil. There's no time to look back. Living in the past is for fools. Better to move on, find new things.'

'But—' Harriet said, watching him carefully as she spoke; this could be her chance to find out exactly what was going on '—you're back here, playing games to buy an overpriced money pit hotel chain. It can't be a coincidence that you've chosen to do something so uncharacteristic in the city you grew up in…'

His expression shut down immediately. Harriet had never realised before just how high the walls were that Deangelo lived behind. Nor just how much he cut himself off from all human interaction. She knew his existence was focused, that he didn't socialise or relax, that he had no hobbies and he had no obvious vices nor any obvious virtues. He ignored the many fundraising messages that crossed her desk—no gala balls for him, no charity concerts. He *chose* to live alone, whereas circumstances had meant that for too many years she had had little interaction with people outside work. The loneliness had nearly broken her. How could he choose to live like this? How could he bear it?

But then again, he had bought her that beautiful cashmere coat last Christmas. It had fitted her like a glove, the colour bringing out the blue of her eyes. It was the most beautiful thing she'd ever owned. For her birthday he'd given her lifetime membership to the London Library, a gift she hadn't realised she'd coveted until she received it. He must have noticed that she always had a book or two in her bag, that her only spending splurges were on books…

He must have noticed her…

She looked across and realised he was watching her intently, warmth suffusing her as his gaze seemed to strip her to the bones, see inside her. She tried to suppress a shiver, the urge to reach out and touch him almost overwhelming her. She wanted to feel his touch again and, God help her, she wanted him to kiss her again.

With the first bite of the herby, cheese-filled bread he was home, seeing his mother balling the dough, slapping away his hands as he had tried to grab the cheese. Grief, for her and the innocent boy he had been, rose thickly in his throat and Deangelo washed the roll down with a swig of beer, almost afraid of the emotions one taste had unleashed, afraid of the urge to confess his sins to the woman opposite him as her gaze snagged his, warmth and understanding in her smile and something that looked very like desire in the depths of her clear blue eyes. His own body responded instantly, blood heating as he allowed himself one long look, one moment of pretending that this was, could be, real before tearing his gaze away. Why would a woman like Harriet, one with so much to give, want a man who was nothing, despite the billions in the bank?

Suddenly he wanted to know the heart of her, even if he could, should, do nothing with that information.

'You told me you left Aion to build a family. What did you mean?'

Harriet picked up another of the cheese balls and began to tear small pieces off it as she looked over towards the sea, her gaze wistful. Deangelo followed her line of sight, his eyes resting on a family playing on the beach, the parents laughing as they threw a ball to their small children, smiles filled with love and pride. 'Like I said, I just wanted a family.' Her voice was so low Deangelo wasn't even sure he'd heard her correctly. He snapped his gaze back to her. The loneliness in her eyes would be like looking in a mirror, if he ever allowed himself to feel anything at all.

'You have a family. Your father…'

'I love my dad more than anything. At least, I love the man he used to be more than anything. I can't help but resent the person he is now.' She ripped another roll to shreds, then pushed her plate away. 'It's like my own dad was kidnapped and replaced with a stranger who looks like him but is in no way my funny, kind daddy. But then occasionally there are glimpses and I know he's trapped in there somewhere. Those moments are the worst of all.' She looked up, stricken. 'I don't mean that exactly…'

'And you have no other family?'

Harriet shook her head. 'Both my parents were only children and already pretty elderly when I was born—it was a second marriage for both of them. Mum said I was her late life miracle. She died when I was eleven, so it was just me and Dad. I do have two half-sisters, but they resented my mother—and me, I think—and I don't see much of them.'

Deangelo couldn't help but see the parallels. One dead parent, one ill parent and a family who weren't interested in helping out. Some stories were universal, and always damaging. 'Don't your sisters help out with your father?'

'No.' There was a world of heartbreak in that answer. Deangelo could have warned her—never put your faith in the goodness of others. But it was clearly too late for Harriet.

'No,' she repeated. 'Like I said, they resented me, resented Mum. They loved the big house Dad provided, their allowances and cars and horses and all the rest of it. Dad was a merchant banker. He worked so hard; Mum was always telling him to slow down. He'd leave for work really early, come back late.' Her face softened. 'On Thursday night he'd always ask us what we wanted him to bring home for the weekend. My mother always asked for flowers and so I did, too; I wanted to be just like her. My sisters laughed at me for that but I loved it when he'd present me with a perfect rose. I'd give anything for him to give me a rose one last time.' She blinked rapidly, before taking a long swig of her beer.

'Anyway, after Mum died he decided he needed to cut his hours, to look after me. He quit his job to become a lecturer at LSE, and sold our house so we could live close to his work. He bought a flat in Crouch End and shared the rest of the money between us; mine was supposed to put me through university. My sisters were appalled; they couldn't bear the loss of their lifestyle but, to be fair, they took that money and multiplied it. They own a chain of tanning and beauty shops; they do really well. But when I asked if they would help out with his costs they didn't even return my calls. They haven't visited him—or me—in years.'

'And your share of the money?'

He was sure of her answer and unsurprised when she answered. 'Oh, well, it was clear Dad was having problems when I was still at school. By the time I was eighteen, leaving him so I could head to university was out of the question so I did a PA course, working part-time so I could look after him. We managed okay for a few years, but then it was more than I could do on my own; he just wasn't safe to leave on his own. I felt so guilty. So guilty.' She stopped, swallowed. 'If I couldn't look after him then he had to have the best and if that meant selling the flat and donating my trust fund to pay for it then of course that's what I would do. Only this meant I needed a full-time job—and to pay rent—so I got a job at Aion. A year later I was promoted to work for you. I thought maybe things would change for me, but they didn't. I'd lost part of myself in those years with Dad. My confidence maybe? Sense of self. Whatever it was, I just seemed to be as lonely as ever.'

She stared out at the beach. 'When you spend your teens and early twenties looking after your dad it's hard to meet people and relationships are pretty much out of the question. I lost touch with my school friends and going out in the evening was impossible anyway. Once I started renting it didn't get easier. London can be pretty anonymous when you don't have money or connections and you have to keep moving because rents are so expensive. And then I met the girls.'

'The girls?'

'Emilia, Alex and Amber. The Christmas after I had just started working directly for you. It was Christmas Eve and we were all free to go at noon, only I had nowhere to go so I stayed.'

Dimly, Deangelo remembered. He usually worked over Christmas, so hadn't thought it odd that Harriet had stayed until six. 'I didn't know.' And if he had what would he have done? Probably nothing. Other people's tragedies weren't his business.

She smiled a brief sad smile. 'How could you? Anyway. I finally left. I was dreading Christmas Eve evening more than Christmas Day in some ways. I had planned a walk, bought some food for the day itself, but the evening seemed unbearably long. And then in the lift I met Alex. I didn't really know her—she's a little intimidating, so posh and cool, you know? Anyway. I asked her if she had any nice plans for that evening and she just looked, for one second, as bleak as I felt and said no. It was a takeaway and an early night. So I gathered up all my courage and suggested a drink. To my shock, she said yes.'

Her mouth softened. 'We gathered up Emilia in the lobby; she was trying to get up the courage to walk out into the lonely night. Amber was outside, fruitlessly trying to find a taxi. We went out for wine and pizza and it was the best Christmas Eve I had had in about ten years. The next day we met and walked through Hyde Park then found a little café selling fry-ups and had bacon and eggs for our Christmas lunch. And somehow we knew. We had found a family, not one of blood but a family nonetheless. A year later we started talking about setting up an agency and here we are.'

The arrival of the *espettos* interrupted anything Deangelo might have said, but he couldn't help but mark the difference between them. Life had stripped all they loved from them, but he had closed himself off and made money, each million, each billion, another brick in the wall separating him from humanity. From feelings. But Harriet? Rejected by what remained of her family, she'd gone out and built herself another one. He had made money but she was the richer by far.

Harriet deserved all the love, all the happiness in the world. He'd lifted her financial burden from her; the least he could do was to make this final fortnight together special too. Show her the real Rio de Janeiro, even if it meant showing her a tiny part of the real Deangelo Santos, too. Show her just how worthy of love and happiness she was. One final gift. Before she walked out of his life for ever.

CHAPTER SEVEN

WHAT WAS WRONG with her? One beach walk and one kiss and she was spilling her guts like a low-level hoodlum with a plea bargain. Harriet cringed. How could she have said so much? It was so unlike her—and so unprofessional. So exposing.

But for a moment there, the amber eyes had been full of empathy, as if he truly knew what it felt like to have nothing, to have no one.

'These are good,' she said a little awkwardly, picking up an *espetto* and waving it around. 'First night and I'm already converted to Brazilian food. What else do I need to do to fit in around here?'

'Sport.' Deangelo nodded at the footballers to one side and the volleyballers on the other just as, as if to prove his point, a gorgeous couple jogged past. 'Football, of course. It's not just the national passion, it's the national reason for existing.'

'I don't mind football. My dad supported Arsenal.'

'Don't mind is better than nothing. But it lacks passion, and passion is one of the most important Brazilian traits. If you want to know Brazil, then you must remember this…' He leaned forward, eyes molten gold, reflecting the evening sun. 'Brazil is a land of hedonism, of pleasure and relaxation and sensuality.'

Harriet swallowed, almost choking on her bread. 'It's *what*?'

'Oh, we don't mind work.' His usually almost imperceptible accent deepened. 'After all, it takes a lot of dedication to look like that.' He waved his hand towards a group of young people drinking at the counter, the girls in tiny dresses showing off lean, toned limbs and dramatic curves, the men all chiselled as if carved by Michelangelo himself. 'But Brazilians don't sweat the small stuff; we like to make sure there's plenty of time to enjoy the finer things in life. Food, music, the outside, love, dance…'

The way he lingered on *love* called to mind something a lot more carnal than romantic, a physicality inherent in the word, and she was instantly transported back to last night, her hand in his, the feel of his shoulder, strong under her palm, the decadent richness of the kiss. Warmth suffused her cheeks, spreading down to touch every part of her.

This was ridiculous. Her love life might have been sedate since she had first found her father looking for the cat that had died several years ago and realised that the loss of words and forgetfulness was not a natural part of ageing but something infinitely more sinister, but she hadn't been in a convent. There had been other kisses, even a two-year relationship that had died a natural death as her father's needs had intensified and she simply had no more emotional give in her. She needed to pull herself together—and then when she got home allow Amber to sign her up to a dating app. Her friend had been trying to persuade her for long enough.

'Dance?' she said, as coolly as she could, despite the intensity in his face, his scar setting off his saturnine handsomeness rather than marring it, reminding her he was both out of her league and her skillset.

'Of course. In Argentina they like to tango. To follow rules, to embody drama and violence and repression. In Brazil we samba. The samba is all about passion. About being free.' His gaze met hers, bold and intense, and Harriet shivered at the wildness in the depths of his eyes.

Passion? Where had this come from? Deangelo was the kind of man who probably slept in his suit. He was organised and predictable and proper. But her body knew full well he hadn't been any of those things last night and, good intentions aside, how could she be anything but intrigued by the dangerous glint in his eyes, the wolfish smile playing on his sensual mouth?

Swallowing hard, she tried to drag the conversation and her mind back on track. 'Samba? That's the dance with the bright costumes, right? All feathers and big hats?' And barely-there outfits, but she wasn't going to mention that.

'Traditionally yes, but samba is more than costume. A samba can be danced in any clothes at any time. It's about rhythm, about intent. It comes from the heart, through the hips.'

'The hips, right. Then I'd better not give it a go. My attempts at baby ballet were not a success. Dance is obviously not for me.'

She was doing the right thing, responding sensibly, not allowing the sensual haze creeping up to envelop her. Last night was a one-off—and Deangelo had ended it before it had gone anywhere. She was putting it firmly behind her to concentrate on enjoying this opportunity to explore Brazil. So why did she feel like a coward, a sense of opportunities lost once again creeping over her?

She was tired of doing the sensible thing—after all, even quitting her job to set up the Happy Ever After Agency had been cushioned by Alexandra's inheritance and the knowledge that, no matter what, she would have a roof over her head. She was in a city known for its laid-back attitude, a city made for fun, for letting go. What was it Alexandra had said, the first time they had discussed working for themselves? 'You can't experience life through books alone, Harriet. At some point you have to go out and start living it.'

Harriet had laughed the comment off, clutching her beloved romance hardback to her, exclaiming that all she needed was in the pages of the book. But the words had stayed with her, came back to her now.

Something had changed in the last twenty-four hours. For her, for them. A line had been crossed and there was no going back, not now she'd finally admitted to herself just how attracted she was to Deangelo. Desire flaring in the pit of her stomach, warming her whole body, setting every nerve on edge with awareness. Awareness of his surprisingly elegant hands, the broadness of his shoulders, the muscles that could make him seem heavyset if he didn't move with such lithe grace, the sensual lines of his mouth, his heavy brows, the utter masculinity of a face that wasn't handsome exactly, but undeniably attractive, the scar running down his cheek adding a rakish sensuality. For the first time Harriet knew why rooms went quiet when Deangelo strode in, why every woman, and plenty of the men, turned as if magnetically pulled in his direction. It wasn't just the money or the power; it was utter sensuality. How had she not noticed before?

Or maybe she had noticed but hid it even from herself.

He sat back, eyes issuing a challenge she knew she was going to accept. 'English people can't samba because they have no idea how to let go.'

Harriet narrowed her eyes at the dismissive comment. 'You live in England now.'

'It suits me. I like the control. I'm not criticising the English; I'm just stating a fact. You said yourself, you couldn't even manage ballet, and ballet is all about rules. The samba twists the rules…'

'So, let me get this straight. You like the rules yourself, but can still let go enough to samba?'

'If I chose to, of course.'

'Okay then.' Harriet pushed back her chair, standing up, nerves competing with an excitement she couldn't quite name. 'Prove it.'

He didn't move for one long moment, only a pulse beating in his jaw showing any sign of life at all. Harriet stood still, watching him, the nerves tumbling in her stomach, her whole body aching with the need to act, to do. This evening was already unusual: the sharing of a meal, the location, the frank speech. Why not carry it on, rediscover the easy intimacy they had shared last night, would need for tomorrow? Then they would, no doubt, move on, to another hotel where they had their own space and normality would resume until they returned home and she walked away once again.

Besides, she was intrigued. This was his home. She knew little more about the enigmatic billionaire than anyone else, despite their close proximity. The opportunity to find out who he really was seemed too good an opportunity to pass up.

But, more than anything, she wanted to keep feeling the way she did right now: full of possibilities and possibility. Attracted and attractive. Desiring and desired. Because there had been a minute there, when his gaze had locked on hers, when something had flickered between them, something new and dangerous.

She'd been good for so very long.

She needed to start living outside the pages of her book.

And it was only one dance.

So she waited, her gaze locked on his, daring, provocative until he nodded. One firm gesture.

'So be it.'

There was only one place to samba. Oh, sure, there were bars all over Rio, even a couple of decent ones here in Copacabana, but to really get to the heart of the dance then they needed to head to Lapa. Without a word to Harriet, Deangelo summoned a taxi, ushering Harriet into the back, joining her as the car headed along the beach.

This was crazy; he knew that. Crazy on so many levels he didn't even know where to begin. To spend an evening together like this under normal circumstances was risky; to do so in the city of his birth, in the city where all his secrets lay buried, was playing with fire.

And that was before he considered the change in Harriet this evening. It wasn't just physical, although he wasn't used to seeing her strawberry-blonde hair loose, her lush curves shown off rather than hidden away by sensible if shapeless office wear. It wasn't the bolder way she interacted with him, her usual reserve replaced with a sharp curiosity and a new openness. It was the way she made him feel: a little protective, a little possessive, as if he wanted to show her his world, impress her. As if he wanted her to know him, the real him. And that was the most dangerous thing of all.

But he was in Rio. Tomorrow the game would begin. Tonight was his.

At one time he'd known all the bars in Lapa. The ones where the tourists were funnelled to, the ones they'd never see. The places where only the best dancers took to the floor, and those where every beginner was welcome. Tiny bars carved into alleyways, large glitzy bars where light glittered from every sequin. Would they recognise him if he went there? Unlikely; back then he'd just been another street rat.

No. Not a bar. He wanted to make this visit special for Harriet; that meant taking her to the very best, most spectacular place.

Harriet didn't speak as they travelled through the darkening streets, staring out of the windows, concentrating on every street scene they passed, absorbing the city, but she let out a gasp as the car pulled up outside the grand stone building. It looked impressive, every window ornately decorated with stone carvings, lights blazing from the open double doors at the top of the wide steps. Deangelo helped Harriet from the taxi, keeping her hand in his as they started to ascend the steps, trying not to notice how much her touch felt like home as he led her into the huge hallway, light bouncing off a dozen chandeliers. Deangelo kept hold of her even as he muttered a few words to the hostess greeting them, and they followed her to a corner table, one both discreet and yet with an enviable view of the dance floor.

It was still early but the room was already half-filled and couples had taken to the floor, showcasing moves that would win awards in Europe, music filling the room from the stage at the other end of the room, the musicians already lost to the beat. Usually he would have ordered the ice-cold beer customary in these establishments but, after glancing at Harriet, her eyes shining as she took in the scene, Deangelo changed his mind and ordered champagne.

'This is incredible.' Harriet took her seat, still transfixed by the dancing in front of her. 'When do the normal people start dancing?'

'These are the normal people.'

'What?' She turned and stared at him. 'They can't be! Look at her feet. And his—and that leg-kick. Normal people can't do that.'

'They can in the *gafieiras*. But everyone is welcome, whatever their level.'

A bow-tied waiter interrupted them at that moment, a bottle of champagne in an ice bucket in one hand, two frosted glasses in the other, and conversation stopped as the cork was popped, the champagne poured and Harriet sat back, glass in hand, to watch the dancing.

The beat swelled, the music thumping through him, every note, every key change calling to him. Almost without noticing, his foot began to tap along, his body to shift in time with the beat. The room was steadily filling and the accomplished dancers on the floor were joined by more and more couples, of much more varying levels, including a few tourists who, although clearly game, had more enthusiasm than ability; they were soon swooped upon by experienced dancers who whirled them away to teach them the proper steps to their evident equal delight and trepidation.

It was time.

Deangelo pushed himself to his feet and held out a hand. 'Come along.'

Harriet clutched her glass. 'What do you mean?'

'You wanted to learn how to be a Brazilian? Right there.' He nodded at the dance floor. 'That's where you'll find out.'

She clutched the glass harder. 'I can't go out there!'

'Why not? If he can—' he nodded at a rotund tourist, furiously jiggling away, his face serious as he tried to remember the steps his partner was teaching him '—you definitely can.'

'But…'

He didn't wait for her to finish the sentence, removing the glass from her hand and drawing her to her feet.

'The thing to remember about samba,' he said, 'is you have to find the rhythm. It's three steps to two beats, the middle step is the quick one. Once you have that, then add bounce, keep your knees soft. So it's back, feet together, forward…' They were on the dance floor and Deangelo swept her into his arms, murmuring the steps to her. 'That's it, back, together, forward, knees bent, let your body roll through the steps, don't be afraid to roll your hips.'

Harriet was clearly nervous, clutching his hand as she shuffled through the steps, her eyes on her feet.

'Look at me,' he murmured. 'Feel the beat; let it guide you.'

The music was getting louder and louder, the beat stronger and more insistent, the dance floor busier and busier. Deangelo lost track of time, knowing nothing but the woman in his arms, the softness of her under his hands, the way his pulse was connected to the music, the light in her blue eyes as she moved, the sheen of perspiration on her forehead as the heat intensified. How had he thought running would be the same as dancing? The solitary sport against this communal celebration of music and passion? No wonder he'd only felt half-alive the last twelve years, replacing joy with monotony, the thud of his feet on the pavement instead of the thud of his heart to the beat. It was necessary, that half-life, but such a relief to let the walls tumble for one night, to let the young man who had loved and laughed and dreamed emerge from the cold professional persona he was caged in. Tomorrow would be time enough to tame him again.

As Harriet got more confident he encouraged her to move in a processional step, her hips moving as if she'd been born to do this, hair swirling in time with the beat. He twirled her, then twirled her back and Harriet lost her footing, falling into him, her face upturned, laughing. Time slowed, each musical note drawn out to an almost unbearable crescendo, every couple moving in slow motion. All Deangelo could see was Harriet's parted mouth, her laughing eyes, all he could feel was her soft weight colliding with his, her breasts against his chest, hip to hip, leg to leg, the heat of her, her pulse racing in unison with his.

He was consumed by her and all she represented—freedom and need and happiness and sensuality—hair around her shoulders, her dress slipping off her shoulders, revealing the deep vee of her breasts, her lush mouth tilted towards his as if offering. How could he resist?

He'd been the king of resistance for so many long years, ruthlessly squashing any need and want that didn't align with his goal. Not for him romance or love. Not for him the false comfort of human relationships. Work and enough exercise to keep his body and mind fighting fit. That was enough. That was all he allowed himself. Harriet represented all that was forbidden. That was what made her so intoxicating.

He could still have walked away, led her back to their table, called a taxi and escorted her back to the hotel, put tonight down to courtesy, if she hadn't moved in a little closer, if her hand hadn't slipped around his waist, if she hadn't put her other hand on his shoulder, aligning herself even closer to him. If she hadn't flicked her tongue nervously over her mouth, her eyes fixed on his. She wanted him and he was powerless to resist, the memory of how sweet her kiss felt consuming him.

His hand slid down her back to the glorious curve

of her hip, his gaze watching her throughout the slow caress, waiting for further permission. She sighed as her eyelids fluttered shut, leaning in to his touch, her own hands tightening their grip. Permission granted.

The first kiss was fleeting, a mere brush of lips. She tasted of champagne sweetened with honey, her mouth soft under his. The second kiss was barely a second longer, Deangelo still needing to know that this was what she wanted.

Once again it was Harriet who made the next move, standing on her tiptoes to press her mouth to his, opening up under him. This was no mere brush, no polite enquiry. Deangelo pulled her tight against him, deepening the kiss, his hands roaming over her body as they moved to the beat of the drums, stepping in perfect time, hips moving, lost in the rhythm they created.

With an effort, Deangelo pulled himself away. 'Want to get out of here?'

'Can we return? Before we leave Rio?'

'It's a date.' The words were out of his mouth before he could stop them and he paused. 'I mean...'

But she laid a finger over his mouth. 'No. You don't have to say anything. I know what this is.'

She knew more than him, then. Deangelo still wasn't sure how he'd allowed everything he'd spent the last twelve years building to be swept away in just a few hours, even if it was temporary. 'You do?'

'Everything has changed. For both of us. That's confusing how we relate to each other, how we interact.'

'So this right now is just confusion?'

She laughed. 'Maybe. No, definitely. But I think we're

two of a kind, you and I. We don't allow ourselves what comes so naturally to others, for different reasons probably, but still. I want to change that, I want to start living like everyone else. To stop being afraid to reach out for what I want. And tonight…' She swallowed. 'Tonight I want you. I'm not looking for more. Good God, I don't think I could handle more, not from someone as intense as you. I need training wheels for a little while longer; I'm very out of practice when it comes to relationships. So I have no expectations, except that tomorrow things revert to normal. But we've a while until tomorrow. And I'd like to spend that while with you…'

Deangelo couldn't imagine the courage it must have taken to be so very honest, to be so very vulnerable, and his lack of worthiness, his inability to be so open hit him. 'Are you sure?'

'Unless you've changed your mind.'

'No,' he said hoarsely. 'I should, I think, but no.'

'Good.' And now it was Harriet's turn to take his hand. 'I was hoping that's what you'd say.'

Stopping to draw her back into his arms, Deangelo banished the doubts still lurking in his mind with another kiss, her ardent response a welcome reminder that this was a two-way sudden attraction. Harriet was right. Tomorrow would take care of itself—and tonight? Tonight was up to them.

CHAPTER EIGHT

HARRIET WAS USUALLY awake with the dawn, trained into early rising by the need to be up before her father and then by the early start demanded by Deangelo's timetable. But, it turned out, Deangelo was an earlier riser still. And when she finally stirred it was to find Deangelo already dressed, seated by the side of the bed.

'What time is it?' she managed to say, her voice embarrassingly croaky with sleep. It would have been easier to wake up alone, or for him to occupy the now cool place beside her, but this halfway house put her at a disadvantage. To look at him, she would have assumed that Deangelo had slept for eight peaceful hours. He was already dressed in blue chinos and a crisp white shirt, the most formal of the informal clothes they'd purchased, his hair still wet from the shower.

But Harriet knew better. Deangelo had had as much sleep as she had—and that wasn't very much. She pulled the sheets higher, horribly aware of her nakedness, the way she ached deep down, that mixture of satiation and too much. Last night had in every way been too much.

And she, uncharacteristically confident, had loved

every sensuous moment. She'd never known sex could be like that, so tender one moment, so fiery the next, pushing her on and on until she wasn't sure where she ended and he began and she didn't care. For the first time in a long time she'd felt that the exaggerated curves of her hips and breasts weren't too much but just right, her fifties hourglass shape fitted into Brazil, fitted into Deangelo's muscled breadth, perfectly.

'It's just past eight. Breakfast is ordered. I'd like to go over our notes during it. Can you be ready in twenty minutes?'

And good morning to you too, Harriet managed not to say, rising onto one arm and pushing the tangle of hair out of her eyes.

'Of course,' she said easily. 'Can you pass me a robe?' She lay watching him as he strode across the room to collect the silk robe she'd bought just two days ago, but when he returned he didn't hand it to her; instead he stood there frowning. Harriet eased herself into a sitting position, sheet high across her chest. She knew what was coming. The talk.

Harriet had been totally honest last night when she'd said she didn't want a relationship with Deangelo. She had such a long way to go to find out who she was when she wasn't spending every moment worrying about her father. She had a business to build. Single-minded, taciturn, control freak billionaires were in no way part of her plan. Last night wasn't her life's purpose, wonderful as it had been, just a memory in the making, so when she looked back she didn't see a grey, solitary, dull existence but glints of fire and adventure.

'Thank you for ordering breakfast.'

For the first time since she'd known him, Deangelo looked disconcerted. 'You're welcome.'

'And thank you for last night. The dancing and, well, everything.' She smiled up at him. 'I know how important today is, and I know what last night was. You don't need to worry. I don't expect you to suddenly be magically in love with me and I'm not magically in love with you—it was just two people exploring an attraction. Maybe a goodbye in a way.'

'Yes.'

'So, if you want me to be ready in twenty minutes you'd better give me some privacy.' She smiled again. 'I promise not to take too long.'

'Right. Okay.' His eyes flicked to the sheet covering her and for one millisecond Harriet could have sworn that his gaze heated up, but immediately his habitual blank expression was right back in place. 'I'll see you soon.'

She breathed a sigh of relief as he handed her the robe and turned and left. So much better for her to deliver the *about last night* speech rather than receive it—and she was a sensible grown-up woman who was not going to feel disappointed that he hadn't argued for a continuance.

It didn't take Harriet too long to shower, quickly washing her hair, bundling it, still damp, into a loose chignon, smoothing on tinted moisturiser, mascara and a little lipstick. She pulled a face as she surveyed her fresh-faced milkmaid wholesomeness in the mirror; she definitely didn't look sophisticated enough to be a naïve but rich investor's wife, but she'd never got the hang of a five-minute full makeover. Her outfit would have to talk for her. She opted for wide silky trousers in navy blue with a white and gold pattern, partnering them with a loose gold vest top, layering up the gold bangles Amber had assured her would make the outfit, and slipping her feet into the kind of wedges that made her relieved that Deangelo usually got chauffeured everywhere.

Exactly twenty minutes later she left the bedroom. The heavy velvet curtains had been pulled back and the French doors opened, allowing the morning light to flood into the overly ornate room. Deangelo was seated at the small table in the dining alcove, his laptop open, ignoring the food spread out before him. An ache in her stomach reminded Harriet that she'd only eaten a couple of the small cheese rolls, some grilled vegetables and prawns last night.

'This looks amazing.'

Deangelo looked up. Had he really been so lost in work he hadn't heard her approach? Was he really as cool as he appeared? It didn't matter, she reminded herself; they had made an agreement. The sort Deangelo always made—brief companionship with no expectations on either side. Harriet just had to act like one of the sophisticated women he usually dated.

'Is that coffee?' she continued in the same overly bright voice. 'Excellent. I need something to wake me up.' At that exact moment she remembered just why she was so tired—and, judging by the heat flaring in Deangelo's eyes as he looked up, he was having exactly the same memories. Cheeks burning, Harriet slipped into the empty chair. The food looked incredible. Whatever the hotel's failings, the kitchen clearly wasn't one of them: freshly baked bread rolls were heaped into a basket, an array of cheeses, meats, jams and fresh fruit spread out on attractive platters, joined by pots of yogurt and a jug of fruit juice. Harriet accepted a cup of milky coffee gratefully, before piling her plate high. Deangelo, she noted, had a few slices of papaya and a black coffee. She looked down at her own teetering pile of food ruefully.

'My sisters are like you. Food to them is a necessity they barely tolerate. Growing up, they were always a little scathing about my appetite. I used to try and eat like they did, then sneak food later. Silly really. I just wanted to be like them, for them to take notice of me in a good way. To include me, as if they were ever going to want to hang out with a half-sister a decade younger.'

She was surprised to see Deangelo's forehead crease as if in pain and stopped abruptly, roll still in hand. 'I'm sorry; you don't need to know this.'

'Half-siblings can be very cruel.' There was a chilling note to his voice and foreboding shivered down Harriet's spine. His face straightened, his expression resolute.

'I'd like to say unthinking rather than cruel.' She stared at her plate. Part of her still hoped that one day Emma and Jayne would act like real sisters. Even after they'd excluded her from their weddings, failed to tell her when nieces and nephews were born, sent Christmas cards to their father only. Even as their visits became more and more infrequent as their father's illness progressed, after they stopped taking her calls and ignored her pleas for help. It wasn't just their financial help she'd wanted. It was their input. For someone else to make the difficult decisions, to reassure her she was doing the right thing. For someone to care.

But someone had. While he still could. Even amidst his own grief, her father had helped her cope with the loss of her mother in every way he could. 'After Mum died I just couldn't eat at all. For weeks. Then one day Dad took me out to Mum's favourite Italian. Nothing fancy, one of those family-run restaurants that are a staple of every small town. The kind where they ply you with garlic bread as soon as you sit down, where every portion could actually feed a family, where they insist you try pudding. And he reminded me that eating together brought Mum more happiness than anything. That cooking together was her favourite pastime.'

Why on earth had she told him all that when the time for confidences was at an end?

'My mother loved to cook too.'

She stilled, barely daring to look at him. She'd never heard Deangelo speak about any member of his family before.

'And she always said breakfast was the most important meal of the day, that you never knew when you'd next get the time or money to eat.' Deangelo said nothing else, but he did add a roll and some cheese to his plate.

Harriet continued to eat automatically, turning that comment over and over in her head. It suggested poverty, not knowing when or where the next meal was coming from.

And the past tense hadn't escaped her either. He'd lost his mother, too. Empathy ached within her, but she didn't know what to say, whether any gesture would be welcomed, last night's intimacy muddying the waters between them, making reaching out to another human being an unwelcome overture rather than a gesture of sympathy.

Neither spoke for the next few minutes. Harriet's appetite had deserted her and she picked at her breakfast, grateful for the bitter coffee. It wasn't until she pushed her plate away that Deangelo looked up again. He picked up a small parcel that lay beside his laptop and handed it to her.

'These arrived this morning; they should be the right size.'

Opening the padded envelope cautiously, she drew out a turquoise ring box and her stomach tumbled with a mixture of fear and anticipation. She'd always dreamt of receiving a box like this, maybe on a moonlit evening by the sea. Never over an awkward breakfast in order to perpetuate a charade.

'I said not to…'

'No one would believe a bride wouldn't wear her wedding ring. Open it.'

With a doubtful glance at him she did, her gasp as much delight as shock as she took in the twisted platinum band and delicate sapphire ring, obviously designed to fit together. They were beautiful. Too beautiful. She'd much rather have worn a huge diamond solitaire or something else not to her taste than the exact same rings she would have picked out for herself.

'These are too much. What if I lost them…?'

'It's no matter.' And of course it wasn't. Deangelo could buy rings like this for every single one of his employees and not even notice. That didn't make it seem right though.

'What about you?'

But he simply shrugged. 'Not all men wear rings.'

'I would never marry someone who didn't want to wear a ring.'

'Then it's a good thing this is not a real marriage. Come on, Harriet, see if they fit. We have a lot to go through.'

Gone was the tender, considerate lover, gone her usually courteous boss. Deangelo's lips pressed tightly together, his forehead pinched with what she assumed was rarely seen annoyance. Harriet gingerly lifted the rings out of the box, swallowing as she held the engagement ring up, admiring the etchings of leaves decorating the delicate band. This was no standard ring. It was *the* ring.

The perfect gift, just like the coat, just like the library subscription. Only this wasn't a gift she could keep and receiving it just made melancholy settle over her. It seemed so wrong that the person who knew her best was the person who would no longer be in her life. The person who lived a life pretty much devoid of any human warmth and liked it that way.

Silence stretched as she slid first the twisted platinum band and then the sapphire ring onto the fourth finger of her left hand. Of course they fitted perfectly.

'Do you like them?'

'I love them,' she half whispered. 'I'll take care of them.'

He waved away her assurance as if it mattered not at all.

Unease sat heavily on her and Harriet stood up, needing to put some distance between herself and the food.

Some distance between her and Deangelo. He was such a stranger this morning, and she didn't know if it was because of the night they had just shared or the meeting they were preparing for. She suspected a little of both; either way it unnerved her. He usually seemed so impenetrable, but then even superheroes had their vulnerabilities, as Achilles had found out in the end. Coming back to Rio was obviously his. The night they'd shared was because of that weakness, not instead of. No wonder he wanted to pretend it had never happened. The sooner she felt the same the better.

But as she turned to look back at him she couldn't help wishing for a little of last night's courage, for the right to take him in her arms, to thank him for the rings, to wipe away the sadness that still lingered in his eyes. She didn't know what his reasons for being here were, but she hoped that whatever he planned would set him free. He deserved love, as did she. Maybe last night was the first step they both needed.

But part of her wished they could take the next step together.

She bit her lip, pushing the traitorous thought away. Maybe sex had addled her brain. She'd better ensure strict boundaries for the next two weeks or she'd start naming imaginary children and picking out dream homes…

'Right—' she was relieved to hear her voice sound so steady '—let's get to work. We have an hour before the meeting; what do you need me to do?'

The initial meeting was to start off in the lobby. The three Caetano siblings had offered a tour of the grand-if-decaying hotel before taking the formalities up to the boardroom. Harriet could feel the butterflies tumbling through her stomach as the lift took them back down to the lobby. She'd sat through hundreds of high-powered business meetings in her time with Aion, many involving much higher stakes monetarily than this, but it was clear this particular deal had nothing to do with money. How could it? It was a terrible investment.

Deangelo was tense as he stood next to her, his hands curled into white-knuckled fists, a muscle beating in his jaw. He looked dangerous, more like a prize fighter than a newly rich businessman, and Harriet, steeling herself, slipped her hand into his. 'We're meant to be on honeymoon, remember?'

Taking his hand wasn't purely about their charade. A casual observer might detect no emotion in Deangelo, but Harriet had never seen him so preternaturally still, apart from that one muscle, as if he was concealing some strong emotion, not, as she often thought, a stranger to it.

Whoever these Caetanos were, there was history here. Personal history. History worth spending a great deal of money and time on.

Deangelo didn't respond as she took a firmer grip of his hand, stiller than she'd ever thought any human could be, until the lift doors opened, revealing the marble lobby beyond. In that moment it was as if he'd flicked a switch, turning himself on, as he strode out of the lift, towing Harriet alongside. His smile was wider than she'd ever seen it, eyes beaming with a frank bonhomie as he slipped an arm around Harriet's shoulders and held her close.

'Senhor and Senhorita Caetano? *Ola*, I'm Marcos Santos and this, this is my beautiful bride, Harriet.' His accent was thicker than usual, and subtly different. A regional accent, she assumed. 'Thank you so much for agreeing to meet me, and thank you for the beautiful suite. It's really made our honeymoon perfect, hasn't it, *querida*?'

Harriet forced a matching smile onto her own face. 'Oh, yes, it's lovely.'

'It's okay if we use English?' he asked. 'My wife—' he squeezed her shoulder proprietarily, and her body jumped to attention, the memory of his touch still imprinted in every nerve '—my wife, she doesn't speak Portuguese.'

The Caetano trio turned to look directly at Harriet as he spoke and she stifled a gasp of shock as they did so. The siblings were all a good fifteen years older than Deangelo, but there was no escaping the similarities in the shape of their eyes, the strong jawline. The arrogant set of all four pairs of shoulders. Maybe a casual observer wouldn't see the resemblance—Deangelo was taller and broader, his hair curled, his mouth wider, his nose more Roman, eyes amber rather than brown. But she knew every inch of him and could see where the similarities overlapped as if laid out on a map.

She'd known this deal was personal, as personal as it could get. She should have known that meant family.

Another squeeze on her shoulder reminded her of her role in this soap opera and she hastily pinned the smile back onto her face, hoping the shock and recognition didn't show in her eyes. There was no answering recognition in the avaricious smiles greeting them, but maybe they saw simply what they wanted to see.

She held out a hand automatically. 'No Portuguese yet. Marcos keeps promising to teach me, but we've just not had a chance. It's all been such a whirlwind.' She forced a giggle.

As introductions continued, Harriet covertly studied the Caetanos, aware that she was being studied in turn. Isabela Caetano was making no secret of her comprehensive summing up and Harriet was relieved that Amber had insisted that she be kitted out so thoroughly. The glamorous older woman would have instantly noted a high street bag or cheap shoes; as it was, her gaze lingered disdainfully on Harriet's rough and ready chignon, her own hair perfectly styled to match her fully made-up face and manicured nails. Her deceptively simple dress was obviously, even to Harriet's inexperienced eyes, haute couture, fitting every dramatic curve perfectly. Her brothers were no less expensively dressed, whereas she and Deangelo were in showy designer labels that screamed money but lacked the old-world class the Caetanos wore as if they had been born to it.

Somehow Harriet managed to keep up her bubbly, if a little naïve and aspirational, persona during the rest of the introductions, making small talk about her first impressions of Rio de Janeiro and how it compared to London and New York. But while she smiled and chatted her mind continued to whirl, adding two and two over and over again but never quite managing to make four. Was she looking at Deangelo's cousins? His uncles and aunt? Why did they not know who he was? Why the secrecy? Did the Caetanos really not see the predator behind the mask? See their own features mirrored in his smile?

Before the day was done she would have answers, whether Deangelo wanted to tell her or not.

The morning went as flawlessly as planned, the Caetanos so busy trying to impress them that they didn't take any time to assess the situation, just as Deangelo had predicted. This was no gamble. It was the execution of a well-honed plan and all the sweeter for it. The only time he had stumbled was when Bruno's gaze had lingered on the scar bisecting his left cheek. Deangelo didn't know whether he was more relieved or angry when his gaze had moved swiftly on. Did Bruno not remember inflicting such a scar? Had Deangelo really been so far below him that he had no memory of the brutal assault? But he remembered clearly how the older man had turned his back the second the whip descended, not caring about what damage he had inflicted or where.

He'd care soon enough.

The tour of the hotel was heavy on prestige and history if light on detail; likewise, the portfolio of other properties in the Caetano empire showcased the symbolism of their name, interspersed with the glossy new resorts developed by Isabela. It was easy to see where the money had gone. Deangelo had barely had a chance to look at the portfolio before the contract was produced. It had already been to both sets of lawyers, this meeting just a formality. Deangelo made a show of flicking through it, aware of the hunger beneath the Caetanos' smiles, the concern and curiosity in Harriet's eyes, the trembling in his own hand as he lifted the heavy fountain pen and stared at the X awaiting just his signature.

This was it. He was not about to make himself part of the family business, whether his siblings wanted him there or not. He was about to become the majority shareholder. The illegitimate street rat was about to be the new Chairman of the Board and they had no idea.

He glanced up at their wide, disingenuous smiles, no doubt gloating as they fleeced the naïve investor for three times what the shares were worth. If they'd just agreed to pay his mother's medical bills that day. If they hadn't literally thrown him out, taking a riding crop to him as they had done so, then he wouldn't be here right now.

But they had and he was.

Deangelo signed *LDM Santos*, the looping script making the initials hard to read.

He pushed the contract over to Bruno, who barely glanced at Deangelo's signature before scrawling his own.

The deal was done. He'd won.

The meeting ended with an offer to send the new shareholder and his bride to one of the new island resorts for a week: an offer Deangelo smilingly accepted.

He needed time to regroup, time to talk to his lawyer and start to put in motion the second part of the plan, which would be implemented at the shareholders' meeting in a couple of weeks. The Caetanos might have realised by then that they had managed to hand over more than fifty per cent of the company, but they would have no idea that they had handed all the power into the hands of one man. He couldn't wait to see the self-satisfied smirks wiped off their faces for good.

Maybe then he would actually feel something. Because right now he still felt numb. As numb as he'd felt the day his mother died, as numb as he'd felt every day since, driven by nothing but cold revenge. The only time he hadn't felt numb was last night.

Last night… He'd lost control and that was unacceptable, especially now, with everything he'd worked for at his fingertips. There was no time for any kind of emotion, not until his siblings were stripped of everything they held dear: their inheritance, their position in society, their good name. Maybe that day he would finally be free.

Harriet said nothing after they'd said their goodbyes and walked back to the lift and to their suite, her thoughtful expression giving little away. She unlocked the door, preceding him into the suite's sitting room, walking straight over to where the French doors were still unlocked, letting the slight sea breeze into the room. She stood with her back to him, looking out towards the sea.

Her shoulders straightened as she inhaled. 'You should have told me,' she said at last.

He didn't need to ask what. 'There was no reason for you to know. You're not here as my guest, Harriet. You're an employee.' Was he reminding her or himself? He strode over to the sideboard and poured some water. 'Here.'

She turned, accepting the glass he held out to her. 'Yes, I am aware of that.' If he'd hurt her with his casual dismissal of last night and all they'd shared she didn't show it. 'I know I'm here because you trust me to do a good job. You trust me so much that you are paying me well over the odds for me to be here...'

He held up a hand dismissively. 'I have more money than anyone can comprehend. The price was irrelevant.'

'Maybe. But you still wanted me by your side for this deal, not because I was the right person to act as your bride—although I am probably the only person you can trust to keep quiet, to not run to the press, but because I am damn good at my job, at looking out for your interests. But your secrets are stopping me from doing that, from doing my job properly. I'm not prepared. If I'd known that the Caetanos were your family...'

'What? What would you have done differently? Because, make no mistake, Harriet, those people back there? They are not my family.'

She stared. 'Of course they are! I can't believe they couldn't see it; it was almost blindingly obvious.'

'You said it yourself—you left Aion to make a family. Families are forged, not made just because we're unlucky enough to share blood with people.'

Harriet flushed, folding her arms as she confronted him. 'I did say it. But you know what? It doesn't matter. Because I don't see you forging anything, not one human relationship at any time in the whole time I've known you. All you forge is more money. What's it all for, Deangelo? What use is all the money in the world if you're all alone?'

It took everything he'd worked at over the last twelve years to stay completely still, to not betray any emotion even though every word she spoke struck him with deadly aim, striking straight through the armour he'd encased himself in, the armour he'd thought was impenetrable, causing physical pain.

'Some of us deserve to be alone, Harriet,' he bit out.

Her eyes softened. 'No one deserves that, Deangelo.'

He stabbed at his chest, contempt dripping from every pore. 'You think money and handmade suits and private jets make a person worthwhile?'

'No, of course not.'

'You want to know what's under this veneer? You want to know who Deangelo Santos is? He doesn't exist. He's a fake.'

'What do you mean?'

'Deangelo's my middle name. My mother called me by it sometimes. It means from the angel. She used it when she wanted me to know she loved me, no matter what, that she didn't regret having me, no matter what. For eighteen years I was Luciano Deangelo Marcos

Santos. But I left Luciano behind me when I moved to London.'

'Why?' She took a step closer.

'Why? Because Luciano was a nothing. He was a no-good street rat. A boy who couldn't save his dying mother, whose failure was carved into his face, who has to stare at it every damn day. A man who deserves that reminder. Who deserves to remember that he came from nothing. That he is nothing. That he failed.'

Harriet didn't move for a long moment and then she took one long step until she stood next to him, and then her arms were around him, holding his unyielding body close. 'That's not true,' she whispered. 'No one is nothing, that boy wasn't nothing, the man isn't nothing. Let me in, Deangelo. Let me help.'

He stood still, trying to ignore her soft curves pressed against him, trying to keep numb. Feeling nothing protected him; it always had. This simmering heat, this need igniting in his veins made him vulnerable. And yet he stayed as Harriet pressed even closer, trailing kisses along his jaw, swift and sweet and tantalising.

'Let me help,' she said again and oh, God, she was so warm, so alive. She was comfort and life and when he'd been with her last night he'd managed to feel, to forget. Dangerous. And so, so seductive, just like her touch, those light kisses.

With a smothered curse Deangelo captured Harriet's hand in his, tilting her chin with his other hand, gazing at her lush mouth and half-closed eyes with a mixture of helplessness and need. Now was the time to step away;

they'd established the rules last night and he never broke the rules.

But he was back in Rio and he'd been a very different person here—and that young man who had everything to prove was still imprisoned inside him; somehow here the walls were thinner, the distinctions blurred.

'Show me,' Harriet said softly, her gaze burning into him, and Deangelo knew he couldn't stop now, not while she was willing him on. He slid his hand round to the nape of her neck, trailing his fingers along her jawline as he did so, splaying his hand wide as he finally gave in to her plea, to the demands of his body and, lowering his head, captured her mouth with his. Her soft moan of satisfaction was all he needed, deepening the kiss ruthlessly, demandingly, knowing she matched him in every way, her hands raking through his hair, down his back.

Revenge was there waiting for him. Let it wait for now. He had the rest of his life to enjoy what he'd put in motion today. Right now there was sensation and heat and, most intoxicating of all, there was hope.

CHAPTER NINE

RIO WAS TURNING out to be more of an adventure than Harriet could ever have anticipated. Over the last few days the mornings had been reserved for work, the afternoons for exploring. Harriet had tried to surf on Ipanema beach, taken the cable car to Sugarloaf Mountain and wandered through the Jardin Botanico. In the evenings they danced until late, returning to the hotel to make love. There was no talk about stopping—just as there was no talk about the future—an unspoken agreement that all rules and plans were to be put aside for this brief spell.

But today was different. Deangelo had mentioned over breakfast that he was planning to visit his aunt and that Harriet was welcome to accompany him if she chose. He'd sounded offhand, as if her decision meant nothing either way, but Harriet was learning to read him and the tightness around his mouth and the muscle beating in his cheek indicated that he did, in fact, care very much.

She hugged that knowledge to herself. She was wanted and needed and even if it was short-term it was glorious. She was living the charade and she was loving it.

It was more than the fun of being a tourist, more than the sex; it was the companionship. The feeling that she understood and was understood in turn. The only cloud was the secrets she didn't quite dare to pry into. She still didn't know how or when Deangelo's mother had died and why he took all the blame on himself or where the Caetanos fitted in. Maybe today would provide some answers.

But maybe it was better for Deangelo's secrets to remain just that, because their existence was a barrier between them, a reminder that, no matter how much fun they were having, it wasn't real.

Walking back into the sitting room, she saw Deangelo standing, staring out of the window, expression utterly inscrutable.

'Hi,' she said. 'I'm ready.'

He turned, eyes darkening to gold as he looked her up and down in a way that made Harriet feel as if her clothes were utterly transparent. One thing was clear; in the unlikely event he ever tried to hire her again, she would never be able to accept. And as Deangelo didn't do relationships, once this trip was over their paths would part for good. She couldn't help a pang of regret at the thought.

But it was done—and she had been equally culpable in instigating the shift in their relationship.

'Are your shoes comfortable?'

She blinked. That was probably the last thing she'd expected him to say. 'Yes. I think so.'

'Good. We have some walking to do. Keep your bag close. You don't have any valuables in it?'

'Work phone and card and a lipstick.'

'The phone's encrypted?'

'Of course.'

'If anyone tries to take your bag, let them. Okay. Let's go.'

'Okay. I thought we were visiting your family.'

His expression didn't change. 'We are.'

Deangelo barely spoke again until they were in the taxi. The sun shone bright with mid-afternoon intensity and the beach and pavements seemed to have taken on a sleepy quality as sun haze mixed with the pollution to produce a shimmering curtain that dulled and slowed the passing scene.

'The Caetanos live in the other direction,' he said at last. 'Past Ipanema and out to the outskirts. They live in the kind of area where the city is like a distant dream, where the rich don't worry about rubbing shoulders with the people who clean their houses and streets. They live in an estate patrolled by security guards, on a street where pampered young *senhors* and *senhoritas* are chauffeured in air-conditioned cars to private schools and exclusive beach clubs so that they too can grow up believing themselves masters of all they can see.'

'Is that where you grew up?'

He'd alluded to poverty and she'd seen its scars in his eyes. But at the same time Deangelo was so at home with his wealth; it didn't seem newly won. Not for him gaudy trimmings or ostentatious displays. Even his watch was discreet: the best Swiss engineering presented in a neat grey package. Tasteful and the very best engineering and craftsmanship. A sneak thief would probably pass it by, but it cost twice as much as the diamond-covered branded watches favoured by the Caetano brothers.

'I grew up there, but I'm not from there.'

He retreated into silence and after a while Harriet turned her attention to the window, watching Rio live and breathe as the car inched its way through busy, noisy traffic away from the beach and into the heart of the bustling, vibrant city. The minutes ticked away but she barely noticed, caught up in the sights and sounds. Eventually the taxi began to make its way up one of the city's steep iconic hills, the traffic lessening as they progressed. The neighbourhood felt very different to Copacabana, the faded mansions and old houses giving the impression of a once fashionable area in decline, although there were enough signs of refurbishment to suggest some regeneration, a suggestion confirmed by the boutique hotels and art galleries they passed as they continued their journey, the trendy little cafés rubbing shoulders with older, shabbier bars.

'This is cool,' she said. 'It makes me think of how Chelsea must have been in the sixties, before it totally gentrified and big money took over.'

'Santa Teresa? Yes, there are parallels.'

Harriet remembered his offhand comment on their first evening that he thought she would like to stay here. She noted a quirky antique shop. He was right. Which once again begged the question—how did he know her so well when for three years he had barely seemed to notice her at all?

At that moment the car pulled up in front of a pink mansion surrounded by vibrant gardens and Deangelo paid the taxi driver before exiting the car, Harriet following suit, joining him outside the imposing wooden gates. 'What a beautiful house.'

'This was built by Marcos Caetano in the nineteenth century. Only one generation actually lived here; my great-great-grandfather joined the exile of the well-heeled to the outer edges of the city, my father moved yet again. But this was where the family empire was built.'

'And now?' She sensed there was much more going on here than some retelling of old family history.

'Now? Now it belongs to me. I bought it five years ago. Anonymously, of course.'

'To you? But you never come here!' Not that it mattered. Deangelo could probably afford a home in every city in the world if he so chose. But in a city where so many had nothing it seemed obscene to own an empty house.

Although, the more she looked, the more signs of life she saw. The gates weren't locked, just closed, and the house looked lived in, signs tacked neatly to outside walls, the formal path running to the front door maintained.

Deangelo raised a surprised brow. 'I don't need to come here. It's a training centre, for teens and young people from the neighbouring *favelas*.'

Of course it was. And another piece was added to the

jigsaw that made up this intriguing man—only every time she slotted in a new piece the jigsaw trebled in size. 'What kind of training centre?'

'Hospitality. It's a budget hotel, and runs like any other hotel except here most of the staff are being trained and that, of course, is reflected in the price.'

'What a great idea.' Harriet smiled brightly, trying to bury her shock. How hadn't she known he was involved in an initiative like this? She'd spent three years handling his correspondence, managing his inbox and yet she'd had no idea. Oh, he was philanthropic, but in a hands-off way. Cheques written and sent, all invitations to gala events declined. But this was personal in every way, located as it was in the house belonging to the family he was trying to destroy. His family.

'I started out funding schools and places at university, I still do, but that kind of study isn't for everyone. This place gives kids a chance; it's not easy to find legitimate employment when you come from the undocumented side of town. We provide training, work experience, first here and then later in other establishments, more specialised to individual skills. We offer maths and languages for those who need or want them, business studies, too. We then help them find their first job.'

'And now,' she teased, 'you own a whole chain of hotels to provide that extra training!'

But her smile wasn't answered, his forehead creasing as if he were trying to find the answer to an insoluble riddle. 'I suppose I have,' he said slowly. 'I hadn't considered that side of things. Come on.'

With that he pushed open the gate and strode into the front garden, Harriet a step behind. As they neared the front door it opened. They were clearly expected, lines of young adults in neat uniforms waiting to greet them like something out of a country house drama. At the front, wreathed in smiles, stood a young woman with abundant hair coiled into a complicated knot and a man of Deangelo's own age who greeted him with a shout of delight and a complicated handshake followed by much backslapping. Harriet stared. She'd never seen Deangelo so relaxed, a smile so warm and real on the usually stern face.

'This is Harriet,' he said at last in English.

Just Harriet. Not 'my PA.' Not 'my fake wife.' Just her name. Even so, the glances the pair flashed her way were frankly curious and Harriet was glad she'd left her new rings in the safe in the hotel.

'Harriet, I'd like you to meet my cousins, Milena and Luis. They run the hotel for me.'

She smiled, but her hands shook as she accepted their welcome embrace. Deangelo was letting her in, showing her who he was and where he came from.

This could change everything, if Harriet was just brave enough to let it. If she could admit to herself that she wanted him, too. Wanted him. It had been so long since Harriet had thought about what *she* wanted, put her happiness first, the agency her first tentative steps towards a future she chose. Falling for someone as intense, as troubled, as enigmatic as Deangelo could derail all her plans.

But as she looked at the welcoming smiles of Deangelo's cousins, looked behind them at the gleaming paintwork and lovingly polished wood in the hotel entrance hall, the pride and dignity of the assembled staff, ready to show off their hard work to the man who made it his mission to provide them with a future, she knew it might already be too late. It wasn't just the sex, the hormones flooding through her newly awakened body, that was the issue here. It was the man who had awakened her.

Let me in, she'd asked just a few days ago. And here he was doing exactly that, or as close to that as he could possibly get. Deangelo glanced over at Harriet as she chatted to Milena and Luis, her face alive with interest and curiosity during the tour of the hotel.

'This half is very simple, more a hostel than a hotel,' Milena explained. 'The students start out here, learning to deal with simple bookings and queries, to prepare buffet meals and snacks. Then, after six months, they move to the other side, which operates as a boutique hotel. Some know by this point whether they prefer the kitchens or hospitality, others are still not sure.'

'It's such a good idea.' Harriet stopped to peek into one of the pristine family rooms. 'I much prefer this to where we're staying, and I love that the tourists get to give back to the community as well.'

'That's Deangelo for you,' Luis said. 'So many schemes, but nothing is just given away. Everything he does is designed to get people to help themselves, whether it's the university scholarships or the schools and childcare or the community centres…'

'That's enough.' Deangelo interrupted his cousin. 'Harriet doesn't need to hear all about this stuff.'

'Oh, but I do,' she said. 'So there are classrooms here on site?'

'Yes, at the back. Practical classrooms—kitchens and a workshop. But also language labs. We try and make sure as many leave here with reasonable English as possible, others also add Spanish and French. The more languages they have, the more employable they are, the more opportunities they have.'

Deangelo was as interested in the tour as Harriet; he might have designed the hotel but this was his first visit. It was incredible, seeing his concept made flesh.

It was the only tangible thing he felt was his. His entire empire was built on shifting networks and clouds. On third parties and their needs for his technology. Whether car sharing or restaurant finding or holiday booking or room letting—he facilitated millions of exchanges every single day, but he owned none of them. There was nothing he could look at and say 'This is mine,' The office block he owned and lived in had been designed by someone else; it was a place of utility, that was all. Not of passion.

Possessions didn't motivate him. He didn't dream of a home or a family. He didn't deserve such things. But he provided thousands of jobs all over the globe and he was making a difference right here in Brazil. Maybe that would be enough on Judgement Day.

But this hotel was filled with passion and pride, not least from his cousins: Luis, whose footballing dreams had crashed and burned like so many thousands of other not-quite-talented-enough boys, leaving his future uncertain, and Milena, widowed too young, left with two small children and no income. He could have housed and supported them without even noticing the spend; instead he had asked them to help him turn his dreams into reality, and in doing so had given them purpose.

The tour ended in the bright sunlit restaurant, tables spilling out onto the flower-filled terrace. Two graduating students served the coffee and delicious little tarts, answering Harriet's questions in near-perfect English as she quizzed them about their futures. Both had jobs lined up, one here in Santa Teresa, in one of the boutique hotels further up in the hills; the other was heading to one of the city's restaurants.

'That is one of the most inspiring things I have ever seen,' Harriet said as they left, promising to return before their visit ended.

'It's nothing.' He shrugged her words off, uncomfortable with her praise, but she shook her head stubbornly.

'It's not nothing. You heard that boy, Paolo, in there. He was living on the street five years ago! On the street. Headed nowhere safe. Now he has an education, a job, a future, and you made that happen.'

'No. He made that happen. I simply provide the place and the opportunity. The rest is down to him.' Her praise made him uncomfortable. It was Luis and Milena and the other staff and teachers who really deserved it; it was the kids themselves, their ability to learn and grow and hope—things Deangelo had never learned despite his degrees and business empire.

He lived locked away. No friends, his family a continent away, no relationships that lasted longer than a few convenient weeks, no ties. Every day he looked in the mirror and his scar would remind him of all he had failed to do. Of who he really was. What he deserved.

But today, visiting the hotel, seeing Harriet's face lit up with interest, seeing his vision come to life, he had felt just a little less of a failure. Every night, Harriet's curves entwined around him, her lips on his, her breathing in time with his, he felt less alone. But he didn't deserve the way he felt with her. And if she knew it all she would agree.

'So where are we going now?' she asked.

'For many tourists the *favelas* are a place to avoid, unless they're on a tour. A few are more sanitised and some tourists even stay there, another tick on their places-to-see list. But many are not safe for strangers, especially strangers with money.'

'Does that mean we're heading to one?'

'It does. But don't worry. You'll be safe with me.'

Her answering smile was unexpected, as was the trust in her eyes. Trust that warmed him even as it warned him to be careful. 'I know.'

It had been twelve years since he'd last walked into the twisty streets of the *favela*, but he still knew his way instinctively. The boys playing football hadn't been born when he'd left, but they had the same hope and determination in their eyes as they tackled each other, performing tricks in the hope some scout might chance by and transform their lives. The old men sitting outside the bar were as familiar as his view from his office window, the noises and smells and vibrancy making his chest ache with a nostalgia he'd thought he'd trained out of himself many years ago.

All the time he was hyperaware of Harriet by his side, taking everything in, her hand in his, her stride matching his. 'I thought you grew up on the other side of the city,' she said.

'I did.'

'But this is your home, too. Unless you've pioneered some navigation chip and that's beaming directions straight to your brain?'

'Not yet, but good idea. I'll get the tech guys to get started straight away.' He stopped outside a bar, newly opened since he'd left, tables and chairs on the terrace looking out over the spectacular view. 'Drink?'

Harriet nodded and he led her through the brightly painted bar and onto the terrace, ordering a couple of cold beers as he did so.

He looked around, admiring the bright, clean decor, the simple menu scrawled onto a board. 'When I lived here places like this, where outsiders could come, just didn't exist. The way some of the *favelas* have been cleaned up is controversial, and not always long-lasting. That's why everything I do is about changing from within, giving the residents the opportunities they need to change things, and to make sure those changes are what they need, rather than what some politician who has never set foot in these streets thinks they need.'

'Like what?'

He shrugged. 'Education, healthcare, community initiatives, jobs and training. The problem isn't that people aren't always documented, or that the settlements have no infrastructure. It's the lack of opportunity and hope. Every boy out there dreams about being a footballer. That's the way out. When it doesn't happen, and for ninety-nine point nine per cent of them it won't happen, they have no backup plan, and the only future they see is in the gangs. And so the cycle continues. I just want to change that cycle.'

The beers arrived then, with a smile and a message that they were on the house. The owner had recognised him, then? The fund he'd set up to help entrepreneurs fund businesses such as this had proved popular. He took a sip of the tart, icy drink, sitting back, his gaze flitting between the incredible view of the city and the girl opposite. She looked so cool and put together, only her eyes betraying her excitement and her curiosity. 'So how did you end up here?'

'My mother was from here.' He took another drink, weighing his words carefully. Nobody, not even the family who still lived here, knew his whole story. He'd kept it within his whole life, but the urge to unburden himself was almost overwhelming, even knowing that she might turn away if she knew it all.

But she should know just who she was sleeping with, that he was no hero.

'So Luis and Milena are cousins on your mother's side?'

He nodded. 'She was a dancer; she used to frequent dance halls just like the ones I have taken you to. She was so beautiful and so talented; she got a lot of attention, including from my father.'

'Augusto Caetano.' It wasn't a question.

'He was a lot older, with three teenage children and a wife he didn't live with. He offered my mother a job as his housekeeper. It was her chance to get out of the *favela*, to earn money, to live somewhere safe, in beautiful surroundings. She had her own cottage in the grounds of his estate, her own car, could use the pool. She said it was like a dream come true, that she felt like a princess when she first went there. And she didn't have to do much manual work; she managed cleaners and cooks. More like the woman of the house than an employee.'

'Did she love him?'

'I don't know. I think so, by the end. I don't know if she went there knowing he wanted her to be his mistress or if it just happened. But she stayed and a couple of years later she had me; she was only just in her twenties.'

'Did you know Augusto was your father?'

'Not in so many words, but as I grew up it was clear. We still lived in the cottage in the grounds, but I went to an exclusive local school, played tennis and learned to ride. Augusto's wife lived in the countryside—she never came to Rio; he always visited her—but occasionally his other children, his other legitimate children, would come and stay and my mother and I would fade into the background. It was clear that they knew, that they hated us, though.' He picked up his beer, needing to touch something tangible, anchor himself to the here and now. 'I worshipped them. Not so much Isabela—she always had a mean streak—but Bruno and Tiago. They seemed so cool, everything I aspired to be. Occasionally, if they were alone, they might be kinder. As if I were a puppy. Play a game of ball. Once Tiago took me to the beach on his scooter. I spent my life hoping it would happen again.'

'Sounds like your brothers would be good matches for my sisters.'

He smiled at that notion. 'Can you imagine?'

'All too well. So you were what—ten when Augusto died? That's very young. I'm sorry.'

'His death would have been hard enough, but what followed was worse. He'd told my mother that he'd made provision for her, for me. Whether that's true or not I don't know. All I do know is that we were thrown out before the funeral was held. That there was nowhere for us to go apart from back here. No more work for my mother, no more school for me. We belonged nowhere, had nothing. My aunt took us in, in her tiny house, gave us a room to share. I had the bed and my mother the floor. I'm not sure I'll ever forgive myself for that.'

'You were a child.'

'I was ten. Round here that's old enough to grow up, to start being a man. But I was too busy feeling sorry for myself, blaming her for the loss of my life, not knowing how to fit in.' He paused, not wanting to relive those months. 'The only way to survive was to forget all I had been. To play football and run errands for the men, knowing that half the time they were illegal. My mother did her best to get me into school, but I didn't see the point. I think I broke her heart. Young, arrogant, entitled fool.'

Harriet reached across the table and laid her hand on his. 'Don't be so hard on yourself.'

'I deserve it. And more.' He took a deep breath. 'But then she got sick. There are no hospitals here, no doctors we could afford. I knew that Bruno was living back at the family estate so I went there to beg him to help. Despite everything, a part of me still worshipped him, still thought that he might have some feelings for me. I even fantasised that he would offer us our old house, welcome me as a brother. Idiot.'

'I take it that your plan didn't work.' Her eyes flickered to his scar as if she guessed the next step in his sorry saga.

'He told me I was nothing, that my mother was nothing, that we deserved nothing, street rats and vermin that we were. He threw me out, but not before taking his riding crop to me—he gave me this.' He ran his finger down his cheek, feeling the ridged skin underneath. 'Told me he never wanted to see me again, gave me one parting lash; he didn't even wait to see where it landed. I went home with my face torn and empty-handed. I'd failed. And she died a few weeks later.'

'Which is not your fault,' Harriet said fiercely. But he shook his head.

'If I'd not run around with the gangs but found a job, if I'd approached Bruno differently, if I'd noticed she was ill earlier. If I had just let her have the bed…'

'Then maybe nothing would have changed. You can't blame yourself, Deangelo.'

But he could and he did. 'After she died I managed to find a school to take me, then got a scholarship to another, better school, and from there the scholarship to Cambridge. I vowed that I would make sure no other woman or child died in the *favela* because of lack of healthcare, that every child would get an education and a chance to be someone. And I vowed that Bruno Caetano will know exactly what it's like to have his life torn apart and be left with nothing.'

'And then what? Will that make you happy?'

'I don't do happiness,' he said softly. 'It's not in my DNA. Come on, I want to introduce you to my aunt. I think you'll like her.'

'Everyone deserves happiness, Deangelo. And I think your mother would want you to have that above all else.'

He didn't need absolution, didn't deserve it, but the warmth in her voice, the empathy in her eyes, allowed the first tendrils of something new to start unfurling. Something that felt like a future.

CHAPTER TEN

'YOU KNOW…' HARRIET said as she rubbed more suntan lotion onto her exposed legs. 'I really liked Rio, but I have to say this is paradise. At least, it will be.'

'Really? What's stopping it from being paradise right now? The hammock is maybe not comfortable enough? The ocean views not quite spectacular enough? Your breakfast not prepared exactly to your liking? Book not gripping enough?'

The teasing tone in Deangelo's voice was new, as was the humorous glint in his eyes. Harriet glanced over, her eyes lingering on every exposed muscle and sinew as he lounged on a large sunbed situated next to her hammock. She knew every inch of that body, how it felt, how it tasted. A week after they'd first made love, it still seemed incredible to her that they had reached this place.

So, they hadn't discussed what happened next, what returning to London would mean for this very new, very delicate closeness. There was still a week to go. They'd figure it out.

She swallowed, a little voice warning her that this

was all too good to be true. She just wasn't a wanton goddess who lay in hammocks on sun-kissed beaches next to gorgeous men. She was even wearing a bikini, shy as she had been to put on something so revealing, but the light in Deangelo's eyes—and the way he had instantly removed it—had emboldened her and now she walked around without wanting to pull on a cover-up, secure in her skin for the first time in a long time. She loved the confidence he gave her, how desirable he made her feel. As if she could do anything, be anyone. If she could just keep that feeling when she returned to London, it was the greatest gift imaginable.

Turning her thoughts firmly back to Deangelo's question, she tried to articulate what she meant. 'The hotel is perfect in many ways. It's in a lot better shape than the Rio hotel, although it should be, it's so new. The location is amazing and the attention to detail is great, but it doesn't utilise the location properly. We're surrounded by all this amazing wildlife; the hotel should educate and protect, not just use it as a backdrop. Plus, as this place is all-inclusive, it does nothing for the local economy. Visitors should be encouraged to explore, not live in a bubble.'

'Some people like a bubble.'

'True, but this place is half empty. Rebranding it as a wildlife paradise, getting the locals involved and supportive, could transform everything. Differentiate this from all the other identikit beach resorts and transform lives.'

She shifted, enjoying the way the sun saturated her very bones with heat. She'd been surprised when Deangelo had taken up Isabela Caetano's offer of a week in one of her island resorts. Although they had two weeks of little activity between signing the contracts and the first shareholder meeting, vacations just weren't his style. It would have been more usual for him to return to London in the interim; she'd assumed that he would spend the two weeks visiting his new acquisitions. As usual he was holding his cards very close to his chest. His broad and bare chest.

She did know that he was planning a big reveal towards the end of the trip—some kind of showdown—and it unnerved her. The anger he felt was completely understandable, but it isolated him, had twisted him into a machine, bent on revenge. Neither of them had done much living over the years, but she had chosen her path out of love and duty. His path was much darker.

But somehow, these last few days, he had seemed lighter. Maybe being back here, confronting some of those demons that haunted him was helping to set him free? The evening they had spent with his aunt had seemed cathartic, but the next day he had decided to leave Rio and head here; she couldn't help wondering if the ghosts in Rio were proving too much.

All she knew was that at some point he was going to have to forgive himself and move on, but his plans for the Caetanos didn't speak of moving on; instead it seemed to root him in the past, and she ached in sympathy when she saw the clouds in his eyes and knew that he was brooding on what might have been.

The rest of the morning passed peacefully. Their room opened straight out onto the beach and Deangelo had retreated to the shady terrace to work, waving away her offer to help. 'I know you want to finish that book,' he said. 'Your eyes keep straying towards it.'

'Yes, but I'm here to work,' she protested half-heartedly, her hands curling around the book.

'Don't worry, I have plenty for you to do later, but right now you are free to read. Take advantage of it.'

'Well, if you insist…'

It was lovely to soak up the sun and read, but as noon approached and she finally finished the last chapter Harriet began to get restless. She rolled out of the hammock and padded over the hot sand. 'Okay,' she said firmly. 'That's enough.'

He looked up, expression confused, and she sighed. 'Do you even know where you are?'

'If you were wearing that bikini back in the office I think HR would have something to say.'

'You could have been anywhere. You were completely absorbed. And that's fine, but we are in near paradise and it seems a shame for you to sit there and stare at spreadsheets. You worked all day yesterday; you should actually spend some time on holiday being on holiday.'

'You didn't mind when you were reading your book.'

'That is called relaxing. You should try it some time.'

Laughing, he pushed his laptop away. 'So what do you want to do?' His gaze slid to the bedroom, visible through the open doors. 'Take a siesta?'

'At some point, definitely, but what I'd really like to do is take a picnic and go to that little beach those Americans told us about. The one you have to sail to. It sounds idyllic.'

Deangelo didn't move for one moment, his narrowed gaze still focused on his laptop, but then he nodded. 'Okay.'

'Okay? Really?'

'As long as you wear that bikini.'

'It's a deal. Yay! I'll order the picnic and arrange the boat and crew. The Americans said they saw turtles and dolphins. Can you imagine?'

'No crew needed. I'll captain and you can be my crew.'

'It's been a long time since I sailed,' she said doubtfully. The ocean looked pretty flat and peaceful, but it was vaster than she could imagine.

'That's why I'm the captain. Give me an hour and I'll be ready.'

'Perfect!'

As she turned to leave, Harriet put her hand on Deangelo's shoulder and absentmindedly he reached up to cover it with his own. She paused, looking down at their entwined hands, relishing the feel of his muscle under her palm, of his strong fingers interlaced with hers. It wasn't just that she couldn't have imagined being this free and easy with Deangelo, she couldn't have imagined it with anyone. The longer between dates, the more terrifying the thought of putting herself out there was. Her last relationship had petered out when her boyfriend had told her that she was always tired, that her lack of willingness to do anything was boring, and she couldn't help but agree with him. She had felt dull and boring. If she was him, she would have broken up with her, too.

But now she felt full of possibilities. Her life opening up before her. She would always thank Deangelo for that.

The little motorboat was so easy to steer that Harriet had no qualms about taking the helm, enjoying the wind whipping her hair and the spray misting over her bare arms. Once they were a reasonable way out to sea she killed the engine and allowed the boat to bob around for a little, enjoying the sensation of just being on the ocean.

'You know…' Harriet said a little wistfully as she trailed her hand in the cool water. 'When I was little we would always go on holiday to Cornwall. Just the three of us. My sisters didn't come, obviously, they deigned to spend time with us when we went skiing or the year we rented a villa in Tuscany, but Cornwall just wasn't glamorous enough, not the part we went to, anyway. But my mum loved it; she'd holidayed there every year of her life. She'd get more and more excited the nearer we got, as if she were the child. We'd always have a competition over who could see the sea first when we drove there and once there we would spend the whole time kayaking and swimming and surfing. But after she died we couldn't bear to go back. We'd holiday in cities instead, gorge on culture and local food. I didn't know just how much I missed the sea until now.' She inhaled. 'The smell just makes everything seem all right.'

Deangelo reached out to touch her cheek. 'We share that, you and I. We both had that before and after. The old and then the new normal, only the new normal would never measure up.'

'Yes. I suppose we did. It's not just losing a parent, is it? It's the loss of everything else. For me a new home, a new school, a father who seemed to have lost part of him—and then he really did lose part of him. For you...' She paused. For him poverty and loss and a physical reminder of the family who had chosen to cast him out. How could she blame him for the anger that palpably drove him? 'For you, everything. But here we are. We survived, moved on.'

'Yes.' But he didn't sound convinced. Was that because he hadn't actually moved on at all? That part of him was still the bereaved boy wondering what he could have done differently to save his mother?

Maybe she could show him another way. She heard her mother as she ploughed on, telling her she couldn't save everyone, but Harriet ignored the remembered warning, as she had done so many times before. 'Yes, and you know, this trip has shown me that I can't keep putting off working out who I am and what I want to be. Who I want to be. The agency is a start, and it's exciting. But we're all frozen in time somehow, me, Alex, Emilia and Amber. That's partly what drew us together, but I wonder if it gives us permission not to try and move on. Well, no more. I'm going to live and love and dance, even if it hurts me. These last few days, life has been in Technicolor. I want it to stay that way.'

Had she said too much? But wasn't that the point, that she was no longer going to be afraid? It wasn't as if she'd made a big declaration of love, begged him to stay with her. She'd just shown him that she had changed. The question was, had he?

She grinned as he shifted closer. Yes, he had changed—he was wearing shorts for a start, *and* a T-shirt. A comfortable cotton T-shirt with a windsurfer emblazoned on the front. His hair was a tiny bit longer, and a lot more dishevelled than his usual neat crop, and stubble darkened his cheeks and jaw. But most telling of all were the laughter lines creasing his eyes and cheeks. She'd barely seen him crack a smile before. Now he seemed to smile all the time.

Was that because being here was cathartic—or did it possibly have something to do with her?

Placing her hand on his, she leaned closer, inwardly thrilling at her daring, at the way she was emboldened to take the lead, the way he let her, amusement warring with desire in his dark gaze. Her mouth touched his in a kiss, soft and sweet, for a moment, then harder and decadently rich as she relinquished the brief control willingly as his hand slid down her bare back and over her hip. She gasped against his mouth, willing him on, her eyes fluttering shut, only to open again as something behind him snagged her attention. 'Deangelo...' she murmured. 'Look!'

Pulling back just a little, he half turned, only to freeze in place as he saw the same dorsal fin she had seen. *'Golfinho...'* he breathed.

Not daring to move, barely to breathe, Harriet just sat, spellbound, as the dolphin swam lazily past them, submerging momentarily, only to leap in the air, twisting as the sun glinted off its sleek purple-black body. 'It's doing tricks!'

It was almost—almost—close enough to touch,

plainly curious about the small bobbing boat and its two inhabitants, swimming away, only to shoot out of the water and twist before swimming back again, treating the pair to an unrivalled display of water gymnastics, clearly enjoying the interaction as much as they were. Harriet was barely aware of Deangelo taking her hand in his, of the way he pulled her close so she sat against him as the dolphin played, the two relaxing enough to laugh out loud at the jumps and games. 'I wish I could swim with him,' Harriet said longingly.

'It's a wild animal, for all it seems so real.'

'I know. And I hate the thought of it being in captivity or tamed in any way. It's perfect wild and free. I feel so privileged it wants to share this time with us.' And as Deangelo dropped a kiss on her head she couldn't help thinking that, although he was the opposite of the dolphin in many ways, constricted by the rules he set himself, imprisoned by the life he chose, she was equally as privileged to share these rare intimate moments with him. Moments to savour, and never to take for granted.

'You know,' Harriet said dreamily, eyes half-closed, 'I take it back. This place *is* paradise. And today was pretty near perfect.'

Deangelo grinned as he ran his hand down her side and felt her gasp. 'Just pretty near?'

'The dolphin was perfect,' she allowed.

'What about what came after the dolphin?' He ran his hand back up, nudging the full underside of her breast, reining in the urge to deepen the touch as she arched ever so slightly.

'You mean the gorgeous beach? And the swimming?'

'The *nude* swimming…' he reminded her, his hand skimming up to her throat and along her jaw. He adored how responsive she was, how uninhibited, how she made him want to worship her completely and unselfishly.

'And the moment we saw the turtle. The dolphin still wins because of the tricks but the turtle comes a really close second in the most-awesome-moment-ever competition.'

'The turtle was amazing,' Deangelo allowed. 'What about after the turtle?'

'The picnic? Yes. That was excellent.'

'Harriet,' he said slowly, drawing one finger down her bare arm, watching the way she shivered under his touch. 'After the picnic…'

'That was excellent, too,' she conceded, rolling over to meet him. 'Almost perfect, in fact.'

'Only almost?' He retraced the path his finger had taken and her chest rose and fell.

'I'm just saying, practice makes perfect…'

'Is that a challenge, Harriet Fairchild?'

'Are you up to it if it is?'

'Always.' As he said the word the reality of it struck home. That this woman, lying languorously next to him, wanted to be there was nothing short of a miracle. Oh, Deangelo attracted women, most drawn to his money, some by success. A few were intrigued by his brawn and scar, suspecting the rough edges under the tailored suit, but none of them knew him. Harriet did, better than anyone. She knew the ugly truth and she still chose to be here.

Even more miraculously, he wanted her here. He never allowed himself to want anything good or warm or real. Just the coldness of success and revenge. And yet here he was. She made him want to be better, do better. She almost made him forgive himself. 'Always,' he said again, tasting the word as he said it.

He saw Harriet swallow, the flicker of her eyes. 'Don't worry. I won't hold you to that when we're back.'

'We agreed just one night and yet here we still are,' he reminded her, unsure why he pressed the point. Of course they would go their separate ways when they returned to London. Harriet had a life to lead, a new business and a world to explore. And he? He had no idea what he would do once his revenge had finally been exacted, but one thing hadn't changed—in the end, people always let you down. If he and Harriet tried to extend this understanding, he'd mess it up. That was what he did. Better to not think past today.

'We agreed no strings. So don't think you have to say nice things to make me feel better, because that really isn't necessary.'

'When have you ever known me to do or say anything nice for the sake of it?' Why was he arguing the point when they both knew it would be over? Was it because he wanted to at least pretend that there might be more—or was it because he wanted Harriet to believe it? To know that if he were a different man he would never let her go. That all the clichés were true. She was a for ever kind of woman for one lucky man. And for the first time in for ever he wished that man could be him.

'You do nice things. You always send your girlfriends an expensive necklace when you break up with them.'

'Dates,' he corrected her. 'They are only ever dates. And I have an account at the jewellers and you order and send the necklaces.'

'True. When you put it that way it isn't quite so nice.'

'Soulless even.' He wasn't sure he wanted her to answer that.

'A little,' she conceded. 'But not always. You paid for Beryl's hip replacement.'

'It was interfering with her work and she cleans the office just the way I like it.'

'With a top surgeon and an all-inclusive holiday to recuperate as soon as she could travel.'

'I wanted her back fit and well.'

'You paid for that guy from Accounts to take his kids to Disneyland.'

'Yes.' He could hear the bleakness in his voice. 'They had lost their mum the year before.'

'It was a nice thing to do.'

'Or a way of salving my own guilty conscience? Buying people things doesn't make me nice, Harriet. It's the easiest thing in the world.'

'Choosing the right thing isn't,' she argued. 'That's far trickier. Dad loved Mum and obviously, compared to you, he might not have been rich, but by normal standards he was really well off. But he never quite got her presents right. A flashy convertible when actually she'd have preferred a vintage vehicle. A diamond necklace when she liked Art Deco beads. He never quite got it. But you get it without being told. Look at that library membership you gave me. That was perfect.'

With a sigh Deangelo pulled himself up to sit next to her. 'You always had your nose in a book when you weren't working and the shared house you were living in was tiny. You always said you had no space of your own. I thought you'd like to be able to hide out there at weekends.'

'I did, I do.'

'So there you go. No miracle. Just observation. That's what I do in business. See what needs fixing and find a solution. It's not as complicated as you make it sound.' Deangelo didn't know why he was trying to downplay the gift, nor the time he had spent trying to find her something really special. He just knew he didn't want her to realise just how much pleasure he had received from giving her something that he knew would make her really happy.

'But that's just it.' Harriet clearly wasn't done, her forehead furrowed as she puzzled out her thoughts. 'I had no idea that was the perfect gift, but somehow you did. It's like the coat. How on earth did you find one to fit me so perfectly?'

'That old coat of yours was no good at all. The colour washed you out; you were always cold in it.'

'How do you know that?'

'Because I know you, Harriet Fairchild. I notice you.'

As soon as he had said the words Deangelo wanted to recall them. Harriet stilled next to him, her eyes the only colour in her suddenly pale face. 'What do you mean?'

'I just told you, I fix problems…'

'No. What do you mean when you say you notice me?'

'You've worked for me for three years. Of course I notice you. If your hip needed replacing then I would have organised that for you too.'

'That's good to know,' she said drily. 'But Deangelo. Those gifts. The membership, the coat. Those ballet tickets—how did you know my mother took me to see *The Nutcracker* every Christmas?'

'Doesn't everyone's mother take them to see *The Nutcracker* every Christmas?'

'No. They don't. They're the most perfect things I ever received. And they're not practical. They don't solve any problems…'

'Nonsense. That old coat could have made you ill.'

'The library?'

'Everyone needs space of their own, Harriet. I spent my teenage years sharing a small house with ten relatives. I know this.'

'The tickets?'

'You deserve to be happy.' Once again words he had no idea he was going to say echoed around the room as once again Harriet froze, as if processing them.

'You were an excellent PA; you made my life run smoothly. You deserved a reward.' He could hear the chilling tone in his voice, feel the walls closing back in as he said the cold words.

'That's all it was?'

'That's all it was. I told you I'm not nice.'

Her next words were so soft he could barely hear

them. 'I know that makes sense. That's what I believed. I mean, nothing else makes any sense. But you know what else makes no sense? Insisting I accompany you on this trip. You need barely any support. Any decent temp could have done it. Any reasonable actress could have pretended to be your wife.'

'I needed someone I could trust.'

'And another thing. Why are you working so hard to push me away? Trying to prove how not nice you are when every gesture tells me something different—when you notice me? When you tell me *always*?'

It was his turn to freeze. For he had said that word not once but twice. He'd told her he'd noticed her. Let his guard down. Why? Because he wanted her to look in the mirror and see what he saw in her. To stop putting herself down and behind, to believe.

He was a man who had everything and possessed nothing. Who made billions from the intangible, using algorithms to profit from other people's work and ingenuity. A man who lived alone, who let no one close. A man frightened of letting anyone in, who deserved nothing. Who didn't trust himself not to let people down. Even now, he was proving himself no better than his father, the man who'd seduced his housekeeper and left her with nothing. He had sworn never to be like the Caetanos and yet here he was, with his PA in his bed.

He knew it was wrong—and yet it felt so right. He also knew he couldn't dent her newfound self-confidence, that to do so would be a crime greater than any his father had committed.

He knew he had to be honest. And that was the most terrifying thing of all.

'I needed you with me on this trip because I couldn't imagine anyone else by my side when I returned to Rio.' He couldn't look at her as he spoke. 'I needed you to play my bride because I couldn't imagine making it seem genuine with anyone else.' She gave a sharp intake of breath but said nothing. 'I bought you the coat because I saw it and knew you would look beautiful in it. I bought you the ballet tickets because I hear you when you talk to me, even when I don't acknowledge it, and one day you mentioned it was opening night and it always made you think of your mother.'

Still she said nothing but she crept a little closer, closing the gap that had opened up between them, and laid her head on his shoulder, her hand finding his and clutching it.

Now he had started he wasn't sure he could stop. 'I liked the way you smiled and said good morning as if you meant it, not because it was a courtesy. I saw you counsel your friends, and heard you speak to your father on the phone three times a day, always patient, even when I could see frustrated tears in your eyes. I saw how you would get lost in a book, even the longest flight an opportunity to read, not a chore, but you always put work first. I saw the way you asked nothing from anyone but gave—and I thought it was time you got put first. I wanted to see you smile. You have a beautiful smile.'

He stopped. There were more words, more feelings, locked up inside but he had no idea how to reach them, if he even dared to try. Harriet lifted her head from his shoulder and turned to him, her eyes damp with tears. 'Thank you. Thank you for saying that.'

'It's true, Harriet. Like I told you, I'm not nice.'

He tilted her chin so that he could look straight into her eyes, imprint his words on her. 'I didn't want you to leave. But it's right you start to live. That you build your family and figure out who you are and where you want to be. I admire that. Respect it.'

'I wish you the same,' she whispered, covering his hand with hers, tilting her chin higher so her mouth brushed his once and then again. 'You need to learn to live as well. To build. Life's far too short to spend it locked away, Deangelo.'

He deepened the kiss, laying her back on the bed, covering her body with his. Deangelo wished that he could believe her words. But some people were safer locked away and times like this nothing but a brief parole. But as her hands travelled down his back, pulling him closer, he allowed himself the indulgence of one wish. That he could be different, that his scars could be external only, that he could be allowed happiness with a woman like this.

CHAPTER ELEVEN

HARRIET STRETCHED SLEEPILY, not wanting to open her eyes quite yet, wanting to stay in this quiet, contented moment for ever. Last night's lovemaking had been like nothing she had ever experienced. Tender, sweet. Loving.

She stilled. Loving?

That wasn't in their agreement, not the formal or the informal.

And yet…

Somehow, over the last week, she had told Deangelo more about herself than any other person, including her friends and her father. And she suspected the same was equally true of him. Was it because they trusted each other, because they had worked together for so long, so intensely, that there were few barriers? She had seen Deangelo tired and frustrated, elated, working tirelessly to solve puzzles. And he? He had noticed her—all those days and weeks and months when she'd thought he saw her as nothing but some kind of competent office robot he had seen straight into the soul of her.

They trusted each other. And this was the last time

they would work together. He would return to his South Bank tower and she to her Chelsea townhouse and it was unlikely their paths would ever cross again. This trip would be a cherished memory for her to examine on those long, dark nights of the soul that seemed to occur far too often. Or better, she could use it as a catalyst to move her life forward in a direction she chose.

She'd been bold and playful and seductive. She'd been open to new experiences. She'd seen this trip as an adventure and grabbed it with both hands. Surely she could repeat that once back in London?

Rolling over, she opened her eyes and allowed herself the luxury of watching Deangelo with no barriers between them. It was rare for him to sleep and her to be awake and she luxuriated in it, starting at the top of the dark head, her gaze moving slowly down the unusually peaceful face, his mouth relaxed in sleep giving him a relaxed air seldom seen in waking hours. She paused as she reached the scar, the visible reminder of his banishment from the family who spurned him, the never-fading reminder of the day he had swallowed his pride to help his mother and failed. That day had changed him, hardened him, driven him. Was he capable of letting go and moving on? She hoped so. Further down, the sensuous mouth and firm chin, broad shoulders and chest, ridged with muscle and yet capable of utter gentleness. Dark silky hair running down to the kind of abs not usually found on deskbound businessmen, then down again…

'Like what you see?'

Damn. How did he do that? Wake so instantly and

alertly. Embarrassed heat flushed through her, although she tried to hide it, meeting his amused gaze full-on. 'It's not bad.'

How she had the *sangfroid* to tease him like that, to lie here, only half-covered by her sheet, utterly comfortable in such intimacy she didn't know. But she had no fear, no worries about her inadequacies, no desire to cover her stretch marks or overly ample curves. From being a skinny child, her hips and breasts had grown in adolescence, giving her an hourglass figure she had no idea how to live in, her height another torment for a girl who just wanted to hide in a reading nook somewhere. With no mother to reassure her, a father who thought of her as a little girl and slender toned half-sisters who looked her up and down—and side to side—with barely hidden scorn, Harriet had spent half her life dressing to hide and shroud. But no more. Deangelo had made her body feel like something that deserved worshipping—and worship it he had. The heat intensified and this time she made no move to hide it, smiling across at him instead.

'That's not what you said last night,' he said, returning her smile with an intimate one of his own, part wolf but with a hint of sweetness that made her chest ache and stomach twist. With lust, yes, with need and want, but with something more.

And she wasn't sure she wanted to face that something more.

'So, what do you want to do today?' she asked, aware she was retreating but unable to do anything about it. 'I thought we might walk into the village and take a look. If you did decide to turn this place from an all-inclusive fortress where guests live in a protected bubble to somewhere that feeds into and helps the local economy it would be a good idea to see what the village actually offers.'

Deangelo's smile disappeared, his expression guarded once more, as if the sweet intimacy had never been. 'You're probably right. But I haven't decided what to do yet.'

'To do about what?'

'About this place, about any of them. This isn't just about gaining control of my father's business, Harriet. It's about justice. I could turn the hotels around, sure, invest in them. But how does that help achieve justice? The Caetanos will reap the rewards without lifting a finger. I want them to lose everything. To know what it is like to see everything they think they are stripped away from them.'

Harriet sat up, chilled despite the heat of the day. 'But how on earth will you do that?'

He shrugged. 'Maybe sell the hotels for nothing. Or let them continue to run them into the ground. I haven't decided yet.'

'Or you could put every penny of profit back into the hotels and make a success of them, despite their mismanagement. Thousands of people work for these hotels; you can't endanger their jobs because of a personal vendetta.' She couldn't quite believe what she was hearing. How could the man who put so much effort into transforming lives be so casual about the people who worked for the Caetanos? 'If not then yes, sell them to someone who will invest and build; don't allow them to wither just to prove a point.'

His expression hardened. 'I would make sure the employees were compensated.'

'Even so…' She lay back down, unease still twisting through her. This wasn't right. 'Compensation doesn't make up for the lack of a livelihood, or purpose.'

'You said yourself this place does nothing for the local economy. No one who comes here enhances the local area at all.'

'No, but they could. And you could drive that.'

'I'm not a hotelier.'

'You own a hotel in Rio, run it as a social enterprise. You could do exactly the same here. Rename them, invest every penny of profit in them and don't hand anything to the Caetanos. You'll achieve the same end but do a lot of good along the way. But, better still, pay them off. Buy the rest of the chain and then walk away, severing all links. Act fair. Show them they are nothing. That's got to be the better win.'

But he had completely shut down. 'I've worked for this for over ten years, Harriet. Everything I have done has been to this end. And you want me to pay them off for their trouble and let them walk away scot-free?'

'I want you to move on.' Suddenly uncomfortable with her state of undress, Harriet slid out of the bed and grabbed the light silk robe she'd bought last week. To play a part, true, but it shocked her how quickly she had slid into accepting the situation, wearing the expensive clothes and accessories as easily as if she had paid for them herself. How quickly her fourth finger had grown used to the rings and how she looked for the flash of blue when the sapphire caught the light. 'You are letting what happened define you.'

'It shaped me,' he said tightly, following her out of the bed and disappearing into the en suite bathroom, closing the door firmly behind him. Harriet's stomach dropped, the feeling of ease and rightness she'd woken up with dropping with it. She should have kept quiet. This was none of her business.

But how could she? Deangelo had always encouraged her to state her opinion, always listened courteously. But that was when their relationship was professional, not personal. When her opinion was purely business-related, not the very heart of him.

Besides, it wasn't as if she didn't know he was ruthless; no one could be as successful as he was without a streak of coldness.

Harriet made sure the robe was firmly tied, slipped on a pair of flip-flops and headed out to the terrace, where she knew their breakfast had been left. Sure enough, a steaming coffee pot sat on the wide wooden table, along with a jug of covered fruit juice and lidded platters which, she knew from experience, contained tiny tasty pastries, slices of fresh fruit and yogurt. But she wasn't at all hungry, unable to stomach anything else but the bitter Brazilian coffee. Pouring a cup, she wandered along the terrace to where her hammock lay, swaying ever so slightly in the faint breeze. Yesterday she had been so happy.

Today reality was beginning to reassert itself and it wasn't a comfortable process. No matter how tender

Deangelo might be, no matter how much they might play the honeymooning couple, nothing had actually changed. Their worlds were miles and miles apart. Not just because of money or position, but because of what they wanted. Harriet wanted a family, not just the friends she had made over the last few years, but a husband and children. She'd just been too scared to articulate that need to herself. To dare to think beyond the next day. She knew all too well what it felt like to lose everything, both instantly and also so slowly that the unthinkable began to be normal.

This last week had shown her just what loving and being loved could be like. Not that Deangelo loved her, she knew that, nor she him…

She placed her coffee cup down, hands shaking, spilling the dark, thick liquid onto the table. Love? Where had thought come from? So she had admitted that she found Deangelo sexy. That she desired him. That maybe, if she was really honest with herself, she had secretly felt that way for a long time. Had been proud of the close relationship they'd shared, that she so often received one of his rare smiles, that he liked her to accompany him wherever he went, whether business trips abroad or the rare occasion he accepted a corporate invitation. That she liked entering rooms by his side, even if her demure shapeless dresses and the tablet she carried rather than a bag made it clear her position. She liked it when he asked her opinion, when he listened.

People thought of him as a soulless, joyless automaton and she would agree. But she'd always known he was more. She'd just been scared to admit it. To admit how much she noticed him.

As he had noticed her. Maybe that was it. Just occasionally he made her feel special and that was so rare in her life she absorbed those moments, holding them close, needing them. But was that love? How could it be? It was all about her, about how she felt. Love wasn't selfish. It shouldn't be.

How could she love the man who tried to change the system that had nearly broken him? The man who quietly made things better, never asking for praise or recognition? The man who danced like the devil and made love like an angel?

How could she not? Because it was hopeless? Because he was so broken there was no way of fixing him? Because he didn't love her, didn't love anyone? If only love worked that way.

Oh, God. She had fallen in love with him. What an utter idiot she was.

Mechanically, she grasped for her bag, realising it was still in the room. She needed her phone, to read HEAA emails and absorb herself in something she had some control over. Rising to her feet, she walked the few yards slowly, still unable to process what had just happened, what she had admitted to herself and what it meant.

The shutter doors were pulled to and she pushed them open, halting at the sight of Deangelo standing in the middle of the large room, a towel looped round his hips, hair wet and slicked back. It was a sumptuous space, a one-room villa dominated by the wooden four-poster, decked in gauzy white curtains. A white sofa and matching chairs were placed on the opposite side of the room, a dining table and chairs behind them. At the back, doors led to his and hers bathrooms. Huge shuttered windows could be un-shuttered to let the outside in, with beach and sea views on three of the four sides. It was the most glorious place Harriet had ever seen.

But, next to him, it was nothing. He dominated the space, not just with his physical size, but with his aura. How could she not love him? But saving him was a whole different matter and one that might just be beyond her.

Harriet didn't speak, just stood by the door staring at him, the morning sunshine framing her, highlighting her strawberry-blonde hair to a golden glow, shining off her lightly tanned skin. She looked like an angel. An angel come to deliver him or to deliver judgement on him. Deangelo wasn't sure which he wanted; he knew which one he deserved.

But hadn't she already begun the process? Taken his certainty and shaken it. He'd come here for revenge, but now he no longer knew if that was the right path.

And after so many years pursuing that path, uncertainty was as unwelcome as it was disconcerting. He had vowed to avenge his mother. How could he turn away now when he was so close?

But Harriet's words rung true, chiming in with the conscience he had been doing his best to ignore. His actions didn't just affect himself. If he was too ruthless, then he was no better than the family who had disowned him, not caring who he trampled in the process, how many lives he destroyed.

'I just wanted to get my bag,' she said, stepping tentatively into the room as if she were afraid of him, afraid of who he really was deep down. As if she could see the unworthiness deep in his soul, even after all they had shared, and at that moment Deangelo knew with cool clarity that the honeymoon was over.

'Of course.'

'I was thinking…'

But he cut in first. She didn't need to say anything.

'I need to get back to the city.'

'Right. Okay. That's…'

'It's time to end this.'

Disappointment clouded her expression for a moment before the polite, bland expression of old reappeared. 'You're the boss.'

Deangelo curled his hands into fists, holding back the words trying to burst out of him. *Try to understand—this is all I have, all I am. Can't you love me anyway? Find me worthy, despite my monstrousness.*

Love? Where had that come from? Love was weakness. If you didn't love then you couldn't lose. If you weren't loved then you couldn't fail someone. He'd spent his whole adult life making sure he never got close enough to anyone for any kind of love, keeping even his mother's family at arm's length, even the aunt who had given him a home, the aunt who had fought tirelessly to get him a scholarship to a good school, to get the education which had led to Cambridge and a new life. Materially she wanted for nothing, although she had elected to stay and work in the *favela*, throwing that same spirit which had propelled Deangelo to school into community projects. But this trip was the first time he had visited her since he had left. She deserved better, but he didn't know how to give her more.

Harriet deserved better. He suspected she knew that. Because she might be able to save him but he was much more likely to drag her down.

'Pack your things. I'll get Reception to order a car…'

'I'll do that,' she said quickly. 'My job, remember? Do you want to head back to Rio? Not the same hotel?'

'Good God, no.' But his reaction wasn't because of the faded glory or the location; it was because he didn't want to return to the suite where he had first made love to Harriet, where they had shared a hot, sweet, fevered night, one that was supposed to be a one and only. If it had been, would the inevitable parting be easier?

'No, I thought not. I'll find us somewhere more suitable. How long do you want to stay in Rio? Or would you like to stay somewhere else until the shareholders' meeting? One of the other hotels maybe, to get a different perspective?'

Deangelo had been born in Rio and stayed there until the day he had flown to England. He'd been born in a vast country full of natural wonders, full of incredible wildlife, and he had never seen more than a few square miles. But what was the point of visiting hotels he had no interest in running, in places he would never return to? His life was over the ocean now.

'We'll stay in Rio for the rest of the allotted time. It'll

take time to put the right compensation packages for workers together, to decide what to do with the hotels.'

'You've made your mind up then?'

'Harriet, it never changed.'

She nodded, a dignified acknowledgement—or capitulation—and his heart cracked, knowing he had just pushed away the one person who might have saved him.

'Fine. I'll get dressed and then book the car and the hotel.' She walked, straight-backed, past him and into her bathroom, the door shutting firmly behind her. Deangelo stood watching the door for a few seconds, wondering what would happen if he was brave enough to tap on it, to ask her to help him be someone new, to help him move on. But as he moved he caught sight of his reflection, the faded scar reminding him of a duty as ingrained as destiny and, turning, he scooped up his laptop and headed out to the terrace and coffee to work.

But as he walked out Harriet's words from the other day returned to him. Was this what his mother would have wanted? She had been fiery, yes. Passionate. Quick to anger, quicker to laugh. And she had loved him. Wholeheartedly. The only person who ever had. Would she have wanted him to lock himself away? If she was looking down, was she proud of all he had achieved—or grieving who he had become?

How could he answer that? All he knew was that revenge had driven him all these years and he had no idea how to stop.

He'd always been able to lose himself in work and today was no exception. Opening his laptop allowed him back into a safe world where all he had to lose was money. He opened a report on potential investments and concentrated on projections and strategies, ruthlessly shutting out the birdsong, the sigh of the waves, the view. This was his life, the rest just a distraction. And if his chest felt hollow and his throat ached, well, he'd just drink some more coffee and carry on. It was all he knew how to do.

The report was absorbing enough to allow him to slip back into his safe space until a cry brought him back to awareness of his surroundings, the sun hot on his back a reminder he wasn't at his desk. Another strangled sob brought him to his feet and back into the bedroom before he was even aware what he was doing, pulse hammering.

'What's wrong? Are you hurt?'

Harriet was sitting on the bed, her phone in her hand, face white, eyes wide in shock. 'I…'

'What's happened?'

'It's my dad. He's had a stroke. The home just called. They said I need to get back straight away. Oh, Deangelo. I think he's dying. I'm going to be all alone. What will I do?'

The next couple of hours passed in a blur, Deangelo ruthlessly taking control, sending Harriet to pack while he organised a car to take her straight to the airport where his pilot would be waiting for her. After her bags were packed she made call after call, to her friends, to the hospital and, fruitlessly it seemed, tried to track down her sisters.

She was making another attempt to find her sisters when Reception alerted Deangelo that the car had arrived and that a porter would be there to collect Harriet's bags in the next few minutes. Deangelo walked back into the room. It looked bare and lonely with Harriet's possessions missing, the suitcases by the door poignant. If he was the kind of man to indulge in poignancy, that was.

Walking over to the sofa where she sat hunched, phone clamped to her ear, Deangelo laid one hand gently on her shoulder. 'It's time,' he said.

Harriet only nodded as she laid the phone in her lap. She sat very still, as if gathering her strength, then rose stiffly to her feet. As she did so the porter rapped gently on the door and, after a quick consultation with Deangelo, took her bags.

'The car will take you straight to the airport. Tony is waiting there for you and will fly you straight back to London, where another car will meet you.'

'Fine. Thanks. Oh, my clothes? My own clothes?'

'Already on board.'

'Great. I'll have these returned to you after…once I'm home.'

'Keep them; they look better on you.' But the feeble joke didn't raise even a glimmer of a smile.

'I can't. It doesn't seem right.'

'Consider them a bonus,' he said, more bitterly than he intended, but she didn't respond. He'd seen Harriet worried before, upset before, but never this bleak. Hopeless, hands twisting as she stood there.

'Oh!' She stilled her hands, staring down at them. 'The rings.'

'They were made for you. Keep them.' He'd ordered them weeks ago, designed them just for her, the entwined branches and leaves symbolising her strength and ability to renew and carry on, the sapphire matching her eyes.

'They are the most beautiful rings I have ever seen. But I can't keep them, Deangelo.' As she spoke she slid them off her finger and laid them in his palm, closing his hand over the delicate circles. 'Right.'

'I'll walk you to the car.'

'No. Please. I can manage.' She touched his cheek, the scarred cheek, with one gentle caress then walked to the door, stopping just before she stepped outside and turned, eyes bright with unshed tears. 'I'm frightened, Deangelo. My father is all I have. Without him I am truly alone. I don't know if I can do this by myself.'

'Hey,' he said roughly, trying to push the emotion away, to stay strong. 'If anyone can handle this, you can.'

'Why do people always leave me?' she whispered, and his heart twisted.

'Harriet, you and I know that the only people we can rely on are ourselves. It's not easy, but that's the way it is. At least we don't get let down this way.'

'If that's true, why did you need me for this trip?'

It was his turn to freeze. 'I knew you'd get the job done. I trusted you.'

'I can't be the only person you trust.'

'It was a business decision, pure and simple.'

But was it, or had it been simply that he couldn't have faced coming home without her? No. That wasn't how he operated; it couldn't be. It would make him weak, vulnerable, to need someone else in that way.

'Come with me,' she said, and his chest thumped painfully at the hope in her voice, in her expression. 'Walk away from revenge and anger. I don't want to do this alone, Deangelo. I want to do this with you. With someone who knows me, who notices me, with someone I trust…' She took a deep breath. 'With someone I love.'

The pain in his chest intensified, the roar of his blood competing with the thud of his heart. For one moment he considered agreeing, leaving Brazil, the Caetanos, his revenge behind, flying back with her, supporting her the way she needed him to. The way she hadn't been afraid to ask him to. He envied her courage. 'Don't waste your love on me, Harriet. I'm not worth it.'

She nodded, one tear falling as she tried to smile. 'That's not how love works, Deangelo. I hope your revenge is worth it.' And then she turned and was gone, leaving him alone once again. Just as he was meant to be.

Only it hadn't hurt this way for a very long time.

CHAPTER TWELVE

'HERE—EAT THIS.'

Deangelo's aunt placed a plate of warm, spicy cookies in front of him, adding a glass of milk, as if he were still the skinny, lost ten-year-old who had come to live with her. Her house was bigger now, thanks to him, but it had the same feel as the old overcrowded cottage clinging to the hillside, her eclectic taste marrying vintage with modern, brightly coloured pictures and ornaments jostling for prominence, the walls and shelves covered with photos of her children and grandchildren. In the centre of the bookshelf was a photo of Deangelo and his mother, a formal one taken when they still lived on the estate. She followed Deangelo's gaze and her face softened.

'She looked so happy. She was so happy. She loved him, your father, never doubt that.'

'But did he love her?'

'I believe so. She believed so. She would never have stayed if she didn't. And she never blamed him for how things turned out. Whether he made a will and it was suppressed, or he forgot to write one we'll never know. But she was never bitter. It was the way things were.'

'She would never have died if she hadn't lost everything.'

'We don't know that. All we can do is live with how things are. Find happiness in what we have. Have you heard from Harriet?'

The last question was shot straight at him. His aunt had taken to Harriet and was sad to hear of her troubles. 'No. I don't want to bother her when she has so much to worry about.'

'Nonsense—why would you be bothering her? She'll want to know you're thinking of her.'

'We're not together, not like that. She worked for me, that's all.' The lies were bitter on his tongue and he wasn't surprised when his aunt laughed.

'You tell yourself that, but I know when two people are mad about each other. I was the eldest of five and I had eight children of my own. You think I haven't seen couples fall in love over and over again? The only thing I don't understand is why you are still here and not back in England, helping her. You know how hard it is to lose your only parent.'

'She lost her father long ago in some ways.' But he knew, despite the illness and the toll it had taken on her whole life, it would devastate Harriet if her father died. 'What did you mean, mad about each other?' His heart thumped as he asked the question. His aunt probably saw what she expected to see in a young couple. But curiosity won out all the same.

She shrugged. 'It's the way you moved, like you were

dancing, always in time. The way you would watch each other, almost surreptitiously, checking you were both okay. Little smiles, little touches, moments when it was as if you were alone in the universe. There's a rhythm with a couple in tune, and you two had it. So why did you let her go alone? Your mother would be very disappointed in you.'

'I let everyone down, Tia Luisa.' As he said the words he saw the sorrow in Harriet's eyes as she had asked him to come with her—and the sorrow when she'd told him she loved him. She'd known it was hopeless, that he was hopeless, but she'd tried anyway. 'She's better off without me in her life.' She'd get over him soon enough. Find someone who loved her the way she deserved. His hands curled into fists at the thought but he relished the pain. He deserved it.

'You're letting her down right now. By doing nothing.' Her voice softened as she sat next to him, one warm hand on his arm. 'You have all the money anyone could want, Deangelo, but if you are too afraid to love then what good is it? Your mother would want you to live, to dare to love, to take that risk. Of course there are no guarantees; humans are built that way. But that's the adventure. Your mother risked it all for your father.'

'And she lost.'

'She didn't lose. She had twelve happy years and she had you. She wouldn't have changed any of that for anything. Believe me.'

'I let her down. I was so angry with her when we came here, acted so badly, couldn't get her the money she needed…'

'All she wanted from you was for you to be happy.

To be the good, honourable man she knew you could be. Maybe Harriet will make you happy, maybe not, but if you don't try, and keep trying, then you dishonour your mother. But you can never dishonour her by love.'

'I promised I would get my revenge, that I would wipe the Caetanos out of society.' He was pleading for his aunt to understand, to sanction his actions.

'Your father was a Caetano. She would want you to preserve his legacy and show his children the mercy they didn't show you. It's your decision, Deangelo, and I will stand by you whatever you decide. That's what families do. But tonight I will pray that you choose love. It's what your mother would want for you. It's what you should want for yourself.'

She squeezed his arm before heading out of the kitchen, leaving him alone with the milk and cookies and wondering if his mother wouldn't want him to pursue vengeance then who was all this really for?

And, more importantly, wondering if Harriet was coping, or if she still had that lost, scared expression in her eyes. His aunt was right—she needed him. Maybe she loved him, maybe not, but he loved her and she needed him. He was doing no good, skulking here, like Achilles withdrawing from battle, revenge no longer the driving force it had once been. If he let Harriet face her father's illness alone then he didn't deserve any happiness. It was time to let go of his hate and his fear. It was time to hope.

'Can I get you anything?' Amber asked, her voice hushed, as it had been since Harriet returned home a week ago.

Harriet shook her head. 'No. But thank you.'

'You haven't eaten anything.'

'I know. I don't mean to be ungrateful; you have worked so hard…'

But her friend waved the comment away. 'When I'm stressed I bake; you know that. I don't know what else to do.'

'It's appreciated, it really is. I just can't seem to get hungry somehow.'

'Don't worry.' Emilia came into the little sitting/dining room they used at the back of the house. 'The rest of us are eating like kings. Or queens. That broccoli quiche was especially good, Amber. Feel free to stress-bake that again. How's your dad doing today, Harriet?'

The churning in her stomach intensified. 'The same. He just hates being in the hospital so much. He has no idea why he's there and why he can't get out of bed. The sooner he gets back to the home the better.'

'Have your sisters been to visit again?'

'No.' Harriet grimaced. 'I'm such a fool. When I saw them I actually thought things might change, that they'd want to be involved, especially when I reassured them that I wouldn't be asking for money any more. But their faces… They were disgusted by him, by their own father. All those years I thought that one day we might be a family again. But now I don't think I can forgive them for their rejection of Dad, even if I can for the way they treated me.'

Amber squeezed her hand sympathetically before retreating to the kitchen, murmuring something about Bundt cakes and a new recipe she wanted to try out. Emilia hovered for a moment, her expressive eyes dark with sorrow. 'Don't let it define you, Harriet. Families are complicated beasts; that's why I am eternally grateful we have each other.'

'Me too,' Harriet reassured her. 'You and Amber and Alexandra are the sisters I chose, and I know how lucky that makes me.' But the anger she felt towards her actual sisters shocked her in its righteousness and heat. She'd spent so long wanting their approval and acceptance, to be part of their closeness, dreaming of weekend barbecues and long Sunday lunches; now she didn't care if she never saw them again. Was this how Deangelo felt? Had he always wanted his older, legitimate siblings to accept him; had their actions not just scarred him physically but emotionally as well? Did his desire for revenge stem from more than his loss of his home, from more even than his mother's death, but from not being thought good enough to be part of their family? Harriet knew how that felt. She'd always known, but she had still hoped.

Without that hope her feelings were dark and murky. It was easy to see how they could harden and warp. She had friends who loved her to steer and guide her, to remind her of what love and real family bonds were, to pull her back into the light. Who had helped Deangelo? His aunt had done her best, with eight children of her own and an uncertain income she had managed to keep him clothed and fed, sorted his education, but would she have had the time to see the hate festering behind his grief?

Probably not. Deangelo needed understanding and

patience, just like she did. Was it too late? For him? For them?

At that moment Amber returned bearing a tray heaped with a teapot and cups, cake and scones and sat it down on the table in front of Harriet. 'House meeting,' she announced.

By the time the tea had been poured and cakes and scones distributed, Alexandra had arrived back and joined them. Looking around at her friends, Harriet felt a twinge of optimism. None of them had had it easy the last few years, yet here they were, planning for the future with hope. Buoyed by the thought, she managed a couple of mouthfuls of scone and a bite of cake, to Amber's beaming approval.

'So,' Emilia said, pushing her plate away. 'Do you want to talk about it?'

'No.' Harriet smiled gratefully at her friends. 'You've all done more than enough, covering my work, coming to the hospital with me, unpacking my bags, even...'

'She doesn't mean talk about your father, although obviously we're here if you need to,' Alexandra added quickly. 'But Em means do you want to talk about your trip to Brazil?'

'You've been withdrawn since you got back, beyond your worry about your father. After all, he was out of danger by the time you landed. I know that's still stressful, but your loss of appetite, the way you keep drifting off into a daydream, the fact you're not sleeping. It's a small house.' Emilia smiled at her apologetically. 'We just want to know you're okay. It's not that we've been discussing you behind your back; it's more that we're all worried and realised that we're worried about the same thing.'

'I'm fine.' But her voice squeaked on the words, the lump in her throat preventing her from saying anything more.

'Harriet, sweetie, did something happen between you and Deangelo?'

'Define "something."'

'I knew it!' Amber said.

'Oh, Harriet. Are you okay? Do you need us to go over there with lighted pitchforks and tear his castle down? Because we will.' Alexandra could be downright scary when she wanted to be.

'No. No, not at all. I am fine. At least, I will be.'

'You fell in love with him,' Emilia said.

'She was always in love with him.' Alexandra reached over and covered Harriet's hand. 'She's just realised it, that's all.'

'Does he love you back?'

How Harriet wished she could answer the hope in Amber's eyes with something positive. 'No,' she said instead. 'At least, he could be. I think he has feelings for me. I know he notices me. But he doesn't know how to love. He's scared to. And I get that. I feel the same way.'

'You deserve more,' Emilia said fiercely.

'I do. But so does he. I just wish I knew how to reach him. I tried. I really tried, Em.'

'Then he's a fool, for all his billions.'

'Maybe.' But as Harriet tried to show her friends how okay she really was she couldn't help but see him as she had walked away—tall, proud, indomitable and so alone it had broken her heart.

As his aunt had predicted, revenge wasn't all it was cracked up to be. Even the big reveal had lacked the piquancy Deangelo had hoped for. Oh, his brothers had blustered and sworn, his sister paled before pleading for her children's share to be preserved if nothing else. But there had been no sense of righteousness. No flaming sword. No resolution. All Deangelo had been able to see was the disappointment in Harriet's face as she had walked away, the hope when she had asked him to come with her. How brave and full of courage she was to have told him she loved him. Harriet, who knew his secrets. Harriet, who knew his fears. Harriet, who feared rejection and hurt and loneliness, had risked all three to try and reach him. And he had failed her, just as he had failed his mother.

For what? For a sense of flatness as he sat opposite the Caetanos and considered devastating their lives as they had devastated his.

Only in the end he hadn't. Because he hadn't been able to go through with it. Oh, he was still the majority shareholder, but the Caetano hotels were still trading. They'd be managed from within Aion, true; his siblings would no longer be able to cream off profits or sell their shares, unless to him, and they wouldn't be penniless, although they would be living on reduced dividends while the hotels were restored to health. He'd even suggested that any nephews or nieces who wanted to be involved could work at Aion. Why? It wasn't as if the gestures had softened his siblings' attitude to him, or made them feel any more familial towards him. But then he hadn't done it for them. He'd done it for Harriet.

He'd done it for his mother. She would never have wanted him to have followed the dark lonely path he had been on for so long, her death the catalyst. He had dishonoured her memory, dishonoured his upbringing, dishonoured himself.

Worse, he had been a fool, let the best chance he had at redemption walk out of his life without a backward glance, let her go alone to face a difficult situation, and the relief her father's stroke hadn't been as bad as first feared in no way negated that.

It had been a long week. The longest, the hardest, the darkest since his mother's death. A week of looking into the darkest depths of his soul and not liking what he saw there. Not some kind of wounded superhero but more a villain, lurking rather than living, contributing nothing except from afar, too scared of rejection from those he respected to reach out.

No more. He needed to start living in the world, not aside from it.

And if it was too late for Harriet—no, he couldn't think that, not just yet.

Deangelo looked out of the window at the darkness. Usually he loved these moments, alone on his plane, the biggest symbol of success there could be, returning to the city he had conquered. But today he was acutely aware of an ache in his chest. Homesickness. A yearning for the dirty, noisy, chaotic streets of Rio and the people who lived there.

But Harriet was in London. So that was where he needed to be.

It was morning when he landed and as usual he bypassed all the usual tedious airport procedures, money and status ensuring he could leave the airport quickly and discreetly. A marked contrast to that very first flight when, cramped from the long journey he had endured in Economy, he had queued for hours to have his visa scrutinised by hostile border agents.

Today he walked to where his car and driver were waiting for him on the airfield, his dual nationality making border controls a quick, respectful formality. Normality resumed.

Except nothing was the same.

He'd sent his instructions from the plane. He was to be driven to Chelsea, after a quick stop across the river in Vauxhall, where Deangelo had arranged for a seller at the famous flower market to stay open especially for him. As the car drove away from New Covent Garden's gates and headed across the bridge he was conscious of a new feeling. Nerves. He couldn't remember the last time he had felt nervous. But then again he couldn't remember the last time he'd had something to win. Or to lose.

The streets narrowed as the driver began to make his way through the well-heeled back streets of Chelsea, the bohemian-looking painted and Georgian houses hiding multi-million-pound makeovers and absentee owners. With a jolt Deangelo realised he didn't want to live alone in his tower any more, nor did he want to live somewhere like this, surrounded by other obscenely rich types; he wanted to be back in a community. Be part of something, contribute to it. No more shutting himself away.

His nerves intensified as the driver turned into the quiet Georgian streets and pulled up outside the freshly painted grey front door of the Happy Ever After Agency. Pots filled with lush green plants stood sentry either side of the entrance. Deangelo stood squarely between them and rang the bell. He didn't have too long to wait before a tall, elegant woman opened the door. She stood there for a moment, shock mingling with worry on her austerely beautiful face.

'Yes?' she said at last.

'Hello…' Deangelo searched his memory. This was the PR girl, wasn't it? Alexandra? He risked it. 'Hello, Alexandra. Is Harriet here?'

'I'll see if she wants to be.' And the door closed in his face. Deangelo blinked. It was a long time since he'd been left out on the doorstep. He set his jaw and waited, shifting as the seconds turned into minutes, acutely aware of his driver, waiting and witnessing this new and much-needed exercise in humility.

After a few minutes the door opened again, a different woman standing there, an identical shocked and worried expression on her face. 'She'll see you. But I need to tell you, she's had a hard week. If you're here to upset her…'

'I'm not,' he interrupted her and she regarded him unsmilingly before nodding.

'Come in then. We're all at home, within calling distance.' The last words were clearly a threat and a promise and Deangelo couldn't help recalling Harriet's words about building her own family.

'She's lucky to have you.'

A surprised smile softened her pretty but solemn face. 'We're lucky to have her. But I suspect you know that, don't you?'

A few strides and he was through the house and back in the sitting/dining conservatory where he had first persuaded Harriet to come and work for him again. Because he needed her in Rio, or because he needed her? He didn't trust his own motivations back then, not now. He suspected he'd loved her for far longer than he knew. All he knew was once he'd realised she was gone he'd have done anything to get her back.

That hadn't changed.

The conservatory door was open onto the large courtyard garden beyond. Looking back, he saw the three other occupants of the house standing grouped in the kitchen, just beyond hearing distance but watching. The smallest—Amber—nodded encouragingly and Deangelo stepped out of the door and into the courtyard. More flower-filled pots ringed the whitewashed walls, a wrought-iron bench set at one end. Harriet sat on the bench, a book in her hands, but for once she wasn't engrossed in it; instead she was gazing unseeingly into the distance.

'Hi,' he said.

She jumped, the book falling from her hands. 'Deangelo? What are you doing here?'

'I came to tell you that you were right. That revenge is no substitution for living. And I came to give you this.' He handed over the large gift bag he carried and she took it in shaking hands but made no move to look inside.

'You already gave me so much.'

'This is different.'

She held his gaze uncertainly before opening the bag and peeking inside.

It was a rose. One perfect white rose. The most perfect rose sold at New Covent Garden that day.

Harriet's hands shook as she drew the rose carefully out of the bag, appreciating the charm of the delicate crystal bud vase, her heart swelling as she looked at it.

'You remembered?'

'When your dad asked what you wanted you asked for flowers. And he would bring you one perfect rose every Friday.'

'You do remember.' She inhaled the rich scent and looked up at Deangelo, blinking back hot tears. Tears of joy, and of an aching nostalgic sadness. 'Nobody has brought me a flower since he started to get sick. I can't tell you how much this means.'

'White roses symbolise a heart unacquainted with love,' he said ruefully. 'That was me. That rose is my heart before I met you.'

Hope, sweet and joyful, began to unfurl inside her. Still holding the rose, Harriet got to her feet and stood in front of him, carefully examining his face, every feature imprinted on her heart. There was something subtly different about his expression, the self-loathing that had always lurked behind the careful mask was gone, as was the mask itself. She'd never seen such candour in his face, nor such tenderness. 'And now?'

'And now I'd need a whole rainbow of roses to express how I feel.' He looked behind him. 'As you can see.'

Harriet stared at the sitting/dining room. A driver was carrying a huge bouquet, so big she was surprised it had fitted through the door, made up of every colour of rose imaginable.

'That's…' She couldn't find the words. 'Thank you.'

'It should be me thanking you. For everything, But for now I just wanted to give you my heart. My cold, unloving heart, if you'll have it, and to tell you that, thanks to you, it isn't cold any more. To tell you that I love you.'

The words hung there, Harriet staring up at him, searching his face for a sign that this was real, that she could believe this was really happening. All she saw was love—love for her. Love, hope and a hint of nerves, which convinced her more than any words, any gesture could that he meant it. 'Deangelo…'

'You don't have to say anything. You don't owe me anything. I just wanted you to know how I feel. To know I'm on your side, always. No matter what.'

Harriet's heart was hammering so loudly she could barely think, her chest tight with suppressed tears—tears and a joy she didn't wholly trust just yet. 'But what about Brazil? The hotels?'

'Still intact. My siblings still have their share and will still have an income—a reduced income as we need to reinvest in the hotels, but a fair one. Not that they believe that. I don't think they'd hate me any more if I had beggared them.'

'Maybe not, but you would have ended up hating yourself.'

'I was halfway there,' he confessed. 'But in the end I didn't want my choices to be born out of hate and fear, but from love and hope. I wanted to make the choices which meant I would deserve you. If you'd have me. To take the path that led me to you. I have more money than I ever dreamed, but it's not brought me one moment's peace or joy. One night with you was worth more than every penny I own. And what I'd like, what I hope you'd like, is to turn that night into a lifetime.'

'A lifetime?' Had she heard him right? Carefully, she set the rose down on the bench. 'Deangelo…' She couldn't finish the sentence, her heart too full for words.

'For several years I went to work looking for a reason to carry on, not seeing that reason was right in front of me. I don't want to waste any more time, Harriet.' And as she watched him with wondering eyes he pulled a familiar box out of his pocket. 'Last time I gave you this it was pretence. I just didn't realise I was pretending to myself, pretending I hadn't picked the perfect ring for the perfect woman. But no more pretending, Harriet. I love you and I want to spend my life with you. If you'll have me.'

She noticed his hands were shaking as he handed her the box, and she opened it to see just the sapphire ring on its bed of white satin.

'The other ring is safe, waiting for the day you do me the honour of becoming my wife. If you will, that is. Will you, Harriet? Will you marry me?'

Harriet stepped close and took his hand in hers. 'Yes. And not because of the perfect ring or the fancy suits or the money. None of that means anything to me. But because you saw me. Because you took care of me. And because I want to take care of you. I love you, Deangelo Santos. So yes.'

She gave him the ring box back, holding out her hand and, with unusually clumsy fingers, he placed the ring on her finger, where it belonged.

'I should have come back with you when you asked,' he said. 'Shouldn't have let my life be governed by fear. Fear of losing people I loved, fear of letting them down, of being unworthy. But in the end I realised that the only thing worse than losing you would be never having you at all.'

'I'm right here,' she vowed. 'I'm not going anywhere. I don't know what the future holds—you and I both know how precarious happiness can be. But I can promise you that I won't hide any more. That I am going to love each day and wring every moment of happiness from life that I can. And there is no one else I want to do that with.'

This was where she belonged—wherever Deangelo was. She smiled up at him, filled with happiness and the sweetness of hope. The tenderness in his eyes nearly undid her as he gently tilted her chin, leaning in to kiss her, and Harriet knew that, whatever obstacles the future held, neither of them would ever know loneliness again.

* * * * *

THE LAWMAN'S ROMANCE LESSON

MARIE FERRARELLA

To
Patience Bloom
And
Gail Chasan
With Gratitude
For Allowing Me
To Live In Forever
A Little
Longer

Prologue

The evenings were the hardest for Shania. Somehow, the darkness outside seemed to intensify the silence and the feeling of being alone within the small house she used to occupy with her cousin.

Before she and Wynona had returned to Forever, Texas, the little town located just outside of the Navajo reservation where they had both been born, noise had been a constant part of their lives.

Joyful noise.

Noise that signified activity.

The kind of noise that could be associated with living in a college dorm. And before that, when they had lived in their great-aunt Naomi's house, there had still been noise, the kind of noise that came from being totally involved with life. Their great-aunt was a skilled surgeon and physician who was completely devoted to her work.

Because Naomi volunteered at a free clinic at least a couple of days a week as well as being associated with one of the local hospitals, patients would turn up on their doorstep at all sorts of hours. When she and Wynona grew older, Aunt Naomi thought nothing of having both of them pitch in and help out with her patients. She wanted them to learn how to provide proper care.

Between the volunteer work and their schooling, there was never any sort of downtime, never any time to sit back, much less be bored.

She and Wynona had welcomed being useful and mentally stimulated because that was such a contrast to the lives they had initially been born into. Born on the Navajo reservation to mothers who were sisters, Shania and Wynona spent their childhoods together. They were closer than actual sisters, especially after Wynona lost her mother. She'd never known her father. Shania's parents took her in to live with them without any hesitation.

Shania herself had been thrilled to share her parents with her cousin, but unfortunately, that situation didn't last very long. Nine months after Wynona had come to live with them, Shania's father was killed in an auto accident. And then less than six months later, her mother died of pneumonia.

At the ages of ten and eleven, Wynona and Shania found themselves both orphaned.

The girls were facing foster care, which ultimately meant being swallowed up by the social services system. Just before they were to be shipped off, their great-aunt Naomi, who had been notified by an anonymous party, suddenly swooped into town. In the blink of an eye, the strong-willed woman managed to cut through all manner of red tape and whisked them back to her home in Houston.

And after that, everything changed.

Shania and her cousin were no longer dealing with an

uncertain future. Aunt Naomi gave them a home and she gave them responsibilities as well, never wanting them to take anything for granted. They quickly discovered that their great-aunt was a great believer in helping those in need. Naomi made sure to instill a desire to "pay it forward" within them.

They had found that their great-aunt was a stern woman, but there had never been a question that the woman loved them and would be there for them if they should ever need her.

Shania sighed and pushed aside her plate, leaving the food all but untouched. Having taken leftovers out of the refrigerator, she hadn't bothered to warm them up before she'd brought them over to the table. She could almost hear Aunt Naomi's voice telling her, *If you're going to eat leftovers, do it properly. Warm them up first.*

Shania frowned at the plate. She really wasn't hungry.

What she was hungry for wasn't food but the discussions they used to have around the dinner table when Aunt Naomi, Wynona and she would all talk about their day. Aunt Naomi never made it seem as if hers was more important even though they all knew that she made such a huge difference in the lives she touched. Each person, each life, Aunt Naomi had maintained, was important in its own way.

When she and Wynona had moved back to Forever, armed with their teaching degrees and determined to give back to the community, for the most part those discussions continued. She and her cousin had been excited about the difference they were going to make, especially since both the local elementary school and high school, for practicality purposes, were now comprised of students who came not only from the town but also from the reservation. The aim was to improve the quality of education rendered to all the students.

But there were times, like tonight, when the effects of that excitement slipped into the shadows and allowed the loneliness to rear its head and take over. Part of the reason for that was because she now lived alone here. Wynona had gotten married recently and while Shania was thrilled beyond words for her cousin, she had no one to talk to, no one to carry on any sort of a dialogue with.

At least, not anyone human.

There was, of course, still Belle.

Just as she got up to go into her den to work on tomorrow's lesson plan, Belle seemed to materialize and stepped into her path. The German shepherd looked up at her with her big, soulful brown eyes.

"You miss her too, don't you, Belle?" Shania murmured to the dog that she and Wynona had found foraging through a garbage pail behind the Murphy brothers' saloon the first week they moved back. After determining that the dog had no owner, they immediately rescued the rail-thin shepherd and took her in.

Belle thrived under their care. When Wynona got married, Shania had told her cousin to take the dog with her. But Wynona had declined, saying that she felt better about leaving if Belle stayed with her.

Belle rubbed her head against Shania's thigh now, then stopped for a moment and looked up.

"Message received," Shania told the German shepherd with a smile. "You're right. I'm not alone. You're here. But there are times that I really wish you could talk."

As if on cue, Belle barked, something, as a rule, she rarely did. It was as if Belle didn't like to call attention to herself unless absolutely necessary.

"You're right. I shouldn't be feeling sorry for myself,

I should be feeling happy for Wyn." Dropping down beside the German shepherd, Shania ran her hands along the dog's head and back, petting the animal. "You really are brighter than most people, girl," she laughed.

As if in agreement, Belle began licking her face.

And just like that, the loneliness Shania had been wrestling with slipped away.

Chapter One

Deputy Daniel Tallchief could feel his anger increasing in waves. He told himself he wasn't going to say anything to the girl sitting in the seat next to him until he calmed down. He didn't want to say anything to his sister that he might wind up regretting later, after he'd had a chance to cool off.

Right now, it felt as if that was never going to happen.

And keeping his temper under control wasn't easy. Not when he wanted to shout into Elena's face and demand to know how she could do something not only so stupid, but so incredibly disrespectful to the memory of their parents as well as to him.

So far, Daniel had been silent. Silent the entire drive home, even though he could feel angry words clawing at his throat, all but choking him in their eagerness to be released.

Elena wasn't much help to him in that respect. His sixteen-year-old only sister was sitting in the passenger seat, obviously fuming. Her very body language, not to mention what she was actually saying to him, were goading him to lose his temper.

"I don't know what you're so mad about," Elena retorted, folding her arms in front of her chest just like their mother used to do when she was displaying anger. "You told me I couldn't have parties in our house while you were gone and I didn't have one," she informed him haughtily. "In case you didn't notice, that was Matthew's house you storm trooped into, not ours. His house is a lot nicer," she deliberately pointed out. "Matthew has a right to throw a party if he wants to and I have a perfect right to be there if I want to." She punctuated her statement by tossing her head defiantly, sending her long, shining black hair flying over her shoulder.

The best laid plans of mice and men, Daniel had read somewhere, *often went awry*—or words to that effect. Right now, that described his plans for waiting until he had cooled off to a T.

So rather than driving straight home in silence—at least *his* silence—Daniel pulled his car over to the side of the road and glared at his angry sister, the person who was responsible, at least in part, for his taking a job as a sheriff's deputy rather than finishing college and getting a degree. Not finishing college put an end to his being able to go on to medical school and to eventually achieve his lifelong dream of becoming a doctor.

It had also wound up putting an end to Lana and him.

The hell with cooling off. "Number one," Daniel enumerated, "Matthew doesn't have the right to have a party loud enough to disturb all his neighbors just because his parents were naive enough to leave him home alone for a week. Number two, *you* don't have the right to attend a party where alcohol was being unlawfully served. From what I could see, everyone there was a minor so if I was as hard-nosed as you seem to think I am, I would have arrested them all on the spot instead of giving them a warning that I'd come down hard on them if this happened again."

Daniel took a breath. It was a real struggle to keep his voice down.

Apparently, his self-restraint was wasted on his sister.

She glared at him. "Not much that they can do in the way of partying now that you took away all their liquor."

"I *confiscated* it," Daniel corrected. "And when Matthew's parents get back and ask about what happened to their incredibly large supply of alcohol, I'll hand the bottles over to them."

Elena's frown intensified. "Along with a lecture, no doubt, about how they should make an effort to be better parents." She fumed, looking at him darkly. "You know, not everyone wants to be like you, Daniel."

"Right now," the deputy told Elena, starting up his car again and heading back to town, "*I* don't even want to be me."

Refusing to appear intimidated, Elena raised her chin defiantly. "Well, it's no picnic being your sister, either."

Daniel bit his tongue to keep back the hot words that were hovering there, aching to be released. Saying them to Elena might very well produce momentary gratification, but he knew that he'd wind up paying for that gratification in the long run. Paying for it with the amount of damage that those words could cause to the relationship he had with Elena.

A relationship that already felt as if it was tottering on its last legs.

He and Elena had been close once. Extremely close. He'd helped raise her because both his parents were so busy trying to provide a decent life for his sister and for him. Despite experiencing the typical wants and desires of a teenager, which included hanging out with his friends and all that entailed, Daniel still doted on Elena and found time to be there for her.

But then the world had been turned upside down. His parents had been in a terrible car accident. His mother had died instantly and his father had lingered for a few hours before he died as well. So instead of graduating college and going off to medical school—he had an early acceptance letter he still carried around folded up in his wallet—he had to drop out and find a job in a hurry in order to be able to provide for Elena and take care of both of them.

And, as hard as giving up his education had been, losing Lana had been even harder on him.

The death of their parents had its effects on Elena as well. Always bright and studious, she'd gradually turned her back on all that. Instead, she just focused on living in the moment.

Partying in the moment.

And frustrating Daniel to the point that he was all but incoherent, like now.

"I don't even know you anymore," he told Elena after another ten minutes of silence had passed.

Exasperated, Daniel pulled his car up in front of the small, three-bedroom, single-story house that had once known such happiness but now stood as a lonely reminder of what no longer was.

"That makes two of us," Elena shot back. "I don't know you anymore, and I can't trust you, either."

He bit his tongue again to keep from saying the first thing that popped up in his mind. Instead, he took a breath, tried to collect his thoughts. "I've got to go to the sheriff's office to log this in," he told her, indicating the bottles of alcohol in the back. He looked into his sister's eyes. "I want your word that you won't leave the house until I get back."

"I thought you didn't trust me," she taunted, her tone haughty and arrogant.

"I don't," he answered honestly. "But I'm hoping you'll want to prove me wrong more than you want to run off to find another party that I'll just have to shut down." He let his words sink in before noting, "That can't be making you very popular, being the girl whose brother follows her around, shutting down the parties she attends."

"It doesn't," Elena snapped, glaring at him. She pressed her lips together, as if going over several things in her mind. "All right, you win. I'll stay home," she pouted.

Instead of getting out, Daniel remained seated behind the steering wheel. Eyeing his sister, he asked, "I have your word?"

Elena blew out a long, dramatic breath. "Yeah, yeah, you have my word."

"Good." Daniel nodded, getting out of the vehicle. "Why don't you study while you wait for me to get home?" he suggested. He saw her roll her eyes. It took effort to hold onto his temper. Taking a breath, he told her, "You used to be a great student."

"And then I got smart," Elena responded sarcastically.

Daniel's eyes narrowed as he looked at her. "Not really," he countered.

Elena uttered a frustrated, guttural sound and then stomped all the way to the front door.

Getting there ahead of her, Daniel unlocked the door then opened it and let her in. For his part, he remained standing outside. "I'll get back home just as soon as I can."

"I can't wait," Elena retorted sarcastically.

Rather than say anything, Daniel quickly closed the

door the moment she was inside the house and then locked it.

"Oh gee, now I can't get out," Elena called out, raising her voice so that it carried to him through the door.

"No, you can't," he informed her. "Because you gave me your word."

Daniel heard another sound, louder and more guttural this time. He could picture the look on his sister's angry face.

He walked to his car and really hoped that he wasn't being an idiot to believe that, despite everything, Elena was going to live up to her promise.

Daniel got into the vehicle.

"Really wish you guys were still here," he murmured under his breath to the parents who were no longer there to hear him.

He would have missed his parents no matter what, but being left to grapple with trying to raise a headstrong, overly intelligent sixteen-year-old teenage girl made everything three times worse. And it *really* made him miss his mother and father.

When Daniel walked into the sheriff's office fifteen minutes later, he was surprised to see Joe there.

Senior Deputy Sheriff Joe Lone Wolf was the reason he had this job. He'd known the older deputy by sight when they were both growing up on the reservation. But then his parents had moved him and his sister into town and the next time their paths crossed, Joe was a deputy, working for Sheriff Rick Santiago. Joe's influence in the scheme of things increased a great deal when he wound up marrying Ramona, the town's veterinarian. Ramona also happened to be Rick's sister. And when Daniel suddenly found himself in need of a job, Joe was the one who not only vouched for him but took Daniel under his wing, teaching him everything he needed to know. It wasn't the job he had dreamed of having, but it was one he felt he could do justice to.

"I didn't know you had the night shift tonight," Daniel said to the other man.

"I didn't. I traded Rodriguez for it. I had a feeling, when you went to answer that domestic disturbance call coming in from the better part of town, that you might wind up coming back." Craning his neck, Joe looked around behind Daniel. "So where's Elena?"

It was unnerving the way that Joe seemed to know about things before they became public knowledge. "She's home."

Joe's eyes never left his face as he rocked back in his chair. "Let me guess, she promised to be on her best behavior."

"I don't think that girl has any 'best behavior' to fall back on any more," Daniel responded. There was no missing the disgusted note in his voice. "But she gave me her word that she wouldn't leave the house until I got back."

Joe laughed dryly. "Then I guess you'd better hurry back before Elena's tempted to break her word again." And then he looked at Daniel, studying him. "Why did you come back?"

"Well, I wanted to log these in at the station," Daniel answered. The next minute, he was going out the front door.

"These?" Joe repeated, following the younger man out.

Daniel paused to reach into the backseat and take out the carton he'd used in order to carry all the liquor bottles out of Matthew McGuire's house.

"These," Daniel repeated as he carried the carton crammed full of bottles back past Joe and into the sheriff's office.

Joe uttered a low whistle as he looked at all the semi-filled and three-quarters-filled bottles stuffed into the carton.

"What was the kid doing? Competing with the Murphy brothers' saloon?"

Daniel glanced down at the bottles in his arms. "I'm guessing these belong to his parents."

"Speaking of his parents, just where are these fine citizens?" Joe asked him.

Daniel thought back, trying to remember. "According to what Elena told me through her clenched teeth and her hostile attitude, I gather that Matthew's parents are away for the week, touring a couple of colleges with his older brother."

Joe smile was grim. "In other words, when the cat's away, the mice'll play."

"And get drunk," Daniel added with a deep, disapproving frown.

"Evidence?" Joe asked, nodding at the liquor bottles and curious as to exactly what Daniel planned to do with all of them.

"My first thought was to get these things out of the kids' reach," Daniel confessed. He put the carton down on his desk. "When Matthew's parents get back into town, they can come by the station and get them."

"My guess is that they're not going to be happy about that," Joe commented.

Joe took a couple of the bottles out of the carton one by one and looked at the labels. He wasn't a connoisseur when it came to alcohol, but he could see that there were some very expensive bottles in the carton.

"I'm counting on it," Daniel told him. "Maybe his parents will think twice before leaving Matthew alone with all this temptation again."

"What did Elena say about you doing this?" Joe asked.

Daniel blew out a breath. "Not anything I feel like repeating right now," he answered.

Opening his desk's middle drawer, he took out a pad and a pen and began to write down the various names that were on the labels.

"Here, let me do that," Joe told the younger deputy, taking the pad and pen away from Daniel. "You go on back to your sister. Like I said, the sooner you get yourself back home, the less tempted she's going to be to fly the coop again."

This was where Daniel would have wanted to say that since Elena had given him her word she'd stay home, he felt confident that she would be there when he walked in through the door. But the truth was that he wasn't confident she'd be there. Not confident at all.

Joe was right. The sooner he got home, the more likely it was that he'd still find Elena at home. Because if she decided to take off again, this time he wouldn't be able to just shrug it off or let it slide. This time, he was going to have to come down on her.

Hard.

And that would do even more harm to their relationship, causing it to splinter and break apart that much more. Maybe even irreparably, because he was only able to hold on to his temper for so long before it exploded on him.

"Thanks, Joe, I owe you," Daniel said, heading for the door.

"Damn straight you do," Joe called out, his voice following the other deputy as Daniel went outside to his vehicle.

How did it all get so confused and heavy-handed? Daniel couldn't help wondering as he got in behind the wheel of his car again.

How did he and Elena go from being practically best friends to being these people who kept snapping at each other and regarding everything the other person did as being suspect?

He wished he knew. Daniel couldn't even remember how it all had started to unravel. All he knew was that somehow, it had. And not just slowly but with what felt like lightning speed. One day he was Elena's confidant, her shoulder to cry on, the next day, he was her enemy, part of "them," otherwise known as a grown-up. And everyone knew that grown-ups or adults were the ones who stood in the way and impeded anything that even remotely looked like fun.

Elena stopped telling him things, stopped confiding in him, stopped looking at him the way she used to. These days, she wasn't proud of him. She was just leery of him and it showed in everything she did, everything she said to him.

How did he go about changing that back to what it had been?

And just as important, how did he get Elena to realize that getting an education was the only way she would ever get out of Forever?

Chapter Two

Shania made sure that she always parked her feelings of doubt and insecurity outside the door before walking into any classroom. It was the one major rule she always abided by. She felt it was her personal mission to inspire her students, to get them to focus on not just their schoolwork, but also on their abilities to surmount any and all obstacles that existed in their daily lives. She did her best to instill a work ethic within them that enabled them to work hard at achieving their personal goals.

On those occasions when things got particularly rough for her, it was then that Shania found herself channeling her great-aunt Naomi.

Early on in their relationship, the gruff, far from soft-spoken woman became her inspiration. To Shania's recollection, there was no problem too big or too taxing to bring Aunt Naomi down or cause her to throw in the towel and give up. No matter what it was, Aunt Naomi had taught them that they could always find a way to deal with it.

Today had been about as taxing a day as she could ever remember enduring.

Usually, on those days when her students turned out to be particularly challenging, she'd go home and then she and Wynona would act as each other's cheering section—or support group—whatever way wound up doing the trick.

But Wynona was no longer here. Right after the wedding had taken place, she and Clint had moved in together at the ranch. For a few minutes after her day had ended, Shania debated picking up the phone and calling Wynona just to unwind for a minute.

She would be *damned* if she was going to call her cousin to complain about today. Wynona didn't need to hear her carping. What her cousin needed was to spend quality time with her husband, not to mention that she was also acclimating to being a mother to Clint's nine-year-old son, Ryan.

No, Shania thought, growing more restless, Wyn had her hands more than full with all that going on, plus teaching. Her cousin definitely had no time to offer her a shoulder to lean on, Shania thought, even though Wynona would if called upon.

She wasn't going to call her. But that didn't mean that she didn't still need at least a willing ear to listen to her, Shania thought as she chewed on her lower lip.

She could only think of one place where she could find that willing ear. An ear that only listened, but didn't feel obligated to give advice.

"No offense, Belle," she said, looking down at the rather diminutive German shepherd that was shadowing her every move and weaving in and out between her legs when she walked, "but tonight I really think that I need a human to talk to."

Belle stopped moving and looked up at her with her big brown eyes. Shania could have sworn that the dog understood what she was saying—and forgave her.

"I won't be long," Shania promised as she grabbed her jacket from the coat rack by the door and shrugged into the garment.

Granted it was only just the end of September, but sometimes the weather took an unexpected turn around seven or eight o'clock, becoming cold. The last thing she wanted to do was to catch a cold. It was bad enough having to deal with low spirits, something she was *not* accustomed to having.

Murphy's, the town's only saloon, has initially been owned by Patrick Murphy, the present owners' uncle. A lifelong bachelor, he had taken in the three orphaned brothers when they were just boys after his younger brother, their widowed father, died. Eventually, since they comprised his only family, Patrick left the establishment that was his pride and joy to them when he passed away.

Although the two younger Murphy brothers occasionally took turns operating it, everyone agreed that the saloon was Brett's baby. The oldest of the Murphy brothers was the force behind its present success and he was the reason that most people in and around Forever would find their way there.

Murphy's had an unspoken agreement with Miss Joan, the woman who owned the town's only diner, which was also its only restaurant. Miss Joan's was where people went for food and, on occasion, for advice. Murphy's was where they went to have a drink amid people they knew. It was also where they went to enjoy some camaraderie and have their spirits lifted.

It was exactly the latter that Shania found herself needing tonight.

The moment she walked into Murphy's, she found herself feeling better. Unlike bars that were located in the larger cities, Murphy's didn't shun ample lighting, opting instead to lean toward atmosphere that was created by a lack of darkness. Because of the bright lighting, there were no shadows to hide in, no dimly lit areas to gravitate toward that would enable the patrons to observe without being observed.

Shania quickly looked around. As usual, she noted, Brett was tending bar. Married to one of the town's two doctors, whenever Alicia worked late at the clinic, Brett was the one who worked late at the bar. In any given emergency, he and his brothers traded off shifts, although Murphy's was doing so well, they could afford to hire a bartender for the nights that none of the brothers could be here.

"Don't usually see you here, pretty lady. I know that my paper's overdue, but I'm still working on it," Brett told her with a wink. Wiping down the bar, he gestured toward a stool directly in front of him.

"I've got a feeling you'll be working on it a long time," she told him, sliding in on the stool.

"You could be right," Brett responded. "So, what'll it be?" he asked, flashing a welcoming smile at her as he retired the cloth he was using. "Or are you just here for some good conversation?"

"I'll have whatever you have on tap," Shania told the man.

"Coming right up," Brett responded. As he spoke, he filled up a mug. There was foam taking up two thirds of the space. Placing the mug down on the bar right in front of her, Brett took a closer look at her expression. "Something wrong?" he asked her gently.

Shania squared her shoulders. "Why does there have to be something wrong?" she asked, drawing the mug closer to her.

"Because it's a school night and you're here, having a beer," Brett pointed out.

"I drink beer," she protested defensively.

"Didn't say you didn't," he answered. "Just not used to seeing you drinking it here."

She couldn't really argue with that. Shrugging off his observation, she told him, "Maybe I just came out to make contact with my fellow man."

The look on Brett's face told her that he knew it had to be more than that, but he wasn't about to challenge her.

"This is the place to do that," Brett agreed. Someone called out to him. Brett glanced over in the patron's direction, then excused himself. "Sorry, Shania, duty calls." He hesitated just for a moment. "You'll be all right?" he asked.

Shania nodded. "I'll be fine. I'm not fragile," she assured him.

"That's good to know," a deep voice behind her told her.

Not so much startled as surprised, Shania turned around to see who the voice belonged to and found herself looking up into the softest brown eyes that she had ever seen. With broad shoulders, a taut, trim waist and standing approximately six one, the rest of the man was even more strikingly impressive.

"Fragile women don't have an easy time of it," the man said.

There was something about the man that looked vaguely familiar, but she was fairly certain that she had never met him.

"And you know this how?" Shana heard herself asking the dark-haired man.

"Years of experience," he answered.

Shania saw the badge he was wearing and she made the logical assumption. The man had to be one of the sheriff's deputies. She also guessed that given the man's high cheekbones, he was also at least part Navajo, which instantly gave them something in common.

But rather than comment on that—it sounded like such a line to her—Shania took another sip of her drink. The beer tasted particularly bitter, but she had gotten it expressly for that very reason. The bitter drink would keep her from having another—if she finished this one at all.

"Are you saving this seat for someone?" Daniel asked her, nodding at the empty stool beside her.

Her hands tightened around the mug she was holding. "No, I'm not saving it." Her voice sounded almost tinny, she thought disparagingly.

"Then you don't mind if I sit down next to you?" Daniel asked, still not making a move to slide onto the stool.

Shania shrugged, doing her best to seem nonchalant. It occurred to her that she had spent so much time looking out for Wynona, she had forgotten how to socialize on her own.

"It's a free country," she replied, taking another sip, a longer one this time.

Daniel slid his long frame onto the stool, setting his drink—a beer—down on the bar in front of him. His eyes skimmed over the woman next to him. The second look was even better than the first. Simply dressed, the dark-haired woman was nothing short of a knockout.

He hadn't come here looking for anything except for people who didn't look at him hostilely the way that Elena had. But, having found someone who definitely captured his attention, he wasn't in a hurry to leave.

"I haven't seen you in here before," Daniel commented.

"There's a reason for that," Shania replied, a smile playing at the corners of her mouth as she faced the long mirror that ran the length of the bar.

Daniel's eyes met hers in the mirror and he said the first thing that occurred to him. "It's your first time here?"

"No." While she didn't frequent the saloon on anything that would have passed as a regular basis, she had been here a few times since her return to Forever. But she'd never seen him during any of those times.

"I'm confused," Daniel admitted.

This time she did look directly at him. And then she smiled. "Happens to the best of us," she told him.

His smile was slow as it spread over his lips—and extremely compelling. She could feel something inside of her responding to it.

"I'm also intrigued," Daniel said.

Finding it disconcerting to make eye contact, she lowered her own. "I can't help that."

"Oh, but you might be able to," Daniel told her. Even though he continued sitting exactly where he was, it felt as if he had somehow drawn closer to her.

Shania had to concentrate in order not to fidget. "Oh? And just how do you propose that I do that?"

"Propose?" he repeated, the smile on his face deepening. He had dimples, she realized. One in each cheek. She found herself growing more intrigued than she wanted to be. "Let's not get ahead of ourselves," Daniel told her. "Although, the evening's still young."

Mention of the time had her looking at her watch. "Actually, it's getting late."

Daniel glanced at his own watch. It was only a few minutes past eight.

"No, it's actually not," he contradicted. "It's still early."

But Shania held her ground and shook her head. "Not really." And then she explained by saying, "It's a school night."

Her response only served to confuse him further. "What's that got to do with it?"

And then he looked down at her hand as a belated explanation for her concern hit him. Was she married and needed to get home? There was no ring on her hand, but in this day and age, that didn't mean that the woman was single.

The shortest distance between two points was a straight line, so instead of beating around the bush, he decided to ask her. "You're not married, are you?"

"No, I'm not," Shania answered. Even as she said that, she felt an atypical pang twisting the pit of her stomach.

What was wrong with her? All these years, she had never once felt that marriage was for her. But ever since Wynona had gotten married, Shania had found herself reevaluating everything, including what she'd thought were her deeply rooted feelings about marriage. Maybe it *was* time to rethink her position on that.

Would it be such an awful thing to get married? Marriage had certainly made Wynona happy.

"The conversation just got more interesting," Daniel said with a smile that unnerved her.

Shania thought of finishing her beer in order to dramatically put the empty mug down on the bar and push it away before she got off the stool. But in order to do that, she'd have to actually drink the brew and she decided that she'd had enough. So she just pushed the mug aside.

"I've got to go," she told him, and started to get up off her stool.

He gave her a long, soulful look. "Was it something I said?"

She needed to avoid looking into his eyes, she silently insisted. He had beautiful, sexy eyes and eye contact had a way of making her thoughts evaporate.

"No, I just have to go," she told him seriously. "I have school tomorrow," she explained.

His eyes narrowed as he studied her more closely, doing his best to see past her beauty even though it wasn't easy.

"No offense, but just how many times have you been left back?" he asked.

"Left back?" she echoed, clearly confused about what he was asking.

"Well, yeah. Because I know for a fact that the Murphys are really strict when it comes to serving alcohol to minors." Then, because she was still staring at him quizzically, he clarified it for her. "They don't, which means that you're not a minor even though you're fresh-faced and pretty enough to pass for one."

"I'm not a minor," she assured him, not sure if she was flattered or insulted by his comment.

"Then why...?" He left the end of his question up in the air, waiting for her to finish it.

"I'm a high school teacher," she told him.

"A high school teacher," he repeated.

He hadn't thought of that. He was slipping, he upbraided himself. But then, he wasn't used to putting moves on a woman. Because Elena had aggravated him, he'd wound up doing something out of character.

"Yes," she confirmed in case there was any doubt. "So you see why I have to go."

But Daniel wasn't quite ready to let this go just yet. Questions popped up in his mind. "What do you teach?"

"Algebra and physics," she answered.

He nodded, impressed. "Ambitious."

"Tiring," she countered.

He thought of what he'd just endured trying to deal with his sister today and he understood exactly what this woman was telling him.

"It's a tough age," he agreed.

"You say that like someone who's been in the trenches," Shania noted. "Were you a teacher?"

"Me?" he asked, surprised that she'd think that. "Hell no." Realizing he might have offended her, he corrected himself. "I mean heck no."

She tried not to laugh and only partially succeeded. "That's okay. I find myself swallowing a few choice words too, especially whenever I'm having a particularly bad day communicating with my students."

Although, she thought, those were happily few and far between.

"Was that what this was all about?" Daniel asked, nodding at her unfinished mug of beer. "A particularly bad day?"

"You might say that," Shania admitted. "There are some times when I really don't think I'm getting through to them."

"If it's only 'some times' then you're doing better than the rest of us," Daniel assured her, thinking of Elena. "Why don't you let me buy you something that you enjoy drinking and we can compare war stories?"

She felt a bit confused again. "But I thought you said you were never a teacher."

"And I wasn't," he answered.

"Then I don't understand. How can you have any war stories?" she asked.

"Because my war stories all involve my younger sister," he answered. "My sixteen-year-old younger sister," he specified, as if that should make everything clear to the woman he was talking to.

"Your parents having trouble handling her?" she guessed.

"My parents aren't there to handle her," he answered, doing his best to mask his reaction to her question. Thinking of his parents always made him feel sad. Then, before she could ask anything further, he told her, "For better or for worse, it's all me. Mother, father and, according to my sister, thick-headed older brother, all rolled up into one big package."

The way he'd worded his response caused something to click in her head. "You said she was sixteen?" Shania asked him.

He nodded and finished his beer. "Yes."

She *knew* the deputy looked familiar to her, Shania thought. Even if she threw the reservation into the mix, Forever was rather a small town.

"What's her name?" she asked.

He narrowed his eyes again as he studied the woman he'd been flirting with.

"Why are you asking me that?" Daniel asked her suspiciously.

Shania tried to sound off-handed as she answered, "I was just curious to find out if perhaps she's in my class."

Bits and pieces of their conversation began to align themselves in Daniel's head, forming an imperfect whole. A whole he didn't really want to own up to.

He suddenly realized that he might have very well just tried to hit on Elena's teacher and, if that was the case, he was fairly certain that if Elena got wind of this, he was never going to hear the end of it.

Chapter Three

He debated his next move—did he mention Elena's name and hope that there'd been some mix-up and this woman *wasn't* her teacher, or did he just not say anything?

At the apex of his debate, Daniel heard his cell phone ringing.

Pulling his phone out of his pocket, he looked down at the screen. Rather than someone's name or a number, he saw that what was vying for his attention was an app. The second he saw it, all thoughts of possibly embarrassing his sister because he was trying to get to know her teacher instantly vanished.

Shaking his head, Daniel frowned at the screen he was watching.

Shania saw the change. "Something wrong?" she asked him.

"Yeah," the deputy answered, closing his phone and putting it away again. "My sister is attempting to escape."

"Escape?" she repeated uncertainly. "Are you holding your sister prisoner?"

"That just might be the next step," he murmured, more to himself than to the woman sitting beside him at the bar. "No, I put up a basic security monitoring camera by the front door while she was at school." He could see by the woman's expression that he needed to explain this a little more clearly. "I grounded her after the last incident—she went to a party during a school night and there was alcohol flowing like the Mississippi River. She's not supposed to go out on school nights for a month and it looks like she's breaking the rules again."

Shania looked at the deputy thoughtfully. A different take on the situation occurred to her.

"Maybe your sister found out about the security monitor and she decided to try to pay you back," Shania suggested.

Daniel's frown deepened. "You sound like you're on her side."

"No," she answered without hesitation. "I just happen to know how the teenage mind works. How *mine* worked for a little while," she added to convince him. "Until I suddenly realized I was being totally selfish and ungrateful."

Shania vividly remembered the confrontation between her great-aunt and herself. The verbal altercation really straightened her out and left her feeling not only very humbled but utterly grateful to the older woman for putting up with her.

"How long did it take you to realize that?" Daniel asked, wondering just how long he and Elena were going to be at odds over absolutely everything from morning until night, because he was *really* getting tired of butting heads with his sister.

"Longer than it should have," Shania admitted ruefully, since she should have realized immediately that Naomi had been under no obligation to take them in, much less put up with her antics.

Daniel saw something in the woman's face that moved him, something that spoke to him even more than the fact that he found her to be an incredibly beautiful woman.

But right now, he had an emergency with Elena to deal with and that took precedence over everything else.

"Look," he told her, "I'd really like to stay here and talk some more with you, but I'm afraid that I've got to handle this."

Shania flashed a smile at him. "I understand perfectly," she told him. Then, on the off chance that she'd correctly guessed whose brother he was, she called after the deputy, saying, "She's a good girl who's just testing you and her boundaries, and being rebellious."

But Daniel had already crossed the floor and gave her no indication that he'd heard her. Within another minute, he was gone.

Shania stared after him, wondering again if she'd accurately guessed who his sister was. She could have very well just been reading into the situation.

"Another one?" Brett asked, standing on his side of the bar right behind her.

Startled, Shania managed not to gasp. Instead, she turned around to look at the bartender. "You really should wear squeaky shoes so you don't scare your customers when you sneak up behind them."

"I wasn't 'sneaking' and squeaky shoes wouldn't help," he told her. "There's too much noise in here to hear anything as understated as squeaky shoes." Brett nodded toward her mug and repeated, "Another one?"

He added, "On the house," no doubt thinking that might sweeten the offer and make it more tempting.

But Shania shook her head. "That's okay. One was enough." Brett looked at her doubtfully. When he went on to tilt the mug she'd pushed aside, emphasizing the fact that there was still some beer in it, Shania added, "More than enough, really."

"I can get you another brand," Brett offered. "Something less bitter," he added.

Shania smiled at the man. Brett Murphy was a decent, down-to-earth man, even more so than his younger brothers, and she appreciated his offer to appeal to her tastes, but that really wasn't the problem.

"Maybe next time," she told him, sliding off her stool. "I really just came in for the company."

Brett nodded. "His name's Daniel Tallchief," he told her, even though Shania hadn't asked. After having been behind the counter for as long as he had, Brett prided himself on being able to read people accurately, at least for the most part.

Tallchief. Shania smiled. She'd guessed right, she thought.

"I thought so," she said aloud, secretly congratulating herself, then quickly added, "I mean, I didn't ask."

Brett's smile deepened. "You didn't have to," he told her.

Rather than become defensive, Shania regarded the man a little more closely, then teased, "You're adding mind reading to your list of talents?"

"I'm not one to brag," he replied, his tone indicating otherwise.

"Okay," she answered gamely. Shania's eyes met his. "What am I thinking right now?"

He studied her for a long moment, then deadpanned,

"You deal with impressionable young minds all day long. Should you be using words like that?"

It took her a second to realize that he was teasing her. "It's how I survive."

"Whatever gets you through the day," Brett answered. He gave her an encouraging grin, then made one final offer. "How about some coffee? It'll get the bitter taste of that beer out of your mouth."

She looked at him, surprised. "How did you know I thought it was bitter?"

"I could just say it's all part of being a mind reader," he said, for a moment falling back on the label she'd given him. "But the truth is you have a very expressive face, at least when it comes to some things." He leaned over the bar, pretending to share a confidence with her. "I wouldn't let myself be drawn into any poker games if I were you."

"No danger of that," she told Brett just before she turned to leave his establishment. "Poker games require money and I'm just a teacher."

"There is no 'just' in front of the word 'teacher,'" Brett called after her.

Shania smiled to herself, her good mood restored as she walked out the door.

That was why she'd come here in the first place, to forget about everything that had happened today. Everything that she *hadn't* managed to accomplish. Meeting Elena Tallchief's brother turned out to be an added bonus.

Don't go there, she warned herself. The last thing she needed was to entertain anything that was even remotely like a daydream about one of the students' relatives.

Belle was waiting for her just behind the door when Shania walked in a few minutes later. The second the dog saw her, her tail began to thump against the floor, underscoring the fact that the dog was very happy to see her.

Shania grinned, responding to the welcome. "I missed you, too, Belle," she told the German shepherd. When the dog paused to look up at her, Shania put her own interpretation to that look. "I know, I know, if I missed you so much, why did I go out without you? Number one, they don't allow dogs in saloons—"

Belle seemed to whimper in response.

"Yes, I know. That's not very nice of them but everyone likes to have rules. And number two, sometimes I need to communicate with other humans. Other *adult* humans," she emphasized because there were times when she could swear that Belle thought of herself as being her equal and human as well.

Belle barked loudly once, as if in response to the last sentence.

Shania ran her hands over the dog's head, petting her. "Thank you, you're being very understanding."

Ready to settle in and continue petting her dog, Shania heard the house phone ring. Because cell phone reception could be spotty, usually at the worst possible times—especially when the weather was inclement—she and Wynona had opted to keep the landline that was in the house when they moved in.

Curious as to who could be calling her at this hour, Shania crossed the room and picked up the receiver. "Hello?"

The voice on the other end didn't bother with a polite greeting but got right down to business, asking her, "Where have you been?"

"Wynona?"

Recognizing the voice, concern reared its head instantly. Because Wynona taught all day at the elementary school, evenings were reserved for her husband and stepson. Shania made it a point not to call her cousin except occasionally on the weekend. To have Wynona call her during the week and at this hour, something had to be wrong.

Shania felt her stomach tightening as she asked, "Is something wrong?"

"Well, if there was, you wouldn't have been home to find out," Wynona answered.

Shania felt obligated to explain why she hadn't been home this one time. "I needed some company."

If Wynona had been harboring as much as a drop of annoyance—which she wasn't—all pretense instantly vanished.

"You could have called here, Shania. Or just come over," Wynona told her.

"That's called intruding," Shania pointed out, then explained, "I'm not about to invite myself over to your place, Wyn. You and Clint are still in the honeymoon stage."

She heard her cousin chuckle softly before saying, "Well, that's about to change."

"Change?" Shania repeated. "Why?" She was back to being concerned. Was there a problem between Wynona and her husband? "You do realize that men require a lot of patience. Whatever Clint's done, he didn't mean it so just forgive him and move on from there. I guarantee you'll both be happier."

Rather than agree with her, Shania heard her cousin sigh—or was she stifling a laugh? "I'm afraid it's not that easy."

This wasn't like Wynona. Her cousin didn't give up this easily. She was exceptionally stubborn. Shania searched for a way to convince her cousin to dig in and fight for her marriage.

"Sure it is. You just have to be the bigger person, that's all. In every relationship, there's always someone who loves more and someone who forgives more. Sometimes, that's the same person," Shania added, hoping she was convincing her cousin to find a way to forgive Clint if that was what was necessary here and give their marriage another try.

And then she heard Wynona laugh. Was her cousin just putting her on?

"Have you ever thought of writing these gems down in a 'how to make a marriage work' book?" Wynona asked.

"Too busy," Shania answered, letting go of the breath she'd been holding. "So, is everything okay then?"

"Well, that all depends on your definition of 'okay,'" Wynona answered.

They were going around in circles, Shania thought. Why?

"Are you like this with Clint?" she asked. "Because if you are, I can see why he might lose his temper with you."

"Lose his temper?" Wynona echoed. "That's not what happened."

Shania took a deep breath, trying to hold on to her patience, which was quickly being shredded. When did her cousin get this trying?

"What did happen?" she asked. "And no more beating around the bush. Tell me straight out why you called or I swear I'm going to drive over to your place right now and ask Clint to tell me what's going on with you."

"Well, if you put it that way..." Wynona said, still hedging.

Shania took a deep breath, struggling to keep her temper under control.

Why did it sound as if Wynona was grinning? she suddenly thought.

"Wynona," she cried, a warning note in her voice. When her cousin still paused, not saying anything, concern returned in spades. Maybe her cousin was too afraid to tell her what was wrong. "Wyn, please. You can tell me anything, you know that."

"You promise not to tell?" Wynona asked in a subdued voice.

There went her stomach again. This had to be worse than she thought. With effort, Shania reined in her imagination, which was on the verge of running away with her. Big-time.

"I promise," she told her cousin solemnly.

Then, to her surprise, she heard Wynona suddenly start to laugh. "That's okay, Shania. You can tell anyone you want."

Okay, Wynona's life wasn't in danger and neither was her marriage. Relieved, she was back to being annoyed. She'd had enough.

"What I'm going to tell them," Shania told her cousin, "is why I committed justifiable homicide if you don't stop this and tell me what's going on."

"You're going to feel bad about threatening me once I tell you."

From the sound of her voice, Wynona was still grinning, Shania thought.

"I'll be the judge of that. Now talk!" she ordered, coming perilously close to the end of her patience.

The words seemed to burst out of Wynona's mouth all at once. "I'm pregnant, Shania!"

This was the one thing that hadn't occurred to her. Shania's mouth dropped open. "Excuse me? Did you just say—?"

"I did," Wynona interrupted her. "And I am. I'm pregnant!" she repeated because she liked saying it and liked hearing it even more.

Still stunned at the news, Shania asked, "When? How?" Realizing what she'd just blurted out, she amended her question. "I mean, I know how. But when?"

"You want the exact moment?" Wynona asked her, laughing. "Because there've been a lot of them and I can't really pinpoint when we—"

"No!" Shania cried, stopping her. "That's okay. That was just the surprise talking," she explained. She took a breath, collecting her thoughts so that she could sound like a coherent person instead of an overjoyed babbling idiot. "Have you seen a doctor? Did he tell you how far along you might be?"

"She," Wynona corrected. "I went to see Brett Murphy's wife, Alicia."

Shania was equally torn between being overjoyed and being impatient to have her question answered.

"And what did she tell you? When am I going to be an aunt—again?" she added belatedly, remembering that Ryan was her nephew now that Wynona had married his father.

All of this was so new to her, Shania thought, trying her best to get used to the idea.

"Well, according to what she said, you've got about a seven-month wait," Wynona told her.

Her mind was already going full speed ahead. "Great, that'll give me a chance to amass some baby clothes and toys for you."

"Don't get crazy, Shania," Wynona warned her with a laugh.

"Sorry." She couldn't stop grinning as the thought of Wynona being pregnant took root. "Too late. So what does Clint say?"

"Well, at first he was speechless," Wynona told her. "And then he couldn't stop grinning. Actually, he's still grinning."

"Grinning?" Shania repeated. She tried to picture that and failed. "Are we talking about the same Clint?"

"We're talking about the new Clint," Wynona corrected. "He's absolutely thrilled, Shania. And so am I."

"Well, that makes three of us. Four," she amended, looking at Belle. Responding to the mood the dog was picking up on, Belle's tail was thumping against the floor again. "The dog's very excited for you."

"Probably not as excited as Ryan is," Wynona told her.

"You told Ryan?" Shania asked, surprised. "And he's not jealous?"

"Jealous?" Wynona laughed. "He's already stacking up his old toys and baseball equipment so he can give it to the baby. He can't wait until he gets here."

"What if it's a girl?" Shania asked. Working with her students had made her anticipate problems.

"It doesn't matter. Ryan'll be happy. Besides, girls play baseball, too."

Pregnant. Wynona was pregnant. Shania couldn't get over the news. "This is really great, you know."

"I think so," Wynona agreed. "Well, enough about me. What about you? How's everything going?"

In the wake of her cousin's news everything else paled in comparison, but since she'd asked, Shania felt obligated to answer.

"Same old, same old," Shania told her. "Mostly I'm too busy to notice much of anything. I've got to drill them to get ready to take their PSATs."

"Are you doing all right?" Wynona asked, more interested in the personal aspect than the scholastic one.

"I wouldn't mind a magic wand that would transform

some of my rebellious students into studious ones. Got one of those lying around somewhere?" Shania asked.

Hearing Wynona laugh was really the best medicine Shania could ask for.

Chapter Four

"Elena," Shania called out the next day as the teenager was just about to shuffle out of her classroom along with the rest of the third period algebra class. When Elena turned around to look at her quizzically, Shania asked, "Could I speak with you for a minute, please?"

Elena remained where she was and regarded her with the excessively bored expression that she had managed to perfect in the past few weeks.

"Do I have to listen?" she asked the teacher.

"That would be the general idea, yes," Shania responded, keeping her voice upbeat and friendly and refusing to rise to the bait.

Elena sighed dramatically, then slowly sauntered over to her teacher. "I'll try to do better on the next test."

"Well, you didn't do all that badly on the last one, but that's good to know since we both know you're capable of doing better," Shania told her. "But this isn't about your test score."

A suspicious look came over Elena's face, subduing her fresh, natural beauty. "Then what is it about?"

Shania gestured toward a desk in the front row, indicating that the girl take a seat. At the same time, she sat down at the desk next to it.

After Elena warily sank down, Shania began to talk to her, continuing to choose her words carefully and with precision.

"I couldn't help but notice that you seemed really upset about something today—even more than usual," she added with a small, encouraging smile. "I was just wondering if there was anything I could do."

Well-shaped eyebrows drew together on Elena's brow. "About what?"

"About whatever it is that's making you scowl so hard," Shania replied. There was no judgment in her voice, just a friendly offer of help.

For a moment, Elena seemed to debate denying that there was anything wrong, that it was all in her teacher's head. "That all depends. Can you turn a narrow-minded, judgmental, know-it-all older brother into a reasonable person?"

"Maybe. What happened?"

Elena waved her hand at her teacher, dismissing the offer. "It really doesn't matter."

But now that Elena had started this, Shania wasn't ready to back off. "Now, there we have a difference of opinion, Elena, because I think that it does."

Elena tossed her head, trying to be the very picture of haughty rebellion.

"Oh? And why would you say something like that?" Elena asked, using her best disinterested, bored voice.

"I've looked at your grades, Elena. Your *past* grades," Shania emphasized before the girl could protest this invasion of her privacy despite the fact that they were talking about something that was listed in her file and was a matter of record. "Until this year, you were on your way to being seriously considered for a scholarship that could pay for all four years of your college education." Her eyes met Elena's. The latter looked away, staring off into the air. Shania wasn't about to drop the matter. "That's not something that you should throw away lightly."

Elena's whole body gave the impression that she was shutting down. There was a defensive expression in her eyes as she lifted her chin, ready for a fight. "Maybe I don't want to go to college."

"Okay," Shania said good-naturedly. "What do you want to do?"

Elena looked even more annoyed as she shrugged. "Why do I have to have a plan?" she demanded.

"Because if you don't," Shania told her patiently, "if you just float along without any kind of a goal, you're really going to regret it someday."

The girl shifted impatiently in her seat. "Yeah, yeah," she said, rolling her eyes. "Can I go now?"

Elena began to rise, but Shania raised her hand, indicating that the teen should remain seated a little longer.

"Not yet," Shania told her.

Elena looked at her watch. "Look, you're making me late. I've got another class."

But Shania knew that was a lie. "No, you don't," she replied simply. When Elena opened her mouth to protest, Shania told the teenager, "I looked up your school schedule."

"You did what?" Elena cried. "Why would you do that? Did my brother put you up to this?" Impotent frustration had the girl suddenly letting loose with a guttural yell. "I can't believe he'd do this."

Shania was quick to set her straight. "Your brother didn't put me up to this. I have no idea who your brother is," she told the girl.

It wasn't absolutely true, but Shania felt that she could be forgiven until she actually confirmed if the man she'd talked to last night was Elena's brother. For now, she felt justified in making the denial.

"Then why would you bother looking up my schedule like that?"

"It's very simple," Shania said. "Because you're really very, very bright and I wanted to talk to you to see if I could help you."

Elena's eyes narrowed again.

"Why?"

"Because I hate to see waste," Shania told her simply. "Because quite honestly you are the brightest student I've ever encountered and, in a way, maybe you kind of remind me of me when I was really mad at the world and almost wound up destroying everything, including the aunt who had gone out of her way to try to save me."

Elena closed herself off as she glared at her teacher. "You're just making all this up," she accused the woman.

Rather than deny the assumption, Shania asked the teen, "Why would I do that?"

Elena threw up her hands. "I don't know. I don't have all the answers!"

The girl appeared ready to bolt. Shania went on talking to her in a calm, even voice, trying to get through to the angry teenager.

"Let's start over," Shania suggested. "What made you so upset? *More* upset," she amended. "You haven't exactly been Miss Sunshine since the beginning of the semester."

"My brother actually set up some kind of a surveillance device so he could watch my every move," Elena cried, seething over what she obviously viewed as an insult.

Rather than act indignant for her, or side with Elena's brother, Shania just asked a simple question. "Why would he do that?"

Elena crossed her arms before her chest, pulling into herself. "Because he doesn't trust me, that's why!"

Shania looked at the girl for a long, probing moment. "Should he?"

"He's my brother," Elena retorted indignantly. "Of course he should trust me."

Now they were getting somewhere. "And you haven't done anything to undermine that trust?" she asked, her eyes meeting the girl's.

"No," Elena protested. But Shania continued just looking at her and finally the teen shifted uncomfortably. "Okay, maybe."

"And how did you do that?" Shania asked her, giving every indication that there would be no judgment attached to anything that Elena said.

Elena glanced away and shrugged. "I might have gone to Matt McGuire's party a week ago," she murmured. And then she quickly added, "But Daniel told me not to have parties at our house and I didn't. I can't tell someone else not to have one at their house."

"No, you can't," Shania agreed. And then she added the part that Elena didn't want to hear. "But you don't have to attend."

"Matt's my friend," Elena protested. "I can't not go."

Shania couldn't help grinning. "That's a double negative, but we'll talk about that later." She got back to the subject under discussion. "Did you ask your brother if you could go to the party?"

The answer came grudgingly and only after a couple of moments. "No."

"Why not?" Shania asked her. Again, there was no judgment in her voice.

Elena's voice grew louder and more assured. "Because I can make up my own mind if I want to go to a party or not."

The girl had to know that wasn't right, Shania thought.

"Elena, like it or not—and yes," she interjected before Elena could protest, "I know it seems unfair—but you are a minor and your brother is responsible for you. That means that you have to ask him for his permission, or at the very least, tell him where you're going to be before you go."

"Why? So he can say no?" Elena challenged her teacher.

"That is his right," Shania informed her. She knew it didn't win her any points with the girl, but it was also true.

"Who says?"

Shania regarded her quietly for a minute before she answered, "You are a very intelligent girl, Elena. More intelligent than most. You already know the answer to that."

"You're on his side, aren't you?" Elena accused. "I knew it!" She was on her feet in seconds, ready to bolt out of the room.

But Shania caught her wrist, holding her in place. "No, I'm on yours. And I'll let you in on a secret. The best way to earn your brother's trust is to be trustworthy."

Elena huffed loudly.

"Did you ever stop to think that he's just worried about you?" Shania asked.

"Well, he shouldn't be," Elena retorted. "I can take care of myself!"

"That might very well be true," Shania allowed, "but you're going to have to prove that to him."

"How? My brother's got me under lock and key like a prisoner," Elena complained, seething. "Can't he be arrested for that?"

"Not unless he's got you chained up. Does he?" she asked, looking at the teen's face.

"No," Elena mumbled. "But—"

"Okay," Shania told her, "since your brother doesn't have you chained up, my suggestion is that you start acting like a model prisoner and he'll slowly start to trust you and give you back some of those privileges that you're missing."

Elena's face clouded over as she snapped, "No, he won't. He's stubborn and pig-headed and he'll just go on treating me like I'm this kid—"

"I think he's probably fairer than you think," Shania countered, assuring the teen. She could see by the look on Elena's face that she needed something more. Shania searched her brain to come up with something. "And until then," she told Elena, "why don't you think about everything that your brother gave up for you just so that he could make sure you'd be all right."

Elena looked at her as if she had suddenly lapsed into a strange language that didn't make any sense to her. "What do you mean what he gave up? He didn't give up anything."

But Shania had done her homework when it came to Elena's background. She'd had a feeling that she was going to need all the help she could get. "Your parents are gone, right?" she asked the teen gently.

Elena's back instantly went up. "That's not my fault."

"I didn't say it was your fault," Shania replied calmly. "But your brother *is* taking care of you, isn't he, Elena?"

Elena kept glaring at her. "So?"

Shania's eyes met Elena's. "He doesn't have to."

"Sure he does," the teenager insisted. "There's no one else to take care of me. Daniel's my brother. He *has* to take care of me."

"Elena," Shania said gently, "people don't always do the right thing, even if they're supposed to. People have been known to just take off when they don't want to face up to their responsibilities. I know a lot of people who would love to be in your place and have an older brother to look out for them, to turn to. You might not think so, but you are very lucky to have someone who cares enough about you to put up with everything you're dishing out and still trying to get you to do the right thing. There are those who, given the circumstances, just might shrug their shoulders and shine you on, letting you do whatever you wanted to."

Elena clearly didn't see that as being a bad thing. "Sounds good to me."

"Maybe," Shania allowed, then pointedly emphasized, "If that person is lazy. Otherwise, it's called not caring."

Elena frowned because her point had somehow gotten away from her. "You just like to twist things around, don't you?"

"No," Shania contradicted, "I like to make things clear. You're smart, you're pretty and you have a great deal of potential. You're luckier than most, Elena. You have it all." She looked into the teen's eyes again, appealing to her common sense. "Don't waste it."

"I'm not wasting it," the girl said stubbornly. "I just want to be able to enjoy it while I still can. While I'm still *young*," she stressed. "I want to have fun, Ms. Stewart. You remember fun, don't you?"

"Yes, I do. I also remember working hard and being

proud of myself for doing a good job. There's no other feeling like that, trust me. Don't rob yourself of it. That kind of 'fun' you're talking about lasts maybe a few hours. On the other hand, what you'll accomplish by applying yourself and putting in all that hard work will last you a lifetime."

"Maybe it just *feels* like a lifetime," Elena quipped.

"I tell you what, Elena, why don't you give my way a try for a couple of weeks? If, at the end of that time, you find that you're not feeling better about yourself, then you can just go back to phoning it in for the rest of the semester."

Elena's brow furrowed. "Phoning it in?"

"Yes. It means just barely squeaking by," Shania explained,

"And no more lectures?" Elena asked, watching her for her reaction.

"It won't be easy, but no more lectures," Shania agreed.

"And you'll talk to my brother and get him off my back?" Elena asked.

Shania thought about the tall, dark, handsome stranger she'd encountered at Murphy's last night. He didn't strike her as someone who welcomed unsolicited advice.

"I'll talk to your brother," she agreed, "but I doubt if my suggesting that he 'get off your back' is going to be well-received."

"But you *will* talk to him?" Elena pressed, her dark, expressive eyes pinning her teacher down.

Shania nodded. "I'll talk to him. And you'll apply yourself?"

Elena frowned, then said grudgingly, "For two weeks."

"That's all I ask," Shania told her with a warm smile.

Hopefully, she thought, two weeks would be enough to do the trick.

Elena muttered something under her breath as she blew out a long-suffering sigh. Shania decided it was best if she didn't ask her to repeat it. Some things were better left unknown.

Chapter Five

Short in stature, large in reputation, Miss Joan had been part of Forever for as long as any of its present citizens could remember, as had the diner that she both ran and owned.

Gruff and abrupt on the outside, soft and understanding on the inside, Miss Joan was also the person that many of the local people went to for advice and guidance when they had nowhere else to turn. On occasion, she was known to take in people, as well as hire them when they found themselves penniless and desperate with no immediate way to rectify that.

What Miss Joan didn't do was coddle people. Instead, she was just as likely to give someone a well-needed kick in the posterior region to get them moving in the right direction. She didn't hold anyone's hand—she didn't want to add to their sense of helplessness. What she did was steer them in the right direction.

In short, due to a variety of different reasons, everyone thought of Miss Joan as the glue that held the town together.

So, whether it was by design or just subconscious motivation, when Daniel felt that he was utterly confused by his teenage sister's rather mercurial behavior, he found himself stopping by Miss Joan's diner to grab a late breakfast—something he very rarely did.

The thin, titian-haired woman, who could make grown men tremble by merely raising a sharp eyebrow, glanced in Daniel's direction the moment he walked in through the diner's door. Topping off a customer's coffee at the far end of the counter, Miss Joan began to move toward the deputy the moment the door closed behind him.

The thin lips curved minutely in greeting. "Well, if it isn't the strong arm of the law."

Daniel took a seat at the counter. "I hate to correct you, Miss Joan, but I think you meant to say the 'long arm of the law,'" Daniel told the woman politely.

Hazel eyes swept over his face. "For your information, Deputy, I always say what I mean," Miss Joan told him. The hint of a smile was gone. "Have you taken a good look at yourself in the mirror lately, Deputy?" she asked.

Despite the concerns that were weighing on him lately, Daniel asked, "Are you flirting with me, Miss Joan?"

The woman didn't answer his question one way or another. Instead, she said, "At my age, Daniel, I get to do what I want."

"What would Harry say?" he asked, referring to the man Miss Joan had finally agreed to marry six years ago after being courted by Harry Monroe for what seemed like an eternity.

"Nothing, if he knows what's good for him," Miss Joan deadpanned. Filling the cup she'd placed in front of him, she got down to business. "So, what brings you here,

Deputy? A sudden desire for a home-cooked meal?" she asked, although one look at her face told him that wasn't what she was really thinking.

He wasn't comfortable admitting that he had sought her out, so he said, "I skipped breakfast and realized that wasn't a smart move."

Sharp eyes took slow measure of him, telling him that the woman was totally unconvinced.

"That doesn't sound like something you'd do, Daniel. What's the real reason you're here?" she asked. Then, seeing him looking at his coffee, Miss Joan asked, "Black, right?"

"Right as always, Miss Joan," he replied.

A spasmodic smile crossed her thin mouth. "Now, we can continue this little stillborn charade and I can get you a plate of scrambled eggs," she said, mentioning the way she knew that he preferred his eggs, gleaned from the few occasions that he had come in for breakfast, "or you can just get down to business and tell me what's causing that deep furrow between those deep, soulful eyes of yours." She looked at him intently. "It wouldn't have something to do with your sister, would it?"

Though he had always been excellent at maintaining a poker face, when Miss Joan's guess was so on target, Daniel couldn't immediately suppress the surprise that flashed across his face.

Belatedly, Daniel managed to recover and murmured, "Yes."

Pleased with herself, although not surprised, Miss Joan nodded. "I thought so."

Daniel paused, looking down at his coffee again, wondering if he'd made a mistake coming here after all. And then he raised his eyes, looking directly into the woman's deep, penetrating hazel orbs.

"You know, someday you're going to have to tell me just how you wound up getting that unnerving sixth sense of yours."

"No mystery, handsome," Miss Joan assured him. "It's just intuition."

"It's a hell of a lot more than that, Miss Joan," he told her.

He had to admit, albeit silently, that he did find it more than a little unnerving at times just how accurate she could be.

Miss Joan waved her hand at his words. She had little time for flattery, even if it was sincerely voiced. "You were going to tell me what's troubling you about your sister."

The word *everything* flashed through Daniel's mind, but he kept that to himself. He'd never had any use for complainers and he wasn't about to start sounding like one himself.

For now, he decided to give the diner owner a little bit of background before getting to the heart of the present problem.

"Elena's been going through this rebellious stage," he began.

Miss Joan looked completely unmoved. "She's sixteen, Deputy. It's to be expected."

But *he* hadn't expected it, Daniel thought. Elena had always behaved herself. Her sense of self-discipline had been inherent.

And then everything changed.

"Until this summer, she was quiet, studious and as close to perfect as anyone could possibly hope for," he told Miss Joan, keeping his voice down so that she was the only one who could hear him. He took a breath and then gave voice to the problem. "And then she changed."

"Because she's sixteen," Miss Joan repeated, stressing her words pointedly.

The look on Daniel's face told Miss Joan that he didn't view what she'd just said as an explanation or an excuse. "The thing is, just as suddenly a couple of days ago, Elena goes back to being the way she was before all this flared up."

Miss Joan waited for him to continue. When he didn't, she posed the logical question to him. "Well, did you ask her about it?"

The memory of that particular exchange was very fresh in his mind and he felt another wave of anger pass over him. "I did, but Elena just rolled her eyes at me and said she didn't have time to talk."

"Let me get something straight," Miss Joan said. "Are you *upset* that she went back to her previous behavior?"

Her question caught him totally off guard. He was surprised that she would ask something like that. "Of course not."

"Then what's the problem?" she asked, not clear why he seemed so out of sorts.

"The problem," he explained as patiently as he could, "is that I want to find out what happened to change Elena's mind and make her go back to her old ways. This way, I'll know what 'buttons' to press to make her revert back to the studious Elena instead of the party girl mode she was in a week ago."

It was all falling into place for her, Miss Joan thought. "My guess is that this all might be the influence of one of her teachers," Miss Joan told him. She let the words sink in and then went on to suggest, "Why don't you try talking to her teachers?"

He knew that made sense, but he had never been the type to seek out a teacher for the sole purpose of having a conference with him or her regarding his sister's progress. Up until now, Elena had been doing just fine and there'd been no need to attempt to "get her on the right path." The extent to which he got involved in her schoolwork was signing her report cards, which had always been stellar.

Maybe he should just let it all just ride, Daniel thought. Maybe Elena would just continue on this path now that she'd gotten back to it.

"That would be butting in," he told Miss Joan, finishing up his coffee.

"Some people would call that taking an interest in Elena's education," Miss Joan corrected. She topped off his cup, then shrugged. "You do what you want, Deputy. But if you really want answers instead of floating along blindly, I'd suggest looking into all the possible influences in Elena's life. If nothing else, that way you could find out if there's any way you could encourage your sister on the home front."

Daniel laughed shortly under his breath, thinking of the recent clashes that had taken place between Elena and himself since school had started this year. Instead of a docile little sister, he'd found himself dealing with a spitfire that challenged everything he said.

"The best way I can encourage Elena to do well," he told Miss Joan, "is to pretend I don't notice she's doing well."

Miss Joan looked at him, something akin to pity entering her eyes. "Trust me, Deputy. Every female wants to be noticed."

"Maybe," Daniel responded, not wanting to contradict the woman outright. "But that rule doesn't apply to sisters."

Miss Joan lowered her head slightly, allowing her eyes

to be level with his. Her gaze held him prisoner. "Is your sister a female?"

Daniel looked at the older woman, thinking he had to have heard her wrong. When Miss Joan continued looking at him, apparently waiting for a response, he finally said, "Of course she is, Miss Joan."

She nodded, a triumphant expression crossing her face as she told him, "Then it applies."

Daniel sighed. Miss Joan had a habit of always being right. He saw no reason to think that this time might be different just because this was about his sister who he'd once thought he knew better than anyone else in the world. It was now obvious to him that he didn't.

Daniel shook his head. "Why are females all so complicated?"

"Because otherwise we'd be boring—and men," Miss Joan answered, softly chuckling to herself. "Now stop wasting time standing here and go call that girl's teachers. When you narrow down which one has been influencing her, ask for a conference. That way you might be able to get some clarity on what's going on with your sister."

It didn't strike him until later that in the space of a few minutes, Miss Joan had taken all of Elena's teachers and zeroed in on just a single one.

As if she knew something he didn't.

But then, he silently admitted, somehow the woman always did.

Right now, however, Daniel was keenly aware that he needed to get going. Just to make sure, he glanced at his watch.

He was right.

It was getting late. He'd wasted enough time trying to get insight into the workings of his sister's mind. If he didn't get going, he was going to be late getting to work.

"Thanks for the help, Miss Joan." Standing up, he dug into his pocket, simultaneously nodding at the empty coffee cup. "What do I owe you?"

"A lot more than you could ever repay me," the woman answered simply. And then, knowing his sense of honor wouldn't allow him to accept a cup of coffee on the house, she told him, "A dollar'll more than cover it."

He placed a five-dollar bill beside his plate. "Consider it a down payment on that debt," Daniel told the older woman as he headed for the door.

"What was all that about?" Cassandra, one of Miss Joan's newest waitresses, asked. She gestured toward the door in case she was being too vague.

"My guess is that we've just witnessed the awakening of Deputy Daniel Tallchief," Miss Joan said. "Now, why don't you follow in his footsteps and get busy with all those dishes?" she told the waitress, gesturing toward the tables that still needed to be bussed.

Cassandra knew better than to sigh. "Yes, ma'am," she answered as she got to work.

Despite what he had said to Miss Joan about being curious about the actual reason behind his sister's sudden reversal in behavior, Daniel was undecided whether or not to take the woman's advice.

Maybe he shouldn't seek out any of Elena's teachers. Talking to them might just be inviting trouble or, at the very least, rocking the boat.

The old adage about leaving well enough alone flashed through his mind.

That was cowardly, he thought the next moment. And he had never been a coward, not even when he'd been a young boy and had stood up to that bully who had been twice his size.

Besides, he'd been serious when he'd said that if there was anything he could do to encourage Elena's sudden renewed interest in studying, he was more than willing to do it. He just needed to be shown the way.

Studying was far preferable to spending time with that Matt kid. That would be a ticking time bomb waiting to go off.

"You're looking more pensive than usual," Joe Lone Wolf commented after fifteen minutes of silence had gone by. Daniel wasn't known to be talkative, but he usually had a few things to say when he came in. This morning the junior deputy had been as silent as a tomb. "Something wrong?"

Daniel was about to say no, then admitted, "I don't know."

"Want to talk about it?" Rick Santiago asked, picking that moment to walk into the room to get himself a cup of coffee. He paused by the space between the two deputies' desks.

"Not particularly," Daniel answered honestly.

Talking to Miss Joan this morning had been something out of the ordinary for him. He usually kept things to himself and at this point, he felt pretty close to being talked out.

However, it looked as if the sheriff had other ideas on the matter.

"Three heads are better than one, Tallchief," Rick told him. "Even if two of those heads are more stubborn than sin," he added.

Daniel thought it might be better for everyone all around if he kept his own counsel for the time being. "I think this is something that I need to work out on my own."

"Whatever it is that you're working out, is it going to interfere with work?" Rick asked.

Daniel gave his superior a look. "You know me better than that, Sheriff."

But the expression on Rick's face was skeptical. "Trouble is, I'm not sure I really know you at all, Tallchief. I appreciate you being self-sufficient and wanting to handle things on your own," he told his deputy, "but you need to know when to ask for help."

Daniel gave it one last try. "I don't need help…exactly," he amended.

The sheriff moved closer to him. "But?" Rick asked, waiting to hear the rest of the man's sentence.

Daniel paused, thinking. He supposed it wouldn't hurt things if he asked a few general questions—just in case he was being too lax about what was going on with his sister's behavior.

"But my sister's driving me crazy," he finally told the other two men.

Rick laughed in response, something Daniel hadn't expected. "Been there," the man told him.

Joe looked at the sheriff sharply. "No offense, Sheriff, but that's my wife you're commenting on."

Rick grinned. "And she's your problem now. Don't mind telling you that you're having a lot better luck getting along with her than I did," Rick admitted. "Of course, Ramona's done a great deal of growing up in the last ten years."

Daniel listened to the two men he'd come to admire and respect over the course of the past couple of years talk. And as he listened, the wall that he kept around himself and his thoughts began to soften and recede to an extent. So much so that he felt that perhaps it wouldn't be interpreted as a sign of weakness if he did ask some questions.

But just before he was about to, he suddenly remembered the woman he'd run into at Murphy's the other night. She'd said something about butting heads with headstrong students. That was the best description of his sister that he'd come across recently. A headstrong student.

"Either one of you know anything about that physics teacher at the high school?" he asked the other two men.

Both men stopped talking and turned to look at Daniel. One smile seemed to spread across two faces.

"Why?" Joe asked.

"You interested?" Rick asked.

Daniel looked at his superior as if the question was too ludicrous to even consider. Instead, he told the two men, "I think she might be Elena's teacher. I was just wondering if she's the kind of teacher to inspire her students to study hard and change their outlook when it comes to doing well."

"I could ask around," Rick told him.

"Might be better if you asked her that yourself," Joe suggested.

Rick nodded, changing his mind about his initial offer. "What he said," he told Daniel.

Daniel had the eerie feeling that somewhere, Fate had just cast a die.

Chapter Six

More than twenty-four hours later, Daniel was still debating whether or not to drop by Forever's high school and introduce himself to the woman he'd probably already met at Murphy's.

Since no names had been exchanged that evening, Daniel was uneasy that Elena's teacher would naturally jump to the conclusion that he was merely trying to complete the pass he had initiated at their first meeting. Therefore, she might not believe that his real reason for going out of his way to talk to her was because he wanted to know what he could do to help encourage his sister with her studies.

But apparently, he realized as he walked into the office, the decision to make that first step had been taken out of his hands.

He had just come back after breaking up a dispute between two ranchers who weren't seeing eye to eye about where one property line ended and the other began. Two steps into the office he became aware that there was someone talking to the sheriff.

A female someone.

Daniel wasn't generally in the habit of eavesdropping, but the sound of the low, melodic voice caught his attention immediately, even before he could make out any of the woman's words.

Going over a report at his desk, Joe happened to look up, and he noticed the attentiveness on Daniel's face. He observed Daniel for a moment before making any sort of a comment.

"If I didn't know any better, I'd say that you look like a bird dog that just realized he'd had a quail walk across his path."

Annoyed, Daniel waved his hand at the senior deputy, implying that Joe should be quiet.

Daniel strained to listen more closely.

The next moment, he realized that it wasn't his imagination playing tricks on him. He would have recognized that voice anywhere. Not to mention that shapely figure.

It was the woman from Murphy's saloon, the one he was almost certain was Elena's teacher.

What was she doing talking to the sheriff? Had something gone wrong at the high school?

Had…?

And then there was no time left for any more speculation. Because the sheriff was escorting the woman out, bringing her into the general area where the deputies sat.

"Tallchief, I need a word." The sheriff beckoned him over to where he and the woman were standing.

Concern ricocheted through Daniel with each step he took as he approached them.

"Sheriff?" he asked, finding it less disconcerting to

center his attention strictly on his superior instead of on the woman standing next to Santiago.

Maybe he could have pulled it off if the woman had been less compelling. But she wasn't. She was the kind of woman who immediately drew all eyes to her whenever she entered a room, even one that might have been filled with other beautiful women—which was definitely *not* the case this time.

Once his eyes met hers, Daniel nodded a silent greeting, doing his best not to focus on the fact that this woman by her mere presence was causing his stomach to pull into itself and all but tie itself up in a knot.

It had been a long time since he'd felt that way—and that had ended in a disaster, he reminded himself.

He felt barriers going up. Protective barriers.

"Ms. Stewart would like a word with you," Rick told Daniel, his expression giving nothing away, including the fact that the three of them had just discussed this woman a little more than twenty-four hours ago. "Why don't you use my office?"

The suggestion was made not to Daniel but to the woman, who it was becoming apparent had come here to speak to him, not the sheriff.

"That's very generous of you, Sheriff," Shania told him, then asked, "Are you sure it's all right? I can just as easily talk to your deputy outside."

"My office will afford you more privacy," Rick answered. "Go ahead. Go right in."

Because there were now questions burning in his chest—was the offer for privacy because the sheriff had anticipated this would hit him hard?—Daniel made no effort to turn down the offer. Instead, he quickly followed the woman into the sheriff's office and closed the door behind them.

The second the reassuring *click* signifying their separation from the others was heard, Daniel couldn't restrain himself any longer. He had to know. "What's wrong?"

Shania looked at him, surprised by his question. "What makes you think that there's something wrong?"

"Well, for one thing, I can't think of a single reason for a teacher to come into the sheriff's office that doesn't have some sort of a dark explanation attached to it," Daniel told her.

Shania smiled. "I can see that you're not the Neanderthal that Elena claimed you are, but you're certainly not given to having optimistic thoughts, are you?"

For a moment, he thought of asking her if she remembered their brief encounter at Murphy's. But given the situation, it really made no difference right now. Instead, he addressed her comment.

"Elena hasn't given me any reason to harbor any optimistic thoughts," he told her, reacting more defensively than he would have thought he would. He ordinarily just allowed things to unfold before him, but Elena was too important for him to merely passively stand by, waiting for questions to be answered.

"Oh, I wouldn't be so sure about that if I were you. Your sister is a very bright girl who exhibits a great deal of potential—"

Daniel swept away the woman's flattering statement to get down to what he felt was the actual crux of the matter.

"Which my sister seems pretty set on squandering away," he pointed out.

She needed him to see that his sister was really trying hard now. "Elena struck a bargain with me that she was going to give studying another try for a short period of time..."

Daniel looked at the attractive teacher, wondering how

well she handled disappointment. As for him, he didn't expect any sort of decent breakthrough to take place. "Emphasis on the word 'short.'" It was more of a statement than a question.

She was beginning to understand why Elena would find her brother's reactions daunting. "I thought that maybe you could encourage her, let her know how proud you are of her for trying so hard."

"You don't know my sister," he told her. "The second I say anything to her that even *remotely* sounds like an opinion about anything, she's going to do the exact opposite."

"Then don't say it," Shania answered simply.

Daniel looked at her as if he thought she was just babbling nonsense.

"How's that again?"

Shania took a breath and did her best to put it in a different way.

"Don't say—do," she told the deputy. But she could see that Daniel still didn't get what she was telling him, so she spelled it out, citing something specific—and positive—he could do. "Take down that surveillance camera you put up by the front door."

"Elena told you about that?"

"Yes, she did. And, more importantly," Shania told him, "I could see how you putting that up made her feel. Like you didn't trust her."

His first instinct was to deny her assumption, but he knew that wouldn't help accomplish anything. Not to mention that it wasn't true.

"I didn't—I don't," Daniel stressed.

"Elena is only going to behave the way you expect her to behave," Shania told him.

He frowned. "Yeah, well, she's already shown me

that she can't be trusted. How am I supposed to build on that?"

"Here's an idea," Shania suggested gamely. "Why don't you trust her and let her live up to *that* image?"

Daniel stared at the teacher as if what she'd just espoused was nothing short of crazy. She *had* to know that, he thought.

"She's a sixteen-year-old girl. Do you have *any* idea what can happen to a sixteen-year-old girl running wild like that?"

The man was allowing his imagination to run away with him.

"I think you might be exaggerating, Deputy Tallchief. Elena wouldn't run wild. Besides, Forever is a decent, quiet little town," she reminded Daniel.

But he shook his head. The woman was obviously missing a very crucial point.

"Teenagers are still teenagers. At sixteen, they all think they're immortal and their hormones run hot."

"Short of putting her in a tower and periodically cutting off her hair, there's not much you can reasonably do." When she saw the deputy's eyebrows draw together over eyes that regarded her in total confusion, she made a guess that her reference had gone right over his handsome head. In his defense, she supposed that the man probably wasn't the type who had ever read any fairy tales when he was growing up.

"Rapunzel?" she told him, but the name, like the reference, meant nothing to him. She tried again. "There's only so much you can do to ensure Elena's safety before she starts to feel like she's in prison. So, instead, why don't you get her to *want* to live up to your standards because it's the right thing to do?"

She could see that he didn't think very much of her

idea, but, on the plus side, he wasn't dismissing it out of hand, either. There was hope.

Shania went over her suggestion again. "Take down the camera. Also, tell her you and I had a parent-teacher conference and that you're proud of the progress she's made."

"In other words, you want me to lie to her."

Instead of answering him, Shania took a folder out of her purse. She spread out a number of papers she had placed inside the folder. "Take a look at your sister's latest tests scores."

Daniel did as she suggested and then he raised his eyes to Shania's. He was clearly surprised by what he'd just seen.

"Elena never said anything about doing well on her tests."

"Your sister's not the type to brag," she told Daniel. "Don't you know that about her?" Putting the pages back into the folder, then tucking the folder into her purse, Shania turned her attention back to Elena's brother. "Did you ever even ask her about her test scores?"

Guilt made him react defensively. "How was I supposed to know she took any?"

"Seriously?" Shania asked. "She's in high school, Deputy Tallchief. She's *always* taking tests. That's what students do. And, just so you know, my students are going to be getting ready to take their PSATs next month. I'll be holding practice sessions for anyone who wants to take them after hours and on Saturdays."

That sounded like a lot of extra work for the teacher, Daniel thought. Didn't the woman have a life? Or was she just really, really dedicated?

He took a guess at why the woman had said anything

to him about the sessions. "And you want me to talk her into taking them?"

"No, I just wanted you to know that she won't be out running around. Elena will be staying after hours to take these practice tests," Shania told him. "She's already signed up."

That *did* surprise him. "She is?"

"She is," Shania answered. "As a matter of fact, your sister was the first one to put her name down on the list."

Daniel didn't even pretend that he wasn't impressed by all this. And he gave the credit where it was due. At this woman's feet.

"You got her to do all this?" he marveled.

"I really didn't 'get' her to do anything," Shania corrected him. "I just made suggestions. Elena's the one who took those suggestions to their logical conclusion. You know your sister well enough to know that I couldn't have made her do anything if she didn't want to."

He laughed shortly. Maybe Elena's teacher did understand what he was up against after all. "Yeah, tell me about it."

"What I will tell you," Shania said, picking up on the deputy's phrase, "is to try to spend a little time with Elena—not telling her to do something," she pointed out, "but just doing something *with* her."

These days Elena had made it clear that she didn't want to do *anything* with him. He was busy with work and she was hardly ever home. And when she was home, she was locked up in her room. Now he knew she was obviously studying in there.

Since this woman seemed to have all the answers, he swallowed his pride and asked, "Like what?"

"Like—" Her voice trailed off for a moment as she

tried to think. "What did you used to do with her when she was younger?"

One thing came to mind and that in turn made him laugh. Shania looked at him quizzically, so he explained, "Elena's a little too big to give her a pony ride on my back."

"True," Shania agreed. "But she's not too big for the two of you to go out horseback riding."

He had no idea how to even get Elena to agree to that idea. "Just like that?"

"Why not?" Shania asked. "My cousin and I used to go out riding on the weekends. It rejuvenates you and gives the two of you the opportunity to talk. Going out like that clears your head, makes you feel closer to nature. And that's kind of important."

Daniel stopped her right there. "Because we're Navajo?"

No doubt about it. Under all that self-assured manliness, the man definitely had a chip on his shoulder, she thought.

"Because we're people," Shania answered simply.

"I wasn't talking about you," he told her. "I was talking about my sister and me."

"I was thinking about my cousin and myself," she clarified. "And before you ask, Wynona and I are part Navajo. Actually," she amended, "we're three-quarters Navajo."

He shrugged. Maybe he did take offense a little too quickly sometimes. "That's none of my business."

"I didn't say it was," she pointed out. "But it's also nothing I'm ashamed of. I'm proud of where I came from and what I've managed to become." Maybe it would help if she shared a little of her own story with this solemn man. "I'm not sure if I would have been where I am if it hadn't been for my great-aunt helping out, but even if she hadn't been there for me, I knew I wasn't going to wallow in self-pity and do nothing my whole life.

"And now that she's been prodded," Shania continued, "neither will your sister. I just wanted you to be aware of what was going on so you could be in her corner and find a way to encourage her." She looked at him for a long moment. "Elena cares about you a great deal."

He didn't believe that for a second. He would have liked to, but he knew better. "Now you're just making things up."

"No, I'm serious," she insisted. "I can see it in her eyes. Even when she's calling you a Neanderthal, there is affection in her eyes."

"Uh-huh." Again, he wanted to believe that, he really did. But he didn't want to set himself up to be disappointed. He'd already been through that shocking set of circumstances.

More than once.

Still, this teacher with the animated expression and flashing bright eyes seemed to be convinced about what she was telling him. Nobody was *that* good an actress.

"All right," Daniel agreed, although far from enthusiastically, "I'll take down that surveillance camera I've got up."

Shania smiled, happy that she'd gotten Daniel to come around. "Good. And be sure to let her catch you taking it down."

He wasn't sure what the teacher was telling him. "You mean point it out to her?"

Shania shook her head. "No, just make sure you're taking it down when you know she's around. That way you'll get credit for trusting her without making a big speech about it. Less is more in this case," she told him. "Trust me, being subtle makes for the best good deeds."

"I don't know how to be subtle," he told her.

"Sure you do. Don't underestimate yourself," she told him.

He supposed, if he thought about it, her advice about being subtle made some sort of sense. "If you say so."

Her smile grew broader as she rose from her chair. She'd done what she'd come to do.

"I do," she told him. She put her hand out to him. "It was nice meeting you—again, Mr. Tallchief."

"It's Deputy," he corrected, then added, "Or Daniel, if you prefer."

"Daniel," she repeated, wrapping her tongue around his name.

He didn't know why, but he felt as if he had just been put on notice—and the odd thing was that part of him didn't mind.

Chapter Seven

Elena's head shot up, listening intently. The sound coming from the front of the house had registered immediately. She knew her brother was at the sheriff's office, working the late shift, which meant she was supposed to be alone in the house.

The faint sound told her otherwise.

Elena crept out of her room where she'd been doing her homework. Leery, not sure what she'd find, she picked up the bat she occasionally used when she played softball at school. Her palm felt damp as she clutched the wood.

The bat had been her brother's, but he never played anymore.

The journey from her room, located all the way at the back of the house, to the front door felt as if it was taking her forever.

When she saw her brother standing on a ladder, taking down the camera he'd put up only a week ago, she let go of both her breath and the bat she'd been holding.

The bat made much more noise as it hit the floor.

The clatter immediately got Daniel's attention. Turning, he caught and steadied himself just in time to keep from falling off the ladder.

"I guess you're not as defenseless as I thought," he commented, going back to removing the camera.

Picking up the bat, Elena leaned it against the wall in the corner and moved in as close to the ladder as she dared.

"What are you doing?" she asked him, looking up as he worked.

"I don't have much time before I have to get back, but I thought I could use my dinner break to take down the camera." Taking out the last screw, he tucked the screwdriver into his back pocket and then climbed down the ladder, holding the camera.

Elena took a step back, getting out of her brother's way. "Why?"

Putting the camera down on the small table just inside the door, he glanced in Elena's direction. "Why what?"

"Why are you taking it down?" He'd made such a big deal out of wanting it up so he could spy on her, she was surprised that he'd take it down so soon after having put it up.

Daniel thought about just saying that the camera was malfunctioning and leaving it at that, but he decided telling his sister the truth was the better way to go.

He shrugged casually, as if this was no big deal. "Because I thought it over and decided I was sending you the wrong message with this camera."

She continued looking at him, waiting to hear something that would explain all this to her. He couldn't just have decided to be a good guy and leave it at that. Could he? "Go on."

She was going to make him say it, wasn't she? He suppressed a sigh. "I don't want you to think I don't trust you."

Elena cocked her head. Her arms remained crossed before her chest. She was a portrait of distrust. "You don't."

He sighed, taking the ladder and bringing it into the living room. He rested the ladder on its side for the time being.

"That's not true. It's other guys I don't trust, not you," Daniel explained. "But that's no reason to make you feel like a prisoner. I *do* trust you, Elena." He could see she didn't believe him. "I trust you to make the right decisions. I raised you right, so I've got to trust that you'll do the right thing."

She was still skeptical, but she was coming around a little. Still, she needed to know something. "Where did this sudden change of heart come from?"

He doled out a little more of the truth to her. "I had a parent-teacher conference with Ms. Stewart."

Now it was starting to make sense to her. Elena nodded knowingly. "And she told you to take down the camera."

He didn't want to lie to Elena, but if he told her that she was right, that could in all probability negate any possible headway taking the camera down may have gotten him.

So instead, he left her question unanswered and focused on something else instead.

"She told me that you signed up to study for the PSATs with her and she also showed me some of your test scores. Why didn't you tell me how well you're doing in school?"

Elena shrugged, noting that he hadn't congratulated her or said anything positive about her grades. "You didn't ask."

She sounded annoyed, but he wasn't going to allow himself to get sidetracked and get into an argument with her.

"True," Daniel agreed. He could see that his answer surprised her. "I didn't want you to think I was trying to force you into studying."

Elena sighed and he had a feeling that she wasn't really buying this, but for the time being, he let it ride.

"I've got to be getting back. I've got the late shift this week," he told her even though he knew that she already knew that. "But I was thinking, maybe you'd like to go for a ride this weekend."

The suggestion caught her completely off guard. "Why?" she asked suspiciously.

He ignored the accusatory tone. "Well, we used to do that all the time and I thought it might be something you'd like to do again."

A bored, intolerant look came over her face. "So you're willing to suffer through it, is that it?"

Why did she have to turn everything into a confrontation? He struggled to hold down his temper. "I like riding, too."

"I've got practice tests to take," she told him, then added, "PSATs."

Daniel nodded. "Yes, I know. On Saturday, but not on Sunday."

That surprised her. "We'll see," she finally answered, not wanting to be pinned down.

Well, he supposed that he hadn't expected her to immediately jump at the chance.

"Right. Just let me know." Daniel began to turn away. "I'll see you in a couple of hours."

"Is that your way of asking if I'm staying home?" she challenged her brother.

He stopped in the doorway. "No, that's my way of saying that I'll see you in a couple of hours." She still looked unconvinced, so he explained, "It's a school night. I figure you're not going out because that's what we agreed on."

Elena tossed her head dismissively. "I don't remember there being an agreement. I do remember there being an order," she added haughtily, her attitude indicating that she didn't have to abide by it if she didn't choose to.

He saw it differently. "Yeah, well, there have to be some rules."

"For my own good?" she retorted, mocking the very idea of what she assumed he was thinking.

He could feel the argument coming but he forced himself not to rise to the bait. Instead, he gave her a somewhat neutral answer.

"And for mine," he told her. "See you in a bit, Ellie."

He saw the surprise on her face. He hadn't called her Ellie in years, not since she was a little girl. Daniel left his sister standing in the living room as he withdrew.

"I sure hope you know what you're talking about," he murmured under his breath, addressing the teacher who wasn't there as he left the house and walked over to his car.

Belle alerted her that there was someone at the door even before that person had a chance to knock. Rising, Shania glanced at the time.

It wasn't exactly late—once upon a time, she would have considered eight o'clock early—but she didn't usually get visitors at this time.

Instantly, she thought of Wynona. That got her moving quickly. She crossed to the door without bothering to even put her shoes on.

Belle wasn't a fierce dog, but no one would guess that based on the show the German shepherd put on before the door was opened. Aside from loud barking, there was leaping involved, as if Belle was warning whoever was on the doorstep that if they had any wrongdoing in mind, they were going to pay for it dearly.

"Easy, girl," Shania told the dog.

One hand firmly holding on to Belle's collar, Shania craned her neck to look through the door's peephole. Any lingering apprehension vanished.

The next moment, still holding on to Belle, she opened the door.

"What are you doing here?" she asked, surprised to see the brooding deputy on her doorstep. "Is something wrong with Elena?"

She couldn't think of any other reason that would have brought him here.

Daniel looked down apprehensively at the dog that had, just a second ago, sounded like an entire squadron of attack animals.

"Do you need to lock her up first?" he asked.

Shania smiled and shook her head. "No, Belle's not dangerous."

"That's not the way it sounds from this side of the door," he told her, still eyeing the dog.

"Let her sniff your hand," Shania urged, nodding at his hand.

He didn't look entirely convinced that this was a good idea. "Will I get it back?" Daniel asked gamely.

"Most likely," she answered, struggling to keep a straight face.

Daniel relaxed a little. He assumed that she wouldn't have told him to do something that would result in his getting bitten. He slowly put his hand out toward Belle to have her sniff it.

Shania kept her hold on the dog's collar just in case.

Then, to her utter surprise, as she watched she saw Belle lick the deputy's hand.

Shania looked at the deputy, clearly impressed. "She's never done that before. I guess that Belle must *really* like you."

A small smile curved the corners of his mouth as he petted the dog's head. "Feeling's mutual," he told Shania. "I like dogs."

Since order had clearly been restored, Shania opened her door wider.

"Come on in," she said, inviting Daniel into her house.

After closing the door behind him, she turned around to see that the deputy had dropped down to one knee and was petting Belle in earnest. For her part, the dog appeared ecstatic.

Although the dog was generally a very friendly animal, Shania had never seen Belle react to anyone like this before—except for Ryan, her cousin's stepson, and even then, there wasn't this effusion of happiness.

She stood there for a moment, watching the interaction between Daniel and her dog. Smiling, Shania asked the deputy, "Would you like for me to leave the two of you alone?"

Daniel brushed off his knee as he rose to his feet. It was obvious that the dog had brought out a softer side to him.

"I had a dog when I was a kid. Chips," he recalled, a fond note momentarily entering his voice. "Chips was a really old dog," he explained. "I found him one day wandering around, looking for food. He had a wicked temper," he remembered. "It took a while until I could get him to trust me." He looked back at Belle, remembering the other dog. "He was a mutt, but I really loved him."

He cleared his throat, thinking that he had said too

much. "Seeing your dog brings back memories," he admitted. Then, realizing that his sister's teacher had to be wondering what he was doing here at her house to begin with, he cleared his throat again. "Look, I know that it's late—"

"Not for some people," Shania pointed out. She wanted to give him some slack in case he was apologizing for being here at this hour.

"Yeah, well, I couldn't come earlier because I just got off my shift," he explained before he could get to the heart of what he was doing here.

"All right," she replied gamely, still waiting for the deputy to actually tell her why he was here. Maybe he talked better once some amenities were in place. "Would you like some coffee?" she asked. "Or some cake? I've got cake in the refrigerator if you're hungry."

"No, that's okay," he demurred. "I don't want to take up your time." He shifted slightly as Belle brushed up against his leg, obviously looking to be petted again. "I just wanted you to know that I took your advice."

She waited for him to be a little more specific. But when he didn't say anything further, she asked, "Which part?"

He wasn't the type to use five words when he felt one would do. But since she wanted details, he obliged. "I took down the camera and I suggested that we go for a ride this Sunday."

Pleased, Shania gestured for him to take a seat on the sofa. When he did, she sat down as well, leaving a little space between them.

Her eyes lively, she asked Daniel, "What did she say?"

He gave her the answer verbatim. "She wanted to know why I was taking down the camera and why I was asking her to go riding with me."

Shania laughed to herself. Elena wasn't a girl to accept things at face value. "I take it that Elena suspected there was something behind you treating her like a human being."

He carelessly lifted a shoulder, then let it drop again. "Something like that. But she wasn't entirely hostile toward me," he added, sounding as pleased as he could, given the circumstances. "I just wanted to thank you for the push you gave me."

Shania grinned, pleased with the result. "Well, Deputy, anytime you want me to push you, just say the word and then brace yourself. Are you sure I can't offer you some coffee or anything to eat?"

Daniel shook his head. "No, I've already taken up too much of your time. I'd better be going now," he told her.

As he got up off the sofa and turned toward the door to leave, Belle moved in front of him, blocking his path to the front door.

Shania laughed as she watched the dog. "I think that Belle has other ideas about you making a quick escape," she told him. "She has really taken a shine to you. I think you might want to reconsider your beating a hasty retreat."

He petted the dog's head, shifting around her. "No offense, Belle, but I've got a sister who, despite popular opinion to the contrary, still might need a little, um…" He paused, trying to find the right word, then gave up. "'Subtle' babysitting."

Shania looked at him, concerned. "You're afraid she might take off?"

"Something like that," he admitted. "The camera's been taken down and I had to work the late shift. There are no eyes on her," he explained. "That's a very tempting scenario." He dared her to contradict him.

"Aside from her regular homework, Elena took home a couple of the PSAT practice tests today," Shania told him, watching his face as he took the information in. "That should keep her busy."

He didn't look completely sold on the idea. "*If* she does them," he pointed out.

He expected her to be judgmental. Instead, he watched a smile bloom on a face that was already compellingly lovely.

"Deputy, you are going to have to work on your trust issues, but the sooner you get those under control," she predicted, "the happier both you and your sister are going to be."

He had to ask her. "Why are you so confident of that?"

She thought of her great-aunt and their less-than-smooth beginning. It had taken her a while to lower her guard—and she would always be grateful that her great-aunt had waited her out. "Because I am living proof that if someone trusts you—if you *realize* that they trust you—most of the time you will try to live up to that trust."

"*Most* of the time," Daniel stubbornly repeated as if that made his argument for him. "But not always."

Shania wasn't ready to surrender the point just yet. "And which category does your sister fall into? The one that says she'll try to live up to your expectations or the one where she'll do whatever she wants to without any regard for you, or your beliefs?"

"A year ago I would have never hesitated answering that question," he told her.

"But you did take down the camera," Shania reminded him. "If you were so sure she was the kind of person who just took off whenever she wanted to, nothing I would have said would have convinced you to remove it."

"Okay," he admitted rather grudgingly. "So I'm guilty of hoping."

Shania shook her head, discarding his explanation. "You, Deputy, are guilty of knowing your sister. And, deep down inside, you know she can be trusted. Especially if you make a point of letting her know that you trust her. Now, go home to spend some time with your sister—as her brother, not her warden," she stressed, walking him to the front door.

Daniel opened it, then paused to look at her. "And she'll know the difference how?"

She put her hand on his shoulder and gently pushed him over the threshold and out of the house. "Because she knows you," she said, then closed the door.

Belle made a mournful noise, then looked up at her mistress.

"Don't worry, Belle. He'll be all right," she assured her pet.

Belle barked again, as if to indicate that she wasn't all that sure about that.

Chapter Eight

Daniel had never been an optimist. It was a given. Part of him was always waiting for something to go wrong, even when everything seemed to be going right.

That was why, even though Elena seemed to have settled down and appeared to have gone back to concentrating on getting good grades rather than bad boys, Daniel felt as if he was coexisting with a ticking time bomb that would most likely, at the most unexpected moment, just go off.

Still, the brooding deputy *tried*, at least outwardly, to maintain a positive outlook on things.

When Sunday finally rolled around, he got up early, got ready and then waited for Elena to wake up.

For her part, Elena slept in, taking advantage of her only day off. When she did stumble her way into the kitchen, her eyes half closed, she looked surprised to see her brother sitting there.

Recovering, she took a deep breath as she sank down at the kitchen table and fixed Daniel with a probing look. "What are you doing here?"

He raised his cup in her direction as if in silent tribute. "Waiting for you to get up."

Elena blinked, still trying to clear the sleep out of her eyes and still somewhat foggy brain.

"Why?"

Although things seemed to have been going along well between them these past few days, deep down inside Elena kept waiting for the next lecture, the next inquisition to suddenly materialize. Each day that it didn't, she just grew that much more tense anticipating what she felt was the inevitable.

"It's Sunday," Daniel answered.

Her eyebrows narrowed together as she tried to focus on his face.

"And…?"

Elena continued staring at him, trying to understand where her brother was going with this. Did he think that because it was her day off from school, she was going to take off somewhere? Do something he inherently disapproved of?

"I'm not going anywhere, if that's what you're thinking," she told him.

She'd forgotten, Daniel thought. "I thought we had a date."

Elena blinked. "Wait, what?" She stared at Daniel, confused. "A date? With my brother?" she asked as if what he was suggesting was as ridiculous as could be.

"And a couple of horses," he added, trying to jog her memory. When she didn't say anything, Daniel made the natural assumption. "You don't remember, do you?"

The cloud began to lift from her brain. Bits and pieces

came back to her. She stared at Daniel as if she was watching him grow another head.

"You were serious?" she cried.

"Of course I was serious."

She thought for a second, then shrugged. She proceeded to let him off the hook—or so she believed. "You don't have to. I know you've been working all week. This is your only day off and you don't have to spend part of it with me."

"You're right," he agreed, his voice totally unemotional. "I don't *have* to. I *want* to. Don't you?"

Daniel had caught her off guard with his question. She looked as if she was torn for a minute.

She wasn't. She liked the idea, but she didn't want him to think he was doing her a favor. That would put her in his debt and she didn't want that.

"Well, if you really want to, I guess I can get dressed and go riding with you," she said with just the right touch of resignation.

"Good. Because I've been looking forward to it all week."

Elena rolled her eyes before she got up from the table. "No, you haven't," Elena said as she left the room to get dressed.

"Yes, I have," he called after her, half rising in his seat.

As he sat back down in his chair and sipped what was left of his coffee, Daniel smiled to himself. Maybe that cute little physics teacher actually did know what she was talking about, he thought. So far, the woman was two for two.

Jake McReedy owned and operated Forever's only stable, simply named McReedy's. He could always be found there, even when the stable was closed for the night. That was mainly because he slept in a tiny room that was located just at the rear of the building. In general, most people thought he had a far better relationship with the horses that were housed there than he did with the citizens of Forever.

The deeply tanned older man had far more hair on his face than he did on his head. That, at times, made it difficult for anyone to see his expression. In addition, his squinty eyes were partially hidden by his bushy eyebrows.

But Jake clearly looked surprised when Daniel came into the stable that morning with his sister.

"What can I do for you, Deputy? Miss?" Jake asked, nodding at Daniel and then his sister. Leaning the straw broom he'd been using to sweep up the small area in front of his office that wasn't covered with straw against the wall, he crossed toward the duo.

"I'd—*we'd*," Daniel corrected himself, sparing a quick glance at his sister, "like to rent two of your best horses for a couple of hours—or possibly longer," he amended, thinking that if Elena didn't start complaining and asking to go back home, they could easily stay out for more than just two hours.

Jake nodded. "We can settle up once you finish your ride and bring the horses back. Something special going on today I don't know about?"

Daniel didn't understand the question. "What do you mean?"

"Well," the older man said, bringing forward one saddle, then a second, "Sundays aren't usually busy until the afternoon, but you're the second and third people to come by so early today. Thought maybe there was something special going on," Jake explained. He began saddling the first horse, a large palomino stallion.

"I just want to go out for a ride with my sister," Daniel told the stable keeper. "We used to do that all the time when she was younger." He stopped there, seeing that he was making Elena uncomfortable.

Jake nodded. Finished tightening the cinch on the palomino's saddle, he prepared to slip on the stallion's bridle.

"Yeah, you can't beat a horse for companionship," he told Daniel. Belatedly, he seemed to realize that could be taken as an insult. He glanced toward the deputy's sister. "No disrespect intended," he mumbled to the teen, awkwardly touching the brim of his hat with two fingers in what passed as a semi-salute.

"None taken," Elena responded.

Wandering toward another stall, she stopped to look at a pinto. The horse was a little smaller than the other horses found in the stable. Saying a few words to him in a very low voice, Elena dug into her back pocket and took out three small lumps of sugar. She subtly offered them to the horse.

Daniel backed up to see what his sister was doing—and was surprised to catch a glimpse of the sugar cubes before they disappeared. He was pleased to see how prepared she seemed to be.

"You brought sugar cubes," he noted quietly.

Her expression indicated that he didn't have to be so surprised.

"I want the horse on my side. I'm not an idiot," she informed him with an all-too-familiar toss of her head that sent her hair flying almost into his face.

"Never said you were an idiot," he reminded her. "You're a lot of other things, including, at times, a royal pain in my butt, but you were never an idiot—and you're still not."

Jake had finished saddling the second horse, the pinto

that Elena seemed so drawn to, while she had been busy bribing it. Taking the reins, one set in each hand, he turned to face the deputy and his sister.

Jake offered them the reins.

"You two want to take these horses out for a ride or are you just going to stand in here, jawing at each other for the next couple of hours?" Jake asked. "Just so you know, the charge is the same either way."

Daniel glanced at Elena, then told the stable owner, "We'll ride."

Elena took the pinto's reins. After eyeing her mount uncertainly for a moment—it had been a long time since she'd gotten on a horse—Elena grasped the saddle horn, put her left foot into the stirrup and fluidly swung herself into the saddle.

For a fleeting second, she looked pleased with herself.

The look wasn't lost on Daniel. "Came back to you, didn't it?"

She'd had her doubts, but that wasn't anything she was about to willingly admit to her brother.

"It never went away," she informed him.

Daniel merely nodded as he swung himself into his own saddle like a man who had been born on the back of a horse.

"I had a feeling," he said, going along with the scenario Elena was trying to create for his benefit.

Now that they were both on their mounts, Jake stepped off to the side.

"If you're of a mind to catch up with that teacher, she rode north," he told them.

Just about to urge his horse forward, Daniel abruptly held himself in check.

"What teacher?" he asked.

"You mean Ms. Stewart?" Elena asked, immediately making the only connection that she could.

Was it just his imagination, or did Elena's voice sound a little higher than it normally did? Daniel wondered.

"Dunno her last name," Jake admitted. "She paid cash," he explained. "She did say that she'd suddenly gotten the yen for riding after spending all week looking over test papers and lesson plans. I ain't got any kids in school no more, but I figured from what she said, she had to be a teacher." He smiled a little wistfully, as if he was thinking about past opportunities that had slipped away. "Pretty little thing. Eyes that made you stand up and take notice. Makes me wish I was a young man—or at least younger," Jake amended with a deep laugh.

He caught the way both Jake and his sister were looking at him. As if they expected him to ride after the woman. He saw no reason to pretend that he had no interest in going for a ride with the woman. After all, she was Elena's teacher and she was the reason that he and Elena were out riding in the first place.

"We'd better get going if we want to catch up with her," Daniel commented.

The next moment, he kicked his stallion's flanks and horse and rider were off in a gallop.

Elena followed suit, quickly catching up to her brother and riding alongside of him. The second they had left the stable—and the owner—behind, she asked Daniel, surprised, "You want to catch up with Ms. Stewart?"

He had a change of heart about honesty and said, "No, I don't. But I got the feeling that if we didn't get out of there, Jake was going to go on talking until both our ears fell off in self-defense."

Elena laughed. He caught himself thinking that he'd

missed that sound. Again he realized that he was in Shania Stewart's debt.

"I thought he liked keeping to himself instead of talking to people," Elena said.

"Obviously you brought out the talkative side of the man," Daniel said, teasing his sister.

"Anyone could see that he was talking to you, not to me," Elena pointed out.

And then, as the situation hit them—the teasing remarks they were exchanging as well as the banter that was going back and forth—they both laughed this time, their voices blending.

Just the way they used to, years back.

"So," Daniel asked as the laughter died away, "where to?"

Elena glanced at her brother. Despite the exchange that had just taken place, she was surprised. "You're leaving it up to me?"

"Why not?" he asked. "We've got the whole day ahead of us if we want and you're just as capable of picking a direction for us to go in as I am."

An amused expression settled in on Elena's face as she slanted a look in his direction. Daniel thought that his sister looked almost devious as she asked, "How about north?"

Part of her waited for Daniel to negate her choice and pick one of the three other directions. Another part of her hoped that he wouldn't.

"All right," he said with a nod of his head. "North it is."

And then he kicked his heels into the horse's flanks as he pointed the animal northward.

The idyllically quiet morning surrounded her like a familiar old soothing melody. The silence was occasionally interrupted by the chirping sound of birds calling to one another.

If she listened very hard, Shania thought, she could make out rustling, signifying some small creature that was scurrying to escape possible danger from a predator. Or maybe just foraging for food.

For the most part, though, there was a harmony about the sounds that were around her and she felt at one with the elements and nature.

Though she rarely had the opportunity to do it, Shania liked going out for a ride in the early hours. Liked pretending that she was the only one around for miles.

Not that she had any desire to become a hermit for any true length of time, but a little "alone time" once in a while could be a really nice thing, she thought now with a smile.

She couldn't help thinking that this was a real change from living in Houston. Houston was all movement and chaos while Forever moved at a far slower, more tranquil pace. It was funny how quickly she had acclimated to both ways of life, Shania realized. When she'd lived in Houston, she couldn't imagine going back to live in a little town like Forever. And now that she was here, she caught herself wondering at times how she had managed to survive all the hustle and bustle that existed within Houston.

Shania sighed. *Stop it!*

She was thinking too much. She had come out here to get away not just from all the demands that she had to deal with, but from her own thoughts as well. She needed to empty her head.

She needed to—

Shania slowed her horse down a little as she cocked her head, listening.

Were those hoofbeats in the distance? And not just hoofbeats that belonged to one horse. From the sound of it, she was certain that she made out the sound of two horses.

Was that—? She crossed her fingers and hoped she was right.

Those hoofbeats were definitely growing louder because they were coming in her direction.

She turned her horse toward the sound of the approaching horse beats.

And then, within less than a minute, she smiled as the two riders came into view.

Shania felt validated that Daniel Tallchief had taken her advice.

Chapter Nine

Butterscotch, the mare that Shania had rented from McReedy's stable early this morning, seemed anxious to resume her fast pace. Shania could feel the horse shifting impatiently beneath her, ready to run.

She leaned in closer to the mare, patting Butterscotch's sleek neck.

"What's the matter, girl?" she asked in a low, soothing voice. "Don't you want to have a little company on this ride?"

The mare shifted a little more, as if she understood what was being asked. Shania knew that all she had to do was give the horse her lead and the mare would take off. But she continued to remain still where she was, waiting for the deputy and his sister to come closer.

She told herself it wouldn't be polite just to take off after seeing them approaching, but the truth of it was that Shania didn't mind having a little company herself. And she was curious to find out what, if anything, the deputy would talk about with her. She had been in Daniel's company and she had certainly been in Elena's company, but she had never been exposed to both of the family members at the same time. She was rather intrigued to find out how the two played off one another in a social situation.

Better, she hoped, than she'd initially assumed they did. Especially now that Elena had settled down and started applying herself.

Though she did try to observe both riders as they came closer, if she was really being honest with herself, Shania would have had to admit that her eyes were drawn toward Daniel.

He cut a magnificent figure astride the palomino, moving as if he and the stallion were one. Daniel's slightly unruly straight black hair was flying behind him and he made her think of a warrior on the move. Watching his strong, wide shoulders and his obviously trim body approaching created an electric current that zipped right through her, making every single inch of her feel alive and alert.

Shania did her best to look unaffected, but she wasn't all that sure she succeeded.

"The stallion's nice, too," she whispered to Butterscotch.

As if in response, although still shifting, Butterscotch seemed to be just a little less agitated, but it could have just been her imagination.

"Hi," Shania called out to Daniel and Elena when the two were almost right up to her. "Nice day for a morning ride."

"Yes, it is," Daniel answered. His voice sounded even more formal to her than it usually did.

"I didn't want to come," Elena told her teacher. And then a shy expression emerged on her face. "I wanted to stay in bed, but my brother thought the fresh air would do me some good."

"Smart man, your brother," Shania commented. Deftly, she turned Butterscotch around so that all three horses and riders were facing in the same direction. "So, did you have any particular destination in mind?" she asked the pair, her eyes moving from Elena to the teenager's brother.

Instead of answering, Elena turned in her saddle and looked toward her brother, waiting for him to say something.

Put on the spot, Daniel shrugged. "Wherever you're going is fine with us."

Now that he was up closer to her, he saw that Shania had no makeup on whatsoever. Another woman would have looked plain or washed out, he thought. But Elena's teacher looked positively radiant and glowing. She made him think of one of those flowers that unexpectedly pop up on a cactus, blooming against all odds and ultimately drawing all attention to itself without actually meaning to.

And then, almost as an afterthought, Daniel's eyes were drawn to something else. Shania had a picnic basket tied against her horse's saddle horn.

She was meeting someone, he thought, raising his eyes to hers.

"Won't Elena and I be interrupting something?" he asked her, not even sure he should be saying that.

Shania looked at him, a bemused expression on her face. "Interrupting?" she repeated, waiting for him to explain.

Daniel nodded at the picnic basket. "Looks like you packed for a picnic," he pointed out.

She'd completely forgotten about that. Glancing down at the basket, she realized how that had to look. "Oh, right. I thought eating out in the open instead of huddled over paperwork at my desk might be a nice change," she told the deputy. "But I have a habit of always packing more than I need in case my appetite suddenly gets out of hand because of the invigorating ride—or I run into someone I know," she added with a grin, looking at Elena. "There's more than enough to share if you two get hungry," she promised them.

Daniel glanced at his sister. Judging by Elena's expression, she looked totally open to the idea of joining up and going riding with her teacher. And, he supposed if he was being completely honest about it, the idea of sharing a ride and some lunch with the beautiful teacher was not without its appeal.

"I guess you've twisted my arm," Daniel told Elena's teacher.

"My brother means yes," Elena told Shania. The girl looked really pleased about the whole thing.

"You two up for a brisk canter or would you rather just go slow?" Shania asked them, looking from one to the other.

Daniel's eyes met hers. "I never go slow," he informed her.

He saw amusement curve the corners of her generous mouth. Something within him responded, but he shut it down.

Been there, done that. Won't go there again, Daniel thought.

"A brisk canter it is," Shania agreed.

Then, as her eyes met Elena's, Shania kicked her heels in Butterscotch's flanks. Instantly, horse and rider took off.

Elena made a gleeful sound as she quickly joined her teacher.

Daniel lost no time keeping pace.

"Wow, you really kept up," Elena cried in admiration when all three of them finally reined in their horses to a full stop an hour later.

Winded, the girl slid off her pinto and sank straight down to the ground.

She appeared surprised and pleased when Shania did the same, sitting down right beside her.

"Were you expecting me to fall off?" Shania asked her with a breathless laugh.

"My sister might have had some doubts, but I knew you wouldn't," Daniel told her, his voice rumbling from deep within his muscular chest.

Holding on to his horse's reins, the deputy joined the other two already on the ground, sitting down cross-legged.

Shania regarded the deputy, wondering if he was pulling her leg or if he was being serious with her. For now, she gave him the benefit of the doubt.

"And why were you so sure I wouldn't fall off?" she asked Daniel.

"Your form," the deputy said simply. "You look like you were born riding," he told her, recalling what she'd said when they first came up to her.

"It was my first memory," she admitted. "My dad put me on a horse before I could walk."

"By yourself?" Elena asked her, surprised that a parent would do something so careless.

Shania laughed, but it wasn't a belittling sound. "No, he got on right behind me. My dad didn't let me sit on a horse by myself until I was three, even though I begged him, telling him I could do it and pouting when he didn't trust me.

"And even when he *did* put me on the horse by myself, he walked right next to the horse, holding on to me until he felt confident that I was old enough to do it all by myself." She grinned, remembering. "I was so excited," she confided.

Her eyes were sparkling, Daniel noticed, intrigued

and mesmerized by the sight. Again, he forced himself to mentally pull back.

"So, do you come out often, Ms. Stewart?" Elena asked.

Shania smiled. "Whenever I get the chance—which lately winds up being about once a week—if I'm lucky. Usually on Sunday morning," she told the teen. Her smile turned nostalgic as she recalled another time. "I used to go riding with my cousin."

"Why did you stop riding with her?" Daniel asked, curious.

"Wynona got married and now she has other priorities." Her cousin had promised to go riding with her again, but somehow it never worked out and after a while, they stopped making arrangements that wound up falling through. "After a while, horseback riding kind of fell by the wayside."

Sharing something so personal made her feel a little uncomfortable. Looking toward the picnic basket, Shania changed the subject.

"So, is anyone hungry?" she asked Elena and the deputy.

"Yes," Elena said with enthusiasm. Then, self-conscious, she toned it down a little. "I guess." Pausing, the teen asked, "What do you have?"

"Well, why don't we see?" Shania suggested with a grin.

She rose to her feet and began to remove the ropes that held the picnic basket in place against the saddle horn.

"How about you, Deputy?" Shania asked, putting the basket down on the ground. "Are you hungry?"

"I'm fine," he demurred.

Daniel assumed that while whatever Elena's teacher had packed might be enough to split between two people as long as neither was very hungry, he sincerely doubted that she could have packed enough to adequately feed three people.

"Yes," Shania murmured, her eyes meeting his. "I know that. But are you hungry?"

Her unexpected teasing response caught him completely off guard. The next second, Daniel cleared his throat as if that could somehow negate the entire exchange, making it unnecessary for him to address it at all.

When he finally did speak, it was in reference to Shania's inquiry about his appetite. "No, thanks," he answered.

She pretended not to hear him. "I've got a small tablecloth in here," she told Elena. "Want to help me spread it out?"

"Sure!"

Elena was already peering into the basket, ready to take the tablecloth out and spread it on the ground the second that her teacher nodded.

Once the tablecloth was taken out and spread on the ground, Daniel casually glanced inside the basket to see just how much Shania had—or hadn't—brought.

He was surprised to see that the basket was filled to the top with wrapped sandwiches, several cans of root beer and, when those were taken out, what looked like a covered tray of brownies on the bottom. The brownies, judging by the aroma, appeared to have been baked fresh early that morning.

As Shania took out the brownies, he raised a quizzical eyebrow in her direction.

It wasn't all that difficult to guess his unspoken question.

"Yes, I'm a closet baker," she admitted. "It relaxes me."

She didn't bother preparing anything out of the ordinary for herself because she felt her time could be better spent otherwise. But today, she had a hunch, would be different.

"I don't usually get a chance to indulge in my passion,

but I decided that there was no reason not to go all out today, so I decided to make my mint chip brownies. You don't have to eat them if you don't want to," she added. "I promise you won't hurt my feelings," she assured them.

"I love mint chip." Elena took a deep breath. "They smell absolutely heavenly," she told her teacher, then asked hopefully, "Can I have the brownies first?"

"You're welcome to the whole tray if you want it," Shania told the teenager. "But I suggest you have one of the sandwiches first."

She noticed that Daniel had quietly reached for one of the sandwiches and was carefully unwrapping it now. Good, she'd won him over. The man was much too rigid. He needed to unwind, not just for Elena's sake, but for his own.

"I think the root beer is probably still cold," she said by way of inviting him to indulge himself.

"It can be warm," Daniel replied. "As long as it's wet, that's my only requirement."

"Then I'd say you're in luck," Shania answered with a warm laugh.

She took a sandwich herself and proceeded to unwrap it.

He waited until the woman had taken a bite of her sandwich before he finally ventured to ask her a question that had occurred to him the moment the tablecloth had been taken out.

"What made you pack so much food in the basket if you were just going to go riding by yourself?" he asked.

Shania regarded him quietly for a moment. He noticed that although she didn't speak, the woman's eyes said volumes.

"Let's just say I had a premonition," she finally admitted.

Still eating, Elena looked at her teacher, clearly surprised. "You *knew* we were coming?"

That sounded a little too pompous and self-assured, Shania thought. "Let's just say that I *hoped* you and your brother were going for a ride this morning."

Finished with his sandwich, Daniel picked up a napkin and wiped his fingers. "What if we didn't come?" he asked.

She glanced at the food that still remained next to the basket. Picking up another sandwich, she quietly pushed it toward Daniel. She was certain that the man had room for more.

"Then I wouldn't have to make dinner," she answered with a smile.

Daniel shook his head. "Got an answer for everything, don't you?"

"I'm a high school teacher," she answered simply. "I'm supposed to have an answer for everything."

There was humor in her eyes as she responded to his statement.

Daniel laughed softly to himself, then let her answer go. Instead, he changed the subject just as she had done earlier.

"So, how do you like being back?" he asked. "You originally came from here, didn't you?" he asked, making sure that he had gotten his facts straight.

"I did and to answer your question, I like it very much," she replied.

"You're going to stay, right?" Elena asked, trying not to appear apprehensive. She'd decided that she had grown to like this unusual teacher, so much so that she didn't want to see her leave.

"Barring something earth-shattering happening," Shania answered whimsically, "I think so."

"Something earth-shattering?" Daniel questioned.

What did she mean by that? He felt it was an odd choice of words.

"You can't count on things being written in stone," Shania explained. "Things have a way of changing. I never thought I'd wind up in Houston to begin with. I had a home, parents who loved me and a cousin who lived with us who was more like a sister. Everything was wonderful," she said. "Until it wasn't," she concluded philosophically. "That's when I learned that nothing was forever—no matter what the town was named," she added with an ironic smile.

"Why did you come back?" Daniel asked.

"Trying to get rid of me?" she asked him, amused.

"Trying to understand why you'd leave Houston," he countered. He opened another can of root beer. "There're more opportunities there."

"Agreed. But not the one I was looking for," Shania told him, looking at his sister. "Let's just say that Wynona and I wanted to pay it forward. Brownies?" she asked brightly, holding the tray up to Elena and her brother and once more changing the subject.

Chapter Ten

"This was fun," Elena announced out of the blue.

Daniel had to admit that he was totally surprised by his sister's reaction. The impatient, hostile teenager he had been living with for the last few months had suddenly receded into the shadows and the sister he loved and would have willingly done absolutely anything for had, at least for the moment, made a reappearance in his life.

"I'm glad to hear that," Daniel told her as they helped finish cleaning up the picnic they'd shared with Elena's teacher and got ready to return to the stable.

Elena cocked her head to get a better view of her brother's expression. "Can we do it again?" she asked.

That question was an even bigger surprise in his estimation.

"Sure." Having packed away the tablecloth, leftover wrappers and cans into Shania's basket, he handed it back to the woman. The latter proceeded to tie the basket to the saddle horn again. Turning toward his sister, Daniel told her, "Next Sunday."

Smiling broadly, Elena barely contained herself as, eyes dancing, she in turn faced her teacher. "Will you come, too?"

Observing this from the sidelines, it was difficult to say which of them was more stunned by Elena's question, her teacher or him.

Probably him, Daniel thought. Now that he took a closer look at the woman, aside from being stunning, Elena's teacher didn't look as if anything could really faze her.

"Don't put Ms. Stewart on the spot, Ellie," he cautioned his sister. Though Shania looked as if everything just rolled off her back, Daniel didn't want to take a chance that Elena's request might cause waves.

Shania put a stop to it before it went too far—the "it" being Daniel's misunderstanding of how she'd react to his sister's question.

It was sweet of the deputy to come to her aid, Shania thought, but it really wasn't necessary.

"She's not putting me on the spot, Deputy," Shania told him. "And if you don't mind my company," she continued, then turned toward Elena to complete what she was saying, "I'd love to come. Riding out here at this time by myself is peaceful, but I have to admit that there's such a thing as *too* peaceful," she confided, lowering her voice as if she was sharing a secret with the girl. And then she really smiled broadly at her student. "I would *love* some company."

"Great!" Elena declared like a proud arbitrator who had just negotiated a new treaty acceptable to all parties involved.

But Shania didn't see this as a done deal—not just yet.

"It *is* all right with you, isn't it?" she asked Daniel in a low voice when Elena doubled back to get her hat before they rode back. "I didn't hear you agree," she explained. Then, because he seemed to hesitate, she came to the conclusion that he was looking for a way out. "I can make up an excuse to beg off. Heaven knows I've got enough work to do to make it sound believable."

For just a single second, Daniel wavered. But by the end of that split second, he realized that he *liked* the idea of going out like this again with Elena and her teacher. It was casual. It was safe. And he got to be around Shania without any accompanying awkwardness—or any expectations on either one of their parts.

"No need to tell her anything," he replied, keeping his voice as low as hers. "Going out for a ride again'll be nice."

"What are you two whispering about?" Elena asked as she rejoined them, her hat firmly planted on her head.

Shania never missed a beat as she replied, "Your brother expressed his doubts about my having made those mint brownies from scratch, so I recited the recipe I used."

It amazed Daniel how quick Shania was on her feet and how easily she came up with a believable lie. He wondered if it was a skill that came from practice and if she did that with any sort of regularity.

There were layers to this woman that bore looking into.

The next moment Daniel reminded himself that he had a lot of responsibilities. The last thing he needed was to take on a new "hobby" that had no future to it and that could only lead him down a path he shouldn't have a reason to follow.

"Daniel's not very trusting," Elena said, referring to Shania's narrative about telling Daniel what ingredients were in the brownies she had made. Elena swung herself into the pinto's saddle.

Responding to what his sister had just said, Daniel couldn't resist saying, "It runs in the family."

Elena's eyes briefly met his. She sniffed. "I don't know what you're talking about," she informed Daniel, then turned her attention back to her teacher. "Home, Ms. Stewart?"

"Home, Ms. Tallchief," Shania responded, doing her best to suppress a grin.

A gleeful laugh escaped her lips as Elena kicked her heels into the Pinto's flanks.

Her horse took off. Shania was right beside her, riding as fast as she could go.

Elena pouted a little because she couldn't seem to pass her teacher by. But on the other hand, she was pleased that the woman had turned out to be so skilled and capable on—and off—a horse. That meant, Elena thought, that her brother had probably met his match.

At least for now, Elena amended.

The three of them got back to the stable all too soon in Daniel's opinion. Reflecting on it, it seemed rather incredible to him that they covered the same amount of distance coming and going and yet it felt as if going had taken far longer than getting back to their starting point.

They caught the stable owner just in time. Jake looked as if he was about to go to the diner to get an early lunch and appeared a little disgruntled that he had to put it off now until he had settled up with the returning customers.

"I see you found each other," he commented, his squinty eyes moving over each of them.

"We did," Shania replied pleasantly. Then, picking up

on the man's impatient body language, she got straight to business. "How much do I owe you, Mr. McReedy?"

"Got your bills right here," he told her, nodding at the bulletin board on the far wall.

There were three separate receipts pinned on it and he took off one of them to hand to her.

Daniel was slightly confused. "I thought you wanted to wait until we got back before you did the calculations."

"If you stay out for more than two hours, there's a flat rate," Jake answered. "It encourages return business."

She thought it spoke in the man's favor to offer deals, but it really wasn't that necessary, either. "It's not like you've got a lot of competition," Shania pointed out.

Jake flushed a little, as if he hadn't really thought the matter out that far. The stable owner shrugged awkwardly. "Still no reason to gouge folks. Miss Joan taught me that."

"Miss Joan's been in business longer than you?" Elena asked him in surprise.

Jake laughed, some of his awkwardness abating. "That woman's been in business just a little less longer than God."

"Better not let her hear you say that, Jake," Daniel warned the older man seriously, "or your days'll be numbered—and there's nothing I can do to help you."

"That old woman's not above the law," Jake reminded him nervously.

But the expression on Daniel's face said otherwise, which just made Jake that much more nervous.

"Oh, she's above a lot of things," Daniel told the stable owner. He didn't particularly care to hear any disrespectful remarks aimed at Miss Joan.

Daniel glanced over toward Shania and then reached for the receipt she had in her hand. "Why don't I just take care of that?" he suggested, then looked at Jake. "Is there a discount for three receipts?"

Jake's small dark eyes looked like marbles as they rolled back and forth between Daniel and the high school teacher.

"You two aren't related, now, are you?" Jake asked them.

This time Daniel didn't bother putting the man on. Instead he gave Jake a very firm "No."

"Then no, there's no discount for three receipts," Jake answered.

Shania reached to take back the receipt that the deputy had managed to slip out of her hand.

"I can pay my own way, Deputy Tallchief," she told him.

But Daniel retained possession of the receipt, holding it above his head. Shania wasn't able to reach for it.

"Nobody said you couldn't," he replied. "You shared your lunch with us, the least I can do is pay for your riding time."

It was obvious that Jake clearly didn't care who won the debate as long as he was paid by somebody. As he listened to the debate, his stomach started to rumble in protest.

Jake sighed impatiently. "This going to take much longer?"

Multiplying Shania's receipt by three, Daniel handed the stable owner the amount owed for all three rides. "Nope, not long at all, Jake," he answered the man.

Money in hand, Jake counted it quickly. He smiled in satisfaction, his grin showing the space between two of his lower teeth before he suddenly remembered it was there. His lips quickly closed over it like a curtain coming down on an unplanned performance.

"Nice doing business with you folks," Jake said, nodding at them. "Come again," he called after the three people as they were leaving his stable.

"See you tomorrow, Ms. Stewart," Elena said, raising her voice as they walked out. They were heading in two different directions.

Shania paused just long enough to look at the girl. Her eyes smiled at Elena as she said, "I look forward to it."

And then she hurried over toward where she had parked her vehicle.

Watching the woman get into her car, Daniel forced himself to start moving. He opened the door on the driver's side of his vehicle, aware that Elena had already opened hers.

"So things are going well between you and Ms. Stewart." It wasn't a question on Daniel's part, but an assumption.

Daniel avoided his sister's eyes as he got into the car. Elena had already climbed in on her side.

He could feel Elena's eyes on him, as if she was debating whether or not to answer his question or just ignore it.

She went with the former, asking a question of her own. "Yeah, why?"

Daniel played along, even though they both knew why he'd ask her the question. "Well, a few weeks ago, you looked like you were ready to spit nails at the woman because she was giving you too much homework and trying to make you dig deep into yourself."

Elena waved dismissively at her brother's explanation. "That's just your imagination."

"Pretty sure it was more than that," he said. "I was just wondering what changed between the two of you."

"Nothing." He heard a defensive note reentering his

sister's voice. "I just decided that it's smart to be smart. Anything wrong with that?"

Daniel allowed himself a small smile. He decided that Shania Stewart was nothing short of a miracle worker.

"Not a thing in the world," he replied. He glanced at her, then looked back at the near empty road. "Would I be ruining something in your opinion if I told you that I was proud of you?"

Elena shrugged, doing her best to look indifferent to his words of praise. "You don't have to say you're proud of me."

"I know I don't have to," Daniel answered. "I *want* to," he said, stressing the middle word. "You know me well enough to know I don't do or say things because I 'have' to."

If anything, Elena seemed to grow a little stiffer. The look his sister slanted at him was one he couldn't quite fathom.

And then she finally said by way of a rebuttal to her brother's argument, "I don't know about that. You're taking care of me."

What was at the bottom of all this? he couldn't help wondering. "Again, it's because I *want* to," Daniel told her.

Elena sighed. "Uh-huh."

It was obvious that she was in the mood to discount what he'd just said.

Daniel decided to drop the subject for now and turned to another one. He glanced at her, then said, "Thanks for going riding with me."

Surprised, Elena looked at him. And then the teen suddenly laughed. "I figured if I didn't, you'd probably tie me up and *make* me come with you."

"Well, as it turned out, luckily, that wasn't necessary,"

he said. "And I think you'll agree that it all turned out for the best—like you getting along better with Ms. Stewart," he couldn't help throwing in again, hoping this time to get his sister to respond the way he hoped she would.

"Yeah, she's all right," Elena answered, adopting a lofty tone. And then she suddenly turned the tables on her brother by telling him, "You sure seemed like you liked her."

Caught off guard, it took Daniel a second to pull his thoughts together. The one thing he knew was that he wasn't about to get pulled into *that* discussion.

Instead, he said, "I like most people."

He didn't expect his sister to hoot at the response. "Yeah, right. What's that fairy tale about that puppet whose nose grew whenever he told a lie?" she asked him innocently.

"Why are you asking me about that?"

She pressed her lips together before she answered his question. "'Cause yours is about to break your truck's windshield."

Unable to maintain a serious expression any longer, Elena grinned from ear to ear, tickled by the image she'd just painted.

She fully expected her brother to vehemently deny her observation. When she heard him laugh instead, she was at first surprised—and then she had to admit that his reaction pleased her a great deal.

They laughed together, something that was thankfully becoming a more common occurrence.

Shania walked into her house and was immediately greeted by an extremely energetic Belle. In her enthusiasm, the German shepherd came perilously close to knocking her down.

"I wasn't gone *that* long, girl," Shania protested, laughing.

But the amount of energy the dog was incorporating into her welcome told Shania that perhaps she'd misjudged the time element—at least as far as Belle was concerned.

"I forgot, you can't tell time very well, can you?" Shania laughed as she rubbed the dog's head. Wynona had once told her that an hour seemed like a day and a day was like an eternity to the dog.

"You know, maybe next time, I'll take you along with me. But you're going to have to do a lot of running to keep up," she warned the dog. Belle barked. "Maybe that'll do you some good," Shania decided. "I know you would have liked who I ran into. Elena, one of my students," she told the dog, then added, "And her brother." She cast a side glance at her pet as she went to refill Belle's water dish and get the dog something to eat.

"You've already met him. It's that deputy you gave a bath to with that big, sloppy tongue of yours," she told Belle.

There was no way in the world the dog could have understood her, Shania reasoned. But Belle seemed to get really enthusiastic when she "heard" Daniel's description.

"You know, Belle, anyone would think that you have a crush on that man," she said with a laugh. "Well, he's all yours, girl."

Belle circled her several times, then plopped down on her back right in front of her.

Shania sank down beside the animal and began petting her. "Rehearsing for when you run into him next time?"

Belle barked.

"I thought so," Shania answered.

Chapter Eleven

In Shania's opinion, as she replayed it, it seemed like an unusual request. But then Miss Joan was an unusual woman by everyone's standards. Still, the owner of the diner had never sent one of her waitresses to ask her to come to the diner after school had let out for the day before.

Until today.

Even so, Shania had demurred at first, citing the fact that she was holding a PSAT class at the high school after hours.

Surprisingly, Violet the waitress seemed prepared for that. She had obviously been coached by Miss Joan for exactly this eventuality. Violet told Shania that Miss Joan wanted her to come whenever she was finished with the class.

Cornered, Shania didn't feel she could really beg off after that. However, she didn't rush through her class, either. Instead, she fielded all the questions that the small group of students in the after-hours class wanted to ask.

Once the last student had left the room, only then did she make her way to the diner. It was a few minutes after five before she was able to show up. The diner was about half full. The dinner crowd hadn't begun to show up in earnest yet.

The minute she walked in, Shania made her way straight to the counter. Now that her class was over, her curiosity finally got the better of her. Why did the woman want to see her?

Try as she might, she couldn't come up with a single reason.

Standing behind the counter, Miss Joan was just pouring some fresh coffee into a cup when Shania reached her.

Miss Joan certainly didn't act as if anything was wrong, she thought. But then, Miss Joan was known to play poker regularly.

"You wanted to see me?" Shania asked the woman. In her opinion this wasn't the time for small talk and she didn't bother with any.

"I wouldn't have sent Violet to fetch you if I didn't," Miss Joan replied, smoothly moving the cup and saucer closer to her.

"About?" Shania asked, curbing her impatience.

What was going on here? When Violet had sought her out, giving her Miss Joan's message, the waitress had made it sound urgent. Yet Miss Joan looked and acted as if she had all the time in the world.

Instead of answering her question, Miss Joan nodded at the empty stool Shania was standing next to.

"Sit," the older woman told her. "Take a load off. Have some coffee."

Since it was obvious that she wasn't about to get the

answer to her question until she complied with Miss Joan's instructions, Shania did as the woman said.

She sat down, loosened her coat and had a sip of coffee. Once she did, Shania looked into the woman's eyes and asked, "*Now* will you tell me what I'm doing here?"

"Sitting and having a cup of coffee," Miss Joan answered as if that should have been very obvious to her.

This *was* a game to the woman, Shania decided. She had no recourse but to go along with whatever this was until it played out. "Violet made it sound urgent," Shania stressed.

"Violet has a tendency to be overly dramatic," Miss Joan answered, waving a thin hand at the idea that this was an urgent meeting.

And then the woman gave her one of her famous long, penetrating looks. The kind Harry, her husband, swore could get a hardened criminal to make a full confession even if he was about to get away with the crime.

It seemed like an eternity later before Miss Joan finally spoke. When she did, she didn't say anything that Shania had been expecting.

"I haven't seen you in a while." The hazel eyes looked at her intently. "Not since Wynona's wedding."

Shania couldn't help thinking that something was definitely up. Miss Joan had never expressed a desire to have her come by before.

At a loss, she made something up. "I've been meaning to drop by the diner, but there never seems to be enough time. I've been kind of busy, what with teaching and holding those extra study classes after hours."

Although everything she was saying was true, Shania couldn't help feeling as if she was coming up with excuses. Excuses that Miss Joan saw right through.

"Uh-huh," the older woman murmured. Probing hazel

eyes swept over her again. “How are you holding up?” Miss Joan asked without warning.

“Holding up?” Shania repeated. She had no idea what Miss Joan was really asking her. “Holding up” sounded as if she was referring to some sort of a crisis and there wasn’t any.

“Well, Wynona’s moved out of the house and she’s busy starting a new life while you’re going on with your old one,” Miss Joan said.

“I’m all right,” Shania replied haltingly, her voice sounding rather tinny to her own ear.

“How about the baby?” Miss Joan asked, the woman’s eyes still pinning her down. “You must be excited about the little one coming.”

For a second, Shania could only stare at the woman. She knew that Wynona had wanted to keep the news under wraps for a few more weeks, which meant that she hadn’t told anyone else. That included Miss Joan.

Yet the woman knew.

Shania suppressed a sigh. She wasn’t about to waste time asking Miss Joan how she’d found out about Wynona’s pregnancy. It was almost a given that Miss Joan *always* knew everything before anyone else did.

In this case, probably before Wynona knew.

She was about to give the woman a vague response when she saw Miss Joan looking around her shoulder toward the door.

It was too much to hope for that someone had come in to divert the woman’s attention away from her, Shania thought.

But, even so, Miss Joan definitely looked as if someone had caught her interest.

If whoever had just walked in came over to engage the

woman in a conversation, she might even be able to make good her escape. Shania crossed her fingers.

But before she could even attempt to slide off her stool, she heard the person Miss Joan was looking at ask almost the same question she just had when she'd walked in.

"The sheriff said you wanted to see me, Miss Joan. Here I am. What's the problem?" Daniel asked the woman before he realized that he was standing one empty stool over from Shania.

Shania turned and their eyes met. Somewhere, she could have sworn she heard electricity crackle.

"I didn't say there was a problem," Miss Joan informed the deputy matter-of-factly. She shook her head. "You'd think that someone like the sheriff would relay messages correctly."

"What message should he have relayed?" Daniel asked her, playing along.

Miss Joan lifted her thin shoulders and let them drop in a careless shrug.

"Doesn't matter," she informed him crisply. "The problem's been resolved." She filled another cup with coffee and moved that cup and saucer toward the empty stool. The one that was right next to Shania's. "Why don't you have this cup of coffee on the house as payment for your time, Deputy?" Miss Joan suggested.

Daniel looked down at the cup, appearing just the slightest bit amused. "You know I can't accept any kind of a payment for services rendered, Miss Joan."

"But you didn't render any services," Miss Joan pointed out.

He tried again. "Even so—"

"Just sit down and drink the damn coffee, Tallchief," Miss Joan ordered. "Didn't anyone ever teach you not to argue with your elders? Take a page out of her book," she said, jerking a thumb at Shania. Then, because the deputy still continued standing there, she asked Daniel, "You do know how to sit, don't you, Deputy? Just bend your knees and let gravity do the rest." Seemingly satisfied that he would do as he was told, Miss Joan was already moving away. "I'll be back in a few minutes to see if either of you needs a refill."

Shania leaned her head toward him as Daniel took his seat. "I think we were just threatened."

"I don't 'think,'" he responded. "I know. That woman gets stranger every year." He took a long sip of the coffee Miss Joan had ordered him to drink. "Lucky thing she makes good coffee."

"Right, because that's the only thing Miss Joan's got going for her," Shania replied, glancing around the diner with an amused smile.

Tempting aromas were wafting out from the kitchen.

"I didn't mean for it to come out like that," Daniel amended. "The woman's got a good heart." There were tons of examples to back that statement up. "But you can't argue that she is rather unique in her approach to things."

Shania laughed. "'Unique' is putting it rather mildly." Following his example, she took a long sip from her coffee cup, then tentatively set it down. "Why do you think she summoned us?"

It was definitely not a coincidence that the woman had asked both of them here at what turned out to be the same time.

His shrug was noncommittal. "Beats me." And he knew that trying to figure it out without the woman's input was just a complete waste of time. "Nobody knows what's on that woman's mind. I'm just happy she's on our side."

"Our side?" Shania repeated, thinking that was rather an odd way for Daniel to phrase it.

Belatedly, Daniel realized his error. "The side of the good guys," he told Shania. "I didn't mean to make it sound as if you and I were on a side."

Now he really had her wondering. Shania studied the man next to her. "We're *not* on the side of the good guys?" she asked him.

"Yes, we are. We're just not there in the full sense of the word." Daniel sighed. His tongue was getting tangled up—just like his thoughts. "This isn't coming out right, is it?"

"Not even close," Shania told him. She made no effort to suppress her amusement. "Don't worry about it," she counseled. "Miss Joan does have that sort of effect on people. She can literally make you forget how to talk."

"You, too?" Daniel asked, surprised.

Smiling, she inclined her head. "Definitely me, too. Not the best thing for a high school physics and math teacher to admit, but there you have it," Shania told him with a self-depreciating shrug.

He supposed he might as well take advantage of this impromptu meeting. "Well, since we ran into one another—" Daniel began.

"Or so it looks," she couldn't help adding, glancing at the far end of the counter toward Miss Joan.

The woman looked as if she was busy slicing up a fresh apple pie, but Shania was convinced that Miss Joan was watching their every move—and reading lips since they were sitting too far away from her to allow the woman to hear them.

But Daniel wasn't looking at Miss Joan, he was looking at Shania. Somehow, he'd allowed himself to be distracted and reined himself in.

"What do you mean?" he asked.

But Shania shook her head. Maybe she was just being paranoid.

"Never mind. Go ahead," Shania urged. "You were saying?"

It took him a second to collect his thoughts and remember what he wanted to tell her. "I just wanted to thank you for what you're doing with Elena."

Shania shook her head. "As much as I love being on the receiving end of gratitude," she told him, "I think you're making a mistake. I haven't done anything with Elena."

Was she just being modest, or was there something he was missing? "I don't understand."

Shania smiled. While she liked the fact that he felt grateful to her, she wanted Daniel to give credit where it was due.

"All I did was point Elena toward the books she needed to be reading and the work she needed to do in order to pass my courses. Your sister did all the rest. She showed up and did the work," Shania summarized. "And she's the one who continues to do the work, walking that extra mile with those practice PSAT tests.

"I could talk until I was blue in the face," Shania concluded. "If Elena didn't want to do it, if she didn't want to get those good grades and to get into college, then none of this would be happening. She's the one who deserves all the credit."

He hadn't expected this degree of modesty. Beautiful, smart and modest. Shania Stewart was a hell of a package. If he were inclined to get involved, she would be the kind of woman he'd pick. But getting involved wasn't on his agenda. He had made a vow to himself that that was never going to happen again. Besides, he had a job that took up all of his time and a sister to raise. Those two things filled a thirty-six-hour day and there was no time left over for anything else.

Still, he was not about to allow the teacher to shrug off the credit that he felt was so very obviously due to her.

"We've got a slight difference of opinion here," he informed her. "You're right in everything you just said—except for one thing."

He saw her lips twitch just a little, trying not to smile. "And that is?"

"If you hadn't been there to inspire Elena—and keep on inspiring her—none of this would be happening right now," Daniel told her simply. "Elena can be an extremely headstrong person—"

"Wonder where she gets that from?" Shania speculated. She stopped trying to hold back her smile.

He was losing his battle to ignore the effects of that smile, he thought, no matter how hard he tried.

"And nothing I said to her was getting through to her even though, until about four months ago, we had a pretty decent relationship." He shook his head as he thought back. "I still don't know what happened to change that," he admitted.

"She turned sixteen," Shania told him simply. She couldn't help being impressed by the fact that despite his busy life, Daniel really cared about his sister and the way she reacted to things. "Consider yourself lucky. Most girls rebel long before that. You were living on borrowed time."

He opened his mouth to argue with her, but then he shut it again. He knew Shania was right. And that made him doubly glad that Shania had happened into his sister's life.

"I guess maybe I was," he admitted.

That was the moment that Miss Joan picked to sweep back to them.

"The booth over in the corner just opened up," she announced.

When, instead of getting up, the two people sitting at the counter just looked at her, puzzled, Miss Joan sighed as she shook her head. "That means hustle your butts over there, you two."

Daniel remained where he was. "Why would we want to do that?"

"Because booths are more private than just sitting out in the open—or at the counter," Miss Joan informed them.

"All right," Shania agreed. Her voice trailed off as she waited for the woman to explain why that should mean anything to either of them at this particular time. They weren't talking about anything that was secretive.

Miss Joan fisted her hand at her waist, waiting for them to comply. When they didn't, she gave them an order. "Now, get on over there. Debbie will be there in a minute to take your order." And then, in case there was still any doubt about the matter, she looked pointedly into the deputy's eyes and said, "You're buying your sister's teacher dinner for all the hard work she's done with that girl." She waited a beat for her words to sink in. "No further questions, right?"

"Miss Joan, Daniel's on duty," Shania protested.

"He's on a dinner break," Miss Joan corrected. "I already cleared it with the sheriff, so don't argue with me. Either of you," she added sharply.

Shania turned toward Daniel. The last thing she wanted was to have him feel as if he was being strong-armed into buying her dinner. While she wouldn't mind having dinner with him, this wasn't the way she wanted it to happen.

"Listen, you don't have to—"

But Daniel cut her short. "No, Miss Joan's right—"

"I'm *always* right," the older woman agreed as she continued to observe the pair.

He could see that Shania was about to voice another protest. He tried to quiet her conscience. "You did put in a lot of work with Elena and the least I can do to show my gratitude is to buy you dinner—unless you'd rather I didn't."

Miss Joan sighed. "Do you two need a fire lit under you? You did the work, he's grateful. He wants to show his gratitude by buying you dinner. Enough said," she declared. "Now, go sit down in the booth."

Shania exchanged glances with the deputy. "Yes, ma'am," they both answered Miss Joan almost in unison.

Daniel allowed himself a smile as he walked behind Shania to the booth.

Chapter Twelve

"I know what you're doing."

Unfazed by the knowing tone, Miss Joan casually looked over to her left to see that her step-grandson had entered the diner. Apparently Cash Taylor, one of Forever's two attorneys, had been quietly observing the interaction between her, the deputy and the high school teacher.

"Running the diner, the way I've always been, Cash," Miss Joan answered, turning back to what she was doing. "No big mystery there."

"That might be true," Cash allowed, making himself comfortable on the stool that Shania had just vacated. "But you're also playing cupid."

Miss Joan continued to keep her eyes on the two people she'd just sent off to have lunch in the rear booth.

"I don't know *what* you're talking about, boy," she informed him. Picking up a cloth, she began to clean a spot on the counter—and then continued rubbing it after the spot had disappeared.

Amused, Cash laughed at Miss Joan's denial. "I just put the pieces together. Not that they were so difficult to figure out. You sent for Shania and Daniel to come here, knowing that no one would ever ignore a summons from Miss Joan."

Miss Joan slanted a confident glance at her husband's grandson, a man she had watched turn into a fine human being after some rocky false starts. "Not if they know what's good for them."

"Exactly." Cash paused in case Miss Joan had anything to add. She didn't, so he asked her, "Now tell me *why* you're playing cupid with these two?" They seemed like an unlikely couple to him.

Miss Joan frowned impatiently. She didn't like having to explain herself.

"Because, Counselor," she informed him, "sometimes even smart people are too dumb to see what's right there in front of their noses. Now, instead of butting into my business, why don't you have some of Angel's fine rib-eye steak before you go home to that pretty little wife of yours?" It was more of an order than a suggestion.

Cash inclined his head and said in a pseudo-docile voice, "Yes, Grandma."

Miss Joan looked at him sharply. "You mind your mouth, boy. It might serve you well when you're in court, but I require a more respectful tone from the people who walk through those doors. Even from you."

Amused, Cash pressed his lips together, doing his best to suppress a grin. "Yes, ma'am."

Miss Joan nodded her approval. "That's better," she told him, then stopped wiping the counter.

Any other questions he might have had, Cash kept to himself.

* * *

"I think that woman would have made one hell of a fine general," Daniel told Shania once they had sat down at the booth.

"Because she's so good at ordering people around?" Shania guessed.

"There's that," Daniel agreed. "But I was actually thinking of the way Miss Joan seems to enjoy mapping out and implementing strategies."

Shania was about to ask him what he meant, but just then Debbie, their waitress, approached their booth. Debbie Wilcox had just recently graduated from high school and that was all due to Miss Joan. Hearing that the girl was about to take off, Miss Joan had kept after Debbie to stay in school.

When things disintegrated at home and her widowed stepfather had thrown her out, Miss Joan had taken her in. It was Miss Joan who had put a roof over the girl's head as well as hired her to work at the diner in order to put money into her pocket.

The woman made sure that the hours she gave Debbie worked around her school schedule. Although she made no attempt to remedy Debbie's home situation, there were rumors that Miss Joan had given Arthur Wilcox a severe tongue-lashing and the kind of dressing-down that left a permanent impression on a man for years to come.

Given all that, Shania was not about to discuss anything regarding Miss Joan in front of someone the woman had so obviously rescued. Instead of continuing her conversation with Daniel, she placed her order, asking for water and a salad.

"What?" she asked, catching the look on Daniel's face.

"A salad?" he asked her. His tone sounded almost mocking.

Shania raised her chin slightly. "Yes. What's wrong with a salad?"

He had a feeling Shania was ordering a salad because she didn't want to have him pay too much for her meal. "Nothing's wrong with it—if you happen to be a rabbit." He gave her a look that told her he was on to her—and that Miss Joan wasn't going to let her get away with it. "I don't think you're going to be able to get out of here ordering anything less than that steak that's on the menu."

Shania didn't need to look toward the counter to know that Miss Joan was keeping an eye on them. She could *feel* it.

"Fine," she relented. "I'll have the steak and mashed potatoes."

"How would you like your steak?" Debbie asked, making notations on her pad.

"Small," Shania answered. When Debbie looked at her in confusion, she amended, "Medium."

Smiling, Debbie nodded, then looked toward the deputy. "And you, sir?"

Daniel frowned. Being called "sir" by someone so young made him feel old before his time.

"Same thing," he told Debbie. "Except make mine rare—just barely dead."

"Got it," Debbie said, happily making the notation. Then, putting the pad back into her apron pocket, she collected the two menus and withdrew.

"It's healthier for you to eat a medium steak than a rare one," Shania told him.

"Not looking to be healthy," Daniel responded. "Just looking to enjoy what I'm eating."

Shania realized that Daniel probably thought she was

lecturing him. Occupational habit. She was spending too much of her time with students, not enough with people her own age.

Taking a breath, Shania changed the subject—or actually brought the conversation back to what they were talking about before the waitress had appeared.

"What did you mean about Miss Joan mapping out a strategy?" Shania asked. "What strategy?"

Daniel looked at her. He'd thought it was obvious, but the woman wasn't playing dumb, Daniel realized. She really didn't see it. She didn't see what Miss Joan was doing.

It had to be wonderful to be that innocent, that unassuming, he couldn't help thinking. Heaven knew he was tired of being so suspicious of everything, and at times so paranoid, always looking for the hidden reasons behind people's actions.

This time, though, there was nothing to be suspicious about in the true sense of the word. He had a feeling that this was just a case of Miss Joan being Miss Joan, overseeing everyone's life in general.

Since Shania was looking at him, apparently still waiting for an answer, he said, "Did Miss Joan ask you to come to see her or did you just drop by?"

"As a matter of fact, she sent Violet as a messenger to ask me to come in. I'd been meaning to come see her," Shania confessed, readily shouldering the blame, "but, well, you know how it is." She shrugged. "Life kept getting in the way."

Daniel merely nodded. "Did she tell you why she asked you to come in?"

"Yes," she answered. "She wanted to know how I was doing on my own, now that Wynona wasn't at the house anymore."

He supposed he might as well follow the groundwork that Miss Joan had set up. It occurred to him that he didn't know all that much about this woman who had become so important in his sister's life.

"And that's it?"

Shania nodded. "That's it."

"Nothing more? She didn't ask anything else?" he prodded.

"If there was more, she didn't get a chance to ask because that was when she spotted you coming into the diner," Shania told him. "Once she saw you, her whole countenance changed."

That just confirmed what he thought. "I don't doubt it," he murmured.

Shania looked at him more closely. There was something in his voice that aroused her interest. "Would you like to let me in on it?"

"Well, Miss Joan called the sheriff and told him that she wanted to see me—same as you," Daniel pointed out. "Then, when I came in, all she said was that whatever reason she'd wanted to see me had taken care of itself. You heard her."

She also heard what the deputy wasn't saying. "You don't believe her."

His eyes met hers and she felt that same warm ripple traveling through her again. "Do you?"

She had a feeling she knew where he was going with this, but she discounted it because it seemed almost silly to think this way.

"It's Miss Joan," she reminded him. "Eccentricity is her middle name."

He laughed then. There was no point in pushing this—and he didn't want to embarrass Shania. If nothing else, the woman was a godsend for his sister.

"I always wondered what it was." Before he could say anything further about Miss Joan's possible middle name, Debbie returned with their dinners.

"My guess is that we'd better not leave anything on our plates unless we want Miss Joan scowling at us," Shania commented to Daniel once Debbie had put their dinners on the table and withdrawn again.

"Not a problem," Daniel assured her. "This smells even better than it usually does. I skipped lunch."

"Dedicated or dieting?" Shania asked. Realizing that it sounded as if she was being critical, she quickly said, "Not that you should. Diet I mean, not be dedicated. You should be that." She stopped herself, pressing her lips together as if to hold back any further torrent of words. She flushed as she raised her eyes toward Daniel. "I don't usually babble like this."

Daniel found the pink hue that had suddenly risen to her cheeks rather sweet. The next second, he realized that he was staring. Daniel forced himself to look away. "I hadn't noticed."

"Yes, you had," Shania contradicted. "But I think that it's very nice of you to pretend that you hadn't." When she heard Daniel laugh softly to himself, she asked him, "What's so funny?" before she could think to stop herself.

"I'm not accustomed to hearing the word 'nice' used to describe me," he admitted.

Didn't the man have any close friends? Someone to bolster him up when he was down on himself? "You're kidding."

The lopsided smile answered her before he did. "Something else I'm not known for."

She pretended that he was a student and she did a quick assessment of the man before her. "You know you're being very hard on yourself."

"Not hard," he contradicted. "Just honest."

She had no intention of letting this slide. If he *had* been one of her students, she would have done what she could to raise his spirits—or maybe it was his self-esteem that needed help.

"Well, *I* think you're nice—and you *do* have a sense of humor."

"If you say so," Daniel replied, not about to dispute the matter. He had a feeling that arguing with Shania would be pointless. "But just so you know, I'm not about to chuck my career and become a stand-up comedian."

She grinned at his words. "See, I told you that you had a sense of humor," she declared happily. The next moment, she looked down at what was left on her plate—just the denuded bone. "I am really glad you talked me into getting this. This steak is really good."

That wasn't his doing. "Angel really knows her way around a kitchen."

"Angel?" she repeated quizzically.

He nodded, then got that she probably didn't know about the woman. A lot of things had happened in the years that she had lived in Houston.

"Miss Joan has her cooking most of the meals. Angel's another one of Miss Joan's secret good deeds. Gabe found her unconscious in a car," he said, mentioning the other deputy who worked for the sheriff. Gabe was also the man who became Angel's husband. "There'd been an accident. When she woke up, she had no memory of who she was or how she got there. Miss Joan took her under that very large wing of hers. When it became obvious that Angel could work miracles in the kitchen, Miss Joan put her to work in the diner."

She appreciated Daniel filling her in on the things that

she had missed while she'd been away. "Did Angel ever get her memory back?"

"She did," he recalled. "But she liked being useful and cooking, and she was so grateful to Miss Joan for all her help that she went on working for her at the diner even after she got married. And before you ask," he said, "the guy she married was the one who rescued her out of her car."

"And did her name really turn out to be Angel?" she asked.

"No," he answered, "but that's the name she goes by because, as she told Miss Joan, she was reborn in this town, so having a new name fit right in with the narrative." Finished with his meal, he pushed aside his empty plate. "Anything else you want to know?"

"Not offhand," she admitted. And then she smiled. "But I now know who to go to if something else occurs to me."

"Fair enough." Daniel paused for a moment as he framed the question he wanted to ask in his mind. "Okay, I've got one for you."

"A question?" she asked. When the deputy nodded, Shania braced herself a little bit then said, "Okay, go ahead."

"Why did you come here?" he asked.

She thought they'd already covered that earlier. "I already told you, Daniel. Miss Joan sent Violet to come get me."

He shook his head. She didn't understand what he was asking. "No, I mean why are you in Forever? Why did you *come back* to Forever?" Daniel clarified.

She would have thought that he of all people would have understood. "Wynona and I were both from here. We saw the kind of life that they don't write about in storybooks. Both of us would have wound up in the foster care system by the time we were eleven and twelve. And then, out of nowhere, a miracle happened," she remembered with a smile. "A great-aunt neither one of us even knew about suddenly popped up in our lives and came to Forever to collect us."

He was curious as to how the dots were connected in this case. "If you didn't know about her, how did she wind up suddenly coming to your rescue out of the blue like that?"

She could see the suspicion in his eyes. He either didn't believe her story, or he was suspicious of this woman who materialized just in the nick of time. A woman who took them in, provided for them and, when the time came, sent them off to get their college degrees so that they could have careers. In her own way, her great-aunt was as tough and demanding as Miss Joan. And she'd had an equally soft heart.

Shania was surprised that he hadn't figured it out already. "Same reason that the two of us are sitting right here, talking to one another."

"Are you talking about 'fate'?" he asked her, sounding even more skeptical about this story than before.

"No, Deputy Tallchief," she informed him, "I'm talking about Miss Joan."

He wasn't sure that he followed her. "Come again?"

She gave him the background behind what happened. "Somehow, Miss Joan stumbled across the information that we had a great-aunt—Great-Aunt Naomi, I think she found it in my mother's papers—and Miss Joan got in contact with her. I don't know exactly what she said to the woman, but whatever it was, it did the trick. By the end of the week, Aunt Naomi was here, snatching us out of the clutches of the foster care system and taking us to her home in Houston. There," she concluded with a smile, dropping her napkin on her empty plate. "I think you're officially all caught up."

Looking at Shania, he didn't quite share that opinion, but for now, he kept it to himself.

Chapter Thirteen

His sense of obligation had Daniel glancing at his watch a number of times, wishing there was a way to make time stand still. But there wasn't. There was no putting it off any longer. He had already lingered far too long over dinner, but sitting here opposite Shania had made the time go by so fast.

"Well, I'd better be heading back to the sheriff's office," Daniel said rather reluctantly. Looking around he saw Debbie and signaled to the waitress to have her bring the bill.

"Right. And I've got a lonely dog to get home to," Shania told him.

Twisting in her seat to see if Debbie was coming, she decided she had enough time to say something else since the young woman was still half the length of the diner away.

Shania turned back to face Elena's brother and told him quietly, "This was nice."

"Yes it was, wasn't it?" Because she'd opened up the door, Daniel felt it was safe to ask, "Would you like to do it again sometime?"

She hadn't expected him to ask that. Caught off guard, her response came out before she could think it through and weigh the pros and cons of telling him *yes* so fast.

"Yes." Then, since she probably sounded way too eager to him, she tried to backtrack and temper her answer. "That is, I mean, I need to check my schedule and see if—"

"Too late," Daniel told her, stopping Shania before she was able to negate her answer. "Sorry, no do-overs allowed."

Staring at him, Shania blinked. This wasn't the response of the serious, semisomber person she had gotten to know. "Excuse me?"

"Your first response was spontaneous," Daniel explained. "In view of this rather…" he hunted for the right word before saying, "*Unusual* first dinner we just had, we could give this another shot, see if this was just a fluke, or if maybe we could guide this into a friendship." He was making this up as he went along. The words that came out weren't really what he wanted to say, but on the other hand, he didn't want to risk scaring Shania away—or himself for that matter. He felt that too much pressure and too many expectations could ruin something before it ever even had the proper chance to evolve.

"A friendship," Shania said, repeating the word he'd used. Daniel wasn't sure if she liked the idea of their having a friendship or if she was annoyed by it.

And then she smiled and he felt as if he had just completed a triathlon and had raced across the finish line to capture first place.

"Sure," she told him. "That sounds good."

Debbie came just then and placed the check facedown in front of Daniel. "I hope you both found everything to your satisfaction," she said, her bright blue eyes sweeping over both of them.

Looking at the bill, he took out a twenty and a ten and placed them on top. He also placed a five on the table as a tip.

"I have no complaints," Daniel told the young woman.

Flattery was definitely not this man's strong suit, Shania thought, amused. It made her reexamine what he'd said to her before Debbie came to their booth. Shania realized that she should be flattered.

Looking at the waitress now, she made a point of saying, "Everything was delicious."

Debbie grinned. "I'll be sure to pass that along to Angel," she said, leaving.

They rose almost in unison. Daniel accompanied Shania to the diner's entrance. He glanced back at Debbie, who waved to them.

"I guess what you said sounded a lot better than what I did," he speculated.

That he even took note of the waitress's reaction in each case meant that there was some hope for the man.

Shania tried to make him feel better about his response. "You're just not an effusive guy," she told him.

Daniel held the door open for her. "I save effusion for the really important things," he deadpanned.

"Got it. Remind me to be there when it finally happens," she told him, walking past him and stepping outside.

They went down the two steps that were in front of the diner, which officially brought them to the diner's parking lot. The temperature had dropped by at least ten degrees since they had walked in. He noticed Shania pulling her coat closer to her. She was cold, he thought.

"Where's your car?" he asked her, looking around the area. He didn't see it.

"In the shop," she told him. A slight sigh accompanied her words. "It decided it didn't feel like running for me. I called Mick and he came by and towed it to his shop." Mick Henley was Forever's exceptionally capable—as well as its only—mechanic. "He told me that it should be all fixed up and running like new in a couple of days. Meanwhile," she concluded, doing her best to focus on the upside of her situation, "walking is good for me."

"Yeah, but freezing isn't," he commented. "C'mon," he urged, "I'll take you home."

She didn't want to be the reason that he got into trouble. "I thought you had to get back to work."

"I do, but it's not exactly like Forever's having any sort of a crime spree," Daniel told her. "In the last week, I had to bring home an inebriated husband who apparently was drinking to forget he was married and I had to break up a fight between two men who couldn't hurt a fly between them if they tried. So," he concluded, "my being twenty minutes late getting back from my dinner break isn't going to make much of a difference. You, however, will definitely feel the difference between walking home from here in this weather or getting a ride home."

The wind was picking up. The weather was definitely on his side. Still, she hesitated just a little. "If you're sure it's okay—"

"Just please get in the car," he told her. His eyes met hers. "Don't make me have to pick you up and deposit you in the backseat," he warned. "Well?" he asked when Shania made no move toward his vehicle.

"I'm thinking about it," she told him with the straightest face she could manage. However, when her mouth began to curve the next moment, Shania gave up her pretense. "Okay, the answer's yes," she told him, then added, "And thank you."

"Just doing my job, keeping the good citizens of Forever safe—and warm," Daniel added as they walked to the extended parking lot that was behind Miss Joan's diner. His car was parked at the very edge.

She looked at him when they stopped next to his vehicle. "I didn't know the 'warm' part was part of your job description."

"My job description envelops everything and anything," Daniel told her, opening the passenger door for Shania.

She slid into the seat and buckled up. Daniel firmly closed her door.

"I appreciate this," she told him once he had rounded the hood of his car and gotten behind the wheel.

Gratitude made him uncomfortable. He never knew how to respond, but this time, at least, he had something to fall back on. "Not nearly as much as I appreciate you going the extra mile with Elena."

"No extra mile," she protested as Daniel started the car. "It's my job."

He had a different view of that. He'd attended the school system in Forever. More specifically, the reservation schools. Anything he had accomplished, he had done on his own. There hadn't been a "Miss Shania" in his life.

"It's your job to show up and to go over the curriculum," he told her, pulling out of the parking space. "According to the manual, finding ways to reach a stubborn sixteen-year-old and get her to buckle down to do her work is not considered to be part of your job."

He'd done his homework, as well, Shania thought.

"Okay, let me rephrase that then. It's what I *consider* to be part of my job."

"And that is the reason why I'm grateful," he pointed out.

Still, she didn't want him thanking her, not until the job was completed. "Save that until after Elena takes her test and passes."

"Why?" he asked as he drove. "Are you expecting there to be a problem?"

A smile played on her lips as she thought back to another time in her life. "I learned a long time ago not to count my chickens until they not only hatched, but took their first steps, as well."

Daniel heard the fleeting grim note in her voice. Pulling up in front of Shania's house, he turned off the ignition and then turned to look at her. "I think that you and I had the same lesson. Except that, for the most part, you came out of it being pretty optimistic."

"I work at it," she told him. And at times, it was a challenge not to just throw her hands up in the air. "I also learned that just thinking dark thoughts gets to be really depressing, so I do my best to think happy thoughts when I can. In other words, I prepare for the worst but hope for the best."

He gave the woman credit, he thought. A lot of the people he had grown up with had gone the other route. More than a couple were dead, having given up and abandoned life altogether.

"I supposed that's a good philosophy if you can manage it," he told her.

"I work at it every day," she told him.

And then she pulled back. She hadn't meant for the conversation to get this serious. There was something about the man that seemed to coax her innermost thoughts out.

There was also something about him that spoke to her soul, making her think things and feel things that she realized were normally buried so deeply, she gave them no thought at all.

Until now.

Shania took a deep breath. "Well, I should get out of your car. I'm keeping you from getting back. And, like I said, I don't want you getting in any trouble on my account."

The space within the car felt as if it had somehow grown smaller. Daniel looked at the woman sitting in his passenger seat for a long moment. Unbidden thoughts and feelings were inexplicably ricocheting madly around inside him.

He thought of what she'd just said. "Might be worth it," he murmured more to himself than to her.

Shania had heard anyway. She felt her face growing hot in response to his words, could almost *feel* the pink color creeping up along her cheeks.

You're past this, she silently insisted, impatient with herself and her reaction. She was a grown woman, for heaven sakes, not some prepubescent girl nursing her first crush.

The word *crush* caught her up short.

Why had she just thought that? Where had it even come from? Had it really been *that* long since she'd had even the mildest form of a relationship in her life?

She suddenly realized that even though she was trying to remember just how long ago that actually was, the truth of it was that she couldn't recall *when* she had been in a relationship. It had been *that* long ago.

Feeling unaccountably nervous, Shania cleared her

throat. "Belle probably thinks that I must have run away from home."

Daniel surprised himself when he told her, "Can't have that."

"No, we can't," she murmured. One hand on the door latch, she still hesitated. What was she waiting for? she asked herself.

Forcing herself to open the door, she heard Daniel call her name.

Turning around to look at the deputy, Shania asked, "What?"

And then she had the answer to the question she'd asked, even though Daniel didn't say anything in response. Instead he slipped one hand behind her, cupping the back of her head just enough to bring her a shade closer to him.

And then he kissed her.

The very air in her lungs felt as if it had backed up as every single nerve ending within her was instantly alert—and waiting for more.

Shania could feel all sorts of feelings waking up within her. Dormant feelings she hadn't even realized had gone to sleep until this very second.

She laced her arms around his neck, absorbing every nuance of what was happening to her.

She couldn't explain what it was—she was only aware that it was, and that she liked it.

Liked *him.*

And that she didn't want this to just be an isolated incident.

Even as Daniel deepened the kiss, he could feel guilt seeping in.

This wasn't like him. He never lost control of himself, not even for a split second. And he read signs first, made certain that he wasn't presuming things. Before he even kissed a woman, he knew for a fact that she wanted him to kiss her.

He didn't know anything here.

He was like a blind man feeling his way around in a world that was completely hidden from him. He'd kissed Shania because he felt this compelling *need* to kiss her and that was all that seemed to matter.

Daniel drew back from Shania even as he felt his heart going into double time.

"Sorry," he apologized.

By all rights, she could have easily read him the riot act if she wanted to, but she didn't. And because she didn't, his own guilt increased.

"I didn't mean to do that," he told her.

Shania stiffened and just like that, a beautiful moment seemed to just vanish into nothingness as if it had never existed.

"I'm sorry to hear that," she told him formally. "Thank you for the ride."

She got out of the car quickly and made it to her front door while Daniel continued to remain sitting where he was, still struggling to figure out what had just happened.

He felt the need to go after her and apologize again, but Shania had already gone inside the house.

There was something very final sounding about the way she'd closed her door.

Idiot! Daniel upbraided himself.

He'd never behaved like that, even in his teens. What had come over him? He had no doubt that he had just single-handedly ruined whatever slim chance he might have had to see Shania socially.

Well, he couldn't sit here and brood about it, he thought, annoyed with himself. If he wasted any more time like this, he would not only be looking at the ashes of a relationship that never even had a chance to take root, but he'd also be out looking for a new job. Forever being what it was, that wouldn't exactly be a piece of cake, even for a former deputy.

He knew that as a last resort, he could take Elena with him and move to one of the larger cities in Texas, but that would probably involve tying his sister up and dragging her with him. And that didn't even take into consideration the fact that unlike so many other people his age in Forever, he had no desire to pull up his roots and plant them somewhere else.

He *liked* the small-town feel of Forever now that he had found his niche in it.

When had things gotten so complicated? Daniel wondered.

Okay, Tallchief, no more thinking. You need to get to work before the sheriff realizes that he can do without you.

Securing his seat belt again, Daniel turned his key in the ignition and felt the vehicle come back to life. Thinking only of the mechanics of driving and nothing more, he turned his vehicle around to head back to the sheriff's office.

Just before he took his foot off the brake to shift it to the gas pedal again, he looked one last time toward Shania's house.

The lights were all on the lower level, but with the drapes drawn, he wasn't able to make out any silhouettes. Or actually, the one particular silhouette he was looking for.

Just as well. He sure as hell didn't need any more visual aids to set him off again.

What he needed, he told himself, was to get his mind back on work as well as his body back to the job.

End of story.

But was it? he couldn't help wondering. Or was there more to the story, something that he was going to find out before too soon?

He really wished that Miss Joan hadn't suddenly decided to play cupid. He liked his life uncomplicated and it didn't look like it was going to be that way, at least not for a long, long time.

Chapter Fourteen

Gabe Rodriguez, the deputy who had been hired before Daniel, decided after watching Daniel for more than a week that he needed to speak up. To him it was like deciding to come to aid a wounded, slightly feral, animal.

He waited until Daniel went to get a cup of coffee from the small lunch nook, gave him until the count of ten and then came up behind him.

Rather than bother with small talk, Gabe went straight for the heart of the matter.

"You know, I don't make it a habit to stick my nose into someone else's business," Gabe said quietly.

"A very admirable quality," Daniel said, commending the other deputy.

Although he was just about to fill up his cup, Daniel left the coffeepot where it was and turned on his heel, heading back to his desk.

Now that he'd made the decision to say something, Gabe wasn't about to just let it go. Abandoning his own unfilled cup next to Daniel's, he followed the other deputy back to his desk.

"But I've been watching you for over a week now—" Gabe continued as if there hadn't been a notable pause.

Daniel sat down at his desk. It was obvious to him that Gabe was not about to cease and desist. He didn't need any more unsolicited advice.

"Maybe you should ask the sheriff to give you something to do that could utilize those special skills of yours," Daniel suggested, hoping Gabe would take the hint and back off.

But Gabe didn't.

"And you've been acting surlier than usual," Gabe told him. "Something crawl down your throat and die there?"

Daniel looked at him darkly. "No, but thanks for asking."

The cryptic comment was meant to end the exchange, but much to Daniel's annoyance, Gabe just refused to take the hint.

"Then what is bothering you, Tallchief?" Gabe asked. "Because something *is* definitely bothering you."

Daniel's look just grew darker. "Other than you?" he asked Gabe.

"Other than me," Gabe replied good-naturedly. The man had a really thick hide, Daniel thought, because Rodriguez just wasn't taking the hint. "Maybe I can help."

"I don't need any help," Daniel retorted, then added, "And nothing's bothering me."

A third party joined the discussion. "That's not what I heard," Joe Lone Wolf said.

Because he'd been quiet as usual and oblivious to the conversation, both men had forgotten that Joe was even there. Now that he had spoken up, Gabe turned to Joe as a potential ally.

Looking delighted that Joe might have something additional that could be used as ammunition, Gabe slid his chair across the common area, using his feet to propel his chair over to Joe's desk.

Gabe's eyes almost gleamed brightly as he asked, "And what was it that you heard?"

The expression on Joe's face didn't change. For all the emotion there, he might as well have been reading that day's menu from the diner.

"That Miss Joan got Daniel to break bread with that really pretty high school teacher, the one who's putting in extra time tutoring his sister," Joe told the other deputy.

Daniel glanced up sharply. "It's not just Elena. There are other students in that class that she's tutoring," he said defensively.

"I'm sure there are," Joe answered mildly, looking back at the report on his desk that he was reviewing. "Shania Stewart's a dedicated educator. Wish we had more like her."

Nodding his head, Gabe turned his attention back to Daniel. "So what's the deal with you two?"

What little patience Daniel had left was quickly evaporating. "There is no 'deal.'"

"Is that the problem?" Gabe asked sympathetically. "There is no deal?"

"If I were you, I'd try to seal one," Joe advised mildly, not looking up this time. "I wouldn't be surprised if a lot of the men in Forever would like to get closer to her, maybe even become teacher's pet," he added.

Daniel didn't welcome having all this attention focused on him, especially given the subject of that focus.

"You two have entirely too much time on your hands," he fairly growled at the other two deputies in disgust. On his feet now, he headed for the door.

"Just looking out for you, that's all," Gabe said, calling after Daniel.

Daniel's parting words just as he crossed the threshold were, "I don't need anyone looking out for me. Clear?"

He thought he heard Joe say, "That's your opinion." But he wasn't about to double back to find out if he was right. Right now, he just wanted to walk off the full head of steam he'd been building up before he wound up saying something they'd all regret.

Daniel chose a path that didn't run through the heart of the town, a path where he could be alone with his thoughts without having to stop to either exchange pleasantries with someone or answer any spur-of-the-moment questions put to him by one of Forever's citizens.

It had been a full week since he'd kissed Shania. A full week since he'd actually seen her, as well. And rather than have things get better—and by better he just wanted it all to fade away—they got worse.

Thoughts of Shania kept invading his mind. The way she'd looked, the way her lips had felt beneath his. The way he had almost felt her body yielding to his.

The only good thing about the incident was that it seemed to have no repercussions, at least not as far as Shania working with Elena was concerned. Shania went on preparing Elena, along with the other students, for her PSATs.

His sister didn't seem to know anything had happened between her teacher and him. If she did, Daniel was certain that Elena would have gone into a full rant about it because of the embarrassment that she'd claim was attached to her brother socially seeing her teacher. That she said nothing proved to him that Shania had not alluded to what had happened between them in his car.

But while he was grateful that she hadn't, it didn't

alleviate what he was feeling. If anything, it seemed to make the itch he was experiencing even worse.

Not to mention that it seemed to confuse things even more.

He needed to resolve this. Now, before it ate away at him any further.

Daniel was back at his desk twenty minutes later. Apparently having gotten the message, Joe and Gabe left him alone and to his own devices, each working on the tedious reports that periodically needed to be filed.

He did the same.

Daniel waited until he was fairly sure that the after-school class was over—and then he tacked on an extra fifteen minutes to that just in case there was a straggler or two who was still in Shania's classroom, asking her questions or working on one of the sample tests.

Pulling up in his official vehicle, Daniel waited outside the school building just in case Shania had decided to leave early, but she hadn't.

The woman was most definitely married to her job, he thought, finally entering the building.

Taking the stairs, Daniel quickly went up to the third floor where Shania's classroom was located. At this hour, the school was almost empty. The building was rather quiet. He could hear the echo of his own footsteps as he went down the hall.

All the classroom doors were closed and presumably locked, except for one. That door was open. He came up to it, knocked on it once before walking in.

Shania was sitting at her desk, busy making notes on a yellow pad. If this same scene was taking place in one of the larger cities where funding was not an issue the way it was here, Daniel had no doubts she would have been plugging entries into a laptop instead of using a pencil and paper.

Finished, Shania looked up. He saw a fleeting look of surprise on her face before it disappeared. "If you're looking for Elena in order to walk her home, she already left," she told him primly. "She went out with Jacquelyn," she added, mentioning one of Elena's friends.

Having informed him of his sister's whereabouts, Shania looked back down at the notes she was putting together.

"I'm not looking for Elena," Daniel told her quietly. "I came to see you."

Shania raised her eyes again. He saw that the wariness was back.

"Well, you've seen me," she replied with an air of finality. "Deputy Tallchief, I have a lot of work to prepare for tomorrow, so unless there is something else, I really need to—"

This wasn't easy for him, but it was the right thing to do and he knew he owed it to her. "I came to tell you I'm sorry."

If possible, she sat up a little straighter, her shoulders braced a little more rigidly. Her voice was distant as she told him, "You already made that clear in your car."

He shook his head. He needed to make her understand. "No, I came to tell you that I'm sorry I said I was sorry."

Shania continued looking at him, a trace of confusion replacing the wariness. "Maybe you could stand to take a refresher course in English when you have the time, Deputy."

He inclined his head. "Maybe I'll look into that." And then he tried one more time to make himself clear. "When I told you I was sorry, I didn't mean that I was sorry I kissed you—I was just sorry that I assumed that you'd want me to."

Shania gave up pretending to work while he was standing there. Pushing the pad and pencil aside, she looked at Daniel, trying her best to untangle what he was having such trouble saying.

"But you *did* want to kiss me?" she questioned.

He released a sigh of relief. Finally. "Yes, I did. But I didn't have the right to just—"

That was all she wanted to hear.

Shania pushed her chair back from her desk. Standing up, she crossed to him in less time than it took for Daniel to realize what she was doing.

"Shut up, Tallchief," she told him a second before she wrapped her arms around his neck and brought her mouth up to his.

His surprise melted away in less than a blink of an eye. Lost in the moment, Daniel went with his reflexes and pulled her closer to him.

In an instant, Shania realized that he wasn't just returning her kiss—he was kissing her with enough verve to completely blot out her mind, erasing everything except for him.

The kiss was well on its way to overwhelming her, creating a tidal wave of feelings and desires that could easily make her forget who she was as well as *where* she was.

Catching herself before that happened, Shania drew her head away.

Looking down into her face, he asked, "Does this mean that you forgive me?"

He could swear that his heart rate had sped up to the point that it was emulating the revved-up engine of a race car. Daniel kept his arms around her as he waited for his heart to slow down enough to allow him to breathe normally.

Shania smiled up at him and he could have sworn that he felt her smile searing right into his heart.

"Let's just say we'll work on it," she told him.

Given that it could have gone a great deal worse, he nodded. "Good enough for me. Can I buy you dinner?"

"I'd like that," she told him, "but I'm going to have to take a rain check for now. I already made plans for dinner tonight." Before he could say anything, or think that she was just brushing him off, Shania explained, "I promised my cousin Wynona I'd come over to have dinner with her and her husband and son." She smiled. "We're officially celebrating the fact that she's pregnant."

And then she paused for a second, debating whether or not to say something. Making her decision, she said, "You're welcome to come if you'd like. You can't pay for anything," she told him, knowing the way he thought. "But you can eat," she teased.

But Daniel shook his head. "No, this is a family occasion. It wouldn't be right to just barge in."

He was surprised to hear her laugh at that. "If you knew Wynona, you'd know that you definitely wouldn't be barging in." Her cousin had been after her to start going out more.

Daniel felt that she was just being nice. "I appreciate the invitation, but, um—"

Shania nodded, reading between the lines. "One step at a time?"

He didn't know if he would have put it that way, but it was as good a description as any. Besides, he felt that they needed to spend a little time alone before they ventured out into the world as anything approximating a couple. Daniel was still extremely leery about taking what to him was a huge step.

"Something like that."

They'd definitely made progress, she thought, and she wasn't about to push.

"Understood," Shania told him. "By the way, Elena is doing great. At the rate she's going, when the PSATs are finally given, she is going to ace them. You should be very proud of her."

Realizing that it was getting late, she gathered her things together, packing everything into her oversize shoulder bag.

"And that's all thanks to you," Daniel told her.

He was giving her way too much credit—and not enough to his sister, Shania thought. "I didn't make her smart."

Daniel followed her out of the classroom. "No, but you made her realize that she didn't have to be ashamed of being smart. And you made her realize that it was okay for her to apply herself so she can go to college instead of just being another example of a rebellious teen who failed to do anything with her life."

Shania paused outside of the classroom and smiled at him. "Okay."

"Okay what?" Daniel asked, not sure exactly what she was saying.

"Okay," she told him, extrapolating, "I'll accept your compliment if you promise to stop making this all about me and realize that it's actually about your sister."

"It's always been about my sister," Daniel assured her solemnly. He waited as Shania locked the classroom door. When she slipped the key into her pocket he asked, "How about tomorrow?"

She fell into place beside him. "I need more of a hint than that."

Daniel flushed, realizing that he'd just jumped ahead. "Dinner." And then he forced himself to be completely clear by using a complete sentence. "How about tomorrow for dinner?"

Shania flashed a smile. "Sounds good."

Daniel had expected it to be harder than this. "Then you can make it?"

"No, but it does sound good," Shania cracked. And then the grin returned. "Of course I can make it," she laughed. "You know, I'm not trying to be difficult, Tallchief."

He looked at her, feigning surprise. "Then it comes naturally to you?"

Shania's grin grew wider. "You made a joke. There really *is* hope for you, Tallchief."

"Do you think you could call me Daniel?" he asked. "When you call me Tallchief it makes me feel like I'm on duty."

She couldn't even summon a serious look at this point, even though she gave it her best shot. "You drive a hard bargain, but I'll give it a try, *Danny*."

"Daniel," he corrected. Only his mother had called him Danny, and hearing himself called that brought back memories he still hadn't learned how to deal with. Memories he kept buried.

"Yes, that, too." And then, because he was looking at her, obviously waiting for her to agree, she obliged and said his name. "*Daniel*."

He nodded his approval.

"Well, now that we've resolved that," Shania said when they reached the ground floor, "and that you're not sorry that you kissed me, what will we have to talk about at dinner tomorrow?"

He knew that she was teasing him and he liked it. The whole situation felt strangely normal even though it had been a very long time since he'd even been in a relationship that was worthy of the label. Since then the women in his life had been few and had left no footprints on his soul.

His main focus once he had laid his parents to rest—and Lana had walked out on him after making it clear that she had no patience for the life he was proposing—was his sister. Providing for Elena and making her feel safe and loved in the aftermath of losing her parents had consumed almost all of his extra time and energy.

Whatever was left over brought nothing memorable or lasting with it.

He had made up his mind that this was what the rest of his life was going to be like.

That was why what he was experiencing now with Shania felt unusual and yet oddly comfortable, as well as exceptionally invigorating.

But he was worried, worried that without realizing it, he was going to do something that would cost him this fledgling relationship before it ever had a chance to take flight.

And he just couldn't go through that again.

Chapter Fifteen

"So, how was it?" Daniel asked as he settled into the booth, taking a seat opposite Shania at Miss Joan's diner.

It was several evenings later and it had taken them this long to finally be able to coordinate their two work schedules in order to carve out some time to share dinner with each other.

Even without any preface on his part, Shania knew Daniel was referring to the dinner at her cousin's house. She wasn't aware of doing it—although Daniel had seen it—but she wrinkled her nose as she recalled the occasion.

"It was a good thing that you didn't come," she told him.

Daniel came to the only conclusion he could. "Then I was right when I said that she'd want it to be a family-only thing."

He couldn't quite read the strange expression on her face. "Not exactly."

Daniel looked at her, confused. "I don't think I understand."

She was trying to find the right way to word this. "You know that old expression about being sick to your stomach?"

"I'm aware of it," he said, still waiting for this to make sense to him.

"Well, now so is Wynona." Shania took a breadstick out of the basket and broke it in half before taking a bite. Parts of that evening were coming vividly back to her. She did her best to block them out. "Everything that went into her mouth came out almost at the same time. I have never seen such a glaring example of morning sickness in my whole life," she told him, feeling very sorry for her cousin. "Except that the poor thing doesn't just have 'morning sickness,' she has 'all day sickness.'" Shania shook her head as she recalled what Wynona had told her. "She even has trouble keeping water down."

Daniel looked concerned. "Shouldn't she be in a hospital then?" he asked Shania. "If she can't keep any food down, she's in danger of starving herself, not to mention possibly harming her baby."

Shania like the fact that Daniel actually seemed concerned rather than just picking up on a few random words so he could make acceptable conversation with her about her cousin's condition.

"Unfortunately, the closest hospital is still over fifty miles away," she reminded him. "But at least some things have changed. They did reopen the medical clinic a few years back and the town has a couple of excellent, up-to-date doctors to turn to."

She knew that Daniel was aware of this, but for her it was still a new occurrence. She knew it made a world of difference to a lot of people who lived here.

"Dr. Davenport ran a few tests on Wynona. He put her on supplements and he did discover that there was one thing Wynona seems to be able to tolerate as long as it's in moderation."

"Which is?" Daniel expected her to say something like chicken soup or boiled chicken, both of which seemed bland enough for a nauseated woman to be able to keep down.

Shania paused, smiled and then said, "Stroganoff."

"What now?" Daniel asked. He was certain that he had to have misheard her.

Shania's grin widened. "I know, I know. It sounds weird since Wyn can't even keep crackers down, but she seems to be able to eat—and keep down—beef Stroganoff served over linguine."

"You're kidding."

Despite the smile on her lips, there wasn't even a hint of a clue to indicate that she was putting him on. "Nope."

Just looking at her was drawing him in, making him want to take her somewhere where they could be alone. Daniel forced himself to just focus on the conversation and not the woman across from him.

He shrugged. "Whatever works."

"Speaking of which," Shania said, picking up on his choice of words, "I know that you have a lot vying for your attention, so you might not know that the PSATs are being given next Saturday."

"No, I didn't know," he admitted, grateful that she'd given him a heads-up. He frowned slightly. "Elena hasn't said anything to me about it."

"I didn't think so." Shania saw the look that came over Daniel's face and guessed what he was thinking. That his sister was reverting back to her old rebellious ways and was shutting him out. "She's just stoic, like her brother.

Plus she told me that you've really been busy lately and she didn't want to bother you with, and I quote, 'trivial things.'"

He didn't see how Elena could think that way. "Her education isn't trivial."

"Yes, I know that," she said, "and I told her that *you* don't think that it is, either."

"And?" Daniel asked, convinced that his sister had to have an opinion about that. "What's the verdict?"

"Jury's still out," she told him honestly, "but I have a feeling that when it does come in, the jury'll rule in your favor."

Daniel never counted on anything going his way, but since Shania seemed optimistic about the outcome, he wanted to do something to help it along.

"So, is there anything I'm supposed to do?"

"Just encourage her and wish her well on Saturday morning," she said, finishing off the breadstick. "She's a very intelligent girl. Short of going off on a bender the night before, she should do just fine on the test."

His face darkened slightly. "She'd better not go on a bender."

"I was just kidding," Shania quickly assured him. "I really don't think there's any danger of her doing that—but just remember," Shania cautioned, "she does better with encouragement than being on the receiving end of dark scowls."

"I don't scowl," Daniel protested.

She congratulated herself for not laughing at him. Instead, she merely smiled knowingly. "Not as much as you used to, but yeah, you do."

Daniel sighed, then unexpectedly pulled his lips back in a wide grin. "How's this?"

"Frightening actually," she answered, giving in and

laughing. Leaning over the table, she patted his hand and promised, "We'll work on it."

He knew that was just a throwaway line that people said, but deep down inside him, he liked the sound of that. Liked the promise that was implied: that this was something that they would be facing together, no matter how minor it actually was.

Daniel thoroughly enjoyed being with her like this and the total lack of privacy kept him from getting ahead of himself before he was ready, he mused as he raised his hand for the check.

They met a couple more times for dinner. Each time they came in, Miss Joan made sure that they were placed at a booth that was tucked into the back. It was as if she wanted to keep them away from prying eyes—other than hers, of course.

It was very evident to both Daniel and Shania that Miss Joan was playing matchmaker, although neither one of them commented on that fact out loud, just in case the other wasn't aware of what was going on.

And then the dreaded Saturday finally came. All the countless hours of studying and taking sample tests came down to this, the moment of truth, otherwise known as taking the PSAT test in earnest.

As expected, Shania was proctoring the test. She had volunteered. As nervous as any of her students, she had gotten very little sleep the night before. She had arrived at the classroom more than an hour before the test was to officially begin. She made sure that all the proper items the students would need were in place so that once the test began, there would be no need to stop for anything.

As the time for the test drew closer, students began to trickle in. She greeted each of them with a wide, encouraging smile. The more her stomach knotted up, the wider her smile grew. At this point, she was certain that she was more nervous than her students, but she also knew that she couldn't show anything except undying confidence that those same students would all do well—or at least pass.

She was aware that they all looked to her and she was not about to let them down.

And then it was time to begin.

It felt as if the minute hand on the wall clock had been covered in molasses and now moved along accordingly, dragging itself from one number to the next.

When the time to take the exam was finally, mercifully over, no one was more grateful than she was.

"Okay, students, time's up. Pencils down," she declared, then looked around the room at the various faces. Some were drawn, some were relieved, but they all shared one thing.

"You all survived," Shania announced cheerfully. "Now come up to the front of the room single file and hand in your papers, then take a deep, deep breath. The worst is over," she told them, her eyes sweeping over a sea of mostly exhausted-looking teenagers.

"When will we get the results?" one lanky teenage boy asked as he handed in his papers.

"Soon enough," Shania answered, then added, "But not today. Today you go out and celebrate the fact that the test is over. Go and have some fun," she urged, adding, "Relax your brain and enjoy yourself."

When Elena came up to hand in her paper, Shania smiled at the girl. "How do you think you did?" she asked her.

"I blanked out on half the questions," Elena complained.

"That happens more than you think," Shania assured her. She lowered her voice slightly to ask, "Were you finally able to focus?"

Elena nodded.

"Good, then you probably did a lot better than you think you did," she assured the young teen. "Now do what I said. Go see your friends, have fun," she urged. "You've worked really, really hard these last four weeks," she reminded Elena, giving her credit for all the hours she had put into studying for this.

The doubtful expression on Elena's face receded, replaced by a glimmer of a smile. She nodded in response to what Shania had said. The next moment she was out of the classroom like a shot, ready to do exactly what Shania had recommended.

But the very next minute Elena recrossed the threshold and came back into the classroom.

"Something wrong?" Shania asked the girl.

"No, nothing's wrong," Elena answered. Then, looking almost tongue-tied, she looked at Shania and murmured, "I just wanted to say thank you."

Surprised, it took Shania a moment to collect herself. When she finally did, Shania smiled at her student and said, "It was my pleasure, Ellie. My pleasure."

Elena returned her teacher's smile. And then the next second, the girl bolted again, and this time she kept on going.

Shania stood where she was, savoring the moment.

"You look really pleased with yourself."

Startled—she hadn't thought that there was anyone left in the building—she immediately looked toward the doorway. Daniel had managed to come in without her realizing it.

"You just missed Elena," she told him, assuming that was why he was there.

"I didn't come looking for her," he said. "I just assumed that after all the hours of studying, Ellie would want to go and unwind with her friends."

She looked at him, surprised and impressed. "I thought you didn't approve of that."

"I don't approve of wild partying and underage drinking," Daniel corrected her, clarifying his position, "but I think I made the boundary lines pretty clear to her—thanks to your influence. Besides, I'm not an ogre. I do think she's earned the right to have some fun with her friends and unwind."

"That's very understanding of you," Shania acknowledged. "All right," she said, accepting his explanation. "Then if you didn't come to pick up Elena, why did you come?"

He smiled at her. "Isn't it obvious? I came to see Elena's teacher."

She could feel her pulse speeding up even as she warned herself not to jump to any conclusions. This might go to an entirely different place than she wanted it to. He might just be here to thank her for all the extra practice classes she'd held.

"Oh?" she asked warily.

"Yeah. I thought that Ms. Stewart earned a little unwinding time, too."

Maybe this *was* going where she wanted it to, Shania thought. "You know, for such a stoic man, Deputy Tallchief, you're pretty intuitive."

"I'm not always so stoic," Daniel told her meaningfully.

Her smile went all the way up to her eyes, which

seemed as if they were sparkling as she looked up at the deputy.

"Oh, sounds interesting," Shania said, then coaxed, "Tell me more."

"I'd be glad to," he answered, then suggested, "Why don't we continue this conversation over a couple of drinks at Murphy's?"

"What kind of drinks?" she asked him.

He had seen too many of his friends have their lives ruined by alcohol, which was why he had never been tempted to surrender himself to it.

"Mild ones," he told her.

She smiled her approval. "You read my mind."

"Not yet, but I think maybe I'm getting closer," Daniel replied.

She took a breath, trying to get her pulse to go back down to normal. It wasn't working.

"Murphy's sounds good," Shania agreed, "but would you mind if we stopped at the diner first so I could get something to eat? Any alcohol on an empty stomach isn't really a good way to go and I haven't had anything to eat all day. Right now I'm hungry enough to eat half a buffalo."

"I don't think Miss Joan serves buffalo," Daniel deadpanned, "but I'm sure she can come up with something you'll like," he told her as he escorted the teacher out of the classroom. "Tell me, why haven't you eaten anything today?"

Shania flushed a little as she admitted quietly, "Nerves."

He didn't quite understand why Shania would be nervous. "You didn't take the test," Daniel quietly reminded her.

"No, but I watched my students take it and I lived every moment of that agonizing experience with them—

through their eyes, so to speak. I remember what it was like," she told him.

Daniel looked at her, impressed, as they came to the stairwell and started walking down to the first floor. Looking back over his own educational experience, most of the teachers he'd had all seemed relatively indifferent. The only time he remembered seeing any of them look eager was when summer vacation approached. He supposed that in that, they were no different than the students they taught.

Shania wasn't like that.

"You really do care about these kids, don't you?" he marveled.

"Of course I do," she said. To her, it was a given. "I couldn't do this job if I didn't."

Walking down behind her, he laughed softly. "I really wish you'd been my teacher back when I was Elena's age."

She didn't want to get too serious right now. That wasn't part of unwinding to her. "If I was, then going out with you like this would be highly inappropriate."

He laughed as they both came to a stop on the second-floor landing.

"Always the clear-eyed one," he said with a touch of admiration.

And then, because they were alone, he gave in to the urge that had been with him since the last time they had kissed.

Pulling Shania to him, Daniel enfolded her in his arms and brought his mouth down to hers. He felt her yielding to him, her lips parting in a spontaneous, unspoken invitation.

But then they both thought that they heard the sound of footsteps coming from just above them. They sprang apart like two guilty teenagers caught in a moment they shouldn't be having.

They heard the door leading to the exit just above them opening and then closing. The sound of footsteps was gone.

Daniel smiled, relieved. Taking her hand in his, he said, "Okay, let's get you fed before we go to Murphy's so we can toast a job well done."

"Well, this is progress," she said, following him down the last staircase.

In Daniel's estimation, he hadn't said anything out of the ordinary. "What do you mean?"

"You're sweet-talking me."

Shania managed to get the line out before she started to laugh. The sound echoed around them as they went down to the last landing, and then opened the door to enter the ground floor of the school.

The rosy feeling tightened around her as she went with him to his car.

Chapter Sixteen

"You must be happy as hell to have those pesky tests behind you," Miss Joan said to Shania as she personally brought Shania and Daniel's order to them. "Careful, the plates are hot," Miss Joan cautioned even as she transferred those same plates from the tray to their table with her bare hands. Miss Joan had been said to have asbestos fingers. "Now you can concentrate on the really major things—like Halloween and Thanksgiving, which are both just around the corner," she reminded the duo needlessly.

Placing two tall glasses of some sort of misty-looking, fruity drink next to the plates, Miss Joan tucked the empty tray under her arm.

Shania looked at the sparkling, light pink concoction and just had to ask. "Miss Joan, what *is* this?"

"Something I whipped up myself." Miss Joan paused for a beat, then added, "Since Murphy's and I have a deal—they don't serve actual food, other than those peanuts of theirs, and I don't serve any spirits—this little number is what I came up with as a substitute. Enjoy," she told them with a wink, then turned away and went back to the rear of the diner.

Taking the glass in his hand, Daniel studied the contents for a long moment. "Looks harmless enough."

"You could say the same thing about Miss Joan," Shania told him, suppressing a grin.

"Oh, not really," Daniel contradicted with feeling. "There is nothing harmless about that woman. Not if you're paying close attention."

"Well," Shania said, wrapping her fingers around the lower part of the glass and psyching herself up, "I'm game if you are."

Daniel raised his tall glass slightly in the air. "All right, we'll both give this a try on the count of three. One, two, *three*."

Shania and Daniel took tentative sips of their drinks at the same time. They looked at each other in surprise as they had the same reaction.

"Not sure what it is," Daniel pronounced, still trying to place the taste and connect it to something, "but it does taste good."

Shania set her glass down on the table. "It does," she agreed, "but right now my stomach is rumbling. It wants food."

Daniel laughed and gestured toward her plate. "Have at it."

And she did.

Quickly.

Without meaning to, Shania wound up finishing the meal that Miss Joan had placed in front of her in what amounted to record time.

Enjoying his own meal, Daniel watched Shania, surprised as well as amused to see how she managed to polish off the meat loaf and mashed potatoes that Miss Joan had brought out.

"Wow," he finally commented, "you weren't kidding about being hungry."

"I never kid about food," Shania deadpanned. And then she looked at Daniel ruefully and apologized. "I'm sorry, I didn't mean to inhale my food like that. Did I make you uncomfortable?" she asked, embarrassed.

"Uncomfortable?" he questioned. "This is admiration on my face. I don't think I could have consumed anything nearly that fast. You must have set some kind of an eating record just now."

Shania laughed. She supposed she had that coming. "Not exactly something a woman aspires to be known for." A flush of red climbed up her cheeks.

It took Daniel a moment to draw his eyes away. "Well, you can rest easy, Shania. You're known for a lot of things."

"Do I even want to know what?" Shania asked him uneasily.

Daniel was surprised that the teacher was displaying a streak of insecurity. He would have thought that of the two of them, insecurity would have been *his* domain.

"Don't see why not," he told her. "Off the top of my head, I'd say you're known for your patience, your dedication, your ability and willingness to go the extra mile for your students—or anyone else who needs help." His eyes swept over her, taking in all of her. "Not to mention you do all this while managing to be the most beautiful woman around."

"Just what did Miss Joan put in *your* glass?" Shania asked, shaking her head. Flattery always made her uneasy.

"Same thing she put in yours," he countered. "I'm just experiencing a bit of clarity at the moment, that's all," he told her. "Happens to the best of us even when we're trying to keep our nose to the grindstone and our eyes on the ground."

Shania looked at him, confused. "What are you talking about?"

"Stuff I shouldn't be," he answered. He knew he'd already said way too much. The problem was she had a way of drawing words out of him. "It's just that, being around you, I just can't seem to help myself."

"Is that so bad?" she asked him, her voice low and intimate despite the fact that the diner was crowded this time of the day, or more accurately, this time of the evening.

Time, he realized, had seemed to slip away from him. Not just at this moment, he thought, but for a good deal of the time now.

"Now that you're not starving," Daniel said, deliberately looking at her empty plate, "do you want to go to Murphy's?"

Shania turned the tables on him and asked Daniel, "Do you?"

Since she'd asked, he did her the courtesy of answering truthfully. "Not really."

She nodded. "Me, neither."

"I've got it. Why don't we just sit here until we finish our drinks, whatever is in these things," Daniel added.

"You talked me into it," she told him.

"So this is what it's like to use my powers of persuasion for good." Unable to get through the line without cracking a smile, Daniel didn't even bother to try.

Shania cocked her head, studying him, doing her best

to get beyond the compelling planes and angles of his handsome face.

"What's so funny?" she asked him.

He knew he should say *nothing* and then grow serious, but it felt so good to smile, so good to just be with her like this, talking about absolutely nothing and making it sound like they were uncovering the secrets of the universe.

And maybe, Daniel thought as he looked into Shania's expressive face, in a strange sort of way, they actually were.

Shania felt as if his eyes were penetrating right down into her soul, seeing every thought, every impulse she had ever had, even though she knew that was impossible.

"What?" Daniel had to ask when he just couldn't ignore the fact that she was looking at him intently any longer.

She was staring and she blinked, trying to erase the moment.

"Nothing," she told Daniel, taking a breath and squaring her shoulders as she tried to clear her head. "Do you want to go for a walk?"

He suddenly found himself wanting to do anything Shania wanted to do, including walking to the ends of the earth if that was what pleased her.

"Sure," he agreed. "Just let me settle up."

Daniel looked around for the waitress who had originally brought them to their booth before Miss Joan took their order. He reasoned that Miss Joan was busy and he didn't want to give the woman anything more to do than she had already done for them.

Seeing the waitress, he waved and caught the young woman's attention. He had also managed to catch Miss

Joan's attention and, the next moment, it was Miss Joan who was making her way over to their table.

"Something else?" she asked, looking from Shania to the deputy.

"No, nothing else," Daniel answered. "We're both beyond full. I'd just like the check."

Miss Joan's eyes narrowed as they pinned him in his place. "Well, that's too bad, because you're not getting one."

Daniel shook his head, unclear as to why she'd say something like that. "I don't under—"

Miss Joan scowled at him. "Don't make me hit you upside your head, boy. Deputy or not, you can't tell me what to charge someone in my own establishment."

She'd really lost him now. "What?"

"You heard me. Go." She waved a thin hand majestically toward the door. "Both of you. Go while the evening—and you—are both still young."

Shania knew how Daniel felt about getting preferential treatment. He's already made that clear and she was ready to try to back him up.

"But—" Shania began to protest.

"Go!" Miss Joan ordered, every inch the ruler of her small kingdom.

Having known Miss Joan for most of his life, he wasn't about to disobey an order when he heard one.

"You heard her," Daniel said, sliding out from his side and coming around to Shania's. "She gave us a direct order."

Miss Joan smiled at Daniel, nodding in approval. "Well, it took you long enough, son, but you're finally learning."

Satisfied that they were leaving, the diner owner walked away.

"But we can't go without paying," Shania protested to Daniel.

"We can if she tells us to," he reminded her.

Helping Shania with her coat, he took her arm and led her to the door. He opened the door and held it for her as she walked out. And then he quickly crossed the threshold and joined her.

Just like the last time, the temperature had dropped once the sun had gone down. Daniel walked slightly behind her so that the wind was at his back, not hers.

"I'll take you back to the school so you can get your car," he offered.

But Shania shook her head. "That won't be necessary," she told him. When he raised an inquisitive brow, she explained, "My car's back with Mick."

That didn't sound right. Usually, when Mick fixed a vehicle, it stayed fixed. "Is there something else wrong with it?"

She sighed. It felt as if it was always something. But she refused to let that dampen her spirits tonight. She'd had a wonderful time at dinner and she was only going to focus on that.

"The alternator cut out on me," she said, answering his question. "Mick's putting in a new one for me at cost, bless him. Although I am beginning to suspect that my car just wants to have Mick baby her."

Bringing her over to his car, he held open the passenger door for her. "Your car's a her?"

"Aren't they all?" she said, surprised that he was asking the question. Didn't men refer to their cars as *she*? "What do you call your car?"

"Car," Daniel answered simply.

She laughed and the light, sexy sound stirred something within him. Something that, no matter how many times he tried to bury it, just refused to remain quiet. He was beginning to suspect that he was fighting a losing battle.

"Then I'll take you home," he said again because she still hadn't gotten into his car. This time, before she could say anything in protest, he sternly told her, "Don't argue with me."

Shania raised her hands in surrender. "Wouldn't dream of it," she told Daniel and then obligingly got into his vehicle.

Pleased, Daniel nodded his approval. "Good."

After a few minutes, Daniel was bringing his car to a stop right before her house. It might just be his imagination, but it seemed like the drive over here was getting to be shorter and shorter. It sure felt that way.

Shania turned toward him after she'd unbuckled her seat belt.

"Would you like to come in for a little bit?" She realized that she'd made it sound more like coaxing than a request so she quickly added, "Belle will be very glad to see you."

Daniel paused as if he was thinking the matter over—and then he nodded. "Sure. Wouldn't be right to disappoint Belle."

"No, it wouldn't," Shania agreed, feigning solemnity. Getting out, she made her way to her door and unlocked it. Turning the handle, she opened the door and gestured for him to go in first.

The dog almost knocked him down in her enthusiasm the second Shania had opened the door and the German shepherd saw Daniel. Without thinking, Shania reached out in an attempt to keep Daniel upright. The next moment, they both wound up going down.

Circling them and obviously thinking this was a new game they were playing with her, Belle starting licking Daniel's face and then Shania's, alternating between the two of them.

Despite being the object of Belle's friendly assault, Daniel managed to sit up.

"Not shy, is she?" he said, laughing. After scrambling up to his knees, Daniel took Shania's hand to help her up.

"That's one thing she's never been accused of," Shania assured him. "Thank you," she said as he brought her up to her feet.

She automatically began to brush herself off. No matter how many times she vacuumed, there always seemed to be dog hair around.

"Nothing to thank me for," he assured her. "If you weren't trying to keep me upright you wouldn't have wound up on the floor like that."

She shook her head. The man was a born lawyer, always arguing.

"Just take the thank-you," she told him. "And you," she said to Belle, "you start acting like you've had some kind of training."

"Has she?" Daniel asked, curious.

Maybe the word *training* would be going a little too far, implying too much, she thought.

"Well, she's housebroken and we're working out the rest of the kinks as we go along," Shania told him.

The pronoun caught his attention. He'd established that she lived alone, but that didn't mean that her status was "single."

"We?" he asked,

Shania flushed a little as she went toward the kitchen.

"My cousin and me," she explained. "I keep forgetting she's not here anymore. We found Belle together." She smiled at the memory. "Belle became our first student. She was our first project, so to speak."

Daniel found himself smiling again. "And how did that turn out?"

The less said, the better, Shania decided. "Like I said, she's housebroken."

"Well, that's a good start," Daniel answered, humoring her.

"How do you feel about beer?" she asked him as she looked into the refrigerator.

Somehow, looking in, she had hoped for a different result from what she remembered seeing in the refrigerator yesterday. But, sadly, there was no hidden fairy godmother to do the shopping for her expressly based on what she'd bought on previous trips to the grocery store.

Why was there never enough time to get everything done?

Daniel raised his voice so that it would carry to her. "Is that all you have?"

"Other than tap water and a container of milk that's probably seen better days, I'm afraid so," she answered, still holding the refrigerator door open.

"Then beer's fine," he told her.

Opening the last two bottles she had, Shania brought them both over to the coffee table and sat down beside Daniel on the sofa.

Daniel picked up his bottle and lightly clinked its neck against hers.

"To a job well done," he told her. When Shania looked at him quizzically, he explained, "Since we didn't get a drink at Murphy's commemorating the end of studying for the PSATs, I thought I'd toast your accomplishment here with this."

Shania inclined her head slightly, accepting his explanation. And then, whimsically, she reminded him, "There's always the SATs next year."

Daniel groaned, feeling a wave of empathy for his sister. "Let's not focus on that."

"I'm a teacher," Shania told him by way of explaining her mind-set. "I always have to focus on the next test that's coming."

"But you don't have to focus on it at this very moment," Daniel stressed.

"No," she agreed. "Not at this moment."

He liked the way her mouth curved as she smiled. He kept his eyes on her lips as he took a long sip from his bottle. He was still looking at her lips as the beer coursed down his throat, moving through his limbs and filling them with a warmth he could only attribute to anticipation.

Chapter Seventeen

Daniel really wasn't sure exactly how it had all happened.

One minute, he and Shania were discussing how she had really earned a little free time to kick back, at least until Monday morning when her week began all over again. The next minute, the space between them on the sofa had somehow just evaporated to nothingness.

And then he was kissing her.

The moment his lips touched hers, Daniel felt the hunger, the hunger that he'd been doing his very best to bury, suddenly explode to life, going off within him like fireworks that were lined up end to end. Fireworks that were shooting into the air with a breathtaking intensity.

Desires and emotions sprang up inside him, full-bodied and demanding to be recognized. Demanding to be satisfied.

Holding Shania against him, Daniel deepened their

kiss layer by soul-vibrating layer until he felt as if he was all but drowning in her.

The enormity of what was about to happen if they continued on this path suddenly, glaringly occurred to Daniel, seizing his attention.

Stunned and chastising himself, Daniel pulled back, even though he was still holding on to her shoulders.

He saw the surprise in her eyes at the sudden separation.

"Something wrong?" she asked, confused.

Daniel couldn't just walk away from her—even though part of him felt it was the right thing to do. But he couldn't just leave without explaining why.

"I've got an awful lot of baggage, Shania," he told her.

What he didn't say was that he felt it wasn't fair of him to bring that burden into a relationship. Lana had done a number on him, giving him trust issues, and that wasn't fair to Shania.

The simple statement was meant to be an apology as well as an explanation, letting her know why he had stopped kissing her—and why he felt it was best to just leave before things went too far.

But Shania deftly aborted his apology with an equally simple statement. "Everyone does."

Was she telling him that was no reason not to continue? Or was she saying that she understood why he'd stopped?

Or was she telling him that she had her demons too and that those demons—his and hers—shouldn't be allowed to stand in the way of their search for happiness?

He didn't know.

The only thing that he did know was that he wanted Shania, wanted her with a fierce, piercing desire that stunned him and rendered him unable to do anything else or think of anything—except losing himself in her.

Still, Daniel wanted to be totally fair to Shania, to give her the opportunity to change her mind at the last moment and just walk away.

"Are you sure?" he asked her, his eyes searching her face for his answer.

Daniel watched in fascination as the smile blossomed on her face.

"You know," she told him, drawing closer again, "for a man of few words, I think you have just used up your allotment for the rest of the month." She paused, letting the words sink in. "So just stop talking and kiss me before I start to think that maybe you've suddenly thought better of the whole thing."

That really surprised him. Did she actually think he thought that? How?

"There is no 'better' than this," he told her with such sincerity, Shania could feel the corners of her eyes moistening.

"Then get back to it, Deputy Tallchief," she "ordered," opening her arms to him in a blatant invitation.

The last of his good intentions were completely dissolved and he had absolutely no strength to keep her—or his own desires—at bay any longer. Pulling Shania to him, Daniel's lips covered hers and he began kissing Shania with such fervor that there was no time to breathe, to reconsider what was happening or to once more attempt to call a stop to what was now so obviously inevitable.

Her head was spinning as she felt him kiss her over and over, each kiss growing in magnitude and scope, more powerful than the one that had come before it. She could feel that there was a fire in his veins, a fire that not only consumed him, but had managed to melt away any of her own resistance, however minor that resistance was. That resistance was completely wiped out before it even had a chance to take form.

Everywhere he kissed her, on her face, on her neck, on her throat, that part instantly joined the symphony of aroused sensations, responding to Daniel and fueling her growing desire for the ultimate fulfillment.

His lips continued gaining more ground, moving ever onward until Shania felt as if all of her had been conquered. She had surrendered to him without even attempting to offer so much as the smallest iota of resistance.

Why would she? Shania now knew that this was where it had all been going since the first moment that they had met one another.

When Daniel suddenly stopped again, her head felt as if it was swirling. That made it difficult for Shania to pull herself together in order to form a coherent thought.

Breathing heavily, she blinked and did her best to focus on him, waiting for Daniel to explain why he had stopped this time.

"We've got an audience," he told her in a low voice, nodding toward Belle.

Turning her head, Shania saw the soft brown eyes that was watching their every move. At any moment, Belle might just push her way between them and easily ruin everything.

Straightening up, Shania said, "Belle, sit," in an authoritative voice.

Daniel was impressed to see that the German shepherd complied, plopping her rear down on the floor, and then she went on to spread her body out like a bearskin rug.

The next moment, Daniel felt Shania get up. His heart

sank as he thought that the interlude was over. But then she was taking his hand.

"Come with me," she whispered.

It never occurred to him to ask where—he just went with her, following wherever she was leading.

Shania led him to her bedroom.

As he continued to watch, Shania closed the door behind them, saying, "So Belle doesn't decide to come and investigate."

His smile was warm as he murmured, "Works for me." Taking her back into his arms, he asked, "Now, where were we?"

Shania rose on her toes, her lips inches from his. "I think if you look very closely, you might just see where you left your place marker."

Daniel grinned just before his lips covered hers again, saying, "You're right. There it is."

And then there was no more need for words, nor room for any because he was kissing her again, picking up just where he had left off. He did so with the same amount of fire and verve he'd built up to just before the feel of small, intense eyes watching him had caused him to stop.

It felt as if any restraints, any of the barriers that might have been there, had all disappeared. There were no more obstacles, no more impedance to get in their way.

When Daniel began kissing her again, it felt as if this was what he knew had been waiting for him all along. He tasted not just surrender in Shania's kiss, but destiny, as well.

His destiny.

Because this wasn't about conquest—it was about finally finding his other half, the woman he had been meant to be with all along.

Don't get ahead of yourself, the voice in his head whispered.

The specter of fear hovered over him in the distance, a ghostly reminder that this wasn't the first time that he had felt that he'd found the right woman, found the one he was meant to be with.

But he'd been a naive kid then. Since that time, he had seen disappointment up close and personal, knew firsthand what heartbreak felt like. Had seen it in the face of the woman he'd believed loved him.

It could happen again, that specter haunting him now whispered. *This one could desert you just the way Lana did.*

Daniel shut out the voice, refusing to allow it back in his head.

He felt as if he was completely drunk on desire. He could practically feel it pulsing in his veins, urging him to continue, to make love with this woman and take what she was offering. And if disappointment was waiting for him in the wings, he'd face it later. Right now, this need he had consumed him.

Daniel began to undress her, drawing away Shania's clothes from her body. He held the urgency that throbbed in his veins in check to the best of his ability so that he could prolong the process, making it last.

Making them both just that much more excited about the end of the journey that waited for them.

As he went on undressing her, Daniel felt her hands on his body, opening up buttons on his shirt, pulling the material off his shoulders. He caught his breath as she pressed her lips against the skin that was revealed beneath.

Slowly she wove a tapestry of warm kisses along the space that was uncovered, branding him.

His breath caught in his throat, then began to come faster until he felt his heart hammering in his chest so much, it almost made him dizzy.

Each movement she made, he matched it, then made one of his own which she in turn mirrored. The game continued like this until there was nothing left to remove, no place left to anoint. They were on her queen-size bed now, free of their clothing, free of any sort of restraints and inhibitions. And they were both on fire.

Daniel worked his way slowly along her body one last time. He began at her throat and moved by small increments along her body as if he was attempting to commit it to memory by touch and by taste. As he skimmed his tongue along her belly, he could feel it quivering beneath him, the invitation crystal clear.

Traveling back up slowly along her damp, palpitating body, he progressed closer by just fractions of an inch until he was almost directly above her.

Daniel looked into her eyes, holding them captive with his own.

Every breath she took he could feel along his own torso. It only fueled his own hunger.

Holding Shania's arms above her head, Daniel slowly threaded his fingers through hers, joining them together before he moved his body the last few increments of an inch closer to hers.

Unable to hold himself in check any longer, Daniel moved his knee between her legs, parting them.

And then he entered her, not quickly but with slow, deliberate determination.

He heard her draw in her breath, felt her heart beating harder a second before he began to move within her.

The dance began slowly, gently, as if he was afraid of disturbing the rhythm that they had just discovered. But when Shania began to echo his movements, then increase them on her own, he joined her, moving with enthusiasm and going faster and faster until they were both racing toward the end that they knew was waiting for them.

Daniel felt her digging her fingertips into his shoulders, felt Shania arching her back as she emulated him thrust for thrust. He could feel the heat coming from her body as they were now racing toward the top of the summit.

Reaching it together, they clung to one another as they felt the wave of fulfillment sweep over both of them, tossing their bodies down the steep incline.

They held on to one another until the very end. And longer.

The sound of labored breathing filled the room that was otherwise nestled in darkness. And they held on to each other, their arms wrapped around one another, until the feeling of ethereal well-being slowly began to recede and fade.

When Daniel was finally able to gather himself together, he turned toward the woman whose body he'd just enjoyed and worshipped and quietly asked, "I didn't hurt you, did I?"

He felt her smile against his shoulder and could feel a longing begin to bud within him again, even though he'd honestly felt that it wouldn't be possible. By all rights, he should have been too exhausted to breathe, much less go another round with her that even remotely approximated what they had just done.

And yet there it was. Desire. Struggling to grow and take over.

"I believe the expression is I'm feeling no pain," she told him with a smile that made her eyes sparkle.

"That usually refers to someone being drunk," he told her.

"Maybe I am," she allowed. "Drunk on a feeling," she added.

"So I didn't hurt you?" Daniel asked. He was worried now that maybe he'd gotten too carried away, been too focused on his own pleasure and not enough on what he was doing to her.

She turned her face toward him. "No, you didn't hurt me. You were miles away from hurting me, Daniel," she assured him. Then, suppressing the smile that was trying so hard to surface, she asked, "Did I hurt you?"

The dark hid her face from him and he didn't see the smile that was there, so he addressed her question as if she'd actually asked him the question seriously.

"No, you didn't."

And then, when he heard the soft laugh, he knew she was putting him on. Daniel responded by pushing her onto her back and looming over her.

"You're slender. You couldn't have hurt me unless you had an anvil strapped to your waist."

"That would have made what we just did almost impossible," she told him. "Picture it," she urged, amused.

The glimmer of moonlight pushing its way into her room allowed him to see the wide grin on her face.

"I have a feeling that we would have managed somehow," he told her.

She didn't even try to hide her laugh this time. "I think we would have, too." She threaded her arms around Daniel's neck, arching her back so that her body was once again close to being sealed to his. "Interested in an encore?"

His mouth curved as he looked at her. "You're giving me a lot of credit."

"I don't think you're giving yourself enough," she countered.

Daniel could feel himself wanting her all over again with an urgency that was impossible to ignore. "I guess we'll just have to see who's right."

She smiled up into his face. "I guess so."

And then the words between them faded away as the dance that they had already shared once now began all over again.

Chapter Eighteen

"So where were you?"

Daniel whirled around, startled to hear his sister's voice as he passed through the living room. He had let himself into the house quietly even though he had expected Elena to be in her bed, asleep at this hour. The one thing he hadn't expected was to be the subject of scrutiny as he entered his own house.

Elena had apparently been waiting for him on the sofa. Closing the TV monitor, she was on her feet and circling him like an old-fashioned version of an interrogator closing in on her subject.

"You were off work today and as far as I know, Forever isn't in the middle of some crime wave, which means that the sheriff wouldn't have suddenly pressed you into service. And that, in turn," his sister concluded, "means you should have been home by now. You weren't." Elena now looked up at her brother's face and repeated her question. "So where were you?"

He didn't care to have the tables turned on him this way. "Out."

"Out," Elena echoed, enjoying herself as she took on the role that her brother normally played with her. "Out where?"

Daniel waved away her question. "That doesn't matter. I thought you'd be home, asleep—or taking advantage of the occasion and celebrating with your friends."

"I was celebrating," she confirmed, never taking her eyes off Daniel.

"And you're back this soon?" he questioned.

The Elena he remembered from not that long ago would still be out there. That she wasn't was something to be grateful for—and he was, but at the same time he wasn't all that happy about her delving into his life like this.

"It's late," Elena said matter-of-factly. "And besides, someone once told me that I shouldn't get carried away celebrating too hard." Concluding her story, she pulled her lips back in a patient smile and, inclining her head, told him, "Your turn."

Daniel frowned at her. "I am not accountable to you, Elena. I'm the adult here, remember?"

But his sister was not about to back off. "Someone once told me that age had nothing to do with it. Family is always accountable to family."

She was right, but that didn't help his frustration level at the moment. "Why is it that you remember these things when it's to your advantage to remember?"

Amused, Elena's grin grew wider. "I'm a fast learner," she told him. And then she looked at him with a knowing expression and asked, "Were you out with Ms. Stewart?"

Her unexpected question caught Daniel completely off guard. Only his years of keeping his thoughts and emotions hidden saved him from giving everything away.

"Why would you even ask that?" he asked.

"Oh, *please*," Elena cried, rolling her eyes. At least *that* was something he was familiar with, Daniel thought. But definitely not happy about. "Everyone knows you two are a couple waiting to happen."

"You sound like Miss Joan's grooming you to be her understudy," he commented, completely bypassing his sister's question.

And then Elena said the second thing that night that completely threw him for a loop.

"Would that be so bad?" she asked him. "I mean, everyone looks up to Miss Joan and she seems to have her finger on the pulse of just about everyone and everything in and around Forever." Because Daniel appeared so stunned, she pounced on her initial question. "Okay, stop stalling, Deputy Sheriff Big Brother. Where were you?"

His eyes met hers. "I'd rather talk about you."

Elena didn't give an inch. "And I want to know where you were." Enjoying this game, she couldn't help but laugh.

He took that as an indication that she was backing off. Daniel softened, sitting down for a moment and nodding at the spot next to him. Elena took the hint and sat down. "How was the test?"

Elena shrugged and then made herself more comfortable on the sofa. "It was okay—thanks to Ms. Stewart." And then she doubled back to her first question. "So, am I right?"

Daniel could only look at her, blindsided by her sudden about-face. "What?"

Elena sighed dramatically as if he was using up her dwindling supply of patience. Slowly enunciating each word, she asked, "Were you out with Ms. Stewart?"

He had just about had it with her questions. This wasn't a topic he was prepared to discuss yet, especially not with his little sister. Certainly not until he knew how Shania felt about their future, or if they even *had* a future.

"Elena—"

"'Cause it's all right with me if you were," Elena assured him brightly.

That managed to momentarily stop Daniel in his tracks. He hadn't expected her to say that. "Oh?"

Elena's smile went from ear to ear. She was convinced that her teacher was good for Daniel, that Ms. Stewart could make him be a happier person. "Yes."

"And why's that?" Daniel asked, turning to face his sister on the sofa. He couldn't remember talking like this with Elena or being this at ease with her, not for a long, long time.

Too long.

Elena didn't even have to pause to think. "Well, for one thing, because she's made you into a nicer person. You're not as grumpy as you've been—at least until just now," she amended.

"Grumpy?" Daniel questioned, then protested, "I haven't been grumpy."

"Yes, you have," Elena insisted, amazed that he could actually deny it. "You've been acting like you had the weight of the world on your shoulders." Until just a little while ago, that would have made her feel guilty. But not anymore. "I know it can't just be me," she told him, "because I don't weigh that much, so it's got to be something else, too. And Ms. Stewart's shown you how to juggle that weight and be a nice guy about it. Like you used to be," she emphasized.

"I could say the same thing about you," Daniel told his sister pointedly.

He watched for her reaction, half expecting Elena's

back to go up. But instead, his sister nodded her head, a small smile playing on her lips.

"Yeah, I guess you could at that," she agreed. "That's Ms. Stewart's doing, too," she admitted. "She worked with me, showed me that I didn't have to turn my back on everything I'd been before in order to be able to grow as a person."

"Is that what you've been doing?" he questioned, trying not to look as if her take on her own previous actions amused him. "Growing?"

"Yes, that's what I've been doing," she concluded with quiet pride and a self-assurance that he hadn't heard before.

Something inside Daniel softened as he realized that she was right. And why she was right. Because the same woman who had touched his life had touched Elena's life, too.

"Yes, you have," he agreed.

Elena raised her chin. "So what are you going to do about it?"

His dark brows drew together in confusion. "All right, you just lost me."

Elena was quick to jump in while her brother was still pliable. "Well, we've just both agreed that we've become the better versions of ourselves that we've always wanted to be. The one thing that's changed in our lives is that we've both spent time with Ms. Stewart, being shown the error of our old ways."

She took a breath, her eyes never leaving his face. "So what are you going to do about keeping Ms. Stewart in our lives? In *your* life?" Elena deliberately specified, watching her brother intently.

"Are you telling me to keep seeing her?" Daniel asked.

Elena sighed deeply and once again rolled her eyes. "I'm telling you to do more than that. I'm telling you not to miss the boat. I'm telling you to get the molasses out of your veins, Big Brother."

"And...?" he asked, still certain that his sister couldn't possibly be saying what he thought she was saying.

Exasperated, she asked him, "Do you really need cue cards?"

He made his mind up to deny the existence of anything between himself and Shania. The disappointment if this fell through would be too devastating for both of them. He'd lived through it once. He didn't want Elena going through it with him if this didn't work out.

"I do when it comes to understanding what you're trying to tell me."

In truth, Daniel was afraid to jump to the conclusion that he *wanted* to jump to because once he did... What if the conclusion he wanted with all his heart turned out to be the wrong one? Continuing the fledgling relationship with Shania would definitely be difficult and challenging.

Moreover, if Elena thought he had romance on his mind with the end result being asking Shania to marry him, and his sister *didn't* want him to, he'd find himself facing a huge dilemma.

Elena's next words were prefaced by another very deep sigh.

"Ask the woman to marry you before one of the other unattached men around here beats you to the punch," she told her brother in no uncertain terms.

Just what did it take to light a fire under him? she silently wondered.

Daniel could only stare at his sister. "You're serious."

"Yes, I am," she willingly admitted. "Aren't you?"

All Daniel could tell Elena was that, "It's complicated."

"Complicated is what people say when they get cold

feet or don't have the courage to face up to something they should," she told him.

His eyes darkened. "Stand down, Ellie."

She ignored what was obviously an order. "Do you love her?"

The last of his patience evaporated. "Okay, Ellie, game time is over," he told her, getting up. "It's late. Go to bed."

"It's a simple question," she told her brother. "Do you love her or don't you?"

He wasn't up to this right now. "If you won't go to bed, I will," he announced, striding toward the rear of the house.

Elena was on her feet, moving quickly and getting directly in front of him.

"Is that a yes?" she pressed.

He looked down into Elena's face, trying to fathom what was going on behind those expressive eyes of hers. "*Why* do you need to know so badly?"

"Because I do," she answered flatly. "Because things are finally coming together in my life and Ms. Stewart's the underlying reason behind it all—for both of us. Now, do you?" she asked, coming back to her question. Her eyes dared her brother to say no.

He debated not saying anything, or lying, and found that he couldn't. Not to his sister.

"Yes," he finally said. "And it's going no further than right here, understand?" he demanded, putting his sister on notice.

He could have sworn that her eyes were gleaming. But her voice was unusually solemn as she repeated, "Understand."

He knew she didn't really understand. Taking hold of Ellie's shoulders, he held her in place.

"Listen to me, Ellie. I don't want you doing anything, saying anything, *thinking* anything that will make Ms.

Stewart suddenly come to her senses and run for her life. *Do I make myself clear?*" he asked, again enunciating each word.

Instead of saying what he wanted to hear, she began to protest. "But—"

He put his hand up to silence her. She stopped talking. "Not a word, Ellie," he warned seriously. "I want you to give me your word."

His sister tried again. "But—"

"Not a word," he repeated, emphasizing each word. "I'm glad you like her and that she's had such a positive influence in your life, but I want to handle this in my own way, at my own pace. In my own time."

She knew that she couldn't change his mind, not when his cadence was this slow, this deliberate. But she still had to tell him what was on her mind.

"I think you're making a mistake," she told him.

"You're entitled to think anything you want," Daniel said. "As long as you remember to keep it to yourself. Understood?" he emphasized again. "Because if you don't, if you decide that you're going to try to butt in like some kind of misguided teenaged Cupid, I swear I'll ground you until you're one hundred and three. Understand?"

Ellie sighed again, frustrated. "I understand."

"Good," he pronounced. "Now I'm going to bed," he told her, once again heading toward the back of the house. "It's been a long day."

Elena was not about to dispute that. "I'll bet it has."

He could hear the grin in his sister's voice even without looking at her.

He just kept going.

"You really are growing up way too fast," Daniel murmured to himself.

He hadn't meant for Elena to overhear, but she had.

"Nothing you can do about that, Big Brother," she responded with an even bigger grin.

"You are my last hope, Miss Joan," Elena said with sincerity.

It was Monday. Though she had wanted to talk to the woman at the crack of dawn, she'd forced herself to wait until school was over. The moment it was, she had made a beeline for the diner, bringing her problem to the only person she knew who could find a way to work through the obstacle that was her brother.

Elena crossed to Miss Joan, asking the woman for a private audience, so to speak. Miss Joan compromised by moving her to the far end of the counter, away from the other customers.

She listened to Elena's story, taking it all in without comment.

Until now.

"What makes you think I can do anything about that stubborn brother of yours?" Miss Joan asked. "If his mind's made up, I can't make it change."

Elena didn't believe that for a second. "Miss Joan, you could make it rain in the middle of a record dry spell in the desert if you wanted to."

Miss Joan's expression remained unchanged. Only her sharp eyes narrowed. "You think flattery's going to turn my head, young lady?"

"No, ma'am," Elena replied solemnly. "I'm just telling you what I believe is true." She took a breath and then forged on. "Everybody knows that you can do anything you put your mind to."

"I can't hog-tie them and make them sit across from each other until your brother proposes," Miss Joan said, sensing that was where this whole plan of Elena's was going.

"You wouldn't need to hog-tie them," Elena promised. "They just need a little push, that's all." She leaned over the counter, her voice lowering as she said, "I can't say anything to Ms. Stewart because Danny made me promise not to."

Miss Joan knew what was coming. "But you didn't promise that I wouldn't."

Elena smiled, happy that Miss Joan understood. "No, I didn't."

"Don't give me that innocent look, young lady," Miss Joan said sharply. "I can see right through you."

Her tone didn't intimidate Elena. "I know. That's why I'm here."

Miss Joan laughed. It was a sound that wasn't heard very frequently. Elena smiled in response, knowing that she had gotten to the woman and that everything was going to be resolved just the way she hoped. Perhaps it would take a while. She knew Miss Joan couldn't be rushed. But she also knew that Miss Joan got results the way that no one else around Forever ever could. And that was good enough for her.

"Go home, little girl. I've got to think about this," Miss Joan told her.

"Yes, ma'am." Elena slid off the stool she was sitting on. "And thank you."

Miss Joan scowled. "There's nothing to thank me for yet."

Elena just smiled back. "But there will be," she replied. "I know that there will be."

Miss Joan said nothing. She had already turned away and was topping off a customer's coffee.

And thinking.

Chapter Nineteen

When he was younger and dealing with something that weighed heavily on his mind, Daniel would take his horse, ride out as far as he could and just lose himself in his surroundings. He'd ride until whatever was bothering him wasn't there anymore. Until all those oppressive thoughts just evaporated.

But he couldn't do that anymore. He had responsibilities. There was his sister, who still depended on him for all the essentials, and his job, which required him to show up every day. Taking off at the spur of the moment just was not an option. Facing up to whatever was out there with his name stamped on it was now what was called for.

So when he discovered that Elena was hell-bent on butting into his life and that his sister had been seen going in to talk to Miss Joan when she should have been on her way home from school, Daniel got the distinct feeling in his gut that he had to get ahead of whatever disaster might result from all this interference and be waiting to take him down.

This was ultimately the reason why, after having kept his distance from Shania for several days, he gathered up his courage and sought her out.

He went to see her late in the day after his shift was over.

Working on next week's lesson plan, Shania didn't hear the doorbell when it first rang. It was Belle, her furry bodyguard, that alerted her to someone being at her door.

Taking hold of the German shepherd's collar, she held on to it as she went to the door and opened it a crack.

When she saw Daniel standing on her doorstep, her first reaction was a flash of happiness. Her next reaction was an equal flash of annoyance, the latter because he had stayed away from her for several days without so much as a word of acknowledgment about their time together.

Torn, she decided to opt for neither and fell back on acting blasé and indifferent.

Belle was pulling, eager to express her joyful reaction over seeing Daniel, but Shania held fast.

"Can I come in?" Daniel asked, still standing on the other side of the threshold.

Shania shrugged, then opened the front door all the way, allowing him to come in.

"Deputy Tallchief, what can I do for you?" she asked him formally.

Daniel heard the touch of iciness in her voice and instantly felt guilty about his part in putting that iciness there.

"How are you doing?" he asked, feeling incredibly awkward.

If possible, her voice grew even cooler. "Well, and you?"

They might as well have been two total strangers who knew one another by sight but nothing more.

Belle was doing her part in attempting to breach that gap by jumping up at Daniel. He petted the dog, but his attention was on Shania.

"I'm all right," he finally answered. The next moment, he shook his head. "No, that's a lie. I'm not."

Shania held herself in check, refusing to let her feelings get the better of her. "I'm sorry to hear that. Maybe you should drop by the medical clinic. I'm sure they'd make room in their schedule to see you, seeing as how you're part of the sheriff's department."

But he shook his head. "It's not that kind of 'not right,'" Daniel answered, sensing that she had to already know that.

Shania abruptly turned on her heel and walked into her living room, and then turned around to look at him. "Oh? Then what kind of 'not right' is it?"

Daniel indicated the sofa, nodding toward it. "Can I sit?"

Shania shrugged again, the picture of indifference. "You can do whatever you want."

Daniel still felt like he was the target of frostbite. He took a stab at explaining what was behind his behavior, even though that sort of thing wasn't his long suit. He was far better at keeping silent than talking.

"Shania, you have to understand that I didn't want you thinking that I was moving too fast," he said.

"Too fast?" she repeated, and for the first time he saw just a flicker of amusement on her lips. "Tallchief, there were schools of *snails* that left you in the dust."

He tried again, rephrasing what he'd just said. "I didn't want to crowd you. I wanted to give you room to breathe."

"You left enough room for an entire major city to breathe," she said, the flicker of amusement gone again. Her hurt feelings ran deeper than she'd realized. "Did you ever stop to think that by giving me this much 'room,' you made me think that you were regretting—deeply regretting—what happened between us?"

"Regretting it?" he repeated, saying the words as if he had absolutely no understanding of what they meant.

"Yes, regretting it," Shania emphasized. "As in trying to pretend it never happened, or at least wishing it hadn't," she concluded, feeling more hurt with each syllable she uttered.

Daniel stared at her in disbelief, momentarily speechless. "That would have made me pretty stupid," he told Shania flatly.

She laughed shortly. "Well, if you're waiting for me to argue with you about that, I'm afraid you're out of luck. Whatever you might feel about that night, I don't regret any of it." She could feel tears forming and she blinked hard to keep them from falling. "I just regret how you feel."

"How I feel?" Daniel questioned, lost again.

"Yes, how you feel." She said the words with seething emphasis, struggling to keep back her hurt and her anger. "Embarrassed, ashamed, I don't know—"

"How about grateful," he interjected, raising his voice so she could hear him.

The thoughts forming in her head came to a dead stop at that single word. "How's that again?" she asked in confusion.

"Grateful," he repeated, his voice low but all the more

compelling. "I feel grateful that it happened. Very grateful."

She didn't believe him. He was just trying to snow her. "Well, if that's supposedly true, why did you go into hiding?"

He told her part of the reason, hoping that was enough. "Because I didn't want you to feel that I was pressuring you into something. Elena gave me the third degree when I got home that night, acting more like an interrogator than I ever did when she got home late.

"And then a couple of days later, someone happened to mention that she was seen talking to Miss Joan. Miss Joan, who'd been the one who'd tried to play matchmaker with us to begin with," he pointed out. He searched Shania's face, trying to see if she understood what he was telling her. "I didn't want either one of them making you feel as if you were outnumbered and being forced to, well, be *receptive* to the idea of 'us.'"

"But I *am* receptive," Shania insisted. She put her hands on her hips. "Did you ever stop to think that maybe you should just come here and talk to me—the way you are right now?"

"In my mind that would have just been part of crowding you," he explained.

"Or making me feel as if you were interested in continuing what you'd started," she said with feeling. "Instead of regretting it with every breath you took."

"I never not regretted anything more," Daniel protested.

Shania winced despite herself. "I'm a physics teacher and I teach math on occasion. I'm not an English teacher, but you've *got* to know that sentence is so poorly worded it hurts." She paused for a moment before saying, "But I'll take it." A grin curved her mouth.

And then she looked at Daniel's face and saw something more. Something he wasn't telling her. Something that was most likely at the bottom of all this.

"What else?" Shania asked.

His eyebrows drew together as he looked at her. "I don't know what you—"

Shania didn't give him a chance to finish or make denials. "The other night, when you said you had 'baggage' and I said everyone does, it's about that, isn't it?" she asked him. "About your 'baggage.'"

When he made no comment, she knew she had guessed right. Now all she needed was for him to trust her enough to tell her just what that baggage he was carrying around was.

"Why don't you unpack it so we can get it out of the way?" Shania told him, watching Daniel intently, looking for a sign that she was getting through to him. "Unless you don't want to talk about it."

He didn't. But again, that wasn't an option here, not now.

Daniel looked at the woman he had made love with for a long moment and knew that if he kept this to himself, he'd lose her. That exactly what he was afraid of happening *would* happen—and that he would be instrumental in doing it himself.

Taking a deep breath, he began to talk.

"You are not the first woman that I've been in love with."

Shania stared at him. He hadn't realized what he'd just said. For him, this was just part of the story. To her, it *was* the story.

But she kept silent because she knew that this—whatever *this* was—had to come out and if she stopped him now, it might just abort itself before it had a chance to see the light of day.

"Go on," she urged quietly.

"There was this girl, Lana." His face softened as he said the woman's name. "She meant everything to me. We were going to get married and move out West to start a brand-new life together. We had everything all figured out." There was a cold cynicism in his voice that she had never heard before, as if he was mocking himself and the idealist kid he had once been. "And then my parents died and I had to leave school to take care of Elena."

He shrugged. "That didn't fit in with the plan that Lana had for us. She put up with the situation for a little while, then told me that I had to choose. It was either her and our new life, or my kid sister and life in Forever. I was angry that she was doing this to me at a time when I was still reeling from my parents' death and I picked Elena."

He looked at her and she could read what was in his eyes. "I thought she'd change her mind, you know, reconsider. But she packed up her things and was gone before I even knew what was happening. It was like my whole world collapsed twice. I swore I'd never put myself in that kind of a position again."

"And then you fell in love with me," Shania said. When he looked at her sharply, she held her hands up. "Hey, you're the one who said I wasn't the first one you ever fell in love with—which means that you *did* fall in love with me. Or was that just something you said to move the story along?"

He frowned, annoyed with himself for not monitoring his words more carefully. "No," he admitted quietly, "I meant it."

She read between the lines—and things began to fall together.

"And now you're afraid I'll become another Lana and just walk out on you whenever you're facing another crisis." She peered into his face. "Did I get it right, Daniel?"

"Yeah," he agreed reluctantly.

She squared her shoulders just a little. "You do realize that's really insulting, don't you?"

He looked at her in surprise. "I—"

"Because it is," she informed him. "All women are not alike and I'd like to think that something inside of you knows that." Her voice grew very still as she informed him, "I'm not accustomed to sleeping with my students' parents or guardians, nor do I have a passing acquaintance with one-night stands. Never had one, never will," she declared with finality. "The only all-nighter I ever pulled was studying for this one Quantum Physics final."

He wanted to apologize for insulting her. "Shania—"

"I'm not finished," she told him. "Now, if you're trying to put up barriers because you don't want to be stuck with me, just say so and you can consider yourself unstuck. Otherwise—"

Taking advantage of the fact that she paused to take in a breath, he asked Shania, "Do you always talk this much?"

She flushed. "Only when I'm very afraid that something that means a great deal to me is about to be forever lost the second I stop talking," she told him.

"I guess then I'll risk getting into this relationship with you," Daniel said.

She looked at him as if she was scrutinizing him. "Haven't you been listening? There is no risk, Deputy Tallchief," she said. "There's only me, forever and always."

Daniel smiled as he took her into his arms. Heaven help him, he believed her. "I can handle that."

"Good answer," she told him, smiling. "And for the record, Deputy, I do love you. More than I ever thought possible."

But he wasn't finished asking questions yet. "How about Elena?" he asked. "We're a package deal."

If he thought that was a deal-breaker, he was wrong, Shania thought with a smile. "Even better."

"Yes, it is," he agreed just before he brought his mouth down to hers and picked up where they had left off the other night.

Epilogue

"You know what would make it feel more like Christmas?" Shania asked out of the blue.

She had taken a rare Saturday off from working on her lesson plans and had devoted the entirety of it to getting some heavy-duty Christmas decorating done with Daniel and his sister.

Daniel thought back to that morning, when he and Shania, along with a number of other people in Forever, had gotten involved in Miss Joan's annual tradition of scouting for and bringing back the town Christmas tree. Putting up the thirty-foot tree in the town square took a good part of the day. Decorating it was usually a three-day affair.

"You mean more than helping bring in that giant tree for Miss Joan, starting to decorate that humongous thing and then letting you talk me into hauling another oversize specimen into my own house?" He looked accusingly at the tree. "The one we're presently decorating?" Daniel asked.

The hour was getting late now and she could see that Daniel was just about decorated out.

"This is not an oversize specimen," Shania protested. She was on a ladder, doing her best to hang decorations on the uppermost branches.

"It's a lot bigger than the trees I usually bring in for the occasion," Daniel countered.

Shania gave him a look. "What you were proposing to bring in wasn't a tree, it was a malnourished twig and it certainly didn't deserve to be called a Christmas tree." She hung up another multicolored ball that caught the light and flashed it around the room. "And if you remember, Elena agreed with me."

That didn't carry any weight in his opinion. "You brainwashed her into agreeing with you."

She wasn't about to concede. "I did not. Your sister has free will. She could have disagreed." Stretching, she hung up another decoration.

"Not likely," Daniel contradicted. "You're her hero. She would have been far more apt to disagree with my choice than yours."

"That's because my choice was better," Shania informed him with what he viewed as a triumphant nod of her head.

Daniel pretended to sigh. "Have it your way."

Her eyes smiled first before the rest of her caught up. "Thanks, I will."

He laughed softly and shook his head. "I never doubted it," he said. Daniel scanned the room, as if suddenly aware that they were alone. "Looks like we lost our helper."

"You just noticed?" Shania marveled, amazed as she went up another step, holding on to the ladder with one hand as she reached up for a higher branch with the other. "I think she ducked out on us and went to bed about forty-five minutes ago." Shania smiled at him fondly. "Not very observant, are you?"

He shrugged, picking up a couple more decorations himself and hanging them on the lower branches. "I save that for work."

She was focusing on hooking a decoration on a branch that was almost out of reach. "I see."

Daniel paused to look up at her. The small box in his back pocket felt as if it was pressing against his skin. "And you."

Shania stopped hanging decorations and looked down at him, replaying his last words. "Why me?"

He knew he had to answer her, but his tongue suddenly felt leaden. "I'm just trying to gauge where we are," he finally said.

"For the record, we're in your living room, creating a proper-looking Christmas tree," she answered, turning her attention back to what she was doing.

It was time, he told himself. "That's not what I meant."

"What did you mean?" Shania asked casually as she hung up the last of the decorations she'd brought up with her. Needing another handful, she climbed down again and went to the worn box that Daniel used to house the tree decorations.

"Where *we* are," he repeated, his eyes on hers as he tried to get his point across without having to spell it out for her.

She looked at Daniel over her shoulder, scrutinizing him. Was something up, or was she reading too much into his words?

"Why is that so important?" she asked.

He put his hand on her arm, stopping her as she started climbing back up on the ladder with a fresh supply of decorations.

"Could you hold still for a minute?" he asked her.

"Daniel, I'd like to get this tree all decorated before next Christmas, so now isn't the time for me to take a break. Besides—" she nodded at the tree "—I'm almost done."

"Shania, Christmas isn't for another three weeks," he pointed out. "What's the hurry?"

"So you and Elena can enjoy the fruits of all this labor longer," she answered matter-of-factly.

He looked at her as if her words had caused him to have a sudden revelation.

"So, doing something sooner allows you to enjoy something longer?" he asked, as if trying to get something straight in his mind.

"In most cases. Certainly in this case." She noticed he was still holding on to her arm. "So could you let go of my arm and let me get back to finishing up the tree?"

Instead of letting her arm go, he continued holding it. "In a minute," he answered. "If I don't do this now, I just might lose my nerve."

She had no idea what he was talking about and why he was still holding on to her. Was he anticipating that she was going to bolt for some reason?

"Lose your nerve about what?" she asked him. "I think it's only fair to warn you that I'm fading fast here and if I don't finish this tree in the next few minutes, it's going to have to wait until tomorrow."

"Would that be such a bad thing?"

Maybe he still had a ways to go before understanding her, Shania thought.

"Perhaps not for someone else," Shania allowed. "But I don't like to leave something only half done."

"Neither do I," Daniel agreed.

"Then you understand how I feel," she said, never taking her eyes off his face. He looked uneasy, she thought. Why?

"I hope so," he told her.

His uneasiness seemed to spread to her. "Are we talking about the same thing, Tallchief?"

"Probably not." Before she could ask him anything else, he reached into his back pocket, closed his hand around the small box and pulled it out. "I'm talking about this."

Shania stared at the box, totally speechless and afraid to allow herself to even *think* that it might be what it looked like.

Daniel used his thumb to flip the lid back, exposing a small, perfect-looking pear-shaped diamond engagement ring. He'd used nearly half the money he had managed to save in the past couple of years to buy it.

"I'm dying here," Daniel finally said, unable to take her silence. "*Say* something."

She was mesmerized by the way the diamond gleamed, creating rainbows and flashing them on the wall. "It's beautiful."

That wasn't exactly what he was hoping to hear. "Say something else."

She raised her eyes to his. "Is that for me?"

"Getting warmer," he told her. Taking the ring out of its box, he slipped it onto her ring finger. "It fits," he said, happy that he had managed to correctly guess her size.

She could have gone on watching the way the light played off the ring for hours, but she raised her head to look up at Daniel.

"I think you're supposed to ask me something really important now," she told Daniel.

And then, amid the nerves that were dancing through him and his fear of possible rejection, Daniel realized that he had forgotten to ask Shania the one question that had been on his mind for the past three months.

Taking her hand in his, he asked, "Shania Stewart, will you marry me?"

She let go of the breath she had been holding this entire time. Her heart slammed against her rib cage as she cried "Yes!" just before she threw her arms around his neck and kissed him.

Daniel's heart emulated hers, hammering just as wildly in his chest as he felt hers was pounding in hers.

He drew back his head just for a moment and asked, "You're sure?"

"Yes, I'm sure!" she cried breathlessly. "Of course I'm sure!"

"That's all I wanted to hear," Daniel replied just before he lowered his lips to hers.

He went on kissing her for a very long time.

The Christmas tree was not finished being decorated that night.

* * * * *

MILLS & BOON

Coming next month

FROM HEIRESS TO MUM
Therese Beharrie

'Still can't get used to this view,' Hunter said quietly as she stopped next to him.

Autumn followed his gaze onto the city of Cape Town. When she'd moved out of her family home—the Bishop mansion, as some people liked to call it—she hadn't tried to find somewhere outside the city she'd grown up in to live. She'd merely been drawn to the Bouw Estate.

It had green fields that exploded with wildflowers; rolling hills beyond the fields; a river that surrounded the estate. The old manor and barn on the property had been renovated into what were now her home and her bakery, respectively.

'You didn't come here at eleven at night to talk about this view.'

His eyes slid over to her, the brown of them a well of emotion, before his head dipped in a curt nod. 'You're right.'

She gestured to the outdoor table she'd lovingly selected when she'd furnished her house. 'Shall we?'

He nodded, pulled a chair out and stepped back. With a sigh, she sat down, thanking him when he pushed it back in. She waited as he sat down opposite her. A long silence followed. She used it to study him. To watch the emotions play over his face.

When his eyes met hers, she caught her breath, and wished she had something to drink to distract herself from how vulnerable all of this made her feel.

'I don't know how to say this,' he admitted eventually.

She let air into her lungs slowly. 'Just…get it out.'

He angled his head, as if accepting her suggestion, but didn't speak.

'Hunter.' She paused. 'Are you in trouble?'

He opened his mouth, and Autumn could almost see his lips forming no, but then he closed it again. Rubbed a hand over his face; took a deep breath.

'I am.'

She straightened. 'Yeah? You're in trouble?'

His eyes shone with an emotion she couldn't quite define. It disturbed her. She'd dated him for two years; they'd been friends for one more. She should be able to tell what he was feeling.

'Yes.'

After a brief moment of hesitation, she laid a hand on the one he'd rested on the table. 'What's going on?'

He took a breath, then exhaled sharply, his gaze lowering.

'I'm a father.'

Continue reading
FROM HEIRESS TO MUM
Therese Beharrie

Available next month
www.millsandboon.co.uk